I stretched my arms above my head, gazing happily into the most striking set of luminescent, turquoise-green eyes I'd ever seen.

They belonged to a breathtaking, masculine face, a face one would expect to see on the cover of a magazine named something like *I'm Way Too Hot to Be Your Man.* Sculpted cheekbones; thick, dark lashes; chiseled jaw; and lips so full they had to be meant for kissing or eating something really juicy. I reached up and ran my fingertip along the ridge of his hard-lined warrior nose.

"Emma, *what* in the name of the gods' creation are you doing?" he said scornfully. "We really don't have time for your immature little fantasies. We're in the middle of a crisis. Do you not remember?"

I blinked and slowly moved my eyes from side to side.

I was in the jungle. And my clothes were wet. My lungs burned, my body felt like it'd been chewed up, and my head was throbbing. So aside from the perfect man with long, damp, wavy, black hair holding me in his arms, none of this felt like a dream.

He pushed himself up off the ground. As he rose, my heart stopped, started, and then went into overdrive. His legs and spine straightened into a towering mass of unforgiving muscles. With shoulders like a lumberjack and thick, powerful thighs, I didn't know if I wanted to run away or climb him like a tree...

PRAISE FOR MIMI JEAN PAMFILOFF'S ACCIDENTALLY YOURS SERIES

"The story really made an impression and she definitely makes me want to continue on with her series... witty and catchy."

—BookMaven623.wordpress.com on
ACCIDENTALLY IN LOVE WITH... A GOD?

"*Accidentally Married to... A Vampire?* remains one of the funniest paranormal novels I've read in a long time."

—Indiebookspot.com

"It was fun, the pace was fast, there were laugh-out-loud funny lines, plenty of pop-culture references, and lots of very sexy moments. I am *definitely* going to be reading the author's other books!"

—SarahsBookshelves.blogspot.com on
Accidentally Married to... A Vampire?

"Hot sex, a big misunderstanding, and a shocker of an ending that made me want the next book in the series now! I can't wait go back and read the other books in the series."

—Romancing-the-book.com on *Accidentally... Evil?*

Cimil has decided NOT to smite the following people because they are awesome and left reviews for Mimi.

"5 Stars! Although I closed my eyes during the steamy scenes and do not approve of the F-word, it was really quite exciting!" —Mimi's mother

"Mimi's books make the naughty side come out of you." —Ashley Swartz

"Her books should come with a warning label. WARNING: MAY BE ADDICTING UPON FINISHING! PRESCRIPTION—MORE NAUGHTINESS FROM MIMI?" —Ashlee Randall

"Mimi makes evil look so yummy *wink*." —Lupe Valdez

"It's hard to say who's crazier, Mimi or Cimil...One talks to voices in her head and the other talks to bugs." —Ally Davis Kraai

"*Accidentally Evil* treated me like a dog—it left me sitting here begging, panting, and wanting more treats!" —Tami Baney

"*Accidentally Evil* makes me like my cat when she paws at the glass trying to eat my hamster." —Michaela Trott

"Reality is the fantasy world of the gods...just ask Mimi; she heard it firsthand from Cimil!" —Cathy Swiger Lincoln

"Really??? Enough with the evil, the dead, and the crazy... No, wait, that's the whole plotline." —Vania Bushman

"The evil woman knows how to turn a phrase to keep you reading. Must be a witch thing!" —Dina Gower

Also by Mimi Jean Pamfiloff

Accidentally Married to... A Vampire?

Sun God Seeks... Surrogate?

Accidentally... Evil? (novella)

Vampires Need Not... Apply?

ACCIDENTALLY IN LOVE WITH...A GOD?

MIMI JEAN PAMFILOFF

FOREVER

NEW YORK BOSTON

This book is a work of fiction. Names, characters, places, and incidents are the product of the author's imagination or are used fictitiously. Any resemblance to actual events, locales, or persons, living or dead, is coincidental.

Forever
Hachette Book Group
237 Park Avenue
New York, NY 10017

www.HachetteBookGroup.com

Printed in the United States of America

Originally published as an ebook

First mass-market edition: October 2013
10 9 8 7 6 5 4 3 2 1

OPM

Forever is an imprint of Grand Central Publishing.
The Forever name and logo are trademarks of Hachette Book Group, Inc.

This book is dedicated to Naughty Nana (whose secret love of men in leather pants provides endless inspiration), the author Phoenix (cheerleader extraordinaire and master of the dreaded comma—don't give up on me), my two pirates in training (Dudes! Stop hitting each other with swords already!), and my alpha-male supreme (words could never describe what a hottie you truly are!). Without each of you, there'd be no dreams coming true in my life.

Special Thanks

You awesome people who bought a book! (I hope I got you to laugh?)

The fabulous people who posted helpful reviews and gave me those happy little stars or sent e-mails! (You know who you are! You're soooo cool!)

ACCIDENTALLY IN LOVE WITH…A GOD?

One

Present Day

Wasn't dating supposed to be fun? Because this was anything but. At any moment, a man I'd never met—approximately six foot three, brown hair, and soul-piercing blue eyes, according to his online profile—would walk through the door of the Conga Lounge, give his name to the hostess, and scream hysterically at the sight of me. Okay. He wouldn't scream…aloud, anyway. Not that I was heinous, but anyone who looked closely enough might notice I was…different.

I eyeballed the door, contemplating a mad dash before he arrived.

No, you can do this, I thought, while staring at the condensation channeling down my glass of water, my leg bouncing under the table. Why had my date picked a corny-themed bar that looked like *Gilligan's Island* threw up? What sort of man goes novelty on the first date?

Bad sign. Bad sign.

At least the other patrons seated around the faux torch-lit room, leisurely sipping Bahama Mamas and mai tais were oblivious to my impending meltdown.

I felt the gentle whoosh of summer evening air as the door swung open, and the noise from the traffic-packed New York street poured in. A tall man with sun-kissed skin, broad shoulders, and tousled brown hair floated inside—yes, floated—as if he'd ridden in on a cloud straight from Hot Man Land. He wore a black, polished cotton shirt, which hugged his well-constructed chest, and low-slung jeans that molded to his lean physique. He wasn't just good-looking, he was Milan runway edible.

"Oh, sweet Virgin of Guadalupe, please be Jake," I muttered under my breath.

Like a cliché from a movie, our eyes met from across the room, and his face lit up with a dimple-framed smile. My heart nearly stopped. "Thank you, Virgin," I said, releasing my breath.

He strutted across the restaurant, a magnet for every female in the room.

"Emma?" he said in a deep, slow-churned voice, then smiled and held out his hand. I stood up in a daze, mentally pinching myself.

"You *are* Emma, right? Curly, shoulder-length, red hair, five three. Several crazed female stalkers for best friends?"

Oh no. What had my roommates done? Since the whole online-blind-date thing was their idea, they assured me they'd carefully "screened" the guy. But I thought they were just joking about breaking into his apartment and rummaging through his underwear drawer. And dammit, they hadn't even bothered to dish.

Tighty-whities or boxers?

I looked down at his outstretched hand. *Oh, shoot. Shake hands.* "Sorry, it's just—I wasn't expecting someone so . . ." I swallowed and placed my palm in his. It was warm and inviting, like his eyes. "Um . . . so tall."

"And I wasn't expecting a woman so"—he paused to look me over like a dog eyeing a giant juicy steak—"adorable."

"Adorable?" said the deep male voice inside my head. *"What kind of moron compliments a woman with the word* adorable*? Does he think you're a goddamned puppy?"*

Couldn't I have one, just one lousy day without the voice? My blood began to boil instantly, but I resisted the urge to snap back with something lame like, "Well, maybe Jake senses I want to lick him from head to toe. Maybe even have a go at his leg." But then I thought better of myself. Because tonight, I was on a mission, and nothing would stop me from climbing my own mental Mount Everest: convince myself that I, Emma Keane, could feel attraction for a real live man with ten fingers, ten toes, arms and legs, and the other necessary, dangly bits needed to make a relationship normal. All I needed was the *right* man.

The catch?

The other person I had to prove this to wasn't exactly a person. Okay, truth be told, he was a mysterious voice only I could hear. Yes, a luscious, deep, velvety voice so intriguing and seductive it could turn me into a quivering mindless puddle of need with one little sigh. I couldn't get enough of it. Sound crazy? That wasn't the half of it. But it was why I had to do this. If I wanted a shot at normal, I had to take this first step and break this annoying, lifelong addiction.

Jake and I held hands for several moments before we sank into our wicker seats. "You must be Jake." Stupid statement, I know, but I had forgotten all of the witty ice-breakers I'd painstakingly memorized.

He nodded and continued smiling.

"So." I paused, trying to think of something clever to say. It didn't happen. "My friends, they didn't do anything crazy, did they?" *Other than a felony B and E?*

Jake shook his head. "Aside from having me followed? No. They just sent an e-mail making it clear they'd remove both my testicles if I did anything wrong."

I cringed inside, but at least he didn't know about the home invasion.

"With a dull spoon," Jake added.

The voice snickered. *"I've changed my mind. I now officially approve of your friends."*

Jake continued, lowering his voice, "I'm glad I came. I thought your profile might have been exaggerating your looks. It didn't."

"What a cretin. You're not falling for this crap, are you, Emma?"

I felt my temper percolating, but I hung on. "Thanks," I said to Jake and then looked down at my hands.

"I hope you like this place." He opened up the piña colada–shaped menu. "The food, I hear, is tiki-licious."

"Right. That's it. This date... is over!"

Percolate went to boiling over. "Jake, I'll be right back."

"Um, okay," I heard him say as I stomped off to the bathroom. I slammed the door shut and checked the two small stalls.

Empty.

"You giant turd! You promised you wouldn't talk!" I hissed. "Not a peep."

"Well, that was before..."

"Before what?"

There was a cricket-worthy pause.

"Fine. You listen to me, Guy." That was my latest name for him since he'd never shared his real one. "We had a deal. You promised you'd behave—"

"And you swore on your soul you'd pull the plug if I said so."

"Oh, no, no, my friend." I shook my finger at the air, even though he couldn't see me. "I said I'd end the date if you sensed anything wrong."

"Yes, and he's clearly deranged."

"Deranged?" I barked. "You're un-bel-ievable! He's said two words—"

"Eighty-five. Or was it eighty-seven? Hell, it doesn't matter. I knew on word three there was something... off."

"Oh my God! You're completely full of it!" *Hiccup! Hiccup!* "Great. See what you did? My night is ruined." *Hiccup!*

"Do you have a paper bag?" he asked.

I continued hiccuping uncontrollably. "No. Doesn't exactly go with my new dress." *Hiccup.* "Besides." *Hiccup.* "That only works for hyperventilating. I'm working up to that next."

"New dress?" he asked, his tone a notch above angry. *"You didn't wear the new green dress, did you? The tight one that shows every curve and 'makes a man instantly hard,' as your friend, Anne, so eloquently stated?"*

The door to the restroom swung open. The woman gave me a nod as she went into one of the stalls.

Christ! I'd forgotten my wireless headset. Again. Without it, I looked like another New Yorker one step away from a Repent Now! sandwich sign. I scrounged through my matching satin evening bag and popped on my prop.

"Answer me! Did you wear the dress? After I expressly prohibited it?"

Should I tell him I secretly wish he could see me in it? No. No! What am I thinking? He could never know what went on inside my head; he'd only use my feelings against me. I hiccuped three times in quick succession. "Yes! I wore it, and it looks fabulous. You should see all the men walking around with colossal erections from looking at me!"

Just then, the woman emerged from the stall and scampered out of the bathroom. She didn't even bother to wash her hands. *Ewww*, I thought.

"You play with fire, little girl."

"No! You play with..." I couldn't think of anything meaty to say. "Uuuh...fire. I'm going out there, and I'm going to finish this date whether you like it or not. And if you make one more peep, just one more, you're going to...uh...get burned!" *I so need to work on my threat technique.* "Got it?"

"And if I don't do as you say?"

Again, I came up empty in the threat department, so I threw out, "I'll go home with Jake and sleep with him! That's right. Wild monkey sex, too! Hanging from the chandelier and everything." *Does Jake even have a chandelier? I'll have to ask.*

He growled. *"You wouldn't."*

"Try me! Not one more peep!" I smoothed down my curls, hiccuped five more times, then took a deep breath, and headed out into the dining area. The woman from the bathroom caught my eyes for a brief moment before looking toward her date and leaning in to whisper something. Her companion shot me a quick judgmental glance over his shoulder. I resisted blurting out that his date was disgusting and had cooties on her hands. Instead, I lifted my chin and walked over to the table where Jake was sitting back, completely unaware of the turbulence he'd invited into his life.

That's when the tsunami of guilt hit me.

I stopped and looked down at Jake, the most beautiful man I'd ever seen in real life.

"Everything okay?" he asked, obviously wondering why I hadn't taken my seat.

Jake's online profile said he was looking for someone special, someone to settle down with. That someone wasn't me. How could it be? I was...complicated. My heart was trapped in some sort of bizarre purgatory, attached to a voice. Or, more accurately stated, attached to the endless images and fantasies my mind had conjured up to go with the stupid voice.

I couldn't go on with the date. There was simply no point. I had to get rid of Guy, or there would be no normal. No boyfriends. No husband. No wild monkey sex.

I hiccuped twice, making Jake jump in his seat.

He stifled a smile. "Oh, here. Try drinking some water."

I smoothed down the front of my dress, barely holding on to my tattered self-esteem. "I'm sorry, Jake, but you don't want me. I've got so much baggage even JFK couldn't handle it. But it was nice meeting you, and I hope you find that special someone."

Jake stared blankly and then nodded slowly.

I bolted outside onto the bustling street filled with people enjoying their Friday night, living their lives while I continued hiccuping uncontrollably.

"Emma, I'm glad you came to your senses. All this bickering is tiresome, especially when you know I'm right. That male was despicable. Why do you even bother to challenge me?"

That's when the doors flew off.

"You're a horrible, egotistical caveman! I'm done! Do you hear me? Done! You. Have. Got to leave!"

Several couples scurried past me. Although I was pretending to be talking to someone on my headset, I still looked like a detonating atom bomb in a green dress, mushrooming with toxic radiation.

"I'm not going anywhere, Emma. Besides, what would you do without me?"

"You can't be serious!"

"Why the hell not? If it weren't for me, some sleazeball would be using you for his sexual pleasure at this very moment. Is that what you truly want?"

"Yes! Wait. No..." I sighed. "Don't you get it?" *I need to move on. I need a normal life. I can't keep obsessing over you,* I wanted to add and thanked my lucky stars Guy could not read my thoughts.

"Once again, you ask this ridiculous question. The answer is no! I do not 'get it.' I do not 'get' your determination to throw yourself into situations that will only cause trouble. And as long as I exist, I have vowed to protect you... even if it's from yourself."

"Protect me?" That was always his fallback line, but he never could explain why that was even necessary. What the hell did I need protection from? "You're not protecting me, you're hurting me and keeping me from having an *actual* life! And if you're not going to tell me why, there's nothing left to talk about."

"I've still got plenty to say, little girl."

"No! This is over! Do you hear me? I'm ending this." I stepped off the curb into the crosswalk, continuing to stomp my way home, determined to find the answer to my million-dollar question: How, dammit, would I get rid of him? I'd researched exorcists, psychotherapy drugs to block him from my mind, and shock treatment, but nothing gave me hope of extracting him without exposing myself and being locked away in a white padded room. Just then, from the corner of my eye, I saw a set of lights barreling down on me and felt my body fly through the air before everything went dark.

Two

"Guy? What happened? Where am I?" I said aloud. I spun several times, looking up, down, in every direction. I was perched on a large balcony jutting from the face of a decadent three-story villa carved into a lush green hillside. *Like a fortress*, I thought. *I feel safe here.*

"Emma, honey? Can you hear me?" a familiar female voice called from beyond the rolling hills.

My head snapped up, canvassing the terrain. I saw nothing but miles of neatly groomed vines heavy with burgundy grapes and almost as beautiful as the red-and-pink bougainvillea bowing over the towering arched windows at my sides. Every inch of the place was breathtaking. But where was I? *Heaven. Yes, must be heaven.*

"Emma, please, baby. Come back." The voice carried on the wind. It was my mother I finally realized, but I didn't want to leave.

Just then, a low hum tumbled down the hills like an

invisible avalanche and began sifting into the air around me, vibrating like a swarm of angry bees. The noise roared inside my head.

I cupped my ears and doubled over, but the sound only amplified. My skull quaked with pain as the buzzing burrowed deep inside and settled in my bones, causing me to collapse into a quivering heap. I could have stayed like that for minutes, hours, or days. Who knows? But when that luscious voice came crashing through the layers of crippling noise, I clung to it like a life raft. It was a voice so soothing, so deep and hypnotic that every cell in my body fluttered with euphoria.

Then the voice began humming, a message embedded in the melody, "Please, my sweet, do not leave me. I'm sorry." The voice repeated the same message over and over again, yet never paused from the melody.

Wait. I recognized that song. It was—it was from... *Madame Butterfly*!

"Oh, God. No! Go away!" My eyes flew open. I wanted to scream, but tubes were wedged in my mouth and throat. I gagged and clawed, then heard ear-piercing beeps and screeches.

My parents, with ghostly pale faces, hovered over me, yelling for the nurse. I was in the hospital, and not just any hospital, but the one where my parents practiced. The powder-blue walls were unmistakable.

"Emma! Baby!" My mother slid the tube from my mouth, threw herself over me, and sobbed with joy.

I winced as someone flipped on the blinding lights directly above. "What happened?" I managed to croak.

My mother's bloodshot brown eyes told me it was something catastrophic. "You were hit by a cab, honey," she said as she smoothed the hair back from my forehead. "The driver said you just... came out of nowhere."

Oh. That. "I was distracted." *By an evil, disembodied dictator who's hijacked my head,* I wanted to add.

"Yes, Dr. Keane?" The nurse entered the room through a panel of pale blue curtains and gasped, her eyes wide. She scrambled to my side and began prodding while my parents moved aside and began hugging each other, crying.

"How long was I out?" I grumbled to the nurse, who checked my vitals.

She gave me a nervous look before she flashed a light in my eyes. "One month."

One month? I'd been out one whole month? I wiggled my toes under the beige blanket covering my lower legs. My body was stiff and sore, but nothing felt broken.

"Blunt head trauma with no signs of brain activity. You were in a coma, but you beat the odds, young lady," the nurse elaborated, checking my IV drip. "A true miracle."

The word *miracle* jarred me. Was it really? Had getting hit by a cab and being in a coma been the magic key to getting rid of Guy? I remembered the dream I'd had before waking up, but it could have been just that, a dream.

I mentally held my breath, hoping the universe had taken pity on me, while the nurse spent the next few minutes observing me like a lab rat before she turned to my still-sobbing parents, who were alternating between hugging each other and making calls on their cells to family.

"Can I speak with you both outside for a moment?" the nurse asked. "I need you to fill out some paperwork."

Frantic, they each kissed me on the forehead. "We'll

be back in two seconds, baby," my mom sputtered. "I love you. Oh, thank God you're okay. We—I, we just love you so much, honey. We'll be right back."

"I love you guys, too," I mumbled.

They disappeared behind the curtain out into the hall. The heavy door made a loud *thug!* as it closed behind them.

"Emma?"

Crap! I jumped. "Holy Virgin of Guadalupe, not you." I covered my face with my hands.

"We have some unfinished business to discuss, you and I."

"Go away," I mumbled with a raspy voice. "Can't you just leave me alone?"

"In fact, no. I cannot, nor do I truly wish to."

"Why did it have to be a cab?" I hissed. "Where's a red double-decker when you need one?"

"Please, my sweetness, do not say such things. Do you know they were ready to pull the plug and dice you into tiny pieces like a pig at the butcher? Damned organ harvesters. It took every ounce of energy I had to bring you back."

How awful that must have been for my parents. They were both doctors. So if they'd made that choice, it was because they had lost any hope for me. "Don't act like my savior. *You* did this to me."

There was a long pause. *"And now I see that you were right . . . this cannot go on."*

Could he be saying what I thought? "You're going to leave?" I whispered. A tiny part of my heart protested; the rest of me rejoiced at the notion.

"Not exactly."

The ratio of protest to rejoice flip-flopped. "What, then?"

There was another long pause, and that's when I noticed my ears were ringing. No, they were vibrating.

"I cannot leave you, but you can free me."

"Do you hear that?"

"Hear what?"

I shook my head from side to side. Maybe it was a side effect from the head injury, but I could've sworn I'd just heard voices. *No. No frigging way! No more voices. Uh-uh.* I refused to buy any more real estate in Crazytown. "Never mind. What did you say?"

"Free me."

He was serious. I could hear it in his voice. I didn't bat an eyelash. He was actually offering me a chance to get rid of him? To get my life back? "What will I have to do?"

"Travel south."

"Florida?"

"Mexico."

"Sorry?"

"Mexico. You know, that little country on the map below yours. Home of tequila and the taco."

"I don't understand. Why there?"

"That is where I am, physically."

Holy crap. "You have"—I swallowed hard—"a body?"

"Is something wrong with your hearing? Yes, I have a body, and you are to go to the jungle and find it."

Holy pickles. This entire time I thought he was some nomadic soul who'd glommed on to me for kicks.

My head began to spin. What did he look like? What if he was like one of those images my mind had dreamed up on hundreds of occasions? There was the one where he stood like a pillar of destruction, donning ancient armor, overlooking a cliff, the wind ripping through his wild ropes of black-as-midnight hair. Then there was my personal favorite where he lay nude across a plush velvet couch next to a fire, his abs rippling under bronzed skin, with golden waves of hair draping down his shoulders as he waited for me.

What was I thinking? Did I have brain damage? Was I really worrying about what he'd look like? "What exactly are you?"

"You are in no danger from me."

"How reassuring. Really. Don't suppose you're going to tell me more? Species might be nice. Or how it's possible your body is in the Mexican jungle yet I can hear you?"

"Those points are not open for discussion."

Of course not. Why should I believe he'd make this easy? "You wouldn't happen to look like a troll or have a body covered in giant warts?" At a minimum I hoped he'd be uglier than sin because that might help end my irrational, unhealthy obsession. Or perhaps not. Because as shameful as it was to admit, something about Guy overrode every ounce of logic known to Emma-kind, which absolutely scared the hell out of me, especially since he was only in my head.

He sighed in that special tone, which sounded more like a groan and made my toes curl. *"Not even close."*

Dammit. "I'm not going anywhere until you tell me who the hell you really are," I said.

He let out a soft, arrogant chuckle, as if he already knew he'd get what he wanted without any concessions. *"Rest, my sweet. You need to heal. There'll be time later to make our plans, but I am truly sorry for putting you in this position when I am supposed to protect you."*

"Protect me from what? Tell me, dammit."

Silence.

"For once, just answer me!" I demanded.

"For starters, yourself."

"I'm a grown woman. I don't need a babysitter." *Except around bright yellow taxis.*

"Heads, Emma. Frozen heads. Twenty of them in his fucking freezer. The bastard."

"Now is not the time for a deranged haiku, Guy." He always did have a bad, bad sense of humor.

"Not a haiku, Emma. That male you went on a date with, Jake. They found heads in his freezer. He was a serial killer."

"I—I don't believe you." I cupped my hands over my mouth. I would have gone home with Jake if he'd asked. Not that I was easy, but I'd been so desperate to make a stand against Guy, and Jake was too hot.

"Just ask your friend, Anne. She was here visiting and spoke of it." His tone was smug, too smug. *"I saved your life. Twice."*

I suddenly felt sick. Not because of the heads, mind you—although that was certainly gross. But because if Guy was telling the truth about Jake being off, which I seriously suspected he had been, then he was also telling the truth about protecting me from that something else he kept alluding to. I was in danger, but from what? Bastard. It was my life. Why wouldn't he tell me what was going on? "Fine. Maybe you're right about Jake, but I don't care. I'd face the fires of hell to be rid of you."

"I do not believe that for one moment, Emma. You. Need. Me. And yet, you might get your wish anyway, little girl."

Three

1940. Bacalar, Southern Mexico

"For the love of all things big and small, which way?" The towering naked god stood alone in the middle of the dense jungle, dripping like a wet dog.

Silence. Not even the waking birds lifted a beak to clue him in.

Votan growled. He didn't have time for petty games. Not when there was killing to do and not when he was in a hurry to return home. Or, more accurately stated, in a hurry to get the hell out of his weak humanlike form. It was nothing shy of annoying.

"Amusing, Cimil. Very amusing. Just remember, I never forget. And worse, I never forgive," he barked into the air above him.

The goddess Cimil, who was on point as his lookout, delighted in tormenting others, and sometimes she simply went too far. Just yesterday, for example, she'd taunted him mercilessly after she had another vision. True to her sadistic nature, she disclosed only enough information to bring about his suffering. She said a female would soon enter his life and emasculate him. "At this very moment..." She chuckled and clapped. "...I'm watching the future version of you in my head, Votan, as you grovel and pine for her." She sighed. "Good times. Good times."

Who was this woman from Cimil's vision? And what sort of powers would she possess? Cimil would not say, but for any female to control him, she'd have to be a force of nature. The thought perturbed him greatly.

He responded by telling Cimil she was a "head case"—an odd colloquialism he learned from her—which she was, but she also struck the fear of the gods into him; everyone knew that Cimil's visions were never wrong.

"Well," he said aloud to himself, "one must face fate head-on."

The cloudless sky rolled with thunder in response.

"We'll just see who gets the last laugh." Votan placed one hand on his bare hip, tapping his fingers impatiently, his golden skin glistening with drops of water. He'd already wasted far too much time climbing out of the wet, slippery portal.

Cenotes, as the Mayans once called them, were deep limestone pools. They were also the only portals to the human world. The active ones, hidden deep in the jungle or veiled inside stalactite-covered caves, were connected to the River of Tlaloc, an underground current of energy flowing between the two worlds. Cenotes were an extremely inefficient way to travel, but they were the only choice.

He looked back up at the sky, trying to gauge the time of day and how many hours of sunlight he had left. He sidled up to a tree trunk and flexed his hands. His new humanlike body still felt a bit weak. Sometimes it took hours for his strength to kick in after the journey, but he didn't want to wait. No doubt their enemies were hard at work causing mayhem. Most recently, they had found a way to shield themselves from being viewed by the gods from the comfort of their own realm. This undoubtedly meant the repugnant priests were up to their usual deadly shenanigans, like being behind a rash of missing and dead young women from the local villages.

Votan wrapped his still-weak hands around a thick branch, careful not to touch the ants scrambling down one side (bugs disturbed him, too many legs) and then pulled himself up. He climbed until he was able to peer above the trees. Like a giant, featherless bird, he perched on a branch, looking for any signs of the priests' encampment—usually a large smoke plume—however, there was nothing beyond the massive span of hazy blue sky and the ocean of treetops.

He shifted his weight to gaze in the opposite direction. Suddenly, the branch gave way as tree limbs lashed at his flesh, hurtling him back toward the earth, where he landed with a hard crunch.

Gods dammit. This was not going to be a quick mission, was it?

Four

Present Day. New York City

"Passport, my sweet?"

"Check."

"Tickets, my sweet?"

"Check. And stop calling me 'my sweet.' "

"Do you have a good map"—dramatic pause—*"my dearest?"*

I rolled my eyes. "I bought a guidebook online. It's got—"

There was a knock at my bedroom door. It was my mom. Sadly I lived at home again after being moved out of my apartment while in a coma. No one thought I was coming back. Ever. And after hearing I was going to die, my roommates and best friends—Anne, Nick, and Jess—couldn't stand to live there. Too depressing, they said. They'd moved out right away.

"Be quiet," I hissed at Guy. My mother couldn't hear

him. No one could except me. But he had an uncanny knack for provoking a response, so I was constantly covering up my seemingly absurd comments.

"Make her go away. You still have to pack, and we must review the plan one last time."

"I'm not leaving until morning. There's plenty of time," I whispered.

"But you must be prepared properly, Emma. We're not going on a picnic."

"Don't you have a nap to take or something?"

"Only if you're…"—he lowered his voice— *"…coming."*

The sexual innuendo wasn't missed. My core fluttered with little waves of warmth. I shook my head, trying to get a grip. I couldn't let him affect me like that anymore. I had to stay in control.

"Right, big man. Like that'll ever happen if you're involved. I bet you're some kind of cave-dwelling, telepathic hobgoblin. I bet you're so ugly even your cooties close their eyes. I bet the only way you can get a woman is by clubbing her over the head."

"Mmm…if I didn't know any better, I'd say you were issuing a challenge. And you know, I cannot resist those. I'm far too competitive. What's the wager?"

Oh, please. "Okay, I'll bite. What do you want?"

"That, my dear, is easy. You will become a nun, never to date again."

"Ha! Nice try. Not in a million years. In fact, as soon as you're gone, I'm going on a slut-athon." Not true, but I hoped he got the point: I hated him trying to control me. And since the accident, he seemed more…intense. More protective, more needy of my attention, and more flirtatious. He reminded me of a caged wolf, a horny caged wolf. Was it a defense mechanism? Was he as nervous as I was about meeting face-to-face?

"My sweet Emma, how you try my patience."

"Eye for an eye, bub," I said.

The knock at my door repeated. *Christ!* I'd forgotten my mom was there. That was the other problem with having Guy in my life. He always distracted me. People thought I was a space case.

I picked up my cell from the nightstand. "Bye. I'll call you later," I said loudly, feigning just ending a call in case my mom had heard me talking. "Come in, Mom."

The door chugged open as it collided with the heap of rejected clothes on the floor. Who knew packing to face my destiny would be so hard?

Her brown bob popped through the crack.

"Sorry, didn't hear you. Was talking to Anne."

"Emma, I was just checking to see if you changed your mind about that ride to the airport?" she asked.

"Be confident, Emma. She cannot sense your deception. The woman has been through enough already."

Guy was right. My parents had been through a lot, first with my grandmother's unsettling disappearance last year and then with my near death. The last thing I wanted was to traumatize them further. And no, I didn't like lying to her, but this was important. This was my life. I had to take this chance if I ever wanted to be free of Mr. Voice.

"No thanks, Mom. I knew you'd be working late tonight, so I've got a car picking me up," I said. The flight was leaving at 6:00 a.m. so it was a good excuse.

"Well…okay, if you want to do it that way," she said.

"Hey, I'm coming back in a week." I squeezed her hand.

The story I told my parents was simple. I had a little money saved and needed to get away for some me time. I told them I needed a break after everything that had happened, including recently graduating summa cum laude from NYU with a BA in marketing, minor in *español*, which was no easy task, but it's amazing what people can do when they don't have a real social life. Once I assured them I'd stay at the resort and only go out on guided tours, they had eased up a bit on the worrying.

Now, if they had any clue I planned to land in the Cancún airport, rent a car, drive five hours toward the border of Belize, and set out to find a dilapidated ruin in the middle of the jungle, they'd handcuff me to my bed. In fact, that wasn't such a bad idea. After hearing the plan from Guy, captivity sounded like the saner choice. According to him, he'd been following some "very bad people." Somehow, they had set a trap, and there he'd been ever since. Cursed.

"You mean, like, magic cursed? They're holding you with some voodoo spell?" I asked.

His only reply was that some things had to be seen to be believed.

No kidding.

I turned to my mom, who had concern written all over her face. "I promise you, Mom, there's absolutely nothing to worry about."

She lifted a brow and crossed her arms.

"You're going to lecture me again. Aren't you?" I asked.

She nodded, and I took a seat. This was going to take a while.

"Finally, I thought she'd never leave," Guy grumbled after an hour of safe-travel talk with my mother.

I sat down on my bed and covered my face with both hands. Was this real? Was this finally going to happen? In twenty-four hours, I'd meet him and be free forever.

I felt the sharp pang of loss in my stomach but mentally shooed it away.

"Emma? Why are you groaning? What's the matter now?"

I didn't want to talk about my irrational conflict. "What do you mean?"

"You're sighing and making funny noises. I know something is wrong. And…why do you insist on calling me Guy? What happened to Mantastic? Which you say with blatant disdain and sarcasm. Or your all-time favorite, a-hole?"

He was trying to make me laugh, but I wasn't in the mood. "You're the one who keeps saying you're just a guy, so tell me your real name, and I'll use it."

"You can call me Hunk of Burning Love or Cupcake."

Okay, that was funny. I laughed. "Those sound like porn stars. And sorry, but I doubt you're fantasy material. How about I call you selfish bast—"

"Guy, it is."

"Fine."

"We need to go over everything one last time," he said in that special voice he used when he didn't want any argument from me. It was stern, yet hypnotic and enchanting. My toes began to tingle along with several unmentionable parts of my body. It was cruel to play with me like that. Why did he do it?

"Stop with the voice thing, or we're done talking."

"I have no clue what you mean, but I love the way your heart accelerates when I do it," he said in the same penetrating voice.

My nipples hardened. *Jerk.* "Good night."

"All right," he said in his normal tone. My body instantly relaxed. *"Did you memorize the phrase I gave you? You can't lift the curse and release me without it."*

He warned that reciting the phrase incorrectly could create some kind of bad energy. This was so hokey. "Yes, and I'm not saying it again." I clenched my fists, preparing to resist his voice if he used it again.

"One more time."

"I've got this. Okay? I'm driving straight through to that little village with the stupid name, Bacaloo—"

"Bacalar," he corrected.

"Whatever." Like it mattered. "Then I'm following the trail into the jungle."

Damn. That sounded crazy. Was I really, really doing this? Yes. Yes, I was.

"And the cardinal rule is no—"

I cut him off. "Deviations." He'd already given me the two-hour lecture about how dangerous that part of Mexico was. Drug dealers were rampant near the border. This made me wonder, were those the bad people who'd trapped him with a spell? If yes, holy crap, the world would be in heaps of trouble. The Mexican feds would have to trade in their guns for Harry Potter books. "I get it. Can I finish packing, take a shower, and get to bed now?"

"You know, I'm eternally grateful for what you're about to do."

I hated when he was nice to me. It made me more confused about my feelings for him; mean was easy to leave.

"Yeah, you keep saying that, but it's not like you gave me a choice. And I'm not doing this for you. It's for me." It was both, actually, but he didn't need to know. After I learned about him being trapped all these years, I felt sorry for him.

"Has it occurred to you?"

"What?"

"That you might miss me once I'm out of your life?"

I can't stop thinking about it, I thought. *I'm terrified. No—relieved. No—terrified.* He'd been a part of me for longer than I could remember. Sure, he was a major pain, but I'd clearly grown attached. "I'll miss you like an ingrown toenail."

He laughed. *"Ouch. Such a nasty bite you have, my little meerkat. But what if I said that our stimulating relationship does not have to end? I know this is what you secretly long for, to be by my side and gaze into my handsome, masculine face,"* he said.

"Don't. This isn't a joke. You've ruined a significant portion of my life, and now you're making me risk it just to get it back."

"It wasn't my intent to hurt you. You know that. You are by far the most important thing in my world. All I've ever wanted is to look after you."

Did he truly see things that way? When I was little, I remember feeling like nothing in the world could harm me as long as he was around. But that feeling quickly ceased when I was six, after the school insisted I get a psychiatric evaluation. My hunch is it had something to do with me inexplicably singing the lines from *Madame Butterfly* in Italian, Guy's favorite opera. I also kept insisting my imaginary friend was real, which sort of freaked people out.

Right after that, he said he had to leave for a while but that he'd stay close in case I ever needed him. I was devastated, and for weeks I begged him to answer me, but he didn't.

When I was fifteen, he finally returned. He wouldn't say why, but I suspected it was because I'd discovered boys. Sadly, they didn't discover me back until I was much older, and by then, it was too late. I was hooked on the mystery of Guy.

Did he have any clue how hard it was to listen to the sound of his dark, melodic voice every day? Or to share my life with him, not knowing what or who he was?

He was an enigma my mind couldn't stop trying to solve, and his refusal to give up the answers drove me to the brink of insanity. That's what made my feelings so... so irrational. How could I pine for someone like that? Part of me loathed him. The other part ached for him.

"I am sorry, Emma. I sometimes forget that I am not the only one trapped."

"What about you? Will you?" I picked up a pair of socks from the bed and began folding them into a ball.

"Will I what?"

"Miss me." I wanted him to say yes. I wanted to know I meant something more to him. I was pathetic.

Several moments passed. *"You see, you love being with me. Admit it, just say the words, woman,"* he gloated.

Arrogant toad. "I think my actions speak for themselves, and they're saying, 'Take a hike.' I'm flying two thousand miles to get rid of you."

"Or they're saying, 'I'd do anything for you.' After all, Emma, you are taking a huge leap of faith to free me. You have no idea what you'll find."

"You're such a..." I paused, trying to come up with

some clever word to knock him down a peg or two, but it was a waste of time. His arrogance was impervious to my insults. "I have something to tell you," I said, changing subjects. I rubbed my palms on my jeans and then continued bundling my clean socks. One could never have too many clean socks or undies when going to meet your fate head-on.

"You're not backing out, are you?"

"No. It's something else. Something I've wanted to say since the accident."

"I know. I know. But you don't have to thank me for saving you."

"Actually, I've started hearing other voices."

"Are you certain?"

Oh yeah. And Crazytown just got a new mayor. "Yes," I replied quietly. I picked up the pile of neatly bundled socks and put them in my backpack.

"Why the hell didn't you tell me?" he asked, his voice more concerned than irritated.

"I don't know. I guess—I thought, maybe I really was going crazy this time. And honestly, I can't understand them. But I've been able to pick out different pitches, kind of like instruments in an orchestra. They all sound like bees. Busy, buzzing bees. I think there are eleven."

There was a long silence. Then he said, *"Sometimes after traumatic experiences, the human brain becomes hypersensitive, and yours is already like a giant satellite dish—one of the reasons you hear me—the noise is probably static, perhaps resulting from your head injury."*

I let out a sigh of relief. *Yes, that's what it has to be.* Besides, the noise hadn't been nearly as bad as during that first week. In fact, most days I didn't even notice it.

"Guy?"

"You're not going to tell me some other secret, such as you now shoot fire from your eyes?"

"No." I snickered and ran my hand through my tangled curls.

"That you're madly in love with me and want to spend eternity listening to the sound of my manly, seductive voice?"

Yes. Definitely yes, I thought instantly. Some days, I wanted to bathe in it. *Wait! No!* "I want to be alone the rest of the night. I need to think."

"Yes, you should rest, my sweet. It's the least I could do for the woman I..."

I waited for him to finish the sentence.

Silence.

"The woman you... what?"

"Good night, my sweet Emma."

Ugh. "Night."

I finished packing in blissful silence and then took a long, hot shower, trying to focus my thoughts away from the trembling in the pit of my stomach. Instead, I basked in visions of my life after he'd be gone. Dates, real conversations, going to the bathroom without wearing my iPod so he couldn't hear anything. God, I could practically taste my new life. I knew the moment I freed him, his hold over my heart—and other body parts—would be severed. I'd finally be free. And then maybe, just maybe, I could confront the neglected skeletons in my closet, like getting over losing my grandmother—a thought never far from my mind.

Five

1940. Bacalar, Mexico

"He's mine!" screamed a woman off in the distance. "I saw him first!"

"Over my dead body!" screamed another. "I'm the oldest. He's mine!"

Several more female voices chimed in, all speaking an ancient Mayan dialect. The voices turned into a blur of death threats and hisses. Slaps and grunts echoed through the air.

"Stop! All of you," a deep, older male voice commanded.

"My brothers found the stranger," screamed the first female. "He's mine!"

"Have you lost your minds?" the male said scornfully. "He is the stranger who took Itzel. He's dangerous. Go warn the others to stay away while I take care of this."

Must get out of here, thought Votan as the footsteps approached. Females tended to go crazy when in his presence; it was a natural reaction to his otherworldly energy. He moved to sit up, but a sharp pain in his head and a warm hand placed firmly on his bare chest prevented him.

"No. You are not well. Lie still," the male commanded.

Disoriented and groggy, Votan finally eased open his eyes, taking note of the dull aches blanketing his body. Bright light poured through the cracks of the walls, but it was the rocking motion that prevented his eyes from immediately focusing. He was lying in a hammock, which he unequivocally hated; hammocks were quite possibly the worst sleeping contraptions since the pea-shuck-filled sacks of the 1400s.

"Wh-where am I?" Votan stuttered, unable to fully control his mouth.

"You are in my village." The old man smiled stiffly. "I am Petén." The muscles of his face moved under his aged skin, causing dark, leathery wrinkles to gather around his eyes and mouth.

"How long have I-I been here?" Votan mumbled.

Petén, who only wore a pair of simple white cotton pants, sat down on a wooden stool in the corner and began picking his teeth with a small twig. "Some boys found you a few hours ago. Your head was split open by a rock, your back broken in two, but you're healing quickly, as would be expected for . . . someone like you."

Votan rubbed the back of his head, feeling a mammoth knot and a slimy wetness in his long hair. He then noticed a brightly colored sarong wrapped around his waist. His chest had also been decorated with red-and-black paint. Votan cocked one brow and looked back at the old man.

Petén shrugged. "The women seem to have gotten carried away when they cleaned your wound."

Votan craned his neck and moved his eyes over the small dirt-floor hut.

Petén cleared his throat. "We weren't expecting you again."

"I've never been here." At least, this is what he believed, though the fall had clearly disoriented him. *Damned human bodies. So weak!*

Petén spoke of another male with a similar appearance and set of turquoise eyes who came through the cenote many years ago. The man demanded several young women, virgins, for sacrifice. When the villagers refused, the stranger scorned them, warning they'd be punished. The very next day, the entire village fell sick, and the man returned.

"Against my wishes," Petén explained, "my cousin, Itzel, who was just nineteen at the time, volunteered to go with him. The man took her, and the village was cured."

The story of the virgins set off alarm bells in Votan's brain. So did the description of the male.

Votan nodded for Petén to continue.

"She came back several months after, changed. Her mind scarred. We thought perhaps you were the man, returning for her."

"No, I am not that man, nor am I here for the woman." *But everything just became much more complex.* Only a handful of males had a similar appearance to his, and if any were stealing women, he had a much bigger problem on his hands.

"So then?" Petén asked.

It was clear Petén knew he was not human, but the gods did not discuss their matters openly with anyone except the Uchben. *Uchben* meant "ancient" in Mayan, and like the name implied, they'd been around for centuries, acting as the gods' human eyes, ears, and muscle.

They were a secret society of highly educated and fiercely loyal people deployed throughout the world. Right now, Votan was kicking himself for not having alerted them to his trip, but there hadn't been time.

"I am only passing through." A sharp pain suddenly racked Votan's head. He winced and moaned.

Petén scrambled away and returned with a bowl. "Try this medicine."

The sweetness ignited a blur of strange images: powdered sugar–dusted cookies, miniature chocolate cakes, and a dozen others. He could see himself standing in an enormous white kitchen, wearing an apron, rolling dough on a board, and singing along with *Madame Butterfly*, which played in the background. A redheaded woman with deep green eyes crept up behind him and slipped her slender, pale arms around his waist, planting a tender kiss on his shoulder blade. Who was she? The woman from Cimil's vision?

His heart filled with warmth as he emptied the bowl and the pain dissipated. "Delicious, may I have more?" Such an odd sensation was running through him. He wanted to see her again. No. He needed to see her again. The loss of the vision ignited an instant hollowness in his chest.

Petén nodded again. "I will return shortly."

Votan lay staring at the thatched roof above, feeling the tingling of his body as it repaired itself, the heat of the tropical air soothing his skin. His mind raced. He had the urge to return to Cimil and beg for more information about the female, but he wasn't going anywhere until he'd dealt with the priests he was after. And now, the situation had become infinitely more complicated; the man Petén described was without a doubt one of Votan's brothers.

Six

Present Day. New York

The hair on the back of my neck stiffened like quills. I was being watched. Should I run? What if the person followed me? No, I couldn't leave. I had a plane to catch, a damned important plane.

"Guy? You there? Someone's watching me."

Silence.

"Guy? Where the hell are you?"

No answer. *Crap.*

A minute earlier, I'd just been enjoying leisurely sips of my icy rum and Coke while people watching—my all-time favorite sport—from a small wobbly table in the airport bar with a view of the terminal. Something about drinking at five in the morning felt trashy, but the flashing neon beer signs and small army of flip-flop-clad fellow rule breakers, kicking off their vacations, somehow made it acceptable. I swiveled in my chair, searching for the discomforting vibe. My nerve endings were tingling.

There, in the corner, I noticed an enormous man with thick waves of long black hair emerging from the shadows. Or at least, I thought he would emerge. Instead, the shadows hugged his body like a heavy cloak as he approached. His eyes, the color of a tropical ocean, suddenly pierced the darkness. Before I could run, we were toe-to-toe, but he wasn't there to dance or buy me another drink.

"I've been looking for you everywhere," he said in a smooth, deep voice.

"You have?" I said, involuntarily rising toward him. I inhaled deeply. He smelled like black licorice.

He reached out his hand and cupped my cheek. His touch was electrifying. "You know you belong to me, don't you?"

My alarm clock shrieked, and I catapulted from bed, drenched in sweat. I ran my hands through my sopping hair. "Jesus H. Christ. What was that?"

"Another hot dream about me, my sweet?" Guy said in a heart-stopping, provocative voice.

It was true; I dreamed about him way too much, but this time it was different. "My only dreams of you involve kicking your man nuggets," I lied. "And by the way, you usually look like that troll from *Lord of the Rings*. I'm sure it's a premonition."

"In about twelve hours, you are going to be very disappointed. I hear a nunnery in your future."

"I never agreed to your wager. Remember? Besides, what's with you and this nun thing? Do you have some weird fetish? Is that normal for decrepit, cave-dwelling creatures?"

Guy laughed, igniting every cell in my body. His laugh was the kind that could melt a polar ice cap. It was powerful yet inviting. It was infectious to the nth degree. I could hear it every day for the rest of my life, and it still wouldn't be enough.

The man from my dream suddenly flashed in my mind.

I sat down on the edge of the bed and rubbed my face. *Oh, God. Maybe it was a premonition.* I'd never had one, but that didn't rule out the possibility. Not only had the man been powerful and irresistibly seductive, even without a face, but he was definitely dangerous.

"Guy, your eyes wouldn't happen to be turquoise, would they?"

Several moments passed before he finally answered. *"Why do you ask?"* he said, his tone irritated.

"Answer me." I grabbed my floral terry cloth robe from the hook behind the door.

"You first."

I suddenly felt my stomach lose altitude. Why was he pushing back? If he didn't have turquoise eyes, then the question was innocuous. "Don't. No games. Not now."

"They are not turquoise. Now tell me, why do you ask?"

Was he lying? I didn't feel the conviction in his tone like I normally did when he spoke. Would it really change anything if he was? I decided it wouldn't. I was committed to seeing this all the way through, even if it killed me. "No reason. The troll in my nightmare had turquoise eyes," I lied.

He hissed with frustration. *"Go get ready. You're wasting time."*

Predictably, General Temper Tantrum wasn't feeling quite so calm about the situation, which meant it really was going to be dangerous. It seemed the closer we got to the airport, the worse his foul language became. He was giving me a massive headache.

Once finally airborne, I slipped the hood of my pink sweatshirt over my hair and turned my head nonchalantly away from the passenger to my side toward the window on my left. "Would you please chill out?" I snapped quietly.

"Chill out? I am perfectly calm!"

I wanted to pull out my hair. "Please?" I begged.

He sighed. *"I'm sorry. Emma? Did I thank you?"*

"About ten times. But if you really want to thank me, how about some of those answers you promised."

"Not yet."

"Why not? We had a deal, remember?"

He growled. *"What do you need to know, my sweet?"*

"What are you?"

"Any question but that."

I huffed in protest. "Fine. Who are you?"

"And that."

Before I protested again, he threw me a bone. *"Do you recall how upset I became when your grandmother disappeared?"*

How could I forget? I remembered every detail from that day. It was when my life went from frustrating and weird to downright miserable. My grandmother was the heart of our family. She was . . . amazing. And I don't mean it in a never-forgets-my-birthday or bakes-the-best-cookies kind of way—although those both applied—but people were drawn to her. They adored her. Maybe it was her wide green eyes or her inviting smile, but I think there was something else. She radiated life, and people flocked to her like moths to a flame. And when she disappeared, it tore me apart. My entire family spent months looking for her, even hiring private detectives, but she was just... gone. The authorities—idiots—officially concluded she ran away. Her passport was missing, and she'd personally cleaned out her bank account. The video at the bank confirmed it. But I don't think any of us, especially my mom, could accept that she'd leave us like that. I knew in my bones she was dead because only death would keep her away.

"I remember. The day is permanently seared in my brain. Why?" I asked.

"I knew her." He was barely audible over the roar of the engines. *"And I'd like to think she and I were friends. So, you see, you have nothing to fear from me."*

My heart stopped. "You're joking," I whispered. *Hiccup!*

"No, I'd never joke about something like that."

I jumped from my seat, hiccuping and ignoring the disgruntled passengers who had to stand to let me into the aisle. I needed privacy for this conversation so that meant the bathroom.

The line was three people long, and the wait felt like an eternity of foot tapping, watch watching, and hiccuping. When it was finally my turn, I slammed the door. "What the hell are you talking about?" I hissed at the wall.

"Like I said, I knew Gabriela."

"How?" *Hiccup!*

"I am not prepared to answer that question."

"Were you in her head, too?" I asked.

"No. You are the only one—"

"You have to give me answers here," I interrupted.

"I just did. Weren't you listening?"

I balled my fists in my hair, pulling from the roots. He was the master of aloof. "Goddammit! How did you know her? Why are you and I connected?"

"Not yet, Emma." His vehemence reverberated through my bones.

Crap. I hated how he tried to manipulate me with his voice like that. "Why can't you tell me?" I croaked, leaning over the tiny stainless steel sink.

"Because you'd never believe me without seeing the truth for yourself. I've explained this many times."

"No. We had a deal. I would 'vow obedience' "—I used his own stupid words—"and you'd—"

"I want to keep you out of danger. Your hot head is hazardous, and the gods only know what you might pull if we get into trouble. As I've explained, Emma, we're not going—"

"On a fricking picnic! Yes!" *Hiccup!* "I get it. But a deal is a deal. I vowed. Now, you speak."

"The deal was that you'd vow to follow my every instruction. No questions asked. In exchange, I will tell you everything I know—about me, about you—right before we meet." He lowered his tone, sending inappropriate shivers down into my core. *"You have yet to meet your end of the bargain. Therefore, I have not gone back on my word."*

"Bastard. That's not what we agreed, and you know it! You're playing with me, you arrogant . . ." I was about to say "monster" when the realization struck me. What if he was one? Maybe that's why he refused to tell me anything. This entire time I'd been blinded by that seductive voice and the fantasy of the body that might go with it. I'd grown attached to him in a sick and twisted kind of way. But what if he was a monster and the moment I freed him, he knew I'd run? Maybe he really never planned to let me go.

"I-I can't do this. I'm sorry. I'm not going, Guy." I felt the panic overtaking me as I realized something worse than death existed: being his prisoner for the rest of my life. "It's too much. I'll help you any other way I can, but I'm not going."

"Emma, you can't back out now! You must release me before I do further damage to your life. I could not live with myself if anything happened to you!"

There was a loud knock on the door as the fasten seat belt sign illuminated.

"I have to go back to my seat." I reached for a tissue from the wall dispenser and patted my face.

"Emma, I can help you find out what happened to Gabriela."

My heart stopped, sank, and then began pounding furiously. "Wha-what did you say?"

"You heard me. I can help you find who took her. I know where to start looking."

"You know something? Why didn't you tell me before?"

"If you want answers, you'll have to free me."

"How could you go there? How could you use my love for her like this?"

"I always intended to find out what happened to Gabriela. I was going to tell you later."

"I don't believe you. You're just saying that."

"Believe anything you like. But if you want to know what happened to her, then get your ass here."

He went there. He definitely went there. He'd pulled the one string that could get me to do anything. It was the only place in my heart that was raw and sad and needed closure. Without a doubt, he couldn't be trusted. And now I had to go to him because if he really could help me find out what happened, it would bring my family closure—peace to my mother—if I survived.

"Fine." I opened the door and slid past the glaring flight attendant, then returned to my seat and popped in my earbuds.

"Emma," he screamed over the music.

I turned up the volume, closing my eyes to hold back the tears.

"Emma, I'm sorry. You left me no choice."

I toggled to "Wake Me Up Before You Go-Go," by Wham! He hated eighties music with a passion. Opera was his thing. I could practically hear him cringing in my head.

"There's always a choice, Guy." And he'd chosen to hurt me. This was not a good sign.

Seven

1940. Bacalar, Mexico

"Hello," said a small voice, startling Votan from his half sleep, causing the hammock to tip. He landed with a soft thump in the dirt and craned his sore neck upward to find a bright-eyed little girl staring down at him.

Her face, with its delicate features, glowed with innocence. And something else. Something familiar. It wasn't her shocking green eyes or the intensity of her gaze. It was the energy radiating from every pore of her body.

"Hi. I'm Gabriela," she said in the same Mayan dialect Petén used. "I'm five." She held out her tiny hand to display five miniature fingers. "Who are you?"

Votan slowly rose, continuing to study the tiny child, unsure of what he was really witnessing. "This cannot be."

The little girl continued staring with her wide, curious eyes. "Who are you?"

Votan blinked. "I am Votan."

Petén entered the hut at that moment, carrying a bowl and then dropping it to the floor.

"Gabriela! Leave here immediately!" Petén screamed. A woman with long, dark hair and equally dark eyes peeked out from behind Petén.

Gabriela began to cry and ran straight for the woman's skirt and buried her face. The woman seemed to be paralyzed and stared at Votan, ignoring the wailing child, gripping a large polished black stone hanging from her neck.

Petén suddenly shook the woman and commanded her to leave. She made an absentminded nod, then scurried away with Gabriela in tow.

Petén turned and eyed Votan cautiously. "You are *the* Votan?" he asked.

Votan ignored the question. "What exactly did the man do to your cousin? That was her, wasn't it?"

Petén kept his distance, clearly shaken. "We are not sure what happened."

"Tell me what you know!" Votan screamed.

Petén held out his hands in self-defense. "I speak the truth. My cousin, Itzel, has told us very little. She was brought to a small village with other females who'd been taken from the south. She will not tell us what happened during those few months, other than one night a group of dark priests, the Maaskab, came and began slaughtering the women."

The Maaskab. Images of priests with black souls and bloodshot eyes, their naked skin covered in a sooty paste, flashed in Votan's mind. Their long, blood-caked hair hung in putrid dreadlocks that dangled to their waists. Their black teeth only served to strain the blood-streaked saliva pouring from their lips as they growled in his mind. He could almost smell the rotting stench of darkness seeping from their pores.

Petén continued, "My cousin escaped. When she returned here, we immediately knew she was with child—our Gabriela."

Votan's jaw dropped. *Of our blood?* he thought, still unsure he could believe what he'd just heard. "Gabriela's father is the man who took your cousin?"

Petén nodded. "Yes, though Itzel will not discuss the matter."

This cannot be. But there she was. Proof. Undeniable proof. One of his brothers had found a way to make a child, with a human no less.

Votan pressed his hands to the sides of his throbbing skull. None of this made any sense whatsoever. His brother was secretly stealing virgins and mating with them. The priests were possibly hunting the women down.

Votan's head hurt, and he could not think straight. *Deal with the priests, and then confront your brother.*

"The Maaskab." Votan ground out the words. "Where can I find them?"

Petén continued staring, seemingly transfixed by the six-foot-nine shirtless man with the massive hulking frame, thick waves of long blue-black hair, and fierce turquoise eyes.

"Are you truly the God of Death and War?" Petén whispered.

Votan nodded.

"I will draw you a map immediately," Petén replied.

Votan crossed his arms. "I'll thank you for some weapons, too."

"Of course, whatever you need." Petén turned to leave.

"And bring me the girl," Votan added. "I want to see her again before I set out."

Petén's weathered face turned pale. He nodded stiffly and left.

As Votan finished anchoring the last leather-sheathed dagger to his bicep, he approached Gabriela and her mother. Votan closed his eyes, tilted his face toward the sky, and recited the ancient prayer of loyalty and protection. Votan intended to bond himself to the girl.

He then grasped the end of his long inky braid and, with one swift motion, drew a dagger. He severed his lock at the nape of his neck and shoved it at Itzel. "Burn this tonight in your fire with a lock of Gabriela's hair. Her light will then be tethered to mine."

He looked down at Gabriela, who was standing happily at her mother's side. The bond would put her under his protection and the protection of the gods—the ones who hadn't turned evil, anyway. The bond would also help him to track the child, if need be, as it allowed him to sense her presence. Gabriela's mother nodded and then accepted the rope of hair.

Votan looked down into the girl's inquisitive green eyes. Suddenly, the world had new meaning. He knew it was odd for the God of Death and War to think of such things, yet it could not be helped. Could he, too, create life, as his brother had, instead of simply taking it? The thought fascinated him.

He crouched and whispered into Gabriela's ear, making her giggle, and then kissed the top of her head. "Goodbye, my little one. I'll be back for you."

Eight

1940. Near Tzolicab. Yucatán, Mexico

"Twenty-two," said Votan as he marched down the path cutting through the dense jungle.

Why the hell did I leave Gabriela behind? I am a fool, he thought.

"Twenty-three." *I should have taken the girl, hid her somewhere safe, and then completed my mission. The others would have*—"Twenty-four"—*understood. Well, maybe not, but who the hell cares.* "Twenty-five. Twenty-six."

Votan stopped and stared up at the cloud of swarming black flies encasing the scalped Maaskab priest hanging in the tree. Like the other twenty-five he'd counted, the man's dreadlocks had been tied into a crude rope and then used to hang him.

"Irritating. This is just irritating." Finding the priests

dead not only meant a delay in returning to Cimil for answers about his vision of the redheaded woman, but now, it prevented his prompt return for the girl, too.

He could only pray nothing bad happened to the child while he was away. The bond was in no way foolproof. And frankly, she was the first true miracle he'd seen during his excruciatingly long life.

Again, he dwelled on which one of his brothers had fathered her. And how? Gods could not be intimate or procreate. Period.

Humans aren't even the same species.

Yes, gods could take a humanlike body, but ultimately, it was only a shell to house their true form. They were made of light, of pure energy. Humans, even those who'd become immortal through the various ways—given the gift by the gods, turned into vampires or other immortal creatures—were still made up of tangible mass.

A god having a child with a human was like fire mating with a log. Sure, they could touch each other, but one would end up cooked to ash.

Votan shook his head and began listening carefully to the animal noises echoing from the green-hued shadows. The creatures were riled, calling out to each other. Votan closed his eyes to listen. He caught fragments of each tiny voice but was unable to piece together any coherent story from them. He just saw flashes of white men with guns and clouds of smoke.

He proceeded cautiously, counting more bodies.

Dammit! What the hell is this?

By the time he reached the smoldering Maaskab village hidden deep in the jungle, he counted thirty hanging bodies. From the markings on their chests, all had been the more senior priests. In their society, one line, one heinous raised scar straight across the chest, equaled one level of rank. The bodies in the trees wore two or three, but none had one—the lowest—or four, the highest. So where had their leader and the others gone?

In the Maaskab village, what was left of it, another fifty dark priests lay scattered across the ground like leaves fallen from a tree, their nearly naked bodies riddled with bullet holes. Whoever had killed them hadn't taken their sweet time like they had with the human tree ornaments. After examining a few bodies, he noticed they had one line across their chests. That answered his question about the peons, but not their leader.

He canvassed the rest of the area and determined no one was left, not one damned bloody soul. The situation was a disaster. Sure, he'd wanted them all to die, but he needed to interrogate them first, find out how they were learning their new dark tricks and confirm why they'd been killing those innocent women.

"Cimil!" he screamed. "A little assistance, please?"

He waited, but there was no reply. "Still behaving like a child, I see."

With the agonizing pain from his earlier fall still coursing freely through his head, Votan clamped his eyes shut. Had someone purposefully murdered the priests to hide something from him? Or had one of the priests' many enemies simply bested them? One thing was certain: The killers had worked over the more senior priests. Ruthlessly. Same damned thing he would've done.

Distracted by pain and frustration, he turned and walked straight into a tree, his nose crunching on impact. "Son of a bitch!" he wailed and kicked the mammoth tree that had toppled over. “I’m sorry. I’m truly sorry,” he said, looking at the decimated tree, cupping his bloody nose.

He wiped the blood across his bare arm and pushed the tree upright. He reburied the roots, covering them with the black, moist dirt while he contemplated his next steps.

Catching a whiff of something out of place, Votan lifted his bloodied nose into the air. Buried among the stench of rotting flesh and burned huts was the smell of something distinctive. He began stalking through the remains of the village, and as clear as day, there were tracks made with boots. The priests barely wore clothes, let alone any form of shoe.

Now what do I do?

When he’d arrived in the cenote, he had thought this mission would be a quick, one-god job so he hadn’t made any arrangements with the Uchben to help him.

But if he turned back now and sent for them, he’d end up losing more valuable time.

“Fine. Alone it is,” he grumbled. “What’s the worst that could happen?”

Three days later. Gulf of Mexico

It was early evening when Votan crouched into the dingy, rancid cabin and slammed the door behind him. “Hello, Captain Pizarro.”

The man with greasy brown hair and hollow cheeks rose, back against the wall, and gave Votan a once-over. Maybe the man was taking stock of his enormous size. Or perhaps he was checking out the bundle of machetes strapped to Votan's back. Or he was looking at the daggers tied to each appendage and the two guns holstered to his sides. Maybe it was the colorful, knee-length man skirt he wore. It had to be the skirt.

"Preparing for a one-man war?" Pizarro asked.

"Always." A grin swept across Votan's face as he propped himself against the door, arms crossed.

"I see," said Pizarro. "And since you know my name, I'm guessing your presence is no accident."

Silly human. There was no such thing as an accident. For three days, Votan followed the killers' tracks from the Maaskab village to the ocean where he watched with intense curiosity as men loaded several small crates onto rowboats and then carefully pulled them aboard their rust-stained cargo vessel. He'd counted sixty heavily armed, contemptible sorts and one evil-looking, shirtless bastard with tattoos—dragons, sea monsters, the works. Votan had heard the men call him Pizarro, a Spanish name.

Traffickers were common in this part of the world, but not Spaniards. Votan could not imagine how they had traveled through international waters; World War II was making ocean voyages very tricky.

Votan had wanted to immediately capture these men and commence interrogating, but they would scatter, and he'd lose more time. So he climbed the anchor chain, hid aboard, and waited for deeper waters.

"Correct, no accident," Votan said to Pizarro. "And you should know I have a strict policy about honesty."

"Honesty? About what?" asked the captain.

"I'm going to kill you. Everyone, actually. Likely today." Votan shrugged casually. "However, if you tell me everything now, I promise not to torture you." He felt his eyes tingle. No doubt they were shifting from a luminescent turquoise to a dark emerald green.

"Well," the captain said. "How very generous of you."

"What can I say? I'm in a good mood today and in a hurry."

The captain's eyebrows pulled together. "Can I offer you a drink?" He inched his way along the wall toward the dilapidated desk in the corner, pulled a bottle from the drawer, and then sat slowly, eyes locked on Votan.

"Thank you. No. But go ahead, rum will help dull your pain."

A large roach scampered across the floor and stopped near Votan's foot. Votan hissed, making the roach flinch. The tiny bug peered up at him with its beady, black eyes and then carefully backed away underneath the bed, not detaching its gaze until out of sight.

Pizarro lifted one scar-split brow, overpouring his tin mug while he watched the exchange. The rum trickled off the desk onto his dirty gray pants.

"Bugs." Votan shrugged again.

"All right, then." Pizarro nervously wiped the beads of golden liquid from his lap and grabbed for the cup. "What answers do you need?"

"The priests. Who sent you to kill them?"

Pizarro's cup slipped from his hand. "Um—I..."

Votan slammed his fist onto the desk, splintering the wood down the middle. He was done wasting time. "Tell me! Or next, I'll crack your skull." His voice sent shards of pain into the captain's ears.

"I don't know! She didn't tell us her name, but she wasn't normal. She was..."

"What?" Votan reached for a machete from the leather bundle on his back.

"Like you! I mean, her eyes."

Votan was startled. One of his own sisters? Dear gods, what next? First Petén's story of women being taken by one of his brothers and now this?

"She paid up front and promised us more money, a lot of money. She wants the jars," he said frantically. "She also told us to take out as many of those dreadlocked demons as we needed to make them confirm the location of the other jars, but they wouldn't talk."

Jars? While hiding in the hold, Votan had seen dark gray jars inside the crates but didn't think much of them. Humans often collected useless objects. His priority was finding out who'd been schooling the Maaskab in the art of manipulating dark energy.

"How did you trap and kill so many priests with only sixty men?"

"We stunned them with tear gas," Captain Pizarro replied. "They never saw us coming."

Ah, yes. Humans were busy inventing all sorts of new weapons and using them in their new war against that nasty Hitler man. Why couldn't Votan have been lucky enough to draw the short straw when that guy's name came up? But nooo. Instead, he got the malodorous, pesky, fanatical Maaskab to deal with.

But this journey led me to the child, Gabriela, he thought. *I cannot forget the importance of fate.*

"Did you at least kill them all?"

Pizarro stared at the floor. "Some got away."

"Dammit all to hell!" Votan screamed. It could take

him months to track them down, including the missing leader, and finish them off.

"What's in the jars?" Votan asked.

"I don't know." He panted. "She made us promise not to open them. She said the jars would kill us."

Idiots. What could possibly be inside that could do that? Killer bees?

"Okay." Votan resisted laughing. He didn't want the captain to think this was some kind of joke.

Next Pizarro told him about the map she'd given them that showed the location of dozens of jars scattered around the globe. They were told to find them and bring them back to Port Rota, Spain, where the woman was waiting.

"Aren't you the least bit concerned about your ship getting blown out of the water by a U-boat or bloody navy ship?"

Pizarro shook his head no. "She told us to stick to the routes she charted on the map. So far, so good."

Votan's mind was a jumble of frustration and anger. None of this made any sense. "What did the woman look like?"

"Flaming red hair, bright turquoise eyes, and a glare to make you wish you were never born. Like yours, actually."

Cimil? No. It simply cannot be. She had been behaving oddly lately, but then again, they all had. The world was gradually spinning out of control. There was so much uncontrolled violence everywhere now. It wasn't supposed to be that way. In fact, once he returned, there was to be a meeting to discuss what to do.

"I've told you everything I know." Pizarro stared at Votan. "So?"

"So, what?" Votan pulled out another machete.

"You're still going to kill me?" Pizarro said with arrogant disbelief. It almost made Votan like the man.

"Of course. You do not deserve the light inside you. You are a cold-blooded killer."

"I could say the same of you," Pizarro said.

"Cold-blooded? Me? Hardly. I'm the ultimate purveyor of justice, an executioner with a flawless track record and crystal clear conscience."

A startling knock at the door caused Votan to glance away. Before he blinked, the captain produced a knife and lunged.

The blade struck Votan's arm. "Hey! That hurt."

A squatty bald man pushed open the door and went slack-jawed at the sight of Votan. He quickly gathered himself and yelled for help as he turned up the stairs toward the deck.

Votan jerked the knife away from Pizarro and rubbed the spot, watching the wound close instantly. He slammed the door shut, turning toward Pizarro, who cowered in the corner of the room.

"What... what are you?"

"Ahhh, now that's more like it!" Votan said, shamelessly contented by the other man's terror. He paused for a moment, his thoughts vacillating between extracting the man's heart with a spoon or making him watch as he executed the crew.

Votan couldn't help but feel grumpy at the whole situation. *Eenie, meenie, miney, mo.* "Perhaps a spoon is a bit harsh—you did kill the Maaskab with admirable ruthlessness. I will be back to deal with you." Votan pointed at Pizarro. "Stay."

Votan marched up the stairs, gripping a razor-sharp machete in each hand. Several large men lunged as he emerged on deck. He could smell the darkness seeping from their pores. No. The Maaskab weren't the first these men had killed. That foul smell only came from a lifetime of dedicated, unrepentant violence. Votan turned into a whirlwind of slicing blades. Before he took one breath, five men lay gasping in a tidy heap, their viscous red blood forming a puddle.

The others stopped their advances, careful to step away from the syrupy crimson pool spreading at their feet. Their bearded faces, dirty and pale, transformed from angry to fearful.

Votan wiped the splatters of blood away from his face and smiled. Feeling a set of eyes on his back, Votan spun to find Pizarro standing behind him, shivering with repulsion at the pile of gory corpses.

The captain hitched up his pants as if rallying his bravery and ran his eyes over the faces of his terrified men. "I-I, uh," he stuttered, "th-th-think this demon has come for our souls, gentlemen, and I do not believe any of us are going to heaven."

"Right you are, my friend. No heaven for you. But I am no demon. I am a god. A very, very cruel one."

Nine

Present Day. Mexico

The bus driver pulled to the side of the highway. It was late afternoon, but with the heat, it felt like high noon in hell. *"Señorita, aquí estamos."*

"Here? You want me to get out here?" I questioned, having no idea where "here" was.

The last road sign said it was still several kilometers to the town of Bacalar and to its nearby lake, but which direction? I was one of those people who immediately lost their sense of direction if I wasn't driving, which, obviously, I wasn't. I'd encountered several mechanical difficulties with my rental Jeep, including not one, but two flat tires and an overheated engine.

Guy immediately accused me of being bad luck, and if I were a superstitious person, I would've believed the universe was trying to tell me something. But it wasn't. Because that would just be crazy talk.

Now, after ditching the Jeep, successfully hailing a third-class, chickens-ride-for-free bus bound for Bacalar—near the Belizean border—and five hours later, I was almost to Guy. This was it. But why weren't my legs moving me off the dang bus?

The other passengers, all locals, turned their heads to dish healthy portions of glare in my direction. The inconsiderate tourist was holding them up.

"*Aquí se puede esperar por un taxi*," said the driver, pointing to the side of the road.

A taxi? In the last hour, I hadn't seen more than two cars on the road.

The driver turned all the way around in his seat and gave me a nasty look. *"Señorita? Se sale, o me voy."*

"What are you waiting for? Get off the bus," Guy pushed.

I quickly glanced out the dust-coated windows, seeing nothing but a long stretch of highway ahead and dense foreboding jungle on either side of the road.

The portly driver revved the engine to make his point.

"I'm going. I'm going! Don't shut the door." The back of my white sticky-wet T-shirt made a *shhhlep* sound as I rose from my vinyl seat. As soon as I stepped out, peeling my sweat-soaked khaki shorts from my rear end, the doors of the silver bus screeched shut. A cloud of black exhaust engulfed me, and the bus rumbled away.

I prayed the driver was right about that taxi, because being dumped on a sad, lonely highway in the middle of the jungle sounded like the plot from a bad horror movie. Or at the very least, a paranormal Lifetime miniseries titled *Things Young Women Shouldn't Do When Traveling Alone in Mexico While Going to Meet a Mystery Being Who Was Trapped in a Mayan Ruin by Evil People; But She Can Hear Him in Her Head and Needs to Set Him Free Because He's Driving Her Batshit Crazy and Might Be the Only One Able to Help Her Uncover the Truth about Her Grandmother's Disappearance.*

"Yeah, let's hope he was right about that taxi."

I slung my red backpack over my shoulder and walked a few yards down the road to take cover from the sun under a large-leafed tree. I could start walking, I thought, but again, I wasn't sure where I was. I just knew where I wanted to be. My guidebook noted there was a lakeside eco resort called the Mayan Sun. It was ideal for bird-watchers and hikers to access the trails around the lake. Those trails also happened to reach several isolated ruins and a few ancient ceremonial pools. Guy and I agreed that would be the best way to pick up the trail leading to him.

I took one long, slow breath. The heat was suffocating, and the dank air smelled like a hot, moldy shower, reminding me that after a five-hour bus ride, I needed to find a bathroom. No way I'd go into that jungle to squat with the critters. No, señor.

"Frigging-a, Guy. You never told me how hot it is here." I moved my ponytail to the top of my head—ignoring how stupid I must look—pulled out my water bottle, splashed a little water in my hand, and ran it over my neck.

"Not where I am; it is cold in here."

"Oh, sorry." I felt my skin crawl. We hadn't spoken about his prison. Not because I didn't ask, but because he wouldn't tell me. He said it was too dreadful to describe, but according to him, I wouldn't have to go inside. I'd just have to stand in the doorway of the temple and recite the phrase he taught me in Mayan.

I shivered. There was still the chance I was heading straight for a trap, and everything he'd ever told me was a bunch of bull. *No turning back now, Emma,* I thought. *You've gone over every angle, and this is the only path with a potential exit. Get it over with.*

I pulled my guidebook from my pack and began thumbing through the pages. "Okay, so you said you're one kilometer northwest of the lake, right?"

"Yes. Yes. Do you see a taxi yet?" he asked.

"Impatient much?" I looked down the road, listening for the hum of a car, but heard nothing except the sound of bugs clicking in the jungle. It was downright creepy. "Guy? How does it feel?" I wondered if he'd say anything to tip his hand.

"Being trapped? It sucks, as you like to say. But you've kept me connected to the world. I'll admit, in your early years, Barney *and* Sesame Street *weren't very exciting. Then you started to grow, and I watched the world change through your eyes. You showed me a side of the world I never knew existed. And..."* His voice became low and pensive. *"I am awestruck by the woman you've become. So aware, strong willed. So pure hearted. It has been an amazing gift, Emma.* You *are an amazing gift."*

I didn't know what to say. Aside from being very direct and unexpected, it was, well, sweet. Quite possibly the nicest compliment anyone had ever given me. "Guy?"

Several moments ticked by before he answered, *"Yes?"*

"Why are we connected? Why me?"

He sighed. *"Because you are special."*

"How?"

"It is something in your DNA."

"What is it?"

"DNA? Well, it is a chain of nucleotides—"

"I know what DNA is, Guy. What makes mine different?"

"We are in a bit of hurry, and explaining could take hours."

"I think I'll head into the pueblo and get lunch." I crossed my arms.

"Fine. Your genes have something... extra."

"Extra? Like what?"

"That, my dear woman, is all I can tell you without going into a science lecture on quantum physics and genetics."

"What? You can't say something like that and leave me hanging."

"You would never believe me, no human would."

"Except you're telling me I'm not a regular human?"

"Even so."

How could he treat this so casually? My head was spinning, trying to put all the pieces together. "Does this have something to do with why you're trapped there?"

"No. I am here because I was tracking a group of men, evil men. They found out and set a trap for me."

"And you're sealed inside of some Mayan ruin in the middle of the jungle. Yes, I heard that part before. But how? How can a man be trapped without food or water for so many years? Are you dead? Am I going to find some scary ghost hovering over an old pile of bones?"

"No."

"Then how?"

"Because." He hesitated and then growled. *"You won't believe me, Emma."*

"Guy, you either trust me or you don't. And the fact I'm here—"

"Because I am not a man. Never have been. Never will be."

Gulp.

"What do you mean 'not a man'? Like, as in, you're a woman? Or"—the words stuck in my throat—"another species altogether?" I always knew he was something... different, but my rational mind steered clear of anything too outlandish. Hearing him say the words suddenly made everything real, made the frightfulness of the situation undeniable.

"Emma, please. No more. You have to trust me."

"Why? You're some...thing who was apparently trapped by evil men—"

"Dark priests, actually. Descendants from the Mayans," he interrupted nonchalantly. *"But they're more powerful and vicious than one might think."*

"Oh, great. Even better!" I threw up my hands. "And you were hunting them? But, of course, you won't tell me why. And I'm the only person who can hear or talk to you on the entire planet, so I have to rescue you. Oh, and you're not human, yet I'm supposed to trust you. Did I get that right, Guy?"

"Yes, you did. And see? I knew you would never believe me."

"You're right. I don't believe any of this."

My grandmother sometimes told stories of the existence of another world, but I thought she was just having fun. And I knew she was a New Age kind of person who believed in energies and spirits. I could swallow those concepts, sort of. But this? His admittance to not being human? What did that mean? Was he an alien? Demon? Monster?

I stood and began pacing under the tree, kicking small pebbles off the side of the road. I still had to go to him; there was no other way out. Doing nothing meant suffering to the point of insanity. Attempting to free him gave me a chance at a normal life and to find out what happened to my grandmother. Then there was that slightly pathetic little part of me that needed to see him, to know what fueled my obsession, even though I knew he couldn't be trusted. Sadly, all roads led to extremely bad places, like this jungle.

"Emma, what more can I do to convince you?"

"Nothing."

"Fine. You win. Leave me to rot for eternity."

"Not a chance because I'm not rotting with you." I opened my mouth to say something else, but then a tiny green dot appeared on the horizon. It was an actual taxi.

"Ha! See! I am good luck. Admit it." I clapped.

The chewed-up lime-green taxi slowed and pulled to the side. *"Buenas tardes, señor, voy a las cabañas Maya Sol,"* I said in my best *español* to the hot and tired-looking driver.

"What was that? Klingon? You really need to work on that accent of yours, Emma. It's embarrassing," Guy said.

Arrogant turd. "I guess I'll never be a master of the universe like you, Guy." I realized that was a stupid comeback. Maybe he *was* master of the universe. Anything could be possible at this point, and he did know a lot about history, science, and math. Let's not forget he spoke almost every language on the planet, according to him.

"Perdón señorita?" asked the driver.

"Oh. Um." I paused trying to think of the word. *"Nada."*

The taxi driver nodded and waited for me to load myself in. We drove for several minutes before the driver told me he passed down the highway every day at the same time to pick up passengers from the bus.

"More like dumb lucky," Guy jabbed at my earlier statement about being good luck.

"Jerk," I said, hoping the driver didn't understand English or wonder why I was talking to myself.

The car continued for several minutes, finally turning down a narrow dirt road that cut into the jungle. The tree branches swiped the sides of the open windows as we passed, flicking small pieces of bark and leaves at my face. After several bumpy minutes, the road opened up into a large, sunny clearing with an enormous thatched-roof structure at one end and several huts at the other.

I left the taxi and was immediately greeted by a sweet-looking old couple. Their faces were dark brown and leathery from the sun, with deep, soulful wrinkles around the edges of their eyes. The woman had long white hair pulled neatly back into a bun and wore a white dress with elaborately embroidered flowers. The man had straggly silver hair pushed under a worn straw hat. They were too cute, in a rustic sort of way.

The man reached out for my bag and spoke in a thick local accent. *"Hemos estado esperandote, mija."*

I did a double take. "Did you say you've been waiting for me? Your daughter?"

"He meant, we're glad you've come to stay with us... my dear," said the woman, plucking a leaf from my hair. "My name is Señora Rosa, and this is my husband Señor Arturo. Will you be staying long?"

"Tell her you're only staying one day, that you're an avid bird-watcher and heard about the toucans."

"I don't know exactly," I said, ignoring Guy. I hated when he barked orders. "I'm just passing through, doing a little sightseeing. Then I have to head back to Cancún to meet my friends," I lied.

They both gave me a peculiar look.

"You've taken quite a detour just to see our quiet corner of the state. What kind of sights are you here to see?" the woman asked.

"The lake, birds...you know, stuff like that. Maybe it'd be nice to see a few of those Mayan ruins I've read so much about."

"Emma, stick to the plan. You childish—"

"Oh, I see." She narrowed her eyes. Was she trying to size me up? "Well, most of those things are an hour or two hike from here, and it's much too late in the day to start out. So you'll have to wait until morning."

"Well, I'm really tight on time, and it looks like there are a few more hours of sunlight—"

"Don't argue with her. Just check into your cabaña *and go. You can still make it!"*

"You're probably right. I don't want to get lost in the dark." I agreed with Rosa to irritate Guy. In reality, I was just as anxious to get this over with as he was.

She nodded. "Good. I'll show you to your cabin." She turned to Arturo and mumbled something in a language I didn't recognize and then started toward a row of thatched-roof huts. "Dinner is at eight if you're hungry, and we sell good trail maps for your hike tomorrow, if you're interested. Oh, and do not forget to bring a walking stick with you."

"A walking stick? Is it a difficult hike?" I asked.

"No, for protection from snakes and other animals. We

even have jaguars, but if you see one, say a prayer. Don't bother with the stick."

Oh, goody. Jaguars.

"Here we are." She stopped in front of the last hut and handed me a small key.

The *cabaña* was simple—palm-frond roof, stone and mortar walls, a few random geckos playing "you can't see me"—but when I turned toward the other direction, I saw a breathtaking view of the water a few yards down the hill. It sparkled like a jewel composed of every luminescent shade of blue, green, and turquoise. The lush shoreline was peppered with wooden docks. "That's a lake, not the ocean?" I asked.

Rosa nodded.

I'd never seen anything like it before. It reminded me of that man's eyes from my dreams. "How come this place isn't infested with all-inclusive resorts?" I asked.

She chuckled. "Oh, the gods would never allow that."

Okaaay. "Thanks, Señora Rosa. I'll probably hop down to the lake for a quick swim and then hit the hay as soon as the sun goes down." I faked a yawn. "It's been a long, hot day, and I want to get started early."

Once again, she narrowed her eyes suspiciously. "Very well. There's a flashlight on the shelf next to the bed. The generator shuts off at nine."

I nodded, tucking a few loose, humidity-crazed curls behind my ear. "Thanks."

"*Hasta mañana*, my dear."

I flashed a polite smile, trying to hide my frayed nerves, and shut the door. "Is it just me, or is that lady a little strange?" I wondered.

"I don't want you to panic, but you need to get out of there."

I dropped my backpack on the cement floor and froze. "Why? What's wrong?" If I wasn't already sopping from head to toe, I would have started sweating; I knew in my bones he'd meant what he said. I felt his fear for me.

"What she said to her husband, it..."

"What?" I was moving quickly into panic mode.

"She said that he needed to go get the others, to tell them that you'd finally arrived."

"Oh, shit. Guy, right about now would be a good time to start talking."

"Emma, I don't know how they could possibly know you."

"Shit. Shit—"

"Stop swearing and get moving. Put your bathing suit on, and pretend you're going down to the lake. Wrap your wallet, map, and water bottle in your towel."

"Okay. Okay." I panted, emptying the contents of my backpack onto the hammock that stretched across the room. I threw off my drenched clothes, which felt fantastic, and put on my bikini. I rolled up a fresh T-shirt and shorts, along with the other items, in my towel. "Guy?"

"What?"

"I really have to pee."

"Oh, Christ, woman. You have the bladder of a guppy."

"It's been over five hours, which qualifies for camel. Can you hum? My iPod's out of juice."

"Now's not the time for modesty, Emma. They could be coming for you any minute!"

Oh, God. How had I gotten myself into this situation? If only I hadn't been so easily manipulated by Guy and that voice. That sexy, deep... *Ugh! Stop it.* "Fine. Did I ever tell you how much I hate you?"

Ten

1940. Pizarro's Ship. Gulf of Mexico

Votan moved the ten waist-high crates to the deck of the ship to make room for the crew in the hold below. He herded them in and locked the door, planning to cull out any souls worth salvaging later. Hell, who was he kidding? There weren't any. He was very much going to enjoy lighting up this dry rot–infested vessel. He'd have to row his way back in one of the dinghies, but it would be well worth it.

First, however, he wanted to learn more about these jars before they ended up on the bottom of the ocean. Why did Cimil want them? Clearly, she was knee-deep in this mess, but he couldn't understand why.

Was it possible she'd been responsible for teaching the Maaskab how to harness dark energy and block the gods from spying on them? But then, why hire the Spanish pirates to kill them? Maybe the Maaskab had turned on her? Maybe she was trying to cover her tracks? She knew Votan was on his way; everyone had been present when he was chosen for the mission.

Votan pried off the already loose top of the crate and lifted out the jar. He stalked around it, inspecting carefully, but saw nothing out of the ordinary.

Votan gripped the round, dark gray ceramic lid with both hands and slowly lifted, bracing for the worst. He wasn't afraid of dying—after all, he was immortal—but he still felt pain, especially when his human body got damaged.

He waited several moments, squinting. Nothing. Why would Cimil go through so much trouble for a silly, useless jar? Had she finally lost her marbles? Or perhaps there were scrolls inside. The jars could contain records, the priests' knowledge of dark energy.

By now, it was pitch-black outside, so he could not see inside the jar. He tilted it forward and reached his arm down the narrow neck. A burning sensation instantly began crawling up his fingertips. He swiftly extracted his hand, screaming in agony as his fingers turned to smoldering ash. The crippling pain continued up his arm, eating the flesh.

His knees buckled, and he watched in horror as the unbearable decay rapidly spread.

When Votan awoke, encased in cool, dark water, it was clear his body had been destroyed, his light sent back to the cenote. The same had happened once before, several centuries earlier when he'd accidentally fallen into a volcano. A long story.

This time, however, something was wrong, alarmingly wrong.

He struggled under the water as he felt the cenote rebuilding his physical form, particle by particle. He tried to break through to the surface, but something blocked him. The process of solidifying, of taking form, wasn't completing itself.

He pounded his fist with every ounce of energy he could muster, but the water held him tightly in its grasp. He looked beneath him and recited the phrase used to open the portal. Not even a flicker of light sparked. It, too, was sealed shut.

There was no going forward and no going back.

Eleven

Present Day. Bacalar, Mexico

I followed the dirt trail down to the lake and then skirted the pebble-strewn shoreline before cutting through the dark jungle, where I picked up the trail exactly where my map said it would be. I was fairly certain no one had followed me, but was that a good thing? If this turned out to be a trap, there'd be no one to save me.

The lonely silence was bone-chilling, especially since I'd expected to see the jungle teeming with life—monkeys, rodents, tarantulas, etc.—but not an animal soul was in sight. Nevertheless, I quickly armed myself with a large stick.

My footsteps made loud crunches as I walked for almost an hour over the leaf-covered path. The angle of the sun, now low in the sky, gave an ominous hue to the trees.

"Guy, no offense, but this is starting to seriously freak

me out, and I'm not sure this is worth the years of therapy I'm going to need."

"I was beginning to wonder how long it would take until the whining commenced."

"Not funny. And have you thought about what's going to happen to me after I get you out of there? That crazy old couple will be looking for me."

"I'll make sure you get home safely. I promise."

Wait. He'd admitted he wasn't human. Images flashed in my mind of me showing up to my parents' house with an Oompa Loompa or perhaps a green alien with glossy black eyes. He couldn't be that strange. Could he? "You're not going to beam me onto a spaceship, are you?"

He sighed. *"No, Emma, I'm not a space alien."*

"You're not into making chocolate by any chance, are you?"

"Emma, focus please."

"Fine, but can you tell me this—after I let you out, what'll happen?" Would I still be as obsessed with him? Would my own curse be broken?

"The people who did this to me should not be too far from here. I plan to find them and find out what they did to your grandmother. Then I plan to kill them."

My heart stopped. "What?"

"I think the people who are responsible for my situation may be involved."

"Why would they want her?" *Wait. Kill? He must mean it figuratively? I hope. Don't ask.*

"As I said earlier, the dark priests had a reputation for. . ." He paused for several moments. *"Killing women from this area. I don't know why, but I will find out."*

He was still hiding something. Was this why he was

afraid for me to come here? And hold the presses. Grandma was from the area where Guy was trapped? I knew she was born in Mexico, but I didn't know what town. Then again, Grandma never talked much about that part of her life. She'd said that after her parents died when she was five, she left Mexico to stay with her only living relatives in the United States. So what reason would she have to go back?

"You think she was near here when she disappeared?"

"Yes."

"But why?"

"I don't know, Emma. It's a hunch."

"But you said you knew her."

"Yes, many years ago, I was traveling through this area, through her village, and I met her. It was right before I was trapped."

Why had my grandmother returned to Mexico, then? Who was she seeing? I stopped in my tracks. The trees suddenly flooded with boisterously squawking birds. "What are those?"

"Toucans. Ignore them."

"Why are there so many all of a sudden?"

"I don't know, just go!"

I swatted at the ravenous bugs encircling my head.

"Not until you tell me!"

"What?"

"Are they going to come after me, too? Is this what you were protecting me from, Guy?"

"Toucans don't eat people, Emma."

I rolled my eyes. "You know what I meant."

He sighed. *"Maybe, but I will protect you."*

"What the hell have I gotten myself into?"

"Too late to turn back now. Move!"

Although he couldn't see, I nodded in agreement and continued marching. After several minutes, I ran my hand over my sweat-slicked neck. "How much farther?"

"About half a mile, my sweet, and you'll have to pick up the pace. It's getting dark."

It was odd to think we were now so close we were under the same sky. "I'm moving as fast as—holy crap." Standing twenty yards ahead was a boy about nine, dressed in all white cotton. His bright turquoise eyes glowed against his deep brown skin. He was staring; he seemed to be expecting me.

"My point exactly. Crap is not very fast."

"It's a boy," I whispered. "With funny-colored eyes."

"That's odd," he said, absurdly unalarmed.

"I thought you told me to run if I saw anyone?"

"I was thinking drug lords or bloodthirsty Mayan priests."

The boy stood motionless, his hands at his sides.

"What do you want me to do?"

"Ask him his name. What else?"

Yes, the obvious answer. "Hi, honey, what's your name?" I called out.

"In Spanish, Emma. We're in Mexico."

"Oh. Right. *Cómo se llama?*"

His lips twitched into a smile. "Chac," he answered and then ran.

"Well, that worked great. He's running away. What do I do now?"

"Follow him! Go."

"Wait! Come back." I followed as quickly as I could, but the branches and vines whipped my face and caught on my feet. "Why am I following him?"

"He will lead you to the cenote."

"Cenote?" *Oh no, bad, bad sign. This must be a trap because we are not heading to where he said.* "I thought I was going to a ruin."

"Just run, woman! The cenote is near the ruin."

"Why does he have turquoise eyes?" It couldn't be a coincidence that they looked just like the man's eyes from my dreams. Could it?

"Christ, Emma, put it on the goddamned question list."

I followed the boy for what seemed like an eternity, but my muscles burned, and finally I had to slow to a fast walk. "I... can't... Guy," I panted, trying to catch my breath. "The air... is way... too thick for any aerobic activities."

"I told you, you need to work out more."

"God. You... are... un... belie... vable," I choked out.

"You have no idea," he replied.

Helplessly doubled over, hands on my knees, I watched as Chac dissolved into the shadows of the thick vegetation. I realized I was no longer on any trail. I pivoted several times. Which direction now? Every damned tree and plant looked the same. Green, green, and more leafy green. It was like being trapped in a huge spinach salad.

"Some guide. Now I'm lost." I grabbed my aching sides.

"No, you're not lost. You are near, Emma. I can hear you."

My heart fell through my stomach, into my knees, and to the bottoms of my feet.

Holy Virgin of Guadalupe. This was it. All of the planning and years of dreaming. And believe me, I'd had every kind of dream imaginable. I had one where Guy turned out to be a gargoyle and swallowed me whole. Then there was the one where he was a poltergeist and pulled me into a giant cave where I was trapped for all eternity with evil spiders, although sometimes the spiders were clowns. I hated clowns. Too happy. That's not normal.

Then there was the dream where his body matched the voice, and I melted into a puddle on the ground and then evaporated.

I cautiously pushed through the next wall of vines and brush. The jungle opened up, and I saw it: the cenote.

The remaining light from the sky filtered through the trees, creating dancing speckles of light over the surface of the deep, dark green pool that sluggishly churned with rotting leaves and other floating debris.

I shuddered at the sight of it.

It was enormous—about fifty yards across with a steep one-story drop to the calm surface. I'd seen photos of cenotes; they were usually covered with tiny plants and vines along the sides. This one was different. It repelled the vegetation, and the limestone walls were perfectly smooth and coated with a thick green slime.

"Hello?" I called out. "Guy? Where are you? I don't see the ruin." *Please don't let this be a trap. Please.*

"Emma, sweetheart, this is the hard part, but I need you to trust me."

"Trust you?"

"Jump in the water."

"Whyyy?" I was frozen on the outside, but inside, a personal apocalypse was going down.

"I'm inside, Emma. You need to be in the water when you say the words."

My whole world inverted once more. Could this get any worse? All this time he'd been lying? "Wait. So there's no ruin? And now I'm supposed to still trust you and jump into the water?"

"Yes."

"No way! I'm not getting in there," I said. Then the reality, the horror of the situation hit me full force. In short, what the hell was I doing rummaging through the jungle in a foreign country, about to free a man whose origins were unknown to me? A man who'd emotionally tormented me in every way possible—a man I couldn't stop feeling I belonged to, yet needed to escape?

Yup. It's official. Emma Keane is insane.

"I'm sorry I lied, but you would've never come if I said the truth."

"Damn straight. Wait. Where...are...you?" I peered over the edge out of morbid curiosity but didn't see anyone inside. I gasped, covering my mouth. "No. No. No." This couldn't be right. It was the one scenario I'd never thought of. All along I believed he was real, that he was not a figment of my imagination. But I was wrong. Flat Earth Club wrong. There was no one there! Had I completely made him up in my mind?

I dropped to my knees and began to bawl uncontrollably. This was bad.

"Why are you crying? You can do this, Emma."

"Because there's no one there. You're not real. I'm a lunatic!"

"No, you're not! Listen to me—"

"Prove it!" I screamed between hysterical sobs. "Prove this isn't some psychotic episode." Had I just asked my imaginary friend to prove he wasn't imaginary? Well, that was silly.

"No, Emma! No. Let me out so I can explain! You're not crazy. I promise."

I ground my fists into the sides of my head. "Now would be a super-duper fucking good time to explain everything, my friend."

"You're being irrational. Let me out. We'll talk this through."

The lightbulb, albeit glaringly red and bursting with giant flames, flickered on. "Oh, I get it!" I screamed at the water. "You never intended to tell me anything! Shit! Why am I talking to a pond? Oh, God!"

I don't know if it was the lack of sleep, the fear, months of stress, or the fact I was talking to an empty sludge pond, but I was certain my head was about to grow rocket boosters and blast off my body.

I. Was. Losing it.

"No. You know what? I don't even care anymore. It doesn't fucking matter. Maybe I should just jump in and die! It would be better than living the rest of my life in a nut farm or with you."

"Emma, calm down. Someone's going to hear you."

"Who the hell is going to hear some crazy woman screaming in the middle of the goddamned jungle?" *Hiccup! Hiccup!* "Oh, great. Just what I needed to complete the moment."

"Emma, I—"

"No, screw you. I'm through with your mind games. Or . . . my mind games? I don't even know anymore!" *Hiccup!*

"Emma, I can prove I'm real, that you're not crazy. Jump in, and you'll see me."

What if I was right? Or what if this was how my grandmother died? Lured by some insane voice to the isolated Mexican jungle, where she was told to jump into a Mayan pool like this one. I envisioned her in my mind, babbling to herself and swatting away the mosquitoes while having this exact same conversation as she stood over the edge of this very same pool.

"No," I said aloud, contradicting my hysterical self. "She wasn't crazy. She was the sanest person I knew. And if she were here now, she'd say, 'Holy Virgin, child. Are you out of your crazy-loca head? Go home, this instant!' "

And, dammit, she'd be right!

"Okay. I'll jump, but on one condition. If you're real, I want you to disappear. I never want to hear your voice again. I don't even want to see you or know what you are. You disappearing from this moment forward will be my proof of my sanity. Got it?"

"You can't mean that. I have answers for you, Emma. I can help you find out what happened to your grandmother. I can make up for all of the pain I have caused you."

Impossible. A lifetime of therapy wouldn't heal the damage he'd done. The best I could hope for was to be able to fake normal.

"Yes, I can mean it." *If you're real, then I can't be whole with you in my life. I'll always be conflicted—wanting to be with you, wanting to be free of you,* I wanted to say but couldn't risk exposing myself for all the obvious reasons.

"For years, I've been your prisoner, and I don't know what I did to deserve it, but it ends today. I don't ever want to hear your voice again. I want you gone. Promise now or I won't take another step."

"Emma, I know I've pushed you, but we've come this far, and so much is riding on you."

"No. Promise now or I turn around."

"I must see you... safely back." There was a long, silent pause. *"I will not promise."*

"I'm out of here! And don't try talking to me anymore

because the first thing I'm doing is checking into the psych ward, where they're going to medicate me so heavily that I won't even hear myself. I bet Mexico has great drugs!"

"Emma, you have to—"

"No. You shut the hell up! You're not even real. You never were!"

"Emma, I'm sorry, but you've given me no other choice."

I felt something soft and furry rub against my leg. "Holy—" I stumbled back, falling to the ground.

Inches from my face, a giant black cat hissed, its bright green eyes boring a hole through my soul. I quickly eyed the water. It was looking much more inviting now; cats didn't like water, right? I slowly rose to my knees, holding out my hands. "Good kitty. Stay, kitty." I inched toward the edge of the cenote. It was a long way down, but maybe I could—

The cat took a small step forward and displayed its incisors.

"Never mind!" I jumped and hit the water sideways with a loud slap, plunging several feet under. My head broke through the surface, where I saw the jaguar leaning over the edge, preparing to pounce in after me. No doubt it wanted to play bobbing for humans.

My heart pounded furiously, and for a moment, I forgot all about my little insanity dilemma.

I looked for something to throw, a fallen branch or magic floating rock, but there were only my sneakers.

Treading water, I awkwardly used one foot to pry off a shoe and chucked it at the furry beast. It hissed as my shoe hit the concave wall of the cenote several feet below. "Dammit!" I slipped off the other and overthrew. "Christ. This can't be happening!" I cried. The cat was leaning over the edge; if it didn't jump, it might fall in anyway.

I did several 360s in the water, hoping to find something, anything, to throw. But there was nothing except...

Near the wall directly behind me, a miniature drum-shaped object bobbed in the water. I swam toward it and tried to hug it into my chest. The jar, ten inches wide and made of a dark gray ceramic material, rolled. I maneuvered the jar closer and got a firm grasp. In one adrenaline-charged motion, I kicked with all my strength and hurled it over my head at the cat.

I nailed it right on the head. "Yes!" The hairy monster scampered away, deciding I wasn't a worthy snack.

I felt utterly ecstatic for two glorious seconds until I realized I was still in hot water...or funky cenote water. Whichever.

I pivoted in the pool, sadly noticing there was no way to climb out. With its ten-foot-high inward sloping walls slick with algae, I was stuck. "Lord love a duck," I muttered. "Can this get any worse?"

Silence.

"Guy? Hello?" But there was no Guy, no humming, no toucans. It was beyond eerie. "Guy? Are you there? What do I do now? I'm stuck here."

Again, nothing but sweet silence. What a lovely way to end my life, except I wasn't ready to die yet.

Something tickled the back of my brain, something I was supposed to do. Something Guy had told me.

Yes! The phrase!

That fleeting thought lasted two more seconds until I realized that ready or not, I *was* going to die. The water began swirling violently like someone had triggered the autoflush—pulling me down. I flopped my arms wildly in the water, but it took less than a minute before it won.

Twelve

When Emma hit the water, Guy poised himself like a racehorse waiting to explode from the gate; the anticipation was almost unbearable. So many years he'd suffered inside the frigid, watery prison of the cenote, cut off from his world, tormented by the physical comforts—air and warmth—just outside his reach.

Worst of all, that torment had deeply scarred him, weakened him. He'd once been free of the smorgasbord of dysfunctional neediness that plagued humans. Now, he was filled with it: the need to kill his enemy, to punish them for hurting Gabriela; the need to see Emma with his own eyes and touch her, perhaps even beg her forgiveness for the pain he'd caused her.

The need to feel the fibers of his world tugging through his soul. Hell, he was even tormented by the need for food. He salivated, thinking about the delectable human treats he'd once prepared in the kitchen of his human home in Italy.

Weak. Weak. Weak, he thought, hoping that time would heal him and return him to his former, heartless deity self.

But he doubted that. Seriously doubted it. Sharing his life with a human female for twenty-two years had drastically, permanently changed him. Fate always took such pleasure in teaching humility, even to the gods.

Right now, for example. A minute had ticked by without incident. Emma had to have recited the phrase already. *Something must be wrong.* The portal remained closed.

But why? Emma had enough of their blood in her veins to open it. Well, so he thought. Could he have been wrong? He was never wrong. He'd had seven sufferable decades to think through every possible explanation of how the cenote's curse functioned, and only one made sense: the Maaskab had used dark energy to shift the chemistry of the water, thereby altering the charge of energy needed to complete the final step of his transformation into a tangible state.

Unable to solidify, he could not move beyond the watery confines of the cenote nor could he create the sound waves necessary to reopen the portal. And while humans didn't have the necessary physical makeup to open the portal, Emma had enough of their light that she should've been able to allow him out of there and not end up trapped herself.

Dammit! He'd been so sure this would work. Perhaps his mind had rotted with cursed water.

Guy screamed and struggled violently under the water, unable to make her hear him. His hand passed through her leg as if he were merely a ghost. They were both in the pool but in two different dimensions. Emma would die in this horrible place, and Guy would watch helplessly, the memory forever branded into his essence. He'd lose the only being in the world he felt truly connected to.

"Emma! Emma!" he screamed, pounding his fists on the underside of the water's surface. He knew his efforts were useless, but he couldn't stop trying.

"Emma, if you can hear me, I am sorry, sweetheart. I never meant for this to happen." He floated at her side, hoping by some miracle of the gods something would change, that she'd somehow sense him. *Useless.*

He watched with intensity while Emma removed her shoes and chucked them at the cat he'd summoned to herd her into the water.

The cat, a lovely female jaguar, had been his only other companion these last years. Birds, toucans especially, and monkeys came to visit every so often, but were more interested in viewing him like an exhibit at the zoo. But the cat, who could hear his words like all other animals, loved to talk about philosophy and the art of the hunt. She was quite entertaining. Luckily, she'd agreed to take part in his backup plan without eating Emma. He knew there was a solid chance Emma's nerves would get the best of her and she would, therefore, need coaxing to take the plunge. He'd been right about that, but not about anything else, and he hated himself for it.

He closed his eyes to send the animal away, but before he gave the instruction, Emma threw something else, and the cat yelped.

Suddenly, the water began to swirl into a liquid tornado, pulling him up. He flailed his arms and kicked with every ounce of anger and frustration stored in his humanlike body.

Breaking free from the water's grip, a scream of joy escaped his lips. Years of being unable to touch the air were suddenly over. His chest heaved. His lungs expanded. His skin tingled to life.

He gazed up at the sky and soaked in the now unmuted colors of the trees. *Green. So much lush, delightful, vivid green!*

"You did it!" He frantically twisted his body, treading water. "Emma? Dammit, woman. Where the hell are you?" She certainly hadn't left the cenote; the walls were too slick. But she no longer bobbed along the surface. Where could she be?

Then the realization struck him. He glanced down into the murky water and cringed. "Son of a bitch!"

Despite the seventy years of constant pain from being imprisoned underwater, he sucked in a lungful of air and dove into the watery abyss. His fingers stretched and clawed, plowing through darkness. All light faded from view as he ran one hand along the jagged wall of the pool as a guide.

Guy felt something fibrous and stringy. *Hair.*

He took hold of the tangled mass until he managed to get a solid grip on her waist. Guy battled his way through the water, kicking hard to reach the light above. As his head broke through the surface a second time, Guy took his first glimpse of Emma, and his heart nearly stopped. She was exactly as he'd imagined. Every lash. Every freckle. Even the tiny dip in the curve of her ear. She was . . . a goddess.

There will be time for admiring her later, he scolded himself.

He took hold of her wrist and then gave a powerful kick, managing to catch the ledge of the pool with his fingertips. She felt like a heavy rag doll, completely lifeless. He gently slid her up over the edge and laid her down in the dirt. Her face, though cold and blue, was exquisite. He pressed his lips to hers (and tried not to think of how he wanted to kill the men who'd looked at them when he could not), then gave her a breath, then another. Her body still had life pulsing inside, but it was fading fast.

"Don't go, Emma. Stay here!" he commanded, prying open her eyes with his fingers. "You can't leave. Do you hear me, woman!"

He breathed into her again before turning her to the side. Using his two hands like a vise, he pushed the water from her lungs and then gave her one more breath before she coughed violently. She cracked opened her eyes.

Dark green, so lovely.

She stared directly into his eyes, and something inside him ignited, froze, stopped, and started all at once. He simultaneously felt rage for having been deprived of the vision of her his entire existence and gratitude for finally having her in his arms. It was all wrong, yet so right. This was not good.

Was Emma the woman from Cimil's vision? Because she most certainly was the one from his, and he could easily see how such a beautiful, smart, feisty woman could emasculate him, as Cimil had put it.

Gods dammit. Yes, yes, throw in pining and groveling, too. I may never be able to let her go, now, he thought. *Then she will truly hate me.*

Long, wet strands of copper curls clung to her face. He cleared them away and gathered her fragile body in his arms. She smiled peacefully, and the most luscious wave of joy washed over him at his realization. They'd done it. She would live, and he was free.

"I'm back," he growled to the sky. "And there will be hell to pay for not coming to my aid. Do you hear me? Hell to pay!"

Thirteen

With his golden face beaming, the man smiled as he stroked my sopping wet hair and cradled me against his warm, smooth chest. "I love this dream," I said with a breathy voice, then stretched my arms above my head, gazing happily into the most striking set of luminescent, turquoise-green eyes I'd ever seen.

To boot, they belonged to a breathtaking, masculine face, a face one would expect to see on the cover of a magazine named something like *I'm Way Too Hot to Be Your Man* or *In Your Dreams, Honey.*

Oh yeah. Without a doubt, I'd topped myself this time. Sculpted cheekbones; thick, dark lashes; chiseled jaw; and lips so full they had to be meant for kissing or eating something really juicy. He was way hotter than the specimen of perfection from my last dream, and bonus, he didn't have that scary vibe. I reached up and ran my fingertip along the ridge of his hard-lined warrior nose.

"Emma, *what* in the name of the gods' creation are you doing?" he said scornfully. "We really don't have time for your immature little fantasies. We're in the middle of a crisis. Do you not remember?"

I blinked and slowly moved my eyes from side to side.

Jungle? I was in the jungle. And my clothes were wet. Come to think of it, for a dream, I didn't feel so hot. My lungs burned, my body felt like it'd been chewed up, and my head was throbbing. So aside from the perfect man with long, damp, wavy, black hair holding me in his arms, none of this felt like a dream. It felt—

"Holy Mother!" I pushed myself away and rolled into the dirt, pointing in disbelief. "Wha—you—you—?"

"Ah...so eloquent as always, my sweet. It is astounding you actually have a college degree, yet cannot find better words." He pushed himself up off the ground.

As he rose, my heart stopped, started, and then went into overdrive. His legs and spine straightened into a towering mass of unforgiving muscles. With shoulders like a lumberjack and thick, powerful thighs, I didn't know if I wanted to run away or climb him like a tree. He was utterly enormous. Jolly Green Giant enormous. Except, obviously, not green. He was a gorgeous, towering mass of golden-brown perfection.

No. Definitely not a cave-dwelling, wart-infested troll. Great. Just great. Now I knew I wasn't crazy—Guy was definitely real—but now I also knew I was in way over my head. He was gorgeous.

I stood in awe, my mouth gaping as my eyes attempted to register every rope of muscle, every capacious curve packed with power. Christ, he had to be at least seven feet tall.

"Six nine actually," he said, guessing my thoughts.

"This can't be possible," I whispered, my eyes continuing to dart up and down the length of his body, stopping right on the dark trail of hair that started just below his navel and continued down, down, down to his enormous beast of a—"Oh! You're naked." I turned sharply, but only to stop myself from reaching out to touch it. No man could be that...that...endowed. Wow. "This can't be happening." I covered my face.

"Emma." He moved behind me, placing his powerful hands on my shoulders. A jolt shivered its way through my body.

I was wrong about the vibe. Way wrong. This man, or whatever he was, radiated hazard. He should come equipped with a set of blinking lights or flares. He was—"Bad. Very, very, bad," I mumbled, pinching the bridge of my nose.

And pathetically, after everything that had happened, all I could think about was this naked, hard-bodied, glorious "man," who'd just permanently seared his image inside the storage compartments of my female DNA. All men, from this day forward, would have to survive a mental side-by-side comparison against him. They'd all lose.

Then a part of my brain, which was now marinating in a pool of whatever hormonal overload he'd triggered, tried to tell me something important. It wasn't ready to capitulate and hand over the keys to the Emma kingdom.

Ah...there it is. "Don't touch me!" I swiveled sharply, pushing his hands from my body, pointing one angry finger in his face. "I asked you for *one* simple thing! One!"

The corners of his delicious lips curled as he arrogantly flipped his dark, wet hair over his bronzed shoulder. "Exactly. You asked." He took one bold step forward, well within my personal-space bubble. Clearly, he was trying to intimidate me with his endless ripples and naked body. How sad. It was totally working, which made me even madder. Mostly at myself.

He bent down to meet my glare, his nose inches from mine. "But I didn't agree. Did I? In fact, my exact words were 'I. Will. Not. Promise.' Sharp emphasis given on the *not*, little girl."

Little girl? Little . . . He so had this coming. I lifted my knee, thrusting squarely in his groin. The almost-seven-foot brawny male fell to his knees cupping himself.

"I am not a little girl. Emphasis on the *not*. And you lied to me! Your eyes *are* turquoise." With the darkening sky, I couldn't see the exact color, but I saw they were in that ballpark. They were also beacons of heaven I wanted to lose myself in. The bastard.

Then I had an extremely poignant moment of lucidity. What was I thinking? This man, only he wasn't a man, could snap me like a twig with his pinkies. He looked like a walking, talking, killing machine, designed to tear me limb from limb . . .

Right after he makes hot, steamy love—bad hormones. Stop that, I scolded myself.

I hated him. He was the embodiment of a male pig. And best not forget that someone out there thought he was dangerous enough to imprison him in an ancient Mayan pool, and I had just freed him. Sure, he'd said they were bad, but that could have been a lie.

Understanding what an idiot I was, I did the only thing I could think of.

I ran.

The darkness had swallowed the jungle whole, leaving me scrambling over vine-covered branches, rocks, and anything else my bare feet could stub a toe on. I really missed my shoes. Damned kitty. I wasn't going to get far, but what other option was there? Guy was... he was... there were no words for him. But now I knew why he wanted me to see him first. Bastard likely thought he could switch from using his guilt trips and voice on me to flexing his biceps or swinging his gargantuan penis in my face.

Why the hell had I set him free in the first place? Oh yeah. Because he said he might be able to find out what happened to my grandmother, and he was slowly driving me insane. And, I'll admit, a tiny part of me wanted to know who or what he really was. Was he a demon? The ghost of gladiator past? I still had no clue.

For certain, he was more beautiful than any living creature should be, which was sufficiently dangerous on its own. Making matters infinitely more perilous, something about him overrode every rational thought in my mind while igniting every female impulse my body was capable of. He was concentrated with an abundance of raw male power, and his body turned me into a dimwitted moth, hell-bent on getting warm and cozy in that nice, bright flame.

I don't know how I found the power to pull away from him, from the need to wrap my legs around his waist, but I was glad I had. He wasn't good for me when he was just an alluring voice in my head, and he wasn't good for me now.

I stumbled my way through the darkness, praying to

God I was heading in the direction of a road or the lake. I reached out to clear away the next wall of terrifying, critter-infested vegetation, hoping I wouldn't haphazardly grope a snake, or worse, that enormous kitty, but instead found a washboard stomach.

"Emma, that wasn't very nice."

"Crap." I turned to run the other way, but he latched onto my shoulders and pulled me against his unnaturally hard body. A crippling vibration moved through me, paralyzing every inch of my body while simultaneously sending my lust into overdrive.

This was just not right. I wanted him to kiss me. Maybe more than kiss me. "Are you going to kill me?" If he didn't, I was about to stop breathing anyway—way too much man. Way too naked.

He let out a low, sinister chuckle—the one I knew all too well. "Kill? What's gotten into you? Although"—he released me and rubbed his groin while I stared wantonly at his thick, long shaft—"if you pull that stunt again, I might be forced to incapacitate you, and trust me, it'll hurt."

I tried to gauge his seriousness, even though it was too dark to see his expression clearly. But really, did I need to see more to know he meant business? For heaven's sake, his touch was like a stun gun. Okay. Time for a different tactic.

"Please," I whimpered. "Just let me go. You promised."

"My sweet, let's get one thing straight. You're *not* going anywhere until I've figured out why those people want you. Got it?"

His scent filled my lungs and pummeled my self-control. He smelled like rich, dark chocolate with a hint of smoky spice.

I nodded my head yes, looking down at my feet. I was so confused. So damned confused.

"Come." He grabbed my trembling hand.

"Where are you taking me?" I stumbled behind him as he yanked me along.

"To see Señora Rosa and her husband."

"What are you going to do to them?" I said.

"Ask them questions, what else?" he said casually.

"Ow!" I fell forward, grasping my badly stubbed toe.

Guy swiftly slung me over his shoulder like a sack of potatoes.

"Put me down," I hissed. "You're hurting me." The vibrations of his touch flowed through me once again, turning my body to mush and my nipples as hard as rocks. Did he have any clue what he was doing to me?

"You've got no shoes, Emma, and I somehow doubt those city girl feet of yours are accustomed to the jungle floor. It's also pitch-black, and there are poisonous creatures lurking," he said, gliding in between the trees, effortlessly ducking and weaving through the vines.

I wanted to snap something back, but what could I say? It figured he could see in the dark. All monsters could.

"I don't know what you are, but…I…still…hate…you."

He made a soft, low chuckle. "You don't hate me. That's impossible. Besides, I already saw your eyes, Emma, and I can feel the lust flowing through your body this very moment. You most definitely want me. It's almost too painful for me to stand."

There was nothing to say to that.

Fourteen

After walking twenty minutes—well, he walked while I tried not to pass out from his touch or from being carried upside down—we arrived back at the Maya Sol Eco resort. Guy gingerly sat me down on a small bench next to a large tree. "Stay there. If you try to get up—"

"What?" I gasped for air as he kneeled in front of me. "You'll kill me?"

He frowned and then swept the damp hair from my face. "No, my sweet, you'll fall over and hurt yourself. It takes a few minutes for the effect to wear off."

"Why does your touch do that?" I stared at the mammoth-sized man as he rose slowly. The light of the nearby cabins gave off a subtle glow, just enough to see the soft shadows of his perfect body. My eyes moved down his powerful lines, stopping right on his large—"Oh, God." I slammed my eyes shut. "Would you please put some clothes on and stop waving that thing in my face?"

"Right. Let's pretend you won't be begging for another peek later."

He was right. I wanted another look already. "Pig," I called out as he turned and stalked off into the night.

Guy reappeared several minutes later wearing some kind of a sarong, which he must have snagged from someone's laundry line. It might have looked silly on any other man, but he looked like a Greek god or some kind of ancient savage warrior. His hair had been tied back, and even in the dark, I could make out the powerful slope of muscles that ran down his neck and faded into the curve of his broad shoulders.

Yum. I hit my forehead in disgust. I so needed to get this guy out of my head. He had to be letting off some kind of debilitating, pheromone-based drug. *Man crack. Yes. Trashy, highly addictive man crack.* There was no other explanation.

"Stop your ogling, Emma," he whispered.

Oh, believe you me, I wanted to. I truly did, but I just couldn't help myself. "Ogling? Don't think so. Just admiring your skirt. Trying to explore your feminine side?"

Guy ignored my comment, grabbed my hand, which turned me to warm maple syrup, and started toward Rosa's cabin. He pressed his ear to their front door. I half expected he'd knock, but instead, he pushed open the door, pulled me inside, and slammed it shut.

The elderly couple was suspiciously unruffled by this sudden intrusion; they merely sat at their rustic wooden table, sipping red wine.

"Ah, Emma. I see you've returned and brought a friend," Rosa said dryly.

"Why aren't you jumping up and screaming? There's

a menacing, half-naked man in your living room, holding me prisoner." *And wreaking sexual havoc on my body.*

Guy frowned. "You're not a prisoner. I'm protecting you." He turned to Rosa. "What do you want with the girl?"

"Girl? You're the one wearing the skirt," I said.

Arturo rose from the table; a cold expression occupied his face. "I don't care what you are. You don't come into our home and bark orders."

I like these people a lot. Going on my Christmas card list.

Guy stalked across the room and then leaned over the old man. "I don't have time for posturing. Start talking or I'll break your wife's neck. Remember who you're talking to and that of all my brothers, I am by far the deadliest."

Did he just say he'd break that old woman's neck? Wait. He had brothers? Run away, Emma, before he drags you to a family reunion or kills you. Either one... bad. Very bad.

Arturo glanced at his wife, who looked irritated but not frightened. Why?

I suddenly felt like they were all part of a secret club I hadn't been invited to.

She gave him a quick nod and said, "We don't want anything with Emma, but the Maaskab do."

Guy's body went rigid. "What do they want with her?"

"Who're the Maaskab?" I asked. Of course, no one answered.

Rosa spoke, cutting off Arturo, who was about to answer. "All I can tell you is that my sister was sent away when she was five. The elders feared she'd be taken." She glared at Guy as she spoke. "Shortly after, the Maaskab began watching our village. They still do. And when we saw Emma, we recognized her immediately and called the other elders to decide what to do."

"Who's your sister?" I asked Rosa frantically.

Guy held up his index finger to silence me. I was about to give him a few choice words, but he cut me off with his powerful, lulling voice. "Are women still being taken"—he paused—"by *the man*?"

The man? Great. More secret code. This is getting ridiculous.

The couple shook their heads. "No," Rosa said. "But we hear the Maaskab have been taking young women from remote villages as far south as Nicaragua."

"Or they hunt anyone who carries the gene," Arturo added, looking directly at me. "Although I imagine there are few left."

I swallowed hard. "Will someone *please* explain what the hell is going on?" I screamed.

Rosa placed a warm hand on my arm. "Your grandmother, Gabriela, was born here. She was my older sister. The Maaskab want you because like her, you are a first-born female. You carry the bloodline of—"

"Enough!" Guy slammed his fist on the table.

Enough? I carried something in my blood. Guy's "bad people," who I assumed were the Maaskab, wanted me for some horrible reason. And this woman was apparently my missing grandmother's sister. I needed to know more.

"You have no right," I screamed. "I want to know what's going on!"

Arturo shook his finger at Guy. "You've brought the girl back here! The Maaskab probably spotted her already, and what they can't see, their wards will detect."

"She's in no danger from a few crazy priests as long as she's with me," said Guy.

"Humph!" huffed Rosa. "You arrogant fool. Where have you been, locked in a cave?"

"Actually, a cenote," I pointed out.

"Since 1940," added Guy.

I turned to him. "Since 1940? Why am I not surprised you left that detail out?" I did some quick math. That would mean he'd met my grandmother when she was a small child.

Guy flashed me an irritated look. "Sorry to have forgotten such an important detail, Princess Emma, but I was busy . . . being cursed underwater!"

"So? Why the hell does that matter?" I replied. "It's not like you were doing anything other than annoying the crap out of me . . ." My speech trailed off as my mind hit a wall. Had he really been trapped underwater for seventy-plus years? What the hell was he? And what the hell was going on? This couldn't be real. It just couldn't be. Maybe I was still back in New York, lying comatose in a hospital, and this was all a dream.

Yes! That's it! I'm dreaming!

Rosa shook her head. "The Maaskab have grown. There are thousands now, not including those who are loyal to them. The only thing keeping this girl safe was that they didn't know she existed. But now, that's likely over, and they'll track her."

"Sure. Why the hell not?" I threw my hands in the air. If I were going to hop on the Crazytown dream train, why not make it extra-super-scary?

"Haven't the *others* been trying to stop them?" Guy asked cryptically.

"Others?" Rosa questioned. "What others? We haven't seen any of you for sixty years, maybe longer."

Guy rubbed his stubble-covered chin. "I need to return," he said. "I have to find out what's happened to them." He stared down at me, his bright turquoise eyes narrowing in contemplation. "I need to put you somewhere safe. You can't stay here."

"This insane conversation is going nowhere. You people aren't interested in giving me any answers, so I see no point in sticking around, either. And since I'm pretty sure none of this is real anyway, I'll just be dreaming my way home now. If I'm not dreaming, then I'll need a good shrink. There are plenty in New York." I started for the door.

"Emma, this isn't a dream," he lowered his voice to that hypnotic, skull-penetrating tone. "And you cannot go home. If they know you're here, they'll follow you."

"Ha! See!" I pointed at his face. "That just proves this isn't real. Why would anyone want me? Me! I mean if anyone thinks this"—I waved my hand down the front of my body—"is anything worth stalking, they're off their frigging rockers."

A wicked little glow flickered in Guy's eyes, then faded. "I am not certain why they want you," he answered, "but the insane do not need a good reason, Emma. The Maaskab are known to kill for sport. They single-handedly brought down the entire Mayan civilization with their bloodlust."

"Thanks. I thought the Mayan alien abduction theory I'd read on the Internet sounded crazy. This makes waaay more sense." I really wished I could have come up with a better line 'cause I so needed to laugh.

"It's not a joke, Emma. These priests are deadly. They are the reason I came—to wipe them out once and for all. And now I've come to the conclusion they've been getting help from a traitor, one of my own. There's simply no other explanation for their power, their ability to use dark energy, including trapping me for seven decades."

A shiver ran down my spine. Something in the tone of his voice made me begin to doubt this dream theory. And my pounding heart sure felt authentic.

"Who's your 'own'?" I asked.

"There's only one solution now," he mumbled to himself and then turned to grab my shoulders. "Emma, I have to go."

Wasn't this ironic? He wanted to leave, and now I didn't want him to. "What are you going to do with me?"

"I'm going to call some people who will take you somewhere safe until I can come for you."

"How long?" I asked.

"I do not know, my sweet." He stared with his hypnotic turquoise eyes and then brushed my cheek. "But you have to promise you won't call anyone you know, and if anything happens, you can't ever come back here. You can't go home, either. Do you understand?"

"No." I felt the tears welling. All I wanted was normal. Friends, a great job, a boyfriend, maybe a little house with a vegetable garden. Normal.

What did I get? Bloodthirsty Mayan priests. A menacing, half-naked, skirt-wearing "man." And living on the run. Forever.

Guy's face contorted as he watched me begin to cry. "Emma, don't do that."

I punched him in the arm. "Don't. I can't help it!

You've so fucked up my life. I'm never going to forgive you, and—"

"What? I'm trying to save your life, woman."

"Then don't leave without telling me."

"Telling you what?"

"Everything! You owe me!" I felt the walls of my sanity crumbling.

"Yes, goddammit! I do owe you. And that means fulfilling my oath to keep you safe until this is over."

"Oath? Wait... You're not going to tell me, are you? You've been living in my head, torturing me with your enormous ego, driving me insane with your jealousy! Then I apparently risked my neck to free you. But what about the truth? You promised me answers! You said you'd help me find out what happened to my grandmother!"

Guy's eyes narrowed. "Right now, there are bigger issues at hand—your irritating, little human life being one of them."

I slapped him hard across the cheek.

A devilish smile crawled over his face. He chuckled. "And lucky for me, I don't answer to little girls, even ones who save me from cenotes. But if you do that again, I'll be happy to bend you over my knee and spank you."

Well. That did it. "Try it, Neanderthal. I'll give your man nuggets another taste of my knee!" I gave him an ineffective push.

Guy grabbed both my arms. A numbing shock rocketed down my spine, causing my knees to buckle.

Oops. I'd forgotten about that.

He lifted me by the shoulders into the air.

Then a grumble came from Rosa's throat. "Will you two stop this childish flirting?"

Flirting? On what planet was this considered flirting? Maybe on Guy's planet. He had called me human, implying that he was not?

He released me, and I shook off the buzzing. "The only place I'm going is away from this troll."

I turned toward the door to find Arturo blocking my way.

Astonishing.

"Seriously?" I scowled. "Now you're on his side? He threatened to snap your wife's neck two minutes ago."

"He doesn't frighten me." Arturo looked at Guy. "You are welcome to leave the half-breed with us. We have family a few hours north that can hide her there."

"Half-breed?" I felt the searing vibration of Guy standing directly behind me, but before I could turn, he'd grabbed my waist.

"I'm sorry, my sweet," he whispered in my ear. "But I made a vow, and the gods do not look kindly on oath breakers." A jolt of pain ran through my body.

Fifteen

Gazing affectionately at Emma's serene face, Guy cradled her limp, flushed body for several moments before concluding the shock was sufficient.

He didn't like using this power, especially given how in the past he'd miscalculated and killed a few unlucky people. Sure, they were deserving of death, and centuries had passed since his last slipup, but nevertheless, it was a crude and dangerous way to gain compliance.

Bloody foolish woman. Why does she never listen to me? Well, he had to do something to get her away from Bacalar.

He gently set Emma down on the dirt floor, propping her in the corner, planting a tiny kiss on her forehead before turning to the elderly couple who stared. To those who knew who and what he was, his presence was never too welcome. These two were descendants from Petén's village and, therefore, wary of his kind.

"I need a phone," he said.

Señor Arturo reached into his pocket and handed Guy a thin, flat, square device with glowing numbered buttons. Guy studied the object, scratching his thick black stubble with his free hand. The last phone he'd seen, with its large black handpiece and numbered rotary mechanism, was in 1940. Sure, during his time with Emma he heard about cell phones and other such modern devices, but that didn't mean he knew how to use them or what they looked like. For the first time ever, Guy felt old.

More weakness, he grumbled in his head.

"How do I use it?" He shoved the phone toward Rosa, who gave a quick demonstration.

Okay, one down. Next: computers, the Internet, and a Porsche 911 GT2. Emma had told him all about the new cars. He couldn't wait.

He dialed, hoping the ancient code might still be the phone number—it was. Speaking in Greek, he gave a few instructions to the person who'd answered and then hung up. "My Uchben have a team three hours from here by plane."

"The Uchben? They're coming here?" Arturo said nervously.

Guy nodded. "Who else?"

"It's that—we thought they were mythological creatures."

The Uchben were hardly in the same category as the Loch Ness Monster or Bigfoot, although they were practically their own race and their society was equally as old. But regardless of their archaic traditions or military-style governance, they were the human embodiment of cultural refinement and enlightenment. They had their own language, religion, schools, and judicial system.

The Uchben's original function was to serve as human muscle, an army of sorts, for the more complex and sometimes violent situations that popped up from time to time. But as their trustworthiness grew over the centuries, the Uchben's role expanded. Since the beginning of the last century, they invested and managed the gods' assets and acted as eyes and ears in the human world. Regardless of what humans believed, gods were not omnipresent, though they could view just about any one spot in the world at any given time.

So what was in it for the Uchben to be the gods' loyal servants? They possessed knowledge no other humans had; their people had inconceivable wealth; and most of all, they had powerful allies. Because of this, their loyalty was fierce, borderline fanatic.

Arturo flashed a glance at Emma's incapacitated body. "What are you going to do to the girl?"

He shrugged. "Protect her."

"Just like your brother protects the women he uses?"

It disturbed Guy beyond belief that anyone believed he'd hurt Emma. Not possible. It was worse, however, to think one of his own had been harming innocent women. But Guy was a product of his environment and the rules of his kind. Meaning he would never believe such an accusation without proof.

The small phone vibrated in Guy's hand. We wait outside. Your efforts will be rewarded flashed across the tiny screen.

These bastards tipped off the Maaskab? Rage filled every square inch of Guy's humanlike body. "Have I ever told you how much I enjoy punishing the wicked?"

Panic flashed in Arturo's eyes as he looked at the

phone. "You are all demons! We are only trying to survive. They have been curing Rosa with their magic."

Arturo's words suddenly clicked in Guy's head. The priests had *already* been healing Rosa. "You helped them get their hands on Gabriela, didn't you?"

Arturo nodded yes. No hint of remorse. No hint of shame. "The Maaskab named their price, so we tracked her down. Gabriela was eager to meet the dying sister she never knew she had. And when we made it clear to Gabriela that letting anyone know where she was going would put her family at risk, she didn't question."

Fury bolted through Guy. "So you let them kill her!" He wanted to hurt the man, to punish him slowly.

His age, instead of buying him leniency, only made him more culpable. Older humans should know better. "You lured her here, took advantage of her goodness. All to save your wicked wife. I hope the pain you're about to feel is wrenching your soul out by the roots, though it's not a fraction of what you deserve."

He wasn't only thinking about Gabriela's and Emma's suffering, he was speaking of his own. Those many months ago, when Gabriela went missing, Guy's world went from a lukewarm torture—the only light being Emma—to a living hell. He'd sensed the moment something had happened; her fear and despair vibrated through the earth and pooled in the pit of his stomach. He'd prayed night and day, pushing with his mind, pleading with his brothers and sisters to save her. They were, after all, compelled to protect her because of the bond. But he hadn't heard from them since he'd come through the portal some seventy years ago. Why? He didn't know. Perhaps they'd turned on him? Or they simply didn't know where he was?

In any case, he was helpless as Gabriela's anguished light slipped away, taking with it the piece of his own, which was bound to her. Emptiness took its place, an emptiness magnified by the pain he sensed from Emma, who carried Gabriela's light, her blood.

"And I suppose Emma was going to be just another payment to the Maaskab? Is that right, you vile little *human*? Tell me now, how many are outside?" Guy asked.

Arturo glanced at Rosa only for a moment. "Three, but more are coming. I hope they take your head and send you back to that cenote." He flashed another glance at Emma. "Stupid girl deserves to die for setting you free. You devil!"

Guy grabbed the man by the collar, lifted him to meet his eyes, and took one last look.

Gray. The light inside his eyes was gray, just one step above black. "I only regret not having time to make you truly suffer, old man."

And with that, Guy snapped Arturo's neck.

Rosa screamed and ran for the door. With lightning speed, he reached her and, with a small motion, snapped her neck, too. She slipped to the floor.

Guy quickly rifled through the small two-room *cabaña*, searching for weapons. He didn't plan to fight the Maaskab because it would be too easy for Emma to get in the way, but he'd be a fool to leave unarmed. Sadly, he only found a few large kitchen knives.

"Let's hope I'm faster than they are." He flung Emma over his shoulder and leaped from the side window.

Sixteen

I woke with a painful, sooty fog rolling through my head, close to what one might expect if they'd sipped tequila mixed with animal tranquilizers. With the accompanying blurriness and the buzzing in my head turned up ten notches, it took several minutes to realize I was somewhere far from the muggy jungles of Mexico.

The bed I lay in was a luxurious, fluffy oasis of down pillows and comforters. The open room was the size of a small country, decorated with red Saltillo tile floors, brightly colored pre-Hispanic paintings, and an entire wall of books. There was even a small sitting area with a soft brown leather couch and a coffee table displaying a stack of fashion magazines.

Where the heck was I? Where was Guy?

The haze of early daylight filtered through the sheer white curtains at the far side of the room. I sluggishly pushed myself from the bed and trudged over, pulling back the cloth panels to find two French doors that opened onto a balcony.

My heart stopped. *Lush, rolling green hills covered in miles of vines heavy with ripe grapes? My dream. This can't be right. I'm dead? Or in a coma again?*

I stepped onto the balcony. "No!" I covered my mouth.

It was the exact same villa, right down to the red-and-pink bougainvillea winding up and around the arched windows. But I wasn't dead. I could smell the earthiness of the vineyard in the wind. I could hear the distant hum of an airplane. This was real.

I stumbled back inside, massaging my temples. The buzzing was almost unbearable.

"Going somewhere?" A well-groomed, disturbingly handsome man, not older than thirty, stood near the doorway, arms folded. He was dressed in a tailored black suit and deep purple shirt. He wore his short black hair stylishly messy. His golden eyes sparkled with a vibrant energy against his light olive skin as he onced—no wait—twiced? Wow. Thriced me over.

I shuddered, realizing he wasn't your average six-foot-two pretty boy; he'd come accessorized with a lethal vibe. *Great. More dangerous men.*

Well, as the wise band Keane—loved their name, by the way—once said, "When your back's against the wall, that's when you show no fear at all."

"Where the hell am I?" I said in my best tough-girl tone.

"You are in Barolo," he said with an accent. Spanish, perhaps?

"Barolo?"

"Italy. You are in Italy." He didn't roll his eyes, but I could tell he sure wanted to.

"Who the hell are you?"

He made a slight bow of the head. "I am Tommaso. I've been asked to keep an eye on you during your stay."

I rubbed the back of my stiff neck. "Well, Tommaso, how long have I been in Barolo?"

"I brought you here last night on Mr. Santiago's private plane."

"Mr. Santiago? You mean Guy?"

He nodded.

Guy had a private plane. No clothes, but he had a plane. *Okay.* "And this place? Is it his?" I asked.

Again Tommaso nodded.

Christ. My coma heaven was Guy's Italian villa? Considering how much I hated him, that was a bit of a buzzkill. Now I'd have to come up with a whole new heaven when I died.

But how had I envisioned it so clearly? Even if he'd described it to me once without my remembering, it didn't make an ounce of logic that I'd dream with such precision. Maybe he and I were more deeply connected than I knew. "And that bastard didn't come with me, did he?"

He shook his head no.

"How about a note mentioning my grandmother?"

"No. Sorry."

It was official. I really, truly hated Guy. Aside from using my grandmother's disappearance to get me to free him, ruining my life, lying to me, and almost getting me killed in the cenote, he'd also messed with my hormones, told me I was in danger from some god-awful witch doctors, knocked me out, and then dumped me with Dr. Evil's handsome twin.

If I ever saw Guy again, I'd castrate the beast with a

dull knife or perhaps a spoon. I'd keep his villa. "Where the hell is he?"

Tommaso smiled, but in a condescending way. "He warned us that you'd ask too many questions."

"I was taken against my will to a foreign country and just lived through the most traumatic event of my life." The fog was still sticking in my head, and the humming of the other voices was louder than ever. I began feeling dizzy.

Tommaso rushed to my side frightfully fast, grabbing my arm to move me to the couch. "Let me help you."

His powerful grip pinched. I was about to yelp but decided a gasp was more appropriate; some pervert had dressed me in a flimsy, see-through white nightgown.

"Oh my God." I quickly sat and covered my chest with my arms. "Did you put me in this?"

"No," he said flatly. "The men got to draw straws. I lost."

I snapped my head up in his direction; he was hovering over me, arms crossed again. It was apparently easier to keep the huge stick up his ass that way.

"Don't worry. You were *well* supervised," he said with a suggestive edge.

Knife. Gun. Atomic bomb. These men were going to die a slow, painful death if I had anything to do with it.

"I want real clothes, and I'll dress myself."

Tommaso bowed his head. "I'll have some brought immediately. And if there's anything else you need—"

"A phone." My parents, who'd been expecting me to call, would have contacted the hotel by now and found out I hadn't checked in. They'd be beyond panicked, especially considering our history with disappearing family members.

"Sorry, no calls. Mr. Santiago said you'd only get yourself deeper in trouble."

Crap. Of all possible scenarios, this was the one I'd feared the most: becoming Guy's prisoner. I couldn't let this happen. I couldn't. I decided to throw a little girl-in-distress Tommaso's way to see if that got me anywhere.

"Me? Did he happen to mention all of the horrific, deceitful things he's done to me? Or how he's almost gotten me killed twice? Did he tell you that he's haunted me my entire life, nearly driving me insane?"

He reached inside his coat pocket and handed me a small pad of paper and a pen. "Anything else you need, write it down." He turned for the door.

Don't give up, Emma. "But my family, everyone's going to think the worst. After what they've been through with my grandmother, they have to know I'm okay."

He paused, gripping the doorknob. A tiny flicker of emotion moved across his face. "If you contact them, they won't have to think the worst. The Maaskab are very skilled at their spying and magic. They will trace the call, and you'll be as good as dead."

"That's not possible. Who would want to hurt me? I'm just some girl from Manhattan. That's it."

"You still don't get it, do you?" He flashed a glare.

"No, matter fact I don't. Even if Guy was right about the priests, how in the world would they know who I am or who my parents are? You guys brought me straight here, right? Not a soul knows I went to the cenote except for that little boy—who has no clue who I am—and . . ."

I stood up, now too confused and shocked to care about modesty. "Unless. Rosa and Arturo? You think they'd help the Maaskab?"

"I don't think, I know," he said.

"No way. That sweet old couple wouldn't do that."

Did I really know that for a fact? Just because Rosa was my beloved grandmother's sister didn't mean she cared about me. I had to believe the blood tie meant something. I had to. I was fully planning to talk to Rosa again and learn all I could about her and any other relatives I might have. There could be a whole slew of second aunts and uncles, even cousins. But why hadn't my grandma told me about them? Or my parents? Did they even know?

Then another thought sprang into my head.

Oh no...

"My parents? Are they okay? Are they safe?"

"You may rely on it," he said with that exotic accent.

"Sorry. I don't speak Magic Eight Ball."

"They are acting like parents who have a missing daughter. If you contact them, if they behave differently, the Maaskab will know and use them as leverage. They are hoping for this."

The situation was far worse than I imagined. How had my life taken such a sad little detour when I was supposed to be on the road to normal?

The tears began streaming down my face. "Why do they want me? Why won't anyone tell me what's going on?" I asked. Yes. Yes. More questions.

He opened the door and stepped out shaking his head. "I should have known getting the short straw wouldn't be worth it. You do ask too many questions."

Short straw? The lying, heartless thug.

An hour later, a nameless, cold-faced man returned with a tray of fresh pasta, warm bread, and a few bags of brand-new comfort clothes: yoga pants, tees, a few sports bras, and...pink thong underwear? Well, of course. Wouldn't want to be held prisoner *and* have panty lines.

I rifled through the bathroom and found tons of other supplies, like the most amazing conditioner, a fresh toothbrush, and a bottle of Flowerbomb. A five-star prison.

But despite the attention to detail and hundred-dollar hair products, I was still being held against my will, and I was very cranky. My parents would be worried sick, and for what? There had to be a way to let them know I was alive and warn them about the Maaskab without putting them in more danger.

Heck, I wasn't even sure I bought this whole Maaskab, evil-threat thing to begin with. When I thought about it, what did I really know? Only what Guy and his evil crony told me. Who the hell were they anyway? For all I knew, *they* could be the bad guys.

Seventeen

Captivity. Day Two

I snuggled deeper inside the covers, grimacing and trying to ignore the buzzing voices; once again the volume had been turned way up. I wished I could understand what they were saying.

My eyes fluttered open. "Christ! Where'd you come from?" Tommaso was lurking at my bedside, staring down. *Cree-py.*

I flicked on the bedside lamp. Needless to say, he looked way better than me. He was dressed in a pinstriped suit with a dark blue shirt that molded perfectly to his sturdy man-model frame. Sickening. Men really shouldn't be so pretty, especially when I had a bad case of bed-fro from tossing and turning for hours.

I sat up, grabbed a stretchy rubber band thing I'd found

in the bathroom, and wrangled my madness of curls into a ponytail.

"Always with the questions," he said, shaking his head.

I glanced down at my clothes just to be sure he hadn't played Barbie and redressed me in a pink negligee.

Relief. Still wearing my tee and yoga pants, and yes, pink thong. "Shove it. What do you want?"

"You looked distressed. Are you not feeling well?" he asked.

How could he . . . "What, you guys are watching me? Are there cameras in here?" My head swiveled around the room.

He didn't answer, so that meant yes.

"Darn it. I'd better not end up on YouTube," I warned. I pulled the white down comforter to my chin.

"Is something wrong with you?" he asked again. I assumed he meant my physical health, but he may have been questioning my overall sanity. In either case, I refused to answer him; I wasn't big on polite lies, so I wasn't going to say no. And whining seemed pointless, not to mention weak. But truthfully, I felt utterly sick; the buzzing from the other voices was getting louder, and I couldn't sleep.

"Do you have any Ambien around here?" I asked. If he said no, my next request would be for a dozen hot dogs or some other equally fattening comfort food.

"Are you not feeling well?" Tommaso asked again robotically.

"I'm the question asker, remember?"

"Mr. Santiago wants you well cared for. So if you're not feeling well, I will send for a doctor. There, not a question."

Was he for real? "Ambien. Please bring some. There, not a question," I said with a deep, mocking voice.

There was no hint of amusement on his face. Perhaps making fun of him wasn't the best tactic. I needed him in my camp so I could find out what was going on, and perhaps even get a message to my parents. If I were super-lucky, he'd help me strangle Guy when the time came.

I had to switch tactics again. "I can't sleep because I'm worried sick. My family thinks something awful's happened, and I'm their only daughter. Can you imagine how that feels for them when I've never been away for more than a few days—"

"This doesn't concern me," he interrupted coldly.

I saw it again, emotion undulating just below the surface. "Of course it concerns you," I argued. "You're the one keeping me here."

"Your family would feel much worse if you were dead. Do you have any idea of how much danger you're in?" he asked.

I shuffled out of bed and planted myself squarely in front of him. "How would I know? No one's telling me anything, even though this is my life. Shouldn't I decide if I want protection? What if I die like my grandmother? For what I don't know because you won't tell me, but then you've robbed me of my last chance to see or speak to the people I love. Don't I deserve to know what's going on, to make the choice?"

His golden eyes looked troubled. I was definitely getting to him. "Please." I grabbed his arm and stared into his eyes, hoping to dig an emotional grappling hook in him. "I don't want to die. I don't want my parents to die, but I'm not a child. Guy has no right to keep me in the dark like this or to keep me prisoner. Let me decide if I should take the risk and tell my parents I'm alive."

He let out a long sigh and ran both hands through his tousled hair. His strong jaw worked a bit, and then, as if someone had pushed a button reactivating robot mode, he went rigid.

He cleared his throat, tugged at one sleeve, and then straightened his square, silver cuff link. "I'm sorry—"

"Emma, my name is Emma Keane." I remembered that the first thing about connecting with people was getting them to remember your full name.

"Miss Keane, I understand everything you're saying, trust me. But I made a vow, and I don't intend to break it. There would be far greater consequences for everyone if I did."

"What sort of consequences? From Guy? Would he hurt you if you helped me?"

"Mr. Santiago would be one of many consequences, yes."

"What would he do? What is he?"

Tommaso's eyes flashed with amusement.

"What?" I asked.

"You really don't know, do you?" He made a small chuckle.

How rude. "Why do you keep asking me that? Obviously I don't. Thus the incessant string of questions pouring from my mouth with an irritated tone."

"Then you'll have to trust me. You don't ever want Mr. Santiago or any of his... associates on your bad side."

"Mr. Guy Santiago can kiss my ass."

Tommaso snickered. "Well, you can tell him when he arrives. I'm sure he'd oblige you since you look like his type."

Guy has a type? "How would you know?"

He flashed a dimpled smile, and I have to admit, even for a jerk, it was a really nice smile. "You're everyone's type, Emma."

Everyone? News to me. Maybe someone should send "everyone" a memo.

He added, "And I doubt he'd go through so much trouble keeping you safe if he didn't feel something for you."

"You're wrong. He's just got some twisted, overly protective father complex."

"Uh-huh," he said condescendingly.

"When will he be back anyway?" I sat back down on the bed, crossing my arms.

"Mr. Santiago doesn't share his schedule with anyone, but he calls once a day to check on you, so I'll advise him that you've asked."

"Please also tell him that he's an arrogant bastard. And if he doesn't get here soon to tell me what's going on, I'm going to kill him."

Tommaso's smile melted away. "Don't say that. Ever. People around here wouldn't take those words lightly."

"What people?"

He turned toward the door. "Trivia hour is over. I'll send the doctor."

Eighteen

"This is bad. Very, very bad. Emma will have my head." Grasping a silver flashlight, Guy sat with hunched shoulders on a boulder at the edge of a large underground cenote. This particular cave, hours from any roads, was the least used of all the portals and, sadly, had been his last hope.

His hands trembled as the gravity of the situation purged all arrogance from his body. In its place, an utterly new sensation flourished: vulnerability. He felt helpless. Him. Votan. One of the most powerful gods in existence shined the light on the surface of the water and didn't know what to do next.

"More weakness." Revolted, he shook his head.

After he'd escaped the Maaskab with a nearly comatose Emma, the Uchben arrived and met them near the old fort by the lake. They quickly debriefed, also confirming the absence of the other gods for nearly sixty years, all except for Cimil, who had been spotted multiple times in the area near several Maaskab strongholds up until about a decade ago.

Then the guards gave Guy the supplies, weapons, and clothes he'd requested, including one of those tiny, square phone devices, and left with Sleeping Beauty, along with his elaborate instructions for her care. Guy traveled back to his cenote—the one he'd been trapped in for seventy years—but when he immersed himself in the water, reciting the ancient words to open the portal, nothing happened. Not even a pathetic little flicker.

Perhaps the curse, which had imprisoned him, somehow sealed the passage to his world, too?

It wasn't until he traveled to another portal and yet another, finally arriving at this last cenote, that he realized they were all impassable. Hexed. He could smell the poisonous energy wafting from the surface. He didn't dare enter.

This can't be. It's impossible.

What disturbed him most was that had the other gods needed to, they could've easily created new portals. Of course, the creation had to be done from their realm, but it took little effort to tap into the River of Tlaloc, the underground channel of energy flowing in this part of the world. But that hadn't happened, and now a startling realization swept over him: those buzzing voices in Emma's head weren't random echoes or meaningless noise she picked up with her powerful, satellite dish–like mind. Those voices *were* the other gods. Trapped.

How had this happened? How was it possible Emma could hear them? Through her connection with him, perhaps? And why couldn't Emma understand them?

Hell, he didn't come close to understanding this connection with Emma. In fact, there was no explanation for their link in the first place; no one had ever inherited a bond. On the other hand, Payals were a completely new breed. There was much to learn.

For now, he had to focus his energy on more important things. "I will be back to free you, my friend," he said to the water, suspecting one of the gods was inside.

His thoughts immediately returned to Emma. She was the whiniest female to ever walk the planet, but she had the heart of a warrior like him. She would be beyond livid for being kidnapped, but she would go ballistic when he told her she'd have to return to Mexico and free the others—a task he couldn't do himself without risking his freedom once again. But Emma had been able to break the water's hold, break the curse. She was the only solution he could think of.

An uneasy pressure began building inside his chest. He didn't want to upset her. He also missed her. Twenty-two years he'd shared his existence with hers. The separation was almost too painful to stand.

"Wait. Am I actually afraid? Of facing a girl? And . . . I miss her?" he said aloud. "I need to get home. Being human is driving me insane."

Nineteen

Barolo, Italy

I stood inside the steaming hot shower, letting the powerful jets pulse at the back of my aching neck. Eyes closed, I began floating the silky bar of rose-scented soap over my body. It was the first time in days that my stomach felt calm. Heaven.

I turned to let the water work on the tightness at the side of my neck.

"Emma, you look irresistible in that outfit," said a melodic voice infused with evil.

I gasped and jumped back against the cold white tile. Standing in the shower, his bright turquoise eyes glowed with amusement, piercing through the dark shadows that hugged his body. "I've been waiting for the opportunity to speak to you again, but apparently, you don't REM sleep much these days."

Sleep? Of course. This is a dream! I let out a sigh of

relief, wondering if I could summon a delicious hot dog to the scene. I hadn't gotten my fix of junk food lately. Or maybe a Belgian chocolate. I closed my eyes but nothing happened. "Darn. Okay then, I'll settle for that black cloud going away."

He made a soft chuckle as the haze began to evaporate. "As you wish."

I stared at his face in shock; he looked almost exactly like Guy. His skin was a silky, smooth golden brown. His long black hair was wetted back, and his stomach rippled all the way down to the ropes of muscles that ran diagonally across the front of his hips, creating a V shape that ended right at his large, thick penis.

Well, hats off to my subconscious for the effort, but somehow, this vision didn't quite stack up to Guy. Don't get me wrong—this man was stunning. It was like comparing crème brûlée to that Belgian chocolate truffle I'd just tried to conjure. I'd blissfully gobble down either one, but only the chocolate made my eyes roll into the back of my head. Guy's skin had a hint more glow to it, and his hair was a bit longer. He was also a bit taller and undoubtedly much huskier. Then there was the size of his man gear—not that I'd measured, but it was pretty substantial. Guy was definitely a Belgian chocolate.

Well, dammit. Now, I officially double hated Guy. Not even my dream men could survive the side-by-side comparison. That just wasn't right.

"Done yet?" His black brows shrugged with amusement.

No, not really. "But since this is a dream and you're not real, can you wash my hair and shave my legs?"

"A dream, yes. But I'm as real as you are. This is the only way I can reach you."

Suddenly I wasn't liking my hot dream so much. Hoping to change the scenery, I squeezed my eyes shut and began thinking of shoes.

"Emma, that won't work," he said. This time the tone had changed. It reminded me of when Guy wanted something. "I need you to promise you won't run," he commanded.

My eyes widened. "Run?"

"I'm sending someone for you, several people, in fact. Their appearance will frighten you, but you mustn't run. If you do, bad things will happen to those you love."

Oh, pickle. That sounded ominous. What a crappy dream. I shut off the water and stepped out, wrapping a fluffy white towel around my body. "What kind of bad things?"

"You want to find out? Then run."

"Why do you want me?" I shoved a towel at him.

"You belong to me," he said coldly, letting the towel drop to the floor without even attempting to grab it.

A prickly shiver quaked through my body. I walked to the bedroom and looked around. Was there something I could use to wake myself up? I didn't like where this was going, and for some odd reason, I was beginning to believe him; this was more than a dream, and my self-preservation radar sensed it somehow. "Sorry, but I belong to no one." I picked up a pen from the nightstand. "Wake up. Wake up, dammit." I jabbed my palm.

Suddenly the man grabbed me and threw me to the bed, pinning me under him. "Promise or I'll have them kill you on the spot." His voice was like a low vibration ricocheting inside my head, leaving behind painful shards.

I squirmed beneath him. "I don't know what kind of sick game this is, but if you're real, then you should know I don't respond well to bullies."

He pushed his upper body up, pinning me with his bare hips. "I don't respond well to humans who don't do as they're told, but keep wiggling. I like it." His cock began to harden, and I realized only my towel stood between us.

My panic mode went into overdrive. I needed to buy time so I could wake up. I needed to divert his attention away from any possible thoughts of the unthinkable. This was not going to happen. No way. No how. Not even in a dream.

I relaxed my body and looked him in the eyes. "Is it true?"

"What?"

"That men who force women to have sex are also into animals, too? I read it in an article. Goats, sheep, you know. Should I *baaah* for you so that you feel more at home? *Baaahh.*"

Okay, that was a really weird thing to say. But it was all I could come up with, and the startled, disgusted look on his face said it all. I'd completely grossed him out.

His expression shifted to anger and then he back-handed me.

Dream or no dream, it stung like hell. Blind, stupid rage burst from inside me. "Fuck you." I tried to position my knee to kick him but was immobilized by his weight. "Tommaso! Tommaso!" I screamed. Maybe, by some miracle of God, I'd scream in real life.

"Shut up!" He gave me another brutal slap across my face; blood gushed from my nose. "If you run, I'll find you and kill you!" he screamed in my ear and began cutting off the air from my lungs with his powerful hands.

"I won't run," I croaked.

"Good girl," he said and then released me.

I curled into a ball and cupped my nose.

"Emma, what the hell? Are you okay?" Tommaso stood above me, a look of horror stretched across his face.

I took a deep breath, relieved to feel the air returning to my lungs. I ran my fingers over my nose and thankfully found it intact, but the painful residue of his strike lingered.

Hands down, that was the most god-awful nightmare I'd ever had. "Just a bad dream." *Hiccup!*

"You sounded like someone was strangling you." Tommaso sat at my side, his hands leapfrogging over the various parts of my body, inspecting for damage. Thankfully, I wore pajamas.

I sat up and buried my head in the oasis of his broad chest.

Reluctant at first, I felt him slip his arms around me and tighten. "What happened, Emma?"

I hiccuped for several moments while trying to wrangle a coherent thought. "I can't explain it."

"Can't? Or won't?" He stroked the back of my head, following the length of my curls.

"Both. But please, don't go. And don't let me go back to sleep."

When I opened my eyes, it was late morning, and I found myself alone. Tommaso had not only left me, but he'd let me go back to sleep. Figured. Why should I expect he'd do me any favors?

I looked over at the bathroom door, almost too afraid to enter. What if I was dreaming again and that monster was in there? And where was Guy? He'd said he'd never let anything bad happen, yet here I was. A mess. Afraid. Being held against my will. Worst of all, he didn't care about me enough to even send a letter or call me. Nothing. He just dumped me off in this place. He didn't care about me. Never did. And it hurt.

I cautiously tiptoed to the bathroom and flicked on a light; letting out a sigh of relief to see the room empty, I looked in the mirror. There were no marks of any kind, but my mind still felt the pain. My neck and nose were tender and sore, like I had invisible bruises.

I ran my hands over my face and then studied red veins in my bloodshot eyes. A tiny sparkle around my neck caught my eye. It was an intricate silver chain with a black stone amulet the size of a nickel. I stared at it for several moments.

"It's supposed to help with the nightmares," said a voice.

Tommaso was standing in the doorway wearing black jeans and a T-shirt that stretched snugly across his chest and the swells of his biceps. If that fabric could talk, it would say, "Lucky me." He wasn't the solid six-foot-nine mass of fiercely intimidating muscles like Guy, but he was a lean, well-built man. The kind any woman could appreciate. Except for me who was too busy hating men.

"I brought you breakfast." He held up a paper bag and gave it a shake. "Fresh bagel and cream cheese."

I didn't know what to say. He was actually letting his guard down, and I was feeling way too fried to resist any act of kindness, even from my captor's minion.

"Thank you," I mumbled.

"I thought it would be a nice day for a walk. Why don't you eat, take a shower, and I'll be back for you. Just knock on the door when you're ready."

"You're going to let me out of this room?" My mind started thinking about plans for escape.

"Don't get any ideas. This entire estate is gated with a hundred motion detectors and a small army of guards."

Oh, shoot. Maybe I could sneak a phone call in then.

"And the only outside lines are safe behind lock and key," he added.

What? Was he a mind reader? "I'm not planning anything. I'm just happy to get out of this room," I lied.

He raised one brow, clearly not believing me. Smart man. "Tommaso?"

"Question time?"

"How did you guess? What exactly are you?"

"Are you asking if I'm human?"

I nodded yes.

"I am," he replied.

"But you know Guy isn't, and that doesn't concern you?"

"No."

"Are there more like him?"

"Yes," he answered.

"Is his kind dangerous?"

"Lethal."

"Oh." How did I figure he'd say that?

"But," he added, "not lethal for you unless you give him a reason."

"You mean lethal but with a conscience?" I could almost grasp that concept—I'd seen *Lord of the Rings* five times. Viggo—yummy.

Tommaso nodded. "Something like that."

"And there's still no way you'll tell me who or what they are?" I asked.

"Not today."

"But why? I mean, why are you so afraid?"

"Emma, I am an Uchben. We're never afraid."

Oh, goody! A real piece of information. He's an Uchben! Wait . . . "What the heck is an Uchben?"

He smiled ever so slightly. "We are an ancient society of warriors who serve Mr. Santiago and his . . . associates."

"Are *you* dangerous?"

He smiled proudly and opened the door. "Absolutely."

My stomach did a flip. "But in a good kind of way, right?"

"Just knock." He turned and shut the door.

⁓

I got the feeling there was a lot more to Tommaso's story, some dissonance stirring just beneath the surface of his immaculate exterior. Whatever it was, however, was his problem. I had my own issues to deal with, like my family's safety and my life being smashed into sad little pieces. Not to mention, I didn't know where Guy was—but he and I had a huge score to settle—and my life wouldn't be fixable until I had answers. Maybe he was out hunting Maaskab. Maybe he'd already found a clue about my grandmother.

I scarfed the delicious, chewy bagel and took the world's fastest shower; I was still in shock from the nightmare. I threw on a pair of jeans—yes, another stupid thong, too—a T-shirt, and flip-flops. They hadn't brought me much in the way of outfit options, but I was more concerned about my life than I was fashion. A first.

I corralled my mass of unruly curls into a knot at the back of my head and then knocked hard on the door. A tall man with thin lips and dark brown eyes opened the door. "This way."

I followed him down the long hallway, passing several closed doors. I wondered if there were other "guests" staying at the villa.

We reached a set of Mexican, blue-and-white tiled stairs that descended into a great room. It had the same brownish-red Saltillo floors and two soft brown leather sofas, same as in my room. In addition, there was a fireplace large enough to park a car inside and a wall made entirely of floor-to-ceiling windows overlooking an expansive patio with a view of endless, rolling, vine-covered hills. I was half expecting to see a man with a snappy black beret painting outside. It was too gorgeous for words.

"Is this really Guy's?" I asked.

"Yes, he's had it for a very long time, though he rarely stays here especially recently, as you're aware. But the Uchben look after all of his assets and have full use of them. This villa is used for training, off-site meetings, and team-building events, you know."

"Oh, sure. Uchben. Team building. Uh-huh. I totally get that." Just like I got how Guy had this house all along and never told me. And a plane. What else had he hidden? Wait. I know. What species he was or what else he knew about my grandmother.

I followed the man outside through a set of double doors and down a tiny set of stone steps that led out to a rose garden. The sky was a spotless blue, and the morning sunlight felt amazing on my face.

"Wait here," he said.

"For what?" I wasn't nervous or afraid, but I wasn't exactly at ease.

"Tommaso. He'll be right here." The man left and went back toward the house. Funny, he wasn't the least bit concerned I'd run off. He probably guessed I wouldn't get far.

I sat down on a cement bench next to a rosebush with

pink blooms the size of salad plates. Gorgeous. Then there were the endless hills covered in vines. More gorgeous. The place just screamed relaxation. Did it really belong to Guy? Because he seemed more like the kind of man who'd enjoy a girl-on-girl mud fight or a relaxing day at the cockfights. Not a vineyard.

I closed my eyes and took a deep breath. The air smelled like potpourri—earth, roses, grapevines, and... Polo cologne?

I heard the low rumble of Tommaso's voice off in the distance. I stood and tiptoed over the path back toward the house. Just around the corner of the villa was Tommaso with his back to me, talking on a cell phone. In his other hand, he had leads with two horses. I was just about to say, *Uh-uh. No way, buddy. No horses for me*, but I realized he was talking about me.

He nodded. "Yes. She liked my gift; she's wearing it." He paused and listened. "He says he's on his way now." Another pause. "Yes. I'll be ready. Everything will be in place. Yes, sir."

He gave one last nod and flipped the phone shut.

"In place for what?" I said.

Startled, Tommaso jumped and dropped the leads. "Jeez. You scared me." He sighed.

"Ready for what?" I asked. "Is he coming?"

His eyes shifted briefly; then he bent to pick up the leads. "Yes, Mr. Santiago's on his way. My chief just wanted to be sure everything is prepared."

Finally. Guy was *sooo* going to get it when I saw him. First, I was going to jump on his head and tear out that long hair of his. Then I was going to visit his groin with my knee. Again.

"So what's this?" I looked at the two horses, one black and the other brown with a white neck.

"They are horses."

I crossed my arms. "Wow. You don't say?"

Tommaso's eyes softened a bit, and then he smiled. "They are the best way to see the entire estate."

"Oh, I get it. You're being nice to me because I cried and made you hug me this morning? Which, by the way, you were horrible at. Possibly the worst hug I've ever had," I said.

He gave a small laugh and shook his head. "No."

"Then why?" I waited, still crossing my arms. I had no reason to trust these people, and this sudden kindness only... well, confused me.

The man who'd led me outside appeared again, holding up a pair of black, knee-high leather boots. He handed them to Tommaso and went back to doing whatever the men did around here.

"Put them on," Tommaso instructed.

"Not until you answer me. I've never been on a horse. I was raised in Manhattan. So before I go and risk my neck sitting on top of that animal, I'd like to know why you're being so nice."

If I didn't know any better, I'd say he suddenly looked ashamed.

"Mr. Santiago called this morning, and I told him how poorly you were doing. He instructed me to make sure you had..."—he swallowed—"fun today. He wants you in a good mood when he gets here."

I was being buttered up for Guy's return? I felt deflated that Tommaso had been told to be kind to me. But why? Tommaso wasn't my friend. He was just some drop-dead gorgeous, lethal überassistant. So why the hell would I care if he was kind to me voluntarily or not?

"Well, tell Guy he can—"

"Let me guess—kiss your ass? You've got quite a mouth, you know that? Were you raised by truck drivers or sailors?"

"No, by doc—" Being suddenly reminded of how much I missed my parents sent me into an angry tailspin. They had no right to be keeping me away from them like this.

Tommaso's face turned from a glowing olive to a pallid taupe as he guessed my thoughts. "I'm sorry, Miss Keane. That was inappropriate. I shouldn't have reminded you." He squeezed my arm.

I jerked it away and turned back toward the house. "I'd rather rot in that room than fraternize with Guy's little whipping boy. You pathetic fuck."

I felt him stalking closely behind. I half hoped he'd say something to retaliate because I needed a good verbal sparring to throw off some tension. Years of living with Guy had made that my instinctual method of release since I wasn't allowed any others.

I marched up the stairs and made it to the door of my room before I felt a firm grasp on my shoulder. I reached for the handle, paused, but I didn't turn it. Somehow, I knew he was very, very angry. Could it be because I called him a "pathetic fuck"?

The air was charged with resentment, and the voices were buzzing in my head like a giant electromagnetic generator. Did they get louder when my adrenaline was turned up? I pushed the noise to the background and, instead, focused on the angry man behind me.

Several moments passed while we both teetered, waiting

for the other to pull the trigger, to push the other over that razor-sharp edge between control and turbulent, unchecked emotion.

Okay. I'll bite. Maybe literally. "Let go, loser—"

He spun me around, pressing me to the door with the weight of his solid body; his golden eyes flickered with anger. "I am many things, Miss Keane, but I'm no one's whipping boy. Best remember that." He pressed his lips hard to mine, and I froze in shock. His lips felt warm and soft and…

Wait! What's wrong with me? I'm letting another man bully me? I was a manhandle magnet, even in my sleep.

Well, dammit, I was getting pretty effing tired of being groped, kissed, flung, bossed, poked, and smacked. "My turn," I snarled.

I backhanded Tommaso clean across the face and punched him squarely in his washboard stomach. He let out a loud groan and doubled over, and when he did, I pushed him back with my foot. He fell over just as I slammed the door shut.

Damn, that felt good. But how had I done it? In any case, it felt earth-shattering! I threw my body against the door and pushed, bracing for him to burst into the room and finish the fight. I almost wanted him to because I was beginning to feel like I could actually kick his ass despite his extra hundred pounds of muscle and eleven inches of height. Okay, maybe I was feeling overly confident because of the adrenaline, but for the love of all things big and small, there's only so much one girl can take.

I waited and waited, until I heard the bolt slide on the opposite side of the door. I guess he didn't want a second helping of Emma.

Twenty

Later that afternoon, after coming off my girl power high, my mind began flooding with thoughts about my little predicament. They weren't good. They were filled with self-pity and worry. Pathetic. I needed a distraction, not to wallow. And since there was no television or computer, exploring the bookshelves was the only way to kill time.

Carefully standing on a small wooden step stool, I picked through each shelf. The place felt more like a hotel—well furnished, but impersonal—so it never occurred to me that these objects might be Guy's possessions.

There was the autobiography of Julius Caesar (someone had comically autographed the front page); the Mayan *Popol Vuh*; the complete works of Kurt Vonnegut; all the Russian classics—Tolstoy, Dostoyevsky, and Pushkin—in their native tongue; and the history of the world in four handwritten volumes. Strange. Very strange.

Then there were the cookbooks. Shelf after shelf, all dedicated exclusively to desserts.

My kind of books.

I plucked out the thickest one, a gray clothbound book over a hundred years old, and thumbed the pages.

Simply put, I didn't know what to make of it. Dozens of recipes had large, greasy fingerprints and notations in the margins: *add extra 1/8 cup butter, too crunchy; replace currants with raisins; bake for additional five minutes at 380.* But only the cookie recipes had them.

How odd. Were these Guy's notes? I tried to visualize him with his massive height; shoulders the width of a side-by-side refrigerator; smooth, deep golden skin; ripped muscles—which cascaded down his chest into what had to be the only ten-pack abs I'd ever seen; shiny, thick waves of long jet-black hair; his exquisitely sculpted cheekbones and angular jaw; fierce turquoise eyes; full, strong lips; and warrior hands the size of Frisbees. Oh, not to mention his extremely firm ass and sinfully large penis that promised to take a girl places only found in the steamiest corners of her sex-starved mind.

Ay yai yai. I fanned myself with my hand and imagined all that man, wearing nothing but a tiny, white apron, baking chocolate chip cookies. I mentally slapped myself. "Jeez, Emma. You've really lost it. Why don't you just cue the cheesy disco music while you're at it?"

A hard knock at the door pulled me away from fantasy land. Maybe it was Tommaso coming to give me an earful. Well, that was just fine because I had a few things to say myself. For starters, what was up with that caveman move? *Me angry. Me kiss you.* Yes, I sort of liked it—I'm sure only because no one ever kissed me, thanks to Guy—but that was beside the point. "Come in," I said loudly, still perched on my step stool.

The door slowly creaked opened and in stepped a petite redhead with bright turquoise eyes, wearing tight black leather pants, a pink angora sweater with a giant glittery heart across the chest, and black leather boots. Her flame-colored hair, straight and flat, was cut in a Cleopatra-style bob, and she wore several jeweled bobby pins at her temples. Stripper meets girl next door?

The room instantly flooded with her presence, and from the look on her determined face, she wasn't here for that double-chocolate fudge brownie recipe I was drooling over.

"Don't just stand there, girl," she whispered coldly, hanging halfway through the door. "Get your ass over here. Let's go." She snapped her fingers and pointed to the floor directly in front of her.

No, she did not just call me like a dog. Okay. Yes. Yes, she did. "Snapping only works if you rub my tummy and give me a treat. Did you bring one?"

The woman stared with confusion.

"Didn't think so," I said. "Why don't you try telling me who you are, then?" I hopped off the stool, considering the option of using it as a weapon.

The room, now stuffed with her ill-omened energy, closed in on me. It was then that I realized she was one of them. Guy's kind. I could feel it in my bones.

"I don't have time for this." She scowled. She walked over and stared at my face. We were exactly the same height. "Listen, you idiot. They'll be here any second, and if you don't want to end up having your throat slit, then you'd better hurry."

"Guy's goon squad?" I asked. "They want to kill me?"

"Not those tame little zookeepers, girl, the Maaskab." She started toward the door, motioning for me to follow.

I felt my skin crawl. I had no idea who this woman was, but she didn't give me warm fuzzies. For all I knew she was working for the Maaskab or for the monster in my dream. *Christ!* That's when I remembered. The monster had said someone was coming for me. How in the world could I have forgotten *that*? "Who the hell are you, and how do you know they're coming?" I asked.

"I've been watching and tracking them. Not so easy, either. They've been learning how to create portals and putting them all over the stupid planet. Not even I can do that! Dammit! Though they're not very good at it yet. The portals don't stay open long, so it makes them easier to corner when I pick them off. And by picking off, I mean I sometimes run them over with my Jeep and lob hand grenades."

She shrugged casually. "Good times." She froze and stared out the window as if listening to something, and then she snapped back to life. "But all play and no work makes me a lazy...fork? Dork?" She scratched her temple. "What word rhymes with work?"

I stared blankly trying to figure out what to do or how to answer. This lady was crazy. "Lurk?" I answered hesitantly, trying to buy a little time to think.

"No! There is no time for lurking," she barked. "There's an army surrounding this place as we speak, and I can't fight them all. We have to run."

Crazy was too kind. She was batshit crazy. "But this place is as secure as the White House—"

"Oh, for the love of gods. If my brother didn't need

you for his eternal happiness, and spiritual growth, and blah, blah, love, blah, blah . . ." She stormed across the room again. I wanted to back away, but there was nowhere for me to go; I was cornered by the wall and the bookshelf. The redhead grabbed my shoulder. I stared into her incensed eyes as they turned confused.

"What the— It's not working." She glared at her hands.

Then I realized she was trying to do that Vulcan grip thing on me like Guy had done. Not good. With my luck, I'd wake up in two days chained to a rock in a cave somewhere. No thanks.

I took advantage of her momentary distraction and slid several large books from the shelf. She let out a tiny curse as they hit her on the head. That split second was long enough for me to sidestep past her and bolt for the door.

"Tommaso!" I screamed as I made it out to the hall. I was almost to the staircase when she sacked me from behind. I landed palms down on the tiled floor.

"No, you don't, little girl," she scathed. "I'm turning up the volume, and you're coming with me." As her hands hit my ankles, a numbing sensation crawled up my legs. She'd apparently gotten her hands working again. Lucky me.

I twisted onto my back and wiggled one leg away, but the sensation was slowly traveling up my thigh. I couldn't kick her like she deserved. That felt very disappointing.

I heard the thunder of loud footsteps rolling through the great room below toward the bottom of the stairs. I knew it was Tommaso and the other men. "Now you're going to get it!" I growled.

The redhead looked down at me, raining irritation. "Yeah, right. I've been wishing for someone to give 'it' "—she made quotation marks in the air with her hands—"to me for hundreds of centuries, and suddenly you think those mongrels can do the job? The only thing I'm going to get is exiled by Votan for hurting his little Uchi-pets and not rescuing his demigoddess."

Was Votan Guy's real name? And did this crazy woman just say "hundreds of centuries"? And was she talking about sex? Who the hell was his demigoddess?

"Cimil, let Emma go," Tommaso ordered from the bottom of the stairs.

"I don't take orders from humans," Cimil hissed. She leaped over me, bounding down the stairs. The grunting and screaming started immediately. As for me, I could barely move. The numbness was spreading through my body like poison.

I managed to flop onto my stomach and drag my way to the top of the stairs, where a tiny *click, click, click* like a marble bouncing caught my attention. The amulet Tommaso gave me had come loose and was rolling down the stairs. I figured I'd retrieve it later if I was still alive, because down below, chaos ensued.

At least a dozen men were being tossed about the room like rag dolls. Oddly enough, they didn't appear to be attacking Cimil, but were instead defending themselves. Well, attempting to defend themselves. Very unsuccessfully. Within sixty seconds, Cimil was doubled over laughing in the center of the room that now looked like the Tasmanian devil hit it. Like the other men, Tommaso was lying on his back, holding his head between his hands.

Cimil crouched over Tommaso, gleefully took him by the neck, and then lifted him with one hand. She shook him violently. "You need to learn your manners. I am your master, too, and don't you ever forget it."

"I have no master!" he croaked, gasping and clawing at her hands.

Her face went stone cold. There was no doubt in my mind she'd kill him. In that moment, something powerful began percolating deep within the pit of my stomach. It was that same sensation I'd had earlier when Tommaso lost his temper and kissed me. It was as if a circuit had been tripped, activating some sort of dormant energy. The numbing pain began to dissipate from my body as my muscles vibrated and tingled with energy.

I swooped down the stairs and struck Cimil square in the face with my closed fist. She released Tommaso, who collapsed on the floor, and flew back.

"Are you okay?" I bent over him, unsure exactly what to do. He was still breathing but unconscious. From the corner of my eye, I saw Cimil rise from the floor. I braced myself for a fight, a fight I was sure I'd lose. But instead of charging after me, she was laughing again.

"You pack quite a punch, little girl," she said, rubbing her jaw. "That's a damned good thing because they're here." She swiveled her head, taking stock of the stunned men. "Get up, you idiots. You're not going to leave us ladies to fight them alone, are you? The gods only know what surprises they'll be bringing for us today." She plucked a gun from the floor.

The guards got up, shaking off their shock, and reached for their weapons.

Was I missing something? She'd just broken into Guy's house to kidnap me, beaten the pulp out of a dozen rather deadly looking men with her bare hands, almost broken Tommaso's neck, and now she was giving orders and they were listening? Not to mention, readying to fight at her side?

What planet were these people from?

Then I remembered I'd just nearly gotten myself killed defending one of my captors. What planet was I from? Everything felt so messed up.

Cimil took several steps toward me and then glanced down at an unconscious Tommaso. "Put him into the closet. He'll be out of the way there until this is over."

"What's going to happen?" It was a stupid question I know. Those Maaskab were coming for me and were apparently bad enough that Guy's men preferred to fight at this crazy redheaded demon's side than take them on alone. It felt like a competition for the evil, eviler, and evilest. I only hoped my team was the evilest. Go team?

I grabbed all two hundred plus pounds of Tommaso by the wrists and clumsily slid him across the tiled floor to a large closet on the far end of the room. I folded his legs and used the door to scoot the rest of him inside. He barely fit.

The other men, all brandishing various guns and swords, gathered around Cimil in a circle. She pointed at the individuals, giving each tactical instructions, before pivoting toward me. "You, girl. Come here."

She didn't snap this time. Smart move. But even if she had, I might have listened; I was scared out of my mind, and she seemed like the only person who knew what to do.

She flicked her thumb over the blade of a hunting knife in her hand, testing its edge. "The Maaskab are exceptionally unpredictable and dangerous. So stay behind us. Understand?" She handed me the knife handle first.

"I can take care of myself," I declared confidently and took the weapon. *And I'm not even hiccuping!*

"If they're dangerous for me, they're deadly for you. Don't argue, you naive child."

This lady was unbelievable. "Who *are* you?"

She paused and puckered her lips before answering. "Some call me Yum-Cimil, others Ah-Puch." She rolled her eyes and then planted one hand on her hip, tapping her fingers in a wave pattern. "I hate that name. Why couldn't they name me Kitty? Or Bubbles? Damned Mayans were so dismal. And anyone can see I'm a magnificent female. Not a man!" She shrugged. "Anyhooo, you can call me auntie, or...oh, oh, I know!" She jumped up and clapped. "Sister!"

"Huh?"

Her smile melted away into a frown. "Do you know how to braid hair? 'Cause if you don't, I'm not going to sleep over no matter how many strippers Ix Chel invites." She scowled.

Batshit crazy did not do her insanity justice. I'd have to come up with an entirely new definition for her. Later, of course. Because there was a pack of evil priests coming.

Suddenly, I couldn't think; the eleven voices filled my head with bloodcurdling screams. I resisted falling to my knees and instead cupped my hands over my ears, which did absolutely nothing, because the Maaskab *were* here.

As best I could, I pushed the howling voices to the back of my mind. I needed to focus if I wanted to survive.

With a potency ten times stronger than Cimil's, an unsettling static filled the air. The hairs on my neck stood up like porcupine quills and goose bumps covered my body, even in the unmentionable cracks—a new one for me. Then the house filled with a smell so vile I retched. "What the hell is that? Month-old roadkill?" I asked, pinching my nose.

Cimil didn't turn to face me as she spoke. "Try centuries

old. They never bathe—they believe it weakens their powers."

Yuck. I hoped I wasn't going to have to touch any of them. And centuries old? What the hell were they? Again, I found myself asking what planet I was on. Yes, my grandmother had spoken of other worlds, but was this what she meant? Why couldn't I get something more like Willy Wonka's candy playground with the chocolate river and gummy grass? This world sucked.

The few remaining unbroken lamps flickered off, and I felt the trickle of nervous sweat channeling down the small of my back. My eyes darted around the disheveled room, trying to anticipate which crevice these monsters would spring from.

There was the enormous fireplace behind me, the floor-to-ceiling windows occupying the entire left side of the room, and a small triangular half wall to my right where the stairs were. Directly in front, across the room, were two open doorways and the closet where Tommaso snoozed. My money was on the window, but Cimil and the men formed a line, facing the doorways.

"Here they come," one of the men whispered as the air in the room began whipping around us with a brutal chill.

Then the first of the Maaskab appeared.

"What...the..." I took several steps back. *Hiccup! Hiccup!*

The almost naked man—if he could be called a man—materialized like an apparition, occupying the entire space of the doorway.

His hair, made of long black ropes, hung to his waist and was caked with the same black mud that clung to his entire putrid-smelling body. Foul vapors rose from his powerful shoulders like steam from a subway manhole in winter. He was wearing nothing but a black animal-hide loincloth, and in each hand he held a machete covered with what looked like *dried blood*? His eyes were pits of black and crimson, and a dark shadow hugged the air around him as he stood, calmly surveying each person in the room.

It was as if he was trying to figure out who he'd kill first.

"Holy..." *Hiccup! Hiccup!*

His feral eyes sifted through the wall of guards and zeroed in on me. The room melted away as he held me in his rabid, bloodthirsty gaze. "We are here for the Payal," he said in a gravelly voice.

Payal?

"I might let you have her," Cimil said cheerfully. "But you'll have to tell me why you want her. She doesn't even braid hair."

The monster's empty gaze crawled toward Cimil. "There will be no negotiations. The Payal belongs to us. Give her to me, or I will kill you all."

Cimil chuckled. "Idiot. You can't kill me. I thought you'd bring a better game than that, Pigpen."

The man reached behind his waist and pulled out what looked like a ball of string threaded with tiny black beads. He held it to his mouth and whispered into it.

"Creepy. Just...creepy." I shuddered.

Then the large glass window shattered to our left, and all hell broke loose. The last thing I remember was the room filling with men who looked like death incarnate and that ball of string being tossed into the air.

Twenty-One

In a fit of rage and agonizing worry, Guy arrived at the villa, finding his worst fears had come true. None of the guards had been answering their phones for hours, and the gate had been left wide open with no one stationed at the entry post.

His black Hummer screeched up the hill toward the house. "No! No! *No!*" He leaped from the vehicle, engine still running, and bolted inside.

The entire villa looked like it had been tipped upside down, rolled down a mountain, and then worked over with a sledgehammer. Every pane of glass shattered. Every door unhinged. Every piece of furniture splintered. And there was a giant gaping hole in the roof above the kitchen.

"Emma!" He scrambled from room to room, searching for any sign of life. There were several dead Uchben lying in the corner draped over a pile of black meat—it was the remains of a Maaskab. "Emma!" he screamed again as he charged through the great room, up the stairs, leaping over several more decimated Maaskab bodies.

He arrived at her slightly ajar bedroom door, bracing for the worst. His heart sank at the thought of losing her, at having failed to protect her. Not once during his entire existence had he ever felt such a sense of loss for a human. But then again, she wasn't just any human; she was *his* feisty little Emma whom he now needed to free the other gods.

He pushed open the door and found something he didn't expect: there, embracing, were Emma and Tommaso. Her face was a picture of contentment; his face was nestled in her soft copper curls. They hadn't even heard him screaming.

She's mine! Blind rage encased him as he stormed over and grabbed the back of Tommaso's black T-shirt, dragging him off her. "I'll kill you! I'll bloody kill you!" he screamed at the disoriented Tommaso.

Emma grabbed Guy's thick arm, trying to tug Tommaso free from the enormous, seething warrior. "Let go."

Panting, Guy turned his head toward Emma, not relinquishing the gasping Tommaso who, though a large man himself, looked like a toy soldier in comparison. "He was supposed to protect you, not fuck you!"

"What the hell is your problem?" Emma screamed, pounding her fists into his upper arm. "He nearly died trying to save me from Cimil, and then those monsters showed up. And where the hell were you? You left me here to die! You fucking bastard! I hate you! The one time I needed you, and you weren't even here!"

He turned his anger toward the woman roaring in his

face and tossed Tommaso to the bed. "Why was he touching you like that?" he yelled.

"So what if he did?" Emma shouted. "You don't own me!"

"Yes, I do! You're mine. And don't ever forget it!" The muscles palpitated in his neck.

"Are you delusional? I'm *not* your damned property! And did you happen to notice there's a pile of dead bodies outside? Or that we're the only two people left standing? That's because he saved me, not fucked me, you stupid, arrogant control freak." She poked him with one defiant finger in the chest and glared with her dark green eyes.

Despite his almost seven feet in height and 270 pounds of pure muscle, he began to feel small. He felt petty and foolish, too. Dammit. Sometimes, he just plain sucked.

Guy's harsh expression softened. He pulled Emma to him and pressed his lips to hers. She squirmed under his immobilizing grasp, but he didn't feel like letting her go. Not quite yet. He desperately needed to kiss her. He'd carried the constant thought of doing so ever since he'd pulled her from the cenote. He'd thought about doing other things to her, too, but now wasn't the time to attempt that impossible mountain. It was, however, time to savor the taste of her lips, the feel of her body pressed to his. Gods, she was delicious. He felt himself beginning to harden for her.

She stopped struggling and her body relaxed, but she still didn't kiss him back. Was it because of the odd sensation she experienced with his touch? He was more or less managing to suppress the flow of energy pulsing through him.

Curious, he opened his eyes and found Emma preparing

to detonate. He released her and then proceeded to adjust his growing bulge.

She briefly fixated on his groin while he did this and then snapped, "Un-effing-believable. Are you done yet?"

Guy flashed a wicked smile and arched one brow. "For now, my little meerkat."

He turned away from her to find Tommaso's livid face. Yes. Something was clearly going on between these two. The room was filled with jealous energy and not all his, either.

Guy stared at the man, sizing him up. Tommaso's commander—or chief as the Uchben called him—had said that Tommaso was one of the smartest, strongest, and most loyal guards. But Guy wanted to punch him right in that pretty-boy face of his. "Tommaso, my apologies for accosting you. As long as you keep your hands off my Emma, I promise it won't happen again."

Emma huffed and rolled her eyes. "The day I'm yours is the day you stop being an arrogant, self-centered tyrant. Never gonna happen."

Guy snickered. "A challenge. I like those." He turned to Tommaso, who was now sitting on the edge of the bed rubbing his red, battered neck. "Tell me what happened here."

Tommaso began debriefing Guy in detail, explaining how he'd blacked out after Emma clocked Cimil. When he woke up in the closet, he'd heard grunts and screams as the Uchben fought the Maaskab outside. He cracked open the door, finding Emma entangled in a net, falling unconscious. The Maaskab were too distracted to notice as Tommaso dragged her inside.

After several minutes, the house fell silent. When he emerged, there was no sign of Cimil, and the remaining live Uchben were gone, too.

"I unwrapped Emma," Tommaso explained, "but when she came around, she started screaming at the sight of all the blood. So I took her up here to the only untouched room in the house." His tone turned apologetic. "I swear, I was only comforting her and maybe using her to keep from falling over. Cimil's touch packs quite a punch."

"Not really," Emma said.

"What do you mean?" Guy asked.

"When she came into my room," Emma elaborated, "she tried to do that thing to me. You know, that feels like being hit with a stun gun. But nothing."

Guy was fascinated. "It didn't affect you?"

Emma shook her head no. "Not at first. Cimil looked kind of confused. Anyhow, she did it again later, and it hurt a little, but she didn't knock me out. In fact, I was able to shake it off completely after a minute."

Guy stared at her, unable to make any conclusion.

"Guy?" Emma asked. "What am I? Please, you have to tell me."

"I'll give you two a minute." Tommaso stood to leave.

"Tommaso," Guy said with a short tone. "Gather up weapons and supplies. We're leaving for the compound. The Maaskab will be back soon for their unclaimed prize." Guy looked at Emma—the prize.

Tommaso nodded and left the room without glancing once at Emma, but she watched him until he was out of view.

Irritated by this, Guy pointed to the couch. "Sit."

"Thanks, but I'd rather stand."

Of course she would. She hated being given orders. *Stubborn little thing.* "I meant, please, sit down. I have much to say, my sweet."

Twenty-Two

I was dumbfounded as I searched in Guy's stunningly surreal turquoise eyes for an answer. Why had he kissed me? Of all the absurd things. We were surrounded by death, yet he felt that was the appropriate response? That and acting like a dog fighting over a bone? Obviously, I was the bone in this analogy.

In any case, his reaction to the hug was *so* over the top. Tommaso was preventing me from wandering off the edge of sanity. I didn't know how to deal with the shock of what I'd just seen: flying knives; guns going off; and blood, limbs, and other body parts exploding. All the while, I was tangled in that net, which drained the energy from my body. I was alert, still able to move, yet I could barely gather the strength to scratch my nose. I just lay there like a wet noodle until Tommaso pulled me into the closet.

The next thing I remembered was Tommaso holding

me, acting as psychiatric glue—the extra-strong, anti-meltdown kind—and then Guy showed up armed to the hilt, doing his impression of Conan the Barbarian on steroids. Only he wore a dark gray commando outfit, complete with black leather boots; military-style cargo pants; and a dark gray, tight-fitting T-shirt. Could Guy possibly look more menacing at a worse time? It was the exact opposite of what I needed to see—more ferocious, scary men. He even smelled angry, like a smoldering, chocolaty campfire. Okay, maybe that part wasn't so bad. Who doesn't love dessert-scented campfires?

Sadly, I should have been infuriated by his misogynist display of insensitivity, but now, now he was staring at me with his docile eyes, his straight, black brows pulled worriedly together. And what was I thinking of all ludicrous things? That I'd die if he never kissed me again. That it had felt way too good being pressed up against his hard body and that I still wanted to climb it like a giant tree. Maybe live there like a little monkey in his branches.

But I couldn't allow myself to go there. No. Not when he'd sent me away like he had. Not when he'd left me in this place to face not just one boogeyman, but fifty. Where had he been when I needed him? Because I did. Need him, that is. And I knew that now because I felt afraid for my life and being with Guy somehow made it all better. Like being home.

"Well? Tell me?" I prodded.

"I—uh." He turned away and scratched the black stubble on his jaw.

"Oh, for crying out loud." I sat on the edge of the leather couch and waited as Guy paced the length of the room.

"I suppose I owe you an explanation—"

"Or two," I added.

He frowned. "But we don't have much time."

"Exactly, so spit it out."

"Right. You remember the story I used to tell you about the evil king who stole the young maidens, and then they were rescued by a handsome prince?"

I nodded, fearing where this conversation was heading.

"Well," he continued, "that's not this story."

"Shocker."

He pulled the thick black braid from the back of his head and began nervously twiddling the end. "This one doesn't have a happy ending for everyone, and the good guys might not win. And the young maidens—well, most of them die."

Was he really doing this to me? Trying to explain this lethal situation in the context of a fairy tale? "Enough! Just tell me!" I exploded. "What the ever-loving hell is going on? Who the hell are you? And where the hell were you?"

He continued pacing, shaking his head from side to side. "Hell, woman, that's a lot of hells."

I stood up and blocked him from pacing, planting my palms flat on his chest. I quickly snapped them away. Touching him felt like shoving a fork into an electrical socket.

"Yes," I answered with a forced calm. "And you can go there if you don't start giving me answers."

"The bond." His eyes drifted off momentarily. "You and I are bonded."

"Bonded? What the hell does that even mean?"

"It means... we are connected and you are under my protection," he elaborated.

For once, I finally understood why I needed protection, but…

"How did we get 'bonded'?" I asked.

"You inherited it from your grandmother. We met in 1940. She was just a child, but I bound myself to her light. It followed her lineage."

"Why her?"

"She was special. I thought it would protect her. It didn't."

This conversation was moving way slower than I liked, and my patience was over. "Guy, Votan—whoever you are…"

Anger flickered across his face. "Who gave you my old name?"

Cimil had said it, but what was the big deal? "Are we playing Rumpelstiltskin now? Unbelievable! Just tell me! What are you?"

He said, "Over the centuries, humans believed us to be many things: fae, aliens, even vampires—since we can't really die—but you'd call us… gods."

"Sorry. Did you just say 'gods'?"

He nodded stiffly.

I was definitely going to need to take up drinking. "Like as in Zeus or Aphrodite?"

"More like Erebus and Gaia—the original primordial gods. But we were never overthrown from Mount Olympus, because there isn't one, and there are only fourteen of us. We also don't marry or have children, except for—"

"Sorry, but did you say 'gods'?" The idea wasn't digesting. Not at all.

"We are very similar to you. We are made of energy; however, our control of it is highly evolved. Like comparing a tree monkey to an ape, if that makes it easier to understand."

Was I supposed to be the tree monkey? Well, at least he was the ape. Fitting. "Where did you come from?"

"We don't know. One day we were here, conscious of our existence but without any knowledge or recollection of how. As best as we can determine, we're simply another species, another miracle of life as you are. Only we're far superior in terms of our abilities, our domain is energy based, and we never die."

"Huh?"

"Emma, I can't give you a physics lesson right now."

"Huh?" My mind reverted back to the word *god.*

He released a slow breath. "Everything in its most basic form is energy. Energy is our realm, our plane of existence. As a result, we can manipulate and use it in many ways. We don't even require bodies to live; although to do our jobs here, we sometimes have to take a form."

"Jobs?" They had jobs. Why wasn't there anyone else here to listen to this?

"Like any living creature, we have a purpose," he elaborated. "Ours happens to be keeping humans from destroying themselves. You wouldn't believe how tiresome it is. Your species is very determined. But even if I wanted something different for myself, I couldn't have it. My role is hardwired, instinctual."

I walked across the room and ran my hands through my wild curls. His answers had only led to more questions. To top it off, my relationship with Guy, which we were now calling a "bond" of all ridiculous things, felt more horrifying, like I was handcuffed to another planet I didn't want to live on.

There was a light knock at the door. "Mr. Santiago, I've got everything loaded in the truck."

"Thank you, Tommaso. We'll be right there," Guy said without shifting his eyes from my face.

I watched Tommaso disappear again. "Why does he call you Mr. Santiago?"

"We have many names, more than I can remember sometimes. And I grew tired of Votan so I changed it."

"Why?" I asked. It seemed odd that after—well, I don't know how many years actually—he'd stop using one name and adopt a new one.

"We have to go now."

He wasn't going to answer? Fine. I had other more important questions. "You didn't finish." I grabbed his arm to stop him from leaving. A jolt of energy shot through the bones in my hand. "What am I?"

"Your grandmother's father is my brother. So I suppose that makes you a little like us, just diluted. However, unlike the gods, your form appears to be entirely anchored in the physical world as a normal human. We remain separate species."

"Brother?" *Holy crap!* That would make Guy . . .

"He is not my brother in the human sense; we have no parents, nor are we related. But he is a fellow deity, my brethren."

"Oh" was all I could manage to say as my mind digested. I knew when Arturo called me a half-breed, it wasn't going to be something good. But I kind of expected I was part gypsy or clairvoyant, maybe even a circus freak. But part supernatural deity? What the heck did that even mean? The only references I had were from Greek mythology or Latin American anthropology.

Could I spit fire?

Or grow corn?

Wait. Come to think of it, nothing good ever happened to the gods in those stories. They were always at war, killing each other, getting broken into a million pieces to become constellations...

All right. This was no time to crumble. I'd been through an excessive amount of terrifying events. So I needed to take that scary little rabbit hole I was about to dive down, fold it neatly in the palm of my hand, and shove it into my pocket—my Can't Deal with This Now Pocket. Later, when I could process this, I'd take that journey. Until then, I needed to remain focused on more important matters.

Just get the answers, Emma, so you can survive this, so you can save your family. "So why did that Scab call me a Payal?" I asked.

"Scab?"

"My new nickname for the witch doctors. Maaskab—Scab."

Guy looked utterly indifferent. "Payal is Mayan for 'key.' I suppose it likens to calling you 'the missing link.' Or perhaps it means the link between gods and humans. In any case, we don't know why they want you."

Missing link? "Whatever the reason, it can't be good," I said.

He nodded. "The Uchben report that the priests have been busy for decades, taking females. We're guessing these women are other Payals or were my brother's mates. And since there are accounts of the priests killing women, we can only guess the Scabs are trying to eliminate our offspring."

"Why? It's not like we've done anything wrong."

"Emma, Maaskab are evil. They're our enemy. The last thing they want is more of us roaming the planet, even demigoddesses like you."

I shook my head; this was all too surreal. "That's why they wanted my grandmother?"

Guy frowned and grabbed my hand. "Come, Emma. We should leave before they return. I need to get you somewhere safe."

It was a simple gesture, holding my hand, but I couldn't help but marvel at it. For so long, he'd been just a voice. Now he was real, standing next to me, touching me. A real, live god no less.

"Hey, you're touching me. Why doesn't it hurt?"

"When I focus and keep my emotions in check, I can turn the volume down." He smiled wickedly. "Or way up if you don't behave."

Great. He had built-in Emma control.

"What happens when you lose focus?" I asked.

He raised one brow as if he was considering saying something flirty and then decided against it. Good choice. I wasn't in a laughing mood. "When the energy inside me flows at full strength, I could kill a human by touching them with my pinkie."

Imagine the obituary on that one: Emma Keane killed by a deadly pinkie. How embarrassing. Then I wondered, with so much power, why did he even need the Uchben? Maybe he just liked having people to boss around. Yeah, that was it.

"I don't get it, Guy. You had the Uchben at your beck and call all these years. Why didn't you just have me go to them to spring you from the cenote?"

"The thought had entered my mind as a last resort only. When I realized there'd be no rescue from the other gods, I began to groom you for the task—to toughen you up mentally. I also needed to wait until you were old enough. I thought, perhaps in another year or two, you'd be ready. Then you pulled that stunt with the cab, and I had no choice."

"I didn't pull anything," I reminded him. "But you shouldn't have waited so long. You weren't the only one suffering."

He nodded and stared at the floor. "I had no idea that when I bound myself to Gabriela, I'd be condemning you to a life with me." He suddenly sounded angry, or perhaps resentful. "You didn't even exist yet, but had I known, I would have made another choice."

He was lying again. I could feel it. "And if I hadn't been able to jar you loose from the cenote, what then?" I asked.

"I would have sent you to the Uchben. Though I'm not sure they could have helped. They don't have our blood and therefore can't open the portal. Second, they're not as strong as you or I, not even your precious Tommaso."

He was still jealous? Figured.

Then I began digesting what he said. He thought I was stronger than someone like Tommaso? I'd punched him as hard as I could in his stomach, and all that did was double him over. On the other hand, I clocked Cimil, and she flew, I mean she really, really flew across that room. Incredible, but it didn't make any sense.

"Honestly," he continued, "I was afraid what might happen if you came into contact with the Uchben. They might've thought you were a Maaskab spy if you just showed up claiming to be my spokesperson. They aren't the most trusting people, they're warriors."

"So? What would they have done?" I asked.

"They would have tortured you to find out the truth," he said flatly.

Torture? His backup plan was me getting tortured? Nice.

Midway down the hall, he abruptly stopped. I collided with his broad back. It was like a brick wall. "What? What's wrong?" I asked, expecting him to say the Scabs were back.

"I forgot something important."

He darted back into the room, reemerging moments later with that enormous, ancient cookbook. "Let's go."

Cookie-baking gods? I couldn't wrap my mind around the fact that he was a deity; he seemed so…human. A flawed, quirky, sexy-as-hell human.

"Pocket. Put it in your Can't Deal with This Now Pocket, Emma," I said.

Twenty-Three

Guy was relieved to find Tommaso had removed the bodies from the stairs and placed sheets over the others lying about the house.

Emma was strong; after all she had the blood of the gods flowing in her veins. And to her credit, she'd taken the news of her heritage rather well. But ultimately she was still human. Bound to the physical world. Fragile. Mortal.

And more news was still coming—the gods were trapped, and Emma was the only one who could free them. Guy had to pace himself, allow her time to process. Human minds were hardy and adaptable if you didn't overload them. The poor female was close to the precipice.

So when the time comes, he wondered, *how will she take the news?*

Would she agree to help or buckle under the pressure? He himself barely tolerated the situation. This coming from someone who'd seen it all over the course of tens of thousands of years: the rise and fall of dozens of empires, entire civilizations disappearing, some into the ocean—countless genocides and wars, the birth of gangster rap and reality television.

Yes. Terrible, awful things.

But nothing was as awful as one of his own helping the Maaskab and teaching them to manipulate dark energy, which was the only explanation. How else could the priests have learned? The power was known only to the gods and sparingly used. When fully employed, the energy didn't simply hover like an acid rain cloud; it rippled and circled the globe until it ran out of steam. The last time they'd employed it—ironically, when fighting the Maaskab—the ripples completed ten entire earthly laps. Plagues and famine broke out on every continent. Civil unrest was rampant for hundreds of years.

Guy and the other gods worked around the clock for decades to prevent humans from annihilation, but they were never able to undo the damage completely. That would've required traveling back in time, something they dared never do. Even primitive humans understood Newton's law of motion: for every action, there's an equal and opposite reaction. And this law particularly applied to altering past events. Move one piece, all of the other pieces must shift to accommodate. Chaos. The outcome, they'd determined, would be unstoppable chaos.

It made what the Maaskab were up to look like child's play, although it clearly was not. They'd developed honest-to-gods weapons: the jar that could devour flesh, which he'd experienced firsthand on Pizarro's ship. And adding an extra-clever diabolical twist—which he had to envy the deviousness of—the priests had figured out how to modify the chemistry of the cenotes, creating an almost inescapable deity prison. So even if they somehow managed to free the other gods, the cenotes were now useless as portals. The gods were trapped in the human world inside humanlike bodies, making them much less powerful.

Damned brilliant, evil bastards.

Gods, he wished he could return to his dimension. He'd produce a massive earthquake right now and open a fiery fissure in the earth's crust directly beneath the Maaskab. He should have done that in the first place long ago and lived with the civilian causalities. If he had, Gabriela might still be alive, and he might not have the constant pang of emptiness in his chest.

But he wasn't going to undo the past, and he wasn't going anywhere, not until he released the others—well, until Emma released the others since he couldn't go in that water—repaired the portals, and located Cimil.

Cimil, he thought. *Is it truly she who turned on us?*

He sincerely hoped he was wrong, but the evidence was mounting. She knew about the jars and never told anyone. She even hired Pizarro to steal them. Yes, she must have been working with the Maaskab. Then they turned on her? Then she tried to cover her tracks?

The pieces weren't fitting. Why work with the Maaskab in the first place? Nothing could incite Cimil to make such a horrible act of treason. And if they'd turned on her, then why would she hire mortals like Pizarro to kill the Maaskab instead of doing it herself? From Emma's account, Cimil had no issues fighting the dark priests. She'd even fled with several Uchben in pursuit, so he guessed. She always did enjoy a good chase.

So what was that goddess up to? Guy's head pounded with frustration. Not a damned piece of the puzzle fit!

He glanced at Emma, who was sitting behind him in the Hummer, staring out the window across the fields of vines. Tommaso was driving, and for once, Guy was pleased to let someone else be in control. He wasn't quite used to handling these machines yet; although he'd enjoyed the rush of going fast during the drive to the villa, he took out a few fences and one very innocent bush. But for the moment, Emma's safety was paramount.

He noticed her expression was solemn, as if she were playing with the same impossible puzzle in her mind. Her reddish-blonde curls shimmered in the sunlight that poured through the open window at her side. Her hair was tied back with some kind of a tiny pink string, and she wore a plain gray sweatshirt and jeans. He couldn't help but bask in her beauty. So many years he'd wondered what she looked like, and now he wished he'd never laid eyes on her.

He also simultaneously thanked the heavens for gracing him with such a vision. Somehow she'd be the death of him, he just knew it. She was just too desirable like Cimil had prophesied. She stole his heart and his balls because he'd do anything for her. Anything. Including letting her go when the time came.

He shook the thought from his mind. "Emma, do you know how the Maaskab and Cimil found you?" he asked, thinking she most likely snuck a call to her parents, allowing her location to be traced.

Tommaso lifted his eyes from the road to glance nervously at Emma in the mirror.

She didn't answer at first, instead fidgeting with her

sleeve. "I don't know. Like I told you, Cimil didn't say anything other than she'd been tracking the Scabs, and she realized they were en route to your villa."

Guy frowned. He wasn't in the mood for more renegade puzzle pieces. "Did she say where she'd come from or why she was following them?"

Emma shook her head and then looked down at her palms. Again she was about to speak, but stopped. Guy had been observing human behavior for what seemed like an eternity, but it didn't take a deity to figure out she was hiding something.

He twisted his large body to face Emma directly. "You called your parents, didn't you?" He'd used his command voice on her, so he knew she'd have no choice but to tell him. No one could resist it.

"No, I didn't. But I'm not talking about this now." Her eyes darted to Tommaso.

What? She'd ignored his voice? How? And the blasted woman wanted to avoid disclosing something in front of Tommaso? She cared about what he thought?

She's mine. A spark of jealousy ignited. He hated that she was giving weight to this other man's opinion of her and that she'd just seemingly ignored his command.

Well then, let him think less of her. Tommaso wasn't worthy of Emma anyway. Frankly, no human man was.

"Emma." He shifted to his persuasion voice; it might work better on her. "Tommaso is one of our most trusted guards. You can say anything in front of him. Besides, we don't have time for this. If you haven't noticed, we've got some serious problems to deal with such as missing and dead guards, and..." He paused. He was going to tell her about the other gods being trapped but pulled back.

Don't give away too much too soon, he reminded himself. "And it would be helpful to understand how they tracked you."

"Not *now*." She folded her arms and glared with defiance.

Again she'd resisted? She was growing stronger somehow.

He stared at her face, observing closely. She was becoming angry. She always hated when he used his voice to control her; it sparked her spiteful, vengeful side. He suddenly felt uneasy.

She blew out a breath. "Fine. I've been having nightmares," Emma said, her voice infused with a subtle wickedness. Yeah, she was mad.

She went on to explain in detail how she'd dreamed of a man several times, not leaving out all of the possessive, seductive things he'd said to her. She explained how she never thought much about them. That is, until this last time when he seemed so real and so violent. When she got to the last part, she looked as though she wanted to cry. The dream had truly frightened her, but Guy wasn't convinced it was anything other than her overactive, human imagination at work.

"The dreams aren't real," he declared dismissively.

"But *you* got inside my head and talked to me. You even woke me up from a coma. So why couldn't someone else talk to me in my sleep? It would explain how the Maaskab found me. The man in my dream could see where I was and said he was sending people, scary people, for me. He said not to run."

"Not real," he repeated.

"Well, why the hell not?"

Guy scratched his rough face.

"Well?" she prodded.

"It's not possible that the man in your dream is a real god because the others are... well..." Then he stopped himself. How much did he really want Emma to know about the gods being trapped? Or that he'd need her to return to Mexico and help free them. She'd already been through so much, and he didn't want to push her over the edge.

"Here we go again! What is it with you? Are you ever going to trust me?" Emma threw up her hands.

Guy snapped. "Everything I say comes under your scrutiny. Nothing's ever right! I don't say enough. I talk too much. I keep too many secrets. I butt in when I shouldn't. Which is it, woman? Am I supposed to be quiet or speak? Do I sugarcoat or be honest? I'm simply trying to protect you, but you don't have enough common sense to see it! You're making my head spin."

Tommaso chuckled, keeping his eyes on the road.

"What are you laughing at?" Emma squawked. "You have no idea how frustrating it's been living with him."

"You two sound like an old married couple," Tommaso said.

Emma's brow creased. "I'd rather marry a Scab. At least the suffering would end quickly."

Tommaso roared for all of four seconds until Guy cleared his throat as a warning.

"Sorry. It's just... she is kind of funny," Tommaso said.

"Thank you." Emma bowed her head and gave Tommaso a wink. "At least *you* get me. He, on the other hand"—she flashed her eyes at Guy—"won't even answer a simple question."

Guy did not like the friendship growing between Emma

and Tommaso one bit. He liked even less that he now felt he had to compete for her trust. *Gods dammit.* "The dream can't be real because the buzzing voices you hear in your head belong to the rest of the gods who're currently enjoying a watery vacation inside those damned cenotes. So even if one could seep through that thick skull of yours, they'd have no way to communicate to the Maaskab and provide your location."

She was silent for a minute, apparently thinking it over, but unfazed. "Okay. You're right there . . . but wait. Didn't you say there are fourteen of you? I only hear eleven voices."

"Eleven? You never said eleven." Guy felt his heart accelerate.

"Yes! Yes, I did. You just don't listen to me. I said it at least half a dozen times."

"No, little girl. I think I'd remember something so important." Of course he would. He was nearly perfect.

"Little girl? Well, I guess compared to an old, crusty deity—"

"Please, would you two stop?" Tommaso interrupted. "I think *I'm* going to marry a Maaskab."

"Emma, are you certain it's eleven?" Guy asked.

"Oh my God . . . yes!" She slammed her fists into the black leather seat at her sides.

"Then that means someone else is on the loose. It's not just Cimil and I who roam free."

"You're a mathematical genius," Emma mumbled.

"Keep it up, Emma. I've always wanted to spank you. Or I could put you to sleep again. Would you like that?"

"If you lay a finger on me, I'll—"

"This I'd like to hear," Tommaso said.

Emma snapped her mouth shut and glared out the window, crinkling her lips into an angry circle. She looked adorable when she was cranky.

"Not that this would validate your theory, but what did he look like?" Guy asked.

Emma took a long moment. Then another.

"Well? We're waiting, Princess Know-It-All," Guy said.

A wicked little smile suddenly made camp on her face. It brought a foldout chair, made a fire, and started roasting marshmallows. Guy suddenly felt uneasy.

"I said, he looked almost exactly like you, but . . ."

"Taller?" Not that any of the gods were taller than him, he thought.

"Not exactly, no." Emma's mean little smile grew bigger.

"Nicer hair?" They might have longer hair, so that was okay. But certainly none had anything as stunning as his blue-black mane of thick waves.

"His hair was a little dull—like yours. And kind of black and wavy."

Dull? She must have hit her head.

"Better looking?" he asked, because such a thing was not possible. He knew he was sinfully handsome.

Emma hesitated for a fraction of a second. "He was definitely worth looking at."

Now he knew she was playing with him.

"What else? Speak woman! I'm growing tired of your game."

"He had a much bigger penis. Gargantuan, actually."

Tommaso burst out in uncontrollable hysterics, and then Emma joined in.

"I mean, compared to you, Guy, it was like night and day!" She held up her pinkie, then roared with laughter.

Guy shook his head, then stared at the roof of the Hummer. “They’re children. I’m stuck with two of the most childish humans on the face of the planet, too stupid to fear a lethal deity. Gods save me.”

Emma and Tommaso continued for several long moments until Guy finally had enough. “Okay, little tree monkeys, can we get back to business? And Tommaso, any time you’d like to play the mine-is-bigger-than-yours game, let me know.”

Tommaso’s smug smile melted away. “No, sir. Sorry, sir. It’s just that...she’s really funny.”

“So he looks *almost* exactly like you. Any idea who he is?” Emma asked.

Guy’s mind worked. “If, in fact, your dream is truly an attempt at communication, I have three brothers who look like me. But I assure you, of the four, I am the most blessed in every way imaginable.”

Emma raised a brow. “Three? Did you say three? Are they all as arrogant as you?”

“They’re worse,” Guy replied.

“Someone, please stop the planet, I’m getting off,” Emma whispered.

“Have the other voices been saying anything recognizable, something that would tell me who’s trapped?”

“Sorry, it’s the same incomprehensible buzzing. But they were getting louder right before the attack. I could barely think. Even now, the volume is way up. I’ve gotten better at ignoring them, but it’s pretty bad.”

Guy faced the road. He didn’t like hearing she was in distress. “I’m sorry, my sweet. It will be over soon, I promise.”

“I hope you mean it.” Her voice was suddenly melancholy. “Because I can’t take much more.”

That's what he was afraid of. "I will make sure of it, my sweet."

Emma looked out the window to her side. She must have realized they'd just driven past the exit for the Genoa Airport. "Where are we going?"

"To Rome," Guy explained. "We have people there, and I need information."

By the time they arrived at the compound, Emma was sound asleep.

Guy was happy to see her resting. She had a long, tumultuous road ahead, and it had also given him a chance to make a few calls to the Uchben chiefs. He needed to coordinate search parties, a cleanup crew, and sadly, a few funerals. He didn't relish the next few days ahead, dealing with the aftermath, the families, and the preparations to rescue the other gods. He found himself wishing he could take Emma somewhere quiet, like his Greek island, to allow her to recoup. After all, she'd been through so much. She deserved a rest before her big job.

Tommaso opened the passenger door to carry Emma.

"Not so fast." Guy dug his hand into Tommaso's shoulder. "I'll take her. You have work to do."

Tommaso ground his teeth. "*You* assigned me to take care of her."

"Yes, when I'm not around. So. Let. Her. Go," Guy said, closing the gap between their faces.

Tommaso gave Guy a discontented nod and waved over several guards to help unload the gear. Guy grunted contently. He was going to have to talk to Tommaso about minding his place, including his interactions with Emma.

On second thought, he'd talk to Tommaso's chief. Tommaso would receive a new assignment, perhaps taking glacial samples in the Sahara.

Guy took stock of the compound, pleased by how it appeared untouched by the centuries. The compound was a villa built in the 1500s just the way Guy liked it. Light gray stone, wide-open courtyards, picturesque sitting gardens, and marble pillars—all the features human homes of this century didn't boast unless the owners were aristocrats stuck in the past or drug dealers.

He'd selected this location specifically because of the statue in the central garden. It was of himself holding a raised sword.

A glorious work of art, he thought proudly. Rome was definitely built for the gods, and now it would be the perfect new home for his precious Payal. Here the Uchben could protect her.

Twenty-Four

I passed out cold from sheer exhaustion during the drive. Luckily, I didn't have any haunting, violent dreams. In fact, I didn't dream at all. There was so much testosterone in the car that no other male, human or otherwise, would dare come near. It was the deepest sleep I'd had in days.

I rolled over in the enormous bed, surveying the room. Had they hired the decorator from the Venetian in Vegas? It was way over the top. The room was the size of a small airplane hangar, complete with brilliant white marble floors, ornate crown moldings, and a domed ceiling with murals of stoic angels and fluffy white clouds. From where I sat, I could see through an arched doorway into a lavish gold-accented bathroom, which appeared to extend the length of a football field. I'd bet my hot Uchben guard that it had a shower for five, steam room for ten, and jet tub for an equal amount of people.

Off to the corner, there was a cozy sitting area near the

front door and, to the side of that, a long, formal dining table and an open, modern gourmet chef's kitchen complete with stainless steel appliances, several convection ovens, black granite countertops, and giant extractor over the gas-burner cooktop.

I looked out the double glass doors at the side of the bed that led to a private walled-in garden. Guy was sitting just outside the doorway, his broad back to me, gazing up at the lavender, early-evening sky. His thick black waves of hair, veined with iridescent blue, cascaded over his shoulders. He truly looked like a mythological creature. Everything about him was larger than life: his size, his power, his arrogance and looks. Even his scent and vibe seemed otherworldly.

Without a doubt, he was a real live god and real goddamned pain in the rear, but something about him felt so raw, so magnetic, so... familiar. Maybe because his voice, correction, *he* had played such a powerful role in my life. He was my constant obsession. My personal enigma.

So why had my feelings for him only grown into something infinitely more complex? The mystery of Guy was now solved. Sure, I still had many questions. Why was I able to hear his voice in my head when he was in the cenote, but not now? What did it really mean to be bonded? Why had he said my grandmother was special? What had happened to her?

Well, at least now I knew what he was and why we were connected. I was free from his mental chains.

Really, now. Then why don't you want to get away from him? Maybe because you just found out you're not normal and never will be? True. Though somehow I didn't feel any different. I was still Emma Keane. And it wasn't like I was a real god or anything. Although they were not what I'd expect gods to be like, they were clearly different from me. They were larger than life. They were powerful and fearless.

I started thinking about how I'd give anything for a day inside Guy's head. What sorts of mysteries of the universe were in there? Where did he go when he wasn't in the human world? Was his real living room a star in the sky? What was it like to watch people living, loving, hating, creating, growing old, and dying? Did it make him feel lonely or was he indifferent?

"Looking for something to throw at me?" he said. He didn't bother to turn around.

I ran my hands over my hair trying to gauge the state of frizz. "How'd you know?"

"I just do."

"What else do you know?" I questioned.

"I know the rhythm of your pulse when you're happy, how you breathe when you're worried, how you've spent every second of your life. I know everything except..." He paused, still not bothering to turn around.

"Except what? The color of my underwear?"

"Pink."

He knew that, too? "Lucky guess."

"Not really. My men did your shopping. They talk."

"Nice," I said.

"Do you care for him?" he asked, his voice low and stark.

I shifted nervously on the bed. "Who?" I knew who he meant, but I needed a second to process. Sure, Tommaso was painfully attractive. Check that box. Strong and mysterious? Check those, too. But was there really something between us? He'd saved my life. Naturally I was extremely grateful. I even trusted him a little—something I couldn't say for Guy.

However, while the insanely horrific events of the last week might be status quo for Guy and his Uchi-pets, they weren't for me. It would take months to digest all this and peel away the layers of raw stress to get to my true feelings. So I guess the truthful answer was I didn't know; Tommaso felt like the man I should be interested in. But he wasn't. Guy was. And I knew I shouldn't be. In any case, I was definitely not going to mention the kiss. Guy would strangle Tommaso or worse.

"Tommaso," he answered. "There's something between you two, isn't there?"

"Let me think about that. Um, I've known him for all of three days. He held me prisoner, yes, on your behalf, but still—"

Guy turned in his chair to face me through the doorway. Gods, he was stunning. "He kissed you, didn't he?" Guy asked like a possessive boyfriend. "I can still smell him on you."

I felt a tiny rush of satisfaction from Guy's jealousy, even though I knew it was an unreasonable response on my part. Besides, it wasn't like Guy really wanted me. To him, I was just some object he felt belonged to him.

"It was just an impulse. And trust me, after I slapped him, I don't think he'll be coming back for more. Besides, look at him," I said. "He's good-looking, dedicated, well-groomed—I'm sure I'm not his type."

Guy smiled. "You're everyone's type."

My heart did a little flutter. Did he mean I was his type, too? "No. Us half-breeds are much too exotic for most men," I said facetiously. "And since you rotted my brain, my chances for any normal relationship are totally ruined, Votan."

Guy stood up and, in the span of a heartbeat, moved to the side of the bed, his boiling hot glare pouring down on me. "Don't call me that, Emma," he growled.

Actually, I had no idea why I'd suddenly used that name. "Why not?" I rose to meet his, well, his chest. After all, I was only five three, but he got the drift.

His bright turquoise eyes narrowed. "Because everything's changed, that's why."

I lifted my chin. "You're right about that. I thought my life sucked before, but now I'm being hunted by crazy Mayan witch doctors—"

"Priests."

"Yeah. Whatever. The point is, my life's over, and for all I know, my entire family's been wiped out. But you're worrying about a stupid name."

"I'm simply not the same being I once was, and the name Votan has memories attached to it. Memories I no longer wish to think about." There was an unmistakable pain in his eyes and I wondered why.

"And as for your family," he continued, "they were the first thing I took care of. They're safe. I made sure of it." He placed his hand on my shoulder sending a shiver through my spine.

"They are?" I suddenly felt warm and gooey inside. He'd protected what I loved most in this world. In fact, he said it was the first thing he'd done. After seventy years of being cursed to live underwater, the gesture meant a lot.

"Your parents," he added, "though unaware, now have around-the-clock security, and they've hired a new maid, one of our Uchben. We've got people at their hospital, too. Even the new neighbors on both sides of them are ours. And they're very excited that the houses on their street have been selling at double the price, but what can I say? We had to persuade the former occupants to move out in one day."

He'd done all that? For me? I suddenly felt that little space in my heart, occupied by Guy, spreading its tendrils. Did he care about me? I mean *truly* care about me? I needed to know. "Why?"

His eyes flickered to a translucent, shimmery blue for a fraction of a moment as he stared deeply into my eyes. "How can you ask such a thing? Did you not listen, my sweet, to one word I've been saying all these years?" His grip pulsed with tension on my shoulders. He brushed my cheek with one hand as if I were his most cherished possession in the world.

Then it hit me. *Crap.* I felt like I'd been punched in the stomach. He really had been trying to protect me. All those years I'd misjudged him. I was wrong. Me. But how could that be? I was the victim. Wasn't I?

Christ. No, I wasn't. He was. He'd been trapped in the water, helpless. And he'd been trapped with me.

I suddenly saw through all of the things he'd done that I'd perceived as evil and realized that I'd behaved like a whiny, spoiled child. Just like he'd always said. I'd been too angry, too focused on the things I didn't have to hear the truth. Of course, his lack of truthfulness didn't help. But still. The threats were real. The priests were real. They had taken my grandmother and had come hunting for me.

Guy really had been watching over me my entire life

despite being trapped in a watery hell, unable to breathe or feel sunlight. And to his credit, he never once complained or whimpered about his effed-up situation. He'd simply focused on doing what he could to keep anything dangerous away from me. Even Jake, the serial killer. Yes. Yes, Guy'd driven me crazy during the process, but I got it now.

Overwhelmed by my emotions, I pulled away from his overpowering touch and began nervously straightening the bed.

"Besides," he continued, "the Maaskab want you, not your parents."

"Why not?"

"Your father is normal, and as Señora Rosa told you, the only ones who appear to be Payals and carry our light, or energy, so to speak, are firstborn female children. We haven't had a chance to understand why yet, but rest assured, your mother is not a firstborn child. She has an older brother."

Yes, Uncle Randy, who lived in Santa Rosa, California. We'd been planning to visit him next Christmas.

Guy's cell phone vibrated. He looked at the screen and shoved it back inside his pocket. "As long as the Maaskab believe your parents can't be used to find you, they are safe. But that doesn't mean they won't always be waiting patiently until you weaken and slip up."

He continued observing me, eyes intense, while I smoothed the white down comforter with my shaky hands. "Guy, I get what you're saying, especially after seeing the monsters for myself, but there has to be a way to safely contact my mom and dad."

"Are you really willing to risk it? Any form of contact

could lead them to you again. Hell, I don't know how they even found you at my villa. There is much about them we do not understand, including the extent of their powers. What we do know is the Maaskab won't stop until they get what they want. Right now, they want you."

"They'd said that I belonged to them." I sighed and then nodded. "I wish I was never born."

"Don't wish that, Emma. Your life is a gift. You shouldn't let fear diminish that," he said.

"That's what my grandmother used to say."

"She was right." He plowed his hands into his pockets and looked down.

I found myself wishing I could talk to her now. I needed someone to help me sort through this mess, especially these mixed-up feelings I had about my life, about Guy.

"I miss her."

"I know, Emma."

"Do you really think the Scabs killed her?" *Please say no.*

He nodded solemnly. "Yes, and they'll pay. I promise. But you can't throw away your life, suffering for those who are no longer with you. You have to move on, my sweet. Leave the revenge to me. It is what I am good at."

Guy watched as I fluffed the pillows and lined them up against the headboard, trying not to cry. I unexpectedly realized how comforted I felt talking to him. It reminded me of when we used to be alone, chatting away while I cleaned my room or folded clothes. Sometimes, we'd talk for hours about life, history, and politics. There were good memories, solidly happy times tucked in between the angry ones. I just hadn't wanted to recall them until now. Oddly, I missed having him inside my mind so close, rubbing intimately against my thoughts. It was so ironic.

"Move on." I considered that. "Easy for you to say. You've never lost anything you deeply cared about."

"I've endured an eternity of sacrifice, pain, and"—his gaze burrowed through me—"never mind."

We stared at each other, the silence emotionally charged. I wondered what was so horrible about his past that it made him want to forget his name. What was so painful that it caused his eyes to turn a deep shade of green? Why wouldn't he tell me? I'd spent so much time hating him, blaming him, but I'd never taken the time to truly get to know him. Now I wanted to.

Even though he was still dressed in his dark gray, military-style clothes, he looked vulnerable. Maybe even a bit sad. Definitely sad. Gods, I wanted to comfort him. To start paying him back for the lifetime of horrible things I'd said to him. Before I knew what I was doing, I dropped the pillow in my hand and took two steps toward him.

He didn't flinch as I looked up into his eyes. I stood on my tiptoes and reached to wrap my arms around his neck to hug him.

He bent to me and pressed those full, mouth-watering, delicious lips to mine. The jolt of energy moved through my body once again, but somehow I'd expected it, wanted it.

A moment passed where we both remained still, lips touching but not moving. We were both assessing what we were doing and were about to do. My assessment happened quickly. *More. I want more.*

His body abruptly shifted, and he wrapped his powerful arms around my waist, pulling me into him. I guess our assessments aligned.

His soft, full lips parted, and his warm breath entered

my mouth, his silky tongue slipping past my teeth. I'd kissed men before, not many, but nothing had been like this, as if I'd plugged myself into him, and the electricity from our bodies merged into one continuous current of elation. Why had I waited so long to do this? His kiss was everything I'd ever needed or wanted. Shoe sale plus hot fudge, orgasm, back rub, lust, power, and crippling neediness—all rolled into one blazing hot man package.

Guy pulled me harder against him, releasing a husky groan. My breasts began to tingle, and I could feel him growing firm against my stomach. Knowing I had that power over him, to create that sort of a reaction, made me melt. Melt. For the first time ever, I literally felt my insides liquefy into a warm, syrupy concoction for a man.

He was male perfection. A god. He could have any woman in the world. And he wanted…me.

Wild lust blazed through my veins and triggered a scalding ache inside my core so consuming that I thought I'd implode if I didn't get him inside me. Images of clawing off his clothes and straddling him flashed in my mind. I wished he was wearing that sarong again; it would make it so much easier to unwrap him like a man treat and tie my legs in a knot around his waist. Even more shocking was how the years of resentment and anger were gone, any residue melting away as his tongue plunged rhythmically into my mouth, each delicious stroke making my body hotter and heavier.

His hands slid to my hips and then smoothly glided up under my sweatshirt, lounging over every curve until he reached my breasts. I gasped from the intensity of his touch as his palms skimmed over my nipples and then began kneading, the speed of his breaths escalating.

"You truly are beautiful, Emma," he whispered in between mind-bending hot kisses as he stroked my pulsing nipples through my bra. "But." He panted. "You and I..."

A painful fire bolted through my mouth as if I'd just bitten into an explosive, spicy chili pepper. The five-alarm fire quickly grew to a ten. I violently shoved away from him, choking and hacking.

His eyes were instantly filled with coldness. "...can never be." He turned and headed for the door. "Get some rest, little girl."

The door slammed shut behind him.

Twenty-Five

As soon as the strange, sharp pain dissipated and I was able to begin processing what had just happened, a new, more horrifying feeling washed over me. I sank down on the bed and stared at the closed door unable to move, unable to speak, unable to cry. How could he kiss me like that? Like he wanted me with every fiber of his being only to then toss me to the curb as if I were nothing?

Because you're human; to him, you are nothing.

The sting of rejection spiked right through my heart, causing those feelings—foolish, idiotic, ridiculous feelings!—to shrivel up and retreat into a deep, gloomy cave where they belonged.

How could I have opened myself up to him like that? Goddammit, how?

Well, I would never let him in again. Ever.

What an idiot! Idiot!

I mentally picked myself up off the floor, dusted the

dirt from my poor, emotionally battered ego, and began talking myself to a better place. *You don't really want him anyway. That's right, your mind had been temporarily blinded by years of sexual deprivation, causing you to throw yourself at Guy.* And who could blame me? I'm only human—sort of—and at least physically, he was a perfect male specimen. A god. Literally.

And who could forget about the stress I'd been under? I once read that stress makes people do all sorts of self-destructive things. Some people go to town on the chocolate or fried chicken. Others pound martinis. I, well, I apparently wanted to commit lewd and indecent acts with Guy.

Impure thoughts aside, he was my one constant, so it was only natural I'd run to something familiar for comfort, even if he was more like a familiar ache from a bad injury that never healed quite right. But after all I'd been through, the familiarity of that ache was almost as comforting as a warm, gooey chocolate chip cookie.

"Shut it, Emma," I said aloud to myself. None of that mattered. Guy was going to throw this back in my face and humiliate me. I'd never hear the end of it. "Emma, you worship me." "Emma, you want to take me to bed." "Emma, you're a little wanton hussy."

Yes. Yes. All true. The residual ache inside left no room for denial. But jeez. What had I done? What was I going to do? Well, there was no going back in time, so I did what any girl would do. I decided to take a long, hot bubble bath in the five-man tub. And yes, I'd been right. The bathroom had a steam room for ten, too.

I soaked in mounds of rose-scented bubbles, trying not to think of the black clouds hanging overhead.

Someone cleared their voice.

"Please don't tell me I've fallen asleep," I prayed aloud with my eyes closed.

"You're awake."

I cracked open one eye to find Tommaso with freshly disheveled, towel-dried hair standing in the doorway of the bathroom. He had changed from his military clothes and was dressed in what could only be described as, well, black silky pajamas, unless that was what he wore to take his evening jog.

I sighed. I was not in the mood for more dangerous, confused men. "Did you get lost on your way to a pajama party for naughty Uchben?"

He shrugged. "Hey, can't a guy pamper himself with a little black silk after a hard day of fighting neurotic goddesses, scraping up dead bodies, and getting his neck wrung twice?"

"Sure, I suppose. But is there any special reason you're in here while I'm trying to bathe in private?" I was covered head to toe in bubbles, but that didn't make it any less awkward.

"I'm your guard, so there are no privacy boundaries. Besides, I've already seen you naked." He flashed a big, bright smile, making his dimples crease. "Just thought I'd stop by and leave you this. I found it at the villa underneath one of those dead Maaskab." He held up the necklace with the black stone pendant.

I'd almost forgotten about it. "I hope you washed it."

"And sterilized it twice," he added.

"Thanks. You can leave it there," I said, flashing a glance toward sink. "Where'd you get that thing anyway?"

He walked over to the white marble counter and set it down. "It's a family heirloom, so take good care of it."

That was odd. Why would he give me something so special?

"Look," he said. "I just want to say I'm sorry."

"For what?" I asked, wondering if he meant the intrusive kiss, the kidnapping, or something else.

"For treating you as badly as I did. I resented you. I saw the assignment as having to babysit Mr. Santiago's little pet. I was wrong. You're anything but his pet—more like a hungry, rabid cheetah that wants to take his arm off."

If Tommaso only knew the truth. I'd just tried to chew off Guy's lips. How sad.

"And," he added, "I want you to know, I truly sympathize with your situation. I lost my entire family in a freak accident. I was never able to say good-bye or tell them I loved them."

"I'm so sorry. That's awful."

"I tried to tell myself it's the way of the universe. Our losses make us who we are, but there are days I'd give anything to undo the past. Anything at all."

I understood exactly what he meant. The pain. The loss. That had to be what my parents were experiencing right now. But I wasn't gone. I wasn't dead. I was taking a damned bubble bath while they suffered. It wasn't right. "Does this mean you'll help me? All I want is to safely contact my parents. There has to be a way."

His eyes narrowed. "No. No matter what, I still owe my obedience and loyalty to the Uchben. They're my family now." His tone left no room for negotiation.

"And to the..." I hesitated. "Gods?" I still couldn't quite say the word *gods* without feeling corny.

He nodded.

"But I'm part... you know," I argued.

He didn't flinch. "I know what you are, but sorry. Doesn't change a thing. I have my orders." The black silk fabric tightened around his biceps as he crossed his arms.

I somehow felt more sorry for him than myself; even though I'd lost my grandmother, my parents were still alive. He'd lost everyone. "Okay. I'll try not to hold a grudge and smite you."

He made a deep chuckle. "Thanks. Because I've taken all the smiting I can handle for one day." He moved to the side of the tub and sat on the edge. "Which brings me to why I'm actually here. I wanted to thank you for standing up against Cimil. I didn't know you'd done that until you mentioned it to Mr. Santiago."

I hadn't had much time to think about that shocking moment, but now that I knew about my ancestry, my sudden burst of strength made a lot more sense. I only wished I'd discovered it sooner and understood how to control it.

"You were pretty out of it when I clocked her," I pointed out. "She only tried to wring your neck because you told her to let me go. So I think we're even."

"Are we? Because I feel like I still owe you something." A mischievous smile swept across his face and I suddenly got the feeling he was flirting. I was in no mood for this.

"Nope. We're all good. Promise. So if you don't mind?" I glanced at the door.

"Of course." He shrugged, making the black silk of his shirt slide over his perfectly sculpted chest. He was almost to the door when he turned around. "Emma, I have to ask you something."

"Okay…I'm sort of naked here. Mind turning around?"

He made a little pout, but then did as I asked before asking his question. "Guy told everyone what happened and how he's bonded to you through your grandmother's blood."

"Yeah. So?"

Tommaso turned to face me again and his expression teetered on discomfort. "Emma, you may not know this, but others are connected to him, yet they weren't able to hear him while he was trapped."

Others? I felt jealous all of a sudden. Did he have a harem of women he was bonded to? He *was* a sexy, powerful god. I bet he bonded every night. Maybe even three times a day with two women at a time. No wonder he'd rejected me. I was just a little girl in his eyes, completely incapable of satisfying a man like him or any man for that matter.

He continued, "That means your connection to him is very strong." He paused, turned back toward the door, and then asked, "Do you plan to stay with him? Do you love him?"

Wasn't expecting *that* question. What was with these men putting me on the spot like this? I swallowed and then nervously cupped a mound of bubbles. "No. I mean—I have feelings for him, but I can't explain what they are. It's not like there's any point of reference for our relationship. He's been a part of my life for so long, but not a day went by that I didn't pray he'd leave. Now that I'm in this situation, I feel almost like he's a necessity, that I won't survive without him."

"Don't let him intimidate you, Emma. And if it's protection you're worried about, there are other options. All you have to do is take your request to the Uchben chiefs, and we'll protect you."

"He'll never allow that. Like he said, we're bonded."

"Then break it. Release him."

My heart stopped. "Can I do that? How?"

"Kaacha'al lu'um, tumben k'iin," Tommaso recited.

"Catch a loom, tomb bent inn?" I repeated with a clumsy tongue. "What does it mean?"

"Literally, 'broken earth, new day.' It's Mayan, from an ancient prayer. It means you wish to break your ties with the past."

"What will happen? Will it hurt when I say it?" I imagined a giant lightning bolt hitting me on the head.

"No, it's a painless procedure." I could see he thought my question was silly but resisted teasing me. Brownie point for Tommaso. "The oath he took to create the bond with your grandmother, which now binds your blood to him—and therefore to other gods—allows them to keep tabs on you more easily. To protect you, of course."

"So it's like having a direct line to the gods?" I asked.

"More like LoJack or twenty-four-hour emergency roadside assistance."

"So it's not some weird force field of protection?" I wondered.

"Nope. Sorry. You're still susceptible to colds, accidents, and horribly psychotic Maaskab. The bond simply creates a connection, a current of energy that links you to Guy."

"Guy mentioned that's why Cimil fought to protect me." It all sounded so strange to me. Bonds, oaths, it was like a supernatural fraternity.

"The gods are compelled to protect you as one of their own since their light runs through you. You saw how Cimil was with the rest of us," he replied.

"You're not under their protection?"

Tommaso tried to turn back toward me.

"Hey! Stop that." I scooped a few handfuls of bubbles and made a larger heap over my breasts.

He cleared his throat. "Sorry. Can't help it. You have very nice bubbles."

Ugh. I bet he used that line on all the ladies. "Time for you to leave."

He looked my way and stuck out his lower lip making an exaggerated pout, his golden eyes sparkling. "Fine, but to answer your question, it's different for us Uchben. We gave our oath to them."

"And you can break it, leave at any time?" I asked.

"Yes, Emma. I'm not a prisoner. I'm an Uchben because this is how I choose to live," he said.

"How did you become one?" I comically imagined them recruiting in malls. Or maybe online.

"My father was an archaeologist, working in Guatemala, when his camp was attacked by a group of Maaskab. He was found by the Uchben barely alive. After he recovered, they made him an offer. I think he said yes, just because he'd have access to so many resources. He became one of the Uchben."

"That's strange. He decided to be a soldier?"

"No, he didn't become a guard. He continued his work. There are Uchben of every imaginable kind: doctors, scholars, politicians, even beauticians."

That explained Tommaso's fabulous haircut.

"Well, whatever you choose to do, Emma, about the oath, just remember, you have other options."

"Options. Do you mean like you?" A very small part of me hoped he'd say yes. Tommaso was smart, mysterious, handsome, strong, funny, and—human. He was clearly a better choice over pining for a god that (a) didn't want me and (b) I didn't want to have feelings for. I deserved better, didn't I? Didn't I deserve a shot at a normal, happy life—whatever the hell that was.

"Absolutely." He leaned down and planted a soft kiss on my mouth, and then left.

Hiccup! That hadn't felt nearly as good as I'd hoped.

Twenty-Six

"Votan, I've heard so much about you. What a pleasure! A true pleasure." The slender, aged man with a graying beard vigorously shook Guy's hand and then practically yanked him through the front door of his Italian countryside–style cottage. Guy had heard many stories about the eccentric Catholic priest, but no one mentioned his exuberance.

"Kind of you to make time for me, Father Xavier. I've heard great things about your work."

"Please, call me Xavier. I don't go by father anymore." He pointed to his collarless neck and chuckled. He wore a blue running suit and slippers.

Father Xavier worked in the Vatican City archives for thirty years until he retired to work for the Uchben. He was one of their most famous scholars. He now lived on the compound and ran the Uchben's Historical Research Department. They'd originally sought him out because he was an expert on Mesoamerican culture, Greek mythology, and the works of Friar Bernardino de Sahagún, the Franciscan missionary who traveled with the early Spanish explorers, documenting the Aztec and Mayan folklore.

"As you wish, Xavier, thank you for making time so late in the evening."

"Sure thing. I can't tell you how excited I am to meet you in the flesh," Xavier said, fervently looking Guy up and down as if he were a rare relic.

It didn't bother Guy much. He was used to being treated like a—well, god. Except by Emma. She treated him like a used doormat. That's right, a used one. Because new doormats were at least shown the respect of being proudly displayed at the front door. Used ones were thrown out back to collect dirt and mud from the yard.

Really, who did she think she was anyway? Toying with him like that. One minute she was throwing herself at that unworthy human, Tommaso. Then she was rubbing her tempting little body all over him. And it wasn't because he had powerful pheromones, either. He'd been suppressing them around her—best he could anyway. After all, keeping his emotions in check was a challenge around her. But did she honestly believe she could manipulate him into letting her call her parents? She must have been able to sense his lust for her through the bond. She thought to control him with it. And what a masterful performance! Nearly had him convinced!

That's not why you left, though, is it? It's because you can't have her, and you know it. And what about at the cenote? You felt her lust then. No faking it there.

He felt the heavy thud of doubt kick him in the gut. *She couldn't—it's not...no. Impossible.* She'd told him a hundred times how much she hated him and wanted him gone. She'd rejected his protection, and even now, she seemed to want nothing more than to return home and take her chances with the Maaskab.

Yet despite the bitter words she'd repeated over the years, his mind couldn't help but toy with the notion of Emma's desire perhaps being genuine.

He swallowed hard.

If it had been, then she'd now be more furious than ever for the way he'd walked out.

She'd be batshit livid.

He needed to know if she'd been pretending. Why was dealing with women so difficult?

Stop your whining and man up! You're a warrior. A god. You were put on this earth to fight and protect. Not fuddle around like a lovesick human. He sighed.

"Oh, manners. Such terrible manners. Please, sit, Votan, or Mr. Santiago? What do you go by these days?"

"You can call me Guy."

Xavier raised one brow. "Guy Santiago, an odd choice for such a being of your stature, but modern. I like it."

Guy shrugged. "That's what Emma calls me. I guess I've become accustomed to it."

Xavier gave one polite nod. "Can I get you tea? Coffee? Oh, I know. A nice Chianti." Xavier swept away a large stack of magazines from the small dining table. They all had a woman named Tyra on the cover.

"Wine will be fine, thank you." Guy took a seat at the table, barely fitting on the tiny cherrywood chair. "Listen, Xavier, I do not need to tell you how sensitive what I'm about to tell you is."

"No. No need. I may not believe your kind is above the

Creator, but I still respect your place—and power—so no need to worry there." Xavier removed a squatty, bulbous wine bottle from the cupboard and poured two glasses.

"Sorry?" Guy asked.

"Well, obviously, I am, or was, a Catholic priest, but I didn't quit simply to serve the Uchben. In fact, I believe the roles might have been complementary to each other. I see you as another one of God's precious creations. Only the other precious creations sharing this world don't know about you. But that's not important. What matters is that we all believe—have faith in his plan."

"I'm assuming you do?" Guy said.

"Oh yes. Yes. Everything happens for a reason."

Interesting man. Guy wasn't much for philosophizing about the Creator or his plans. It wasn't that he hadn't thought about it over the tens of thousands of years. But he'd come to the conclusion that like all beings, he would never really know the truth. And sharing his assumptions was pointless because it didn't change his circumstance or purpose. He could believe he was the Easter Bunny himself, and it wouldn't make him warm or fuzzy!

"So what can I do for you?" Xavier asked. "I heard the latest in this morning's debrief."

The Uchben were excellent at communication. So much so that they proudly called their network the Bee Hive. All it took was one message to one Uchben, and everyone else was as good as informed. It was one of their key strengths.

Guy took a small sip of wine and rolled the ruby-red liquid over his tongue. Gods how he'd missed the taste of it. "Then you already know about the jars I found on that ship and the portals being blocked?"

"Yes, fascinating. Isn't it? The Maaskab have certainly honed their skills. And since you've been gone so long, I guess you can only imagine the progress they've made. If we'd only found out sooner—"

"Yes," Guy said. "Well, that couldn't be helped. My communication channels were a bit limited while I was on vacation."

"Ha!" Xavier snorted. "Yes. Vacation. Funny."

"Right. So before we attempt to free the other gods, I need you to do a little homework for me—find out how the Maaskab are sealing the portals."

"We're already on it," Xavier said. "I've got several people combing through the database." He leaned across the table. "I even called in a few favors at the Vatican," he whispered.

"Thank you. I want to know everything, even if it might seem irrelevant."

"We'll be very thorough as usual. However, we'll need more than a day."

"How many? I can't afford to leave my brothers and sisters festering much longer, especially now. The Maaskab must know I'm free and that I've figured out what's going on. They're probably preparing for our return to Mexico now."

"More the reason for you to know what you're walking into, my friend. I promise, we'll do everything we can to move quickly. But something like this—well, I could be studying it the rest of my life! A real live Pandora's box."

"Pandora?" Guy knew the stories of the Greek gods; after all, he'd inspired many of their stories. In fact, it was around the time of the Greeks that the gods had to implement more stringent controls over the way they'd been interfering with the human world. If they weren't careful, people might resolve to leave their fates in the gods' hands, and that was never their intention. The gods could influence, sway the odds, even perform minor miracles. At the end of the day, humans drove the fate of their world. Fourteen gods could do little to control billions of people like tiny robots. Thus, they implemented their policy of surgical intervention, only stepping in when events were leading toward an irreparable path. Like any good parent, the gods needed to nurture humans to evolve and mature on their own, not by brute force, which would only serve to create a species of dependent nonthinkers. That would be wrong, not to mention annoying and impractical.

"Well, yes," Xavier explained. "I mean, the contents don't sound the same. Your jar only contained one ingredient. Did you know Pandora's box was actually a jar and—"

Guy interrupted, "This is something quite different than a plague, famine, or good old-fashioned evil. The contents instantly incinerated my entire body when I reached inside. Of course, I ended up back in the cenote where there was a pleasant trap waiting for me—made from the same dark energy. It had the same smell, for lack of a better word, and it was powerful. Only a god could have taught the Maaskab to do this."

"Hmmm..." Xavier nodded. "Did the jar do anything when you took the lid off?"

"No. Nothing happened until I reached my hand inside." He suddenly felt foolish for admitting his curiosity had gotten the best of him. His confidence was sometimes both a blessing and a curse. Usually it was a blessing.

"And how many jars did you say there were?" asked the ex-priest.

"Pizarro showed me the map Cimil had given him. At the time, I saw at least two dozen scattered around Latin America and Europe. It was as if someone purposefully tried to make it laborious to collect them all. I don't know if Cimil wanted them because she had a hand in all this and needed to cover her tracks or for some other motive. It's anyone's guess."

"But why wouldn't she send the Uchben to retrieve them?" Xavier asked.

It was the same question Guy had, and the only conclusion was that she didn't want the other gods to know.

"When we release the other gods, we'll catch her and find out," Guy stated coldly. That said, there was still the matter of another god roaming free. Emma had counted only eleven voices out of fourteen. Both he and Cimil were apparently free. So who was not trapped? Was this the god working with the Maaskab? They'd soon find out.

Guy rose from the table, almost knocking his head on the chandelier. "I'll expect an update tomorrow."

"Of course." Xavier followed him to the door. "Oh, and what about the girl?"

Guy turned casually. "What *about* Emma?"

"I ask purely out of academic interest—since her kind is relatively new. How is she adjusting to the news of being a demigoddess?"

Guy shrugged. "It's hard to say. She's had to face more than her fair share of shocks this week. Who's to say how she'll truly feel when the dust settles."

"And your plans for her?"

Keep her. Maybe forever. And find a way to bed her.

Yes, I'd definitely like that. "She will go home. We may perhaps even erase her memory, though I'm not sure it is possible. She's got a lifetime of them with me."

"Erase her memory?" He scratched his gray beard. "Oh. How unfortunate. I'd so hoped to study her."

"Well, we'll make the final call when we return from Mexico."

"Yes. Yes, of course," Xavier responded. "Well, in that case, could I have some time with her while she's still here? Perhaps interview her?"

Guy nodded. "As long as she has no objections."

"Good, it's settled then. I'll see you tomorrow. Will you be bringing the girl to the dinner?"

"I plan to, yes. She deserves a little fun," Guy said.

"Good. I'll introduce myself then."

Guy nodded and reached for the door, pausing. "Xavier, one last thing," he said, facing the door. "I'd like to learn how she was made."

"Excuse me? Made?"

Guy took a deep breath. "Yes. How my brother, whichever one it was, managed to make a child. Specifically, sleep with a human."

Xavier's face blushed as he cleared his throat. "Um, I will let you know what we come across."

"Naturally, this is not to be discussed with anyone, and all information should be brought to me first."

"As is our protocol." Xavier nodded and closed the door.

Twenty-Seven

The next morning, I sprang out of Guy's king-sized bed, feeling like the previous day—all five of them, in fact—had been nothing but a nasty dream. Sadly, they weren't. But at least now I had options with the new bond-breaking chant Tommaso gave me. Not that I would release Guy because my life was on such shaky ground, but knowing I could helped me see the light at the end of my surreal little tunnel. Thank you, options.

Wanting to see how they felt, I began trying on the possibilities as I meticulously brushed my teeth in the ostentatious bathroom. I could go with a pack of armed Uchben to retrieve my parents, take them somewhere safe—like Rome—tell them what happened, and live happily ever after. Maybe even go on a date with Tommaso to see how it felt. If anyone could help me overcome my irrational attachment for Guy, he could. Right?

Wrong.

Well, perhaps you need time.

Perhaps.

I rinsed and spit into the sink. *Or I can become an Uchben and fight Scabs—Emma the Exterminator.* "Yeah, right. Emma the Delusional."

I quickly showered, threw on my last clean outfit—jeans and yet another T-shirt and flip-flops—wrangled my wet curls into a knot at the nape of my neck, and then headed out the door. I expected to see a particular guard waiting for me, perhaps reading a book about the history of the ninja or Armani. Yet instead of Tommaso, there were two blond men dressed in plain khaki cargos, T-shirts, and dark blue fleece vests. Old Navy warriors? I guess it worked. "Where's Tommaso?"

The taller of the blond men shrugged. "I think he had some stuff he needed to do."

Stuff? But I really wanted to talk to him about that kiss. He needed to know it wouldn't be that simple for me to turn off my emotions for Guy, nor did I intend to break the bond. Being friends was a good place to start and miles ahead of where I stood with Guy.

"His chief asked us to fill in and take you shopping."

"Shopping?" Usually nothing brightened my day like shopping, but given the situation, that sounded mildly absurd; clothes just didn't feel important anymore—except for the obvious reasons like modesty, warmth, and hiding the fact I'd gone two days without shaving. "I'm really not in the mood. Besides, I don't have any money."

As if I'd said something foolish and naive, they both gave each other a look. "Not an issue," said the taller blond. "Mr. Santiago will take care of everything and said to let you spend as much as you want."

"Is this some strange consolation prize?"

"Sorry?" the taller man asked.

"Never mind. Let's go."

I caught a glimpse of a gun holstered underneath one of the men's vests. "Won't people be concerned if they see you wearing a gun?" I asked.

"That's the point," responded the taller man.

So true.

As we walked to the car, I got my first glimpse of where we were. The compound was more like the Oxford campus, not that I'd been there, but there was a huge central courtyard, fountains, walkways filled with people going in every which direction, and dozens of gorgeous gray stone buildings that looked like pieces of old Italian castles. It was more like a small city.

"How many people live here?" I asked.

"Maybe a few hundred. Then there are the dorms for those staying for meetings and training. During the day we have another thousand or so who work here."

"What do they all do?"

Again, both men looked at each other. Had I spoken Martian or duck? "What?" I said defensively.

"We're surprised no one's told you all this."

Apparently, I hadn't received my Uchben welcome package. "Sorry, I've been a little preoccupied since my arrival from the massacre at Guy's villa."

Both men suddenly looked solemn. Had any of the dead been their friends?

"Not to worry," said the shorter man. "We've got all day. We'll fill you in."

They took me to a quaint little plaza tucked away from the center of the city in a quiet neighborhood. I begged them to drive by the Coliseum, but they insisted on keeping their heads attached to their bodies. Guy made it clear that would be the penalty for putting me in any danger.

In between buying shoes, clothes, makeup, and a really gorgeous little black dress they said I needed for some dinner that night, the two men—Robert and Michael—explained all about the Uchben. Surprisingly, they held nothing back. I guessed because of my half-breed status.

The most shocking thing I learned was that the Uchben had existed for a thousand years or so, concealing their existence from the world, while most lived and worked in normal jobs. They were like some elite Rotary Club, except they had their own 401(k), owned their own country—two actually, but they wouldn't tell me which ones—and had their own army.

By the time we returned, two thousand dollars later, I'd learned all I ever wanted to know about the Uchben, but the answers I needed most were still missing. Did the Maaskab kill my grandmother like Guy said? And why did they want me? If I broke my bond with Guy, would I really be safe? Would my heart ever heal from his rejection?

I opened the door to the suite, finding it empty, but I saw an envelope on the table by the door.

Dear Emma,

Do not be angry, my sweet. I care for you more than you could possibly imagine. Give me a chance to explain and make it up to you.

See you at eight.

G.S.

I read the note three more times. Was he for real? And why did I suddenly feel like I was being buttered up? It was bad enough that he'd rejected me. I could understand why—I was a child in his eyes—but it was insulting that he didn't trust me enough to ask if he wanted something.

Questions whirled through my head. The more I thought about it, the more I needed to extract the truth from him, once and for all. What was I to him? His duty? A friend?

If I didn't find out, I'd never be able to move on, even if I released him.

For once, my hair decided to play the role of ally. My strawberry blonde curls hung past my shoulders in perfect spirals. My skin was smooth and soft from the hour-long sauna, and since I'd barely eaten in the past week from nerves, my little black dress couldn't possibly look better—it was the only consolation I had, so why not enjoy it? I'd even managed to buy a fantastic black satin bra during my spree that made my respectable Bs look and act like naughty Cs. Thank you, underwires.

I didn't have any fancy jewelry, so I just wore Tommaso's necklace and tried not to be angry at it. It wasn't the necklace's fault that he'd ditched me for "stuff" all day when I'd needed to talk to him.

By eight o'clock, I looked like a new woman. Complete with shimmery pink lip gloss, smoky eye shadow, and thick black lashes. It seemed silly to take time out to play dress-up, but I sorely needed to have a break from the drama. So as the saying goes, "When in Rome . . ."

Right on cue, Guy entered and time seemed to move

in slow motion. He wore a tailored black suit—Italian, no doubt—with a turquoise shirt and tie that matched his iridescent eyes. His hair fell in loose black waves, framing his high cheekbones and perfect full lips. All of it sensuously complemented his cinnamon-dusted skin. Even for a man his size, he looked lean and elegant. A refreshing change from deadly and annoyed.

He gave me a hungry look and mouthed a word—was it "mine"?—while his eyes lounged over my body. "You look absolutely lovely tonight," he said, and then swallowed.

"Thanks for the dress," I said coldly. Just because he looked mouthwatering didn't mean I wasn't still angry with him for rejecting me so coldly the night before or for the years of torment.

"So?" I said, raising one brow, expecting answers.

"I'd hoped we could have dinner first and then talk. I don't want us to be interrupted, and unfortunately, the dinner begins in ten minutes."

I resisted kicking his shin. I didn't know if I could take more waiting. "You must really hate me or really want me to hate you."

"I promise, it's neither. I'm ready to tell you anything you want to know, but after we eat."

I could see that the stubborn man had made up his mind and wasn't going to change it. "Fine. What's the dinner for anyway?" I asked.

Guy stared appreciatively at my chest before answering. "We will honor the dead with a celebration feast. The Uchben do not believe in funerals." He held out his arm. "My return is also being toasted. Shall we?"

"Fine. But when we come back, you and I are having a long talk, and I want answers."

"You, my sweet"—his eyes ran down the length of my body and then looked at my face—"can have anything you want."

My stomach did a little cartwheel and those stupid feelings returned with a vengeance. *Back! Back. We are so not going there again.* I'd be a complete idiot to fall for his pseudo affections after what happened the last time. A complete idiot.

I smiled sweetly. "Answers will do just fine. Thank you."

Dinner was held in a giant medieval-looking ballroom on the compound. The open room was dimly lit by several wrought iron candelabras and rustic sconces mounted in between life-sized portraits of men, who apparently earned their places of honor by looking or being virulent and brutal.

There were paintings of a blood-spattered redheaded Viking standing on a cliff, an Attila the Hun–looking guy, and even one of a bare-chested Aztec wearing a feather and jade headdress, gripping a severed head in his hand.

Classy. Where could I get prints for my living room?

Speaking of heads, the headcount easily exceeded two hundred tuxedo-clad men of all ages and their dates. So naturally, Guy and I were precariously seated smack in the middle of a long, U-shaped table, where we could be easily seen. And stared at. And talked about like live centerpieces or animals on exhibit at the zoo. Awkward.

After the nerve-racking meal, which Guy ate none of with the exception of dessert—cookies, oddly enough—there were toasts and cheers, ceremonies, and songs for the recently deceased. It was like a giant antediluvian frat party.

Somewhere between the wrap-up dinner speeches, I noticed Tommaso enter through the side door and take an empty seat. He shot a tiny twitch of a smile my way when he noticed me glaring at him.

Not surprisingly, he looked fashion shoot unbelievable. Tailored dark gray suit, black shirt and tie, and hair combed neatly back. Absurdly, I found myself wondering what it might be like if I had serious feelings for him. I'd probably be much happier.

I noticed he was trying not to stare, but it was almost impossible not to look my way. Guy was at my side being the boisterous center of attention, laughing and playfully heckling the speakers with his deep, velvety voice that filled the room. When Guy stood up and told one final story about his time with Buddha—I had a hard time with that one, I have to admit—even I was fascinated by this new, crowd-pleasing side of him.

Afterward, everyone moved into the larger hall next door for after-dinner drinks and music—compliments of the live orchestra. I think an additional five hundred or so showed up, and Guy was obviously the guest of honor. I was clearly his arm candy since he kept me pinned to his side. Was that why he'd invited me? For show? Or perhaps he'd been afraid that Tommaso might've asked me and didn't want me—aka his possession—hanging out and socializing with another male. That was the sort of sadistic crap Guy would pull.

See. You're much better off without him.

I tried to keep up, politely nodding and shaking hands with person after person, but it was impossible to remember everyone's names, except for the Alexanders. There were at least fifty of those.

"Why so many?" I asked Guy.

"I asked the chiefs the same question when I reviewed the new soldier roster," Guy explained. "Apparently, he is—was—our most famous Uchben."

"What did he do?"

"He killed Hitler," he whispered.

"Oh. I thought Hitler committed suicide."

"No. Ixtab was indisposed that day."

Ixtab? "Huh?"

"Never mind." Guy scanned the room, practically glowing with pride. "The Uchben have truly become such impressive killing machines. They make me feel very proud."

What an odd yardstick this man carried. "Sure. Okay. Hey, since you and the other gods have been locked away, who's been giving them orders?" I asked.

"They have directives they follow at all times," he replied. "That's what the chiefs' roles are for, enforcing them. It's a very efficient system. We only provide occasional oversight, and the directives can only be changed by a unanimous vote of the gods."

I didn't know what to say to that. The foreignness of this new world made me feel uneasy. It was as if my reality was nothing but a thin sheet of ice, and every time I took a step, another crack appeared. But I didn't want it to shatter; I liked my reality. Well, maybe I didn't like it, but at least I'd become accustomed to it. *Better than the devil you don't know . . .*

Guy's attention quickly moved back to the crowd gathering around, anxiously awaiting yet another anecdote, so

I slipped away to the bathroom for a break. Being near him all night was too intense.

I'd almost arrived to the ladies' room doorway when I heard a deep voice say, "Going somewhere?"

I turned to find Tommaso leaning casually against the wall, arms crossed, smiling at me.

"Hi," I said and kept walking.

"Are you enjoying yourself?" he asked.

"Did you enjoy your *stuff* today?"

"What 'stuff'?"

I perched one hand on my hip. "It was *your* 'stuff.' Why don't you tell me?"

"Oh, I see. Did Mr. Santiago tell you that?"

"Maybe. Or maybe your stand-ins, Robert and Michael, who had time to take me shopping all day, did." I was seriously annoyed he'd ditched me.

"Emma, I don't know what kind of garbage they've fed you, but that's not what happened." His face turned red, and he looked like he was ready to explode.

"Then?" I asked.

"I spent the day getting a physical and outfitted for my new assignment—Siberia."

Siberia? What the hell? I didn't want him to go; he was the one person I knew I could trust in this crazy new world. "When do you leave?" I asked.

"I was supposed to go tonight, but my visa won't be ready until morning." He didn't look happy.

That soon? I hoped it wasn't because of the fact I hadn't jumped all over him when he'd kissed me. I simply wasn't in a place where I could offer him anything more than friendship, even if I wanted to.

"But why? Why are you leaving?" I said.

"Emma, I was given a choice: leave the Uchben or take this new assignment. I'm pretty sure you can guess why." His eyes flickered across the room toward Guy, who was busily chatting with a large, redheaded man wearing a kilt. He sort of looked like the bloody Viking in the painting. Maybe a descendant?

"He's forcing you?" I asked. Well, that figured. The one person I could call a friend and Guy was sending him away.

"Apparently."

Well, in the words of the great band Placebo, I said, "Someone call the ambulance."

"Why? Is something wrong?" Tommaso asked, confused.

"Because there's going to be an accident." I turned and started pushing through the crowd toward Guy, who was about to have a deep conversation with my knee.

"Emma, wait!" Tommaso called, but I was determined to bulldoze my way to Guy.

Then a thinly built older man with a grayish beard stepped in my way. "Emma, it's so nice to meet you!"

"Excuse me—don't mean to be rude, but I have to talk to someone." I stepped to one side, and he matched my move. I stepped again, and he followed. It looked like we were doing a bad box step.

"I just wanted to introduce myself and ask if we could have coffee tomorrow?"

"I'm sorry, who are you?" I asked, my eyes looking past the man and hatefully zeroing in on Guy.

"I am Xavier. Votan—I mean, Guy—told me about you, so naturally I'm eager to study you while I have the chance. I'm what you'd call the in-house historian and spiritual guidance counselor—a long story—but your help could assist others of your kind acclimate to their situation, if we find any."

"I'm sorry, what? Acclimate?" I tried to focus on the quirky little man, but all I could think about was punishing Guy.

"Yes," he said. "I realize my request may seem callous after everything you've been through, but I figure a few questions wouldn't bother someone as strong as you. After all, you've been the constant companion of the God of Death and War."

"Yeah, interesting." I nodded while glaring across the room.

"But we're so pleased you've brought him back to us, my dear," he rattled on. "Things tend to spiral out of control without the gods' help. For example, have you seen that terrible show, *The Real Housewives*? That wouldn't have existed if the gods hadn't been locked away." He chuckled.

"Sorry?" My attention bounced back.

"I was making a joke, but, uh, I guess old, retired priests aren't so funny these days."

"No. I mean…sorry, can you repeat that part about God of Death and War?"

Xavier's face flushed. He tugged at the collar of his tux. "Oh, heavens. I thought you knew."

The room melted away. "Tell me, please?"

The priest looked at me sideways. "I—uh—really sh-shouldn't," he stuttered. "It's not my place."

"Did you just say that Votan—Guy—is the God of Death and War?"

He hesitantly replied, "Well, well, yes. I did, but—"

"What does that mean exactly?" I was going to throw up.

"It means his special talent, what he's best known for, is..." He cleared his throat. "Death and war, my dear."

Well, great. Now my life was just perfect. And how stupid of me not to see it before. Anyone who looked at the man knew he was lethal, not to mention tedious and annoying. Of course, he was the God of Death and War.

My world froze, but the little old man didn't seem to notice because he continued to ramble on. "They all have many special talents, you know. Dozens in fact. But they're usually known best for the ones they excel at or by what the adoring culture values most. For example, Votan, Guy, is also known as Coquenexo, the Lord of Multiplication and the God of Drums. It's quite funny when you think about it." He removed his glasses and rubbed his nose. "And the Norse, well, they called him Odin; they worshipped him for his skills at poetry and killing. Quite odd. Then there were the Germanic who called him Wotan—"

"Excuse me." My face went cold, and blood had pooled in my feet. I turned away from the little man and headed for the door. I needed to get out of there.

All this time, I'd been living with a killer. The Grim Reaper.

Could things get any worse?

I paced back and forth in Guy's quarters, thinking through my options. I could play it calmly and not let on that I was in a hysterical panic, then break our bond and run away.

Okay. That wouldn't work. Maybe he'd snap my neck before I got to the door or chain me up in some dungeon. Surely this place had one. Or ten. Then there was choice number two. Cry. Yes, crying always helped when I felt overwhelmed. No. No. That was no good. I could—

The door swung open. Guy entered, smiling like he'd just come back from the best night of his life.

Of course, having seven hundred people groveling all night, worshipping him for being a ruthless killer was glorious fun.

Guy's eyes met mine, and his bright white smile melted away.

"Is it true?" I asked, standing at the farthest end of the room at the foot of the bed.

"Is what true?" He removed his jacket.

"What do you think?"

"Honestly, Emma, I'm not one for games." He sat down on the couch in the small sitting area with his back to me and started removing his shoes.

"Are you really the God of Death? Is that your special talent? Killing people?"

Guy glanced over his shoulder at me. "And don't forget war."

"No. Who could forget that?"

"Oh, come on, Emma. You can't define me by that silly title. You of all people should know better."

"How many people have you killed?" Just looking at him now made me imagine battlefields littered with bloody masses while Guy hovered over them in his flaming chariot, laughing. A bit dramatic. I know. But that's what my imagination came up with.

He stood up and took a few steps toward me. I noticed he'd removed his socks. Even his perfect toes looked powerful and lethal. Could he throw star darts with them?

"Emma, please don't look at me that way. It's not like

that." Was that disappointment I saw in his eyes? Mr. Arrogant Killer felt bothered by my disapproval of his profession?

"How many?" I said, chewing my thumbnail.

"What difference does it make, woman?"

"It just does. I want to know."

"If I tell you ten thousand or a million, you'll still see it the same way, and it doesn't address the fact that every time I take a life, it's the right thing to do. It's what I must do, even if I don't want to." He slowly unbuttoned his shirt, leaving on the plain white tee underneath.

I tried not to notice the swell of his biceps or the rise of his pecs, which created two crescent-shaped shadows beneath them. I tried not to notice how the line of his body started at his broad shoulders, tapered down into a tight waist, and then flowed out into two powerful thighs. I tried not to notice when he ran his fingers through his thick blue-black waves and how they fell around his wickedly handsome face. Because if I did, I might find myself wanting him past the point of no return. So, nope. Wasn't looking. I was going to cup my hands over my lust and sing, *la-la-la-can't-hear-you*, because I knew better now. I needed to remind myself of the night before and the unforgettable humiliation of being rejected, not to mention he was death personified.

"How do you know you're not killing good people?" I argued. "And what about redemption? What about people making mistakes and deserving second chances?"

"That's a very altruistic perspective, and sweetly naive, Emma, but the difference between good and evil is easier to determine than you think. Sadly, you would never understand such a thing because you're human. You can't see into their souls like I can."

"I'm not just a human. Remember? But I guess you're right—the numbers don't really matter. It's simply what you are that disgusts me."

"Disgusts you?" His face lit up with resentment, and for once I wasn't so sure it was a good idea to push his buttons. Oh—wait. Yes, it was. It would be easier to get him to let me go.

"Yes. I can't be around a killer. I want out, Guy. I want my life back, and you have no right to continue hijacking it under the guise of protecting me. You have no right to keep me, treating me like your plaything and forcing me to share your sick little world!"

He crossed the room and stood boldly in front of me, glowering down. "Don't I? Don't I have every right if it's for the greater good?" The air around us radiated with his energy.

"Holding me hostage and keeping the truth from me, is that for the greater good? Or controlling me with fear to feed that gargantuan ego of yours?"

"I'd never do that. I always put my responsibilities first. I've always put you first," he growled.

"Is trying to remove Tommaso from my life for the greater good, too? Is it!? Because I'm pretty damned sure that falls into the category of just plain old jealousy."

"Oh, I see. This is all about him, isn't it?" he scathed.

"Did you get Tommaso assigned to Siberia?"

"Maybe." Guy crossed his arms.

"Afraid of a little competition?"

Guy's eyes narrowed. "I simply didn't want you to get hurt."

"You arrogant, bloated— The only one who's hurt me is you!"

"You know, Emma, I didn't create you or the Maaskab.

I'm not the bad guy, and this victim of Guy crap is getting pretty old."

"I'm glad you agree because there's nothing more pathetic than an ancient, bloodthirsty deity who feels the need to control a scared young woman whose only flaw is being born with the wrong bloodline—"

"You're just bitter because of last night," he said with a raised voice. "But you never let me explain—"

"You're right," I snapped. "I am bitter. Someone I love very much was taken from me, and I still don't know why!" Did I mean Grandma or . . . Guy, who'd rejected me? Both? I was so confused! "Now those psychos want to hurt me and the rest of my family. You—you keep me in the dark about everything, even though you promised me answers. Even after I endured years of being branded a freak because of you! And now, well, stupid me! I'm bitter because I'd started to believe in you. That you had a heart and even, call me crazy, genuinely cared about me. But now I see it clearly. You don't care about anyone."

Guy's jaw muscles tightened; his bright turquoise eyes undulated with ripples of black. "That's not true. I've given you my oath to look after you—"

"Really?" I screamed. "That's what you call it? Well, then why am I still sitting here, heartbroken and wondering what happened to my grandmother? Why can't you tell me what you know? And why are you sending away Tommaso, the one person I trust?"

His one eye ticked.

That made him mad. Good.

"Sometimes," he growled, "withholding information is for your own good. Why should I make you suffer for that which you cannot change?"

"Because I need to know the truth! And if treating me like a child is your version of looking after me, I don't want your protection."

"You ungrateful—"

"This ends right now," I interrupted. "I don't want you in my life. I don't want you anywhere near me."

"You're just angry, but if you let me—"

"No. It's over. I don't want your protection. Do you hear me? I. Don't. Need. You."

The room was so silent that I could hear his blinding fury vibrating through the air. His face was as hard as stone.

Then, I recited, "*Kaacha'al lu'um, tumben k'iin*," the words Tommaso taught me, and braced for his divine wrath.

Twenty-Eight

Guy's first thought was that he wanted to take the woman and finally give her that spanking he'd always dreamed of. She was whiny, hotheaded, and too naive for her own good. She was also filled with a delightful, fiery, unstoppable life force and would stand up to anyone, even the most powerful being on the planet. Even one whose gift was killing.

So brave. So full of light. Adorable.

His second thought was how badly he wanted her to understand. If he could get her to calm down, he could start explaining how things worked in his world. For gods, mankind came first. Responsibility came first. He truly didn't mean to hurt her, but something about Tommaso made him uneasy. Maybe he simply wasn't good enough for her, but then again, no one was.

Guy had been ready to tell her everything, including why he'd rejected her. He felt she deserved the truth. But when she broke the bond, something snapped. It wasn't simply the hit to his male ego because, yes, he'd never been rejected in such a monolithic manner. Instead, it was the excruciating pain as she ripped her essence away. A piece of their souls dwelled inside the other's. That's how the bond formed. Severing something so strong was like cracking an atom. His atoms.

Worst of all was the giant gaping hole left behind. Her light was the only piece of him that felt peaceful and warm. Without this tiny fragment of Emma, he was nothing but a savage, a coldhearted deity.

I need her, he finally realized. More than he cared to admit and for reasons he'd yet to fully understand. He needed her. And she needed him, too; he'd felt it through their connection on endless occasions. So why did she torment him like this? Why couldn't she understand that everything he was doing was to protect her? "You're always so full of surprises, my sweet." He reached out and roughly stroked the light copper spirals that framed her delicate face and vibrant dark green eyes—eyes that were, at the moment, filled with a cocktail of anger and lust.

She turned her head away from him.

"Can't you feel it now?" he said in a low voice. "The emptiness? You. Need. Me."

"No. You're a killer, a demon. You forced yourself into my life and don't ever forget it."

"Emma, I am the darkness that makes light possible. I kill because someone has to destroy those born soulless and evil, those who rape, murder, and breed darkness. And for this, you reject me? Judge me? You have no clue what I've endured, what I've sacrificed for humanity."

Her gaze was white-hot. "No, I don't. But how could I? You never tell me anything!"

"Because I want to shield you from such drudgery. Trust me, I have given everything!" His anger quickly spiraled as more of Emma's calming essence abandoned him and returned to her.

Guy pushed her against the wall, pinning her with his hard body. "Say it again, Emma," he snarled in her ear. "Say it, dammit. Say you don't need me to keep those Maaskab from finding you and tearing out your heart or keeping them from killing your family. Say. It. Because without the bond, without me, you're as good as dead, just like Gabriela."

She tightened her lips and ground her teeth before stiffly turning her head to meet his smoldering glare. "I will never fucking need you. You're nothing but a medieval bastard. The Uchben will still protect me. *Tommaso* will protect me."

Guy could feel her slipping further away and his savage side becoming more dominant. He could take no more. He pulled back his body a fraction of an inch and pinned her arms above her head to peer into her eyes. Her pupils were wide and inviting.

Yes. Lust and anger, matching his own, he thought. He could smell the intoxicating cocktail of emotions wafting from her skin.

He sucked in a deep breath, wanting to pull some piece of her, any piece of her back inside him. Thoughts of their bare, sweaty flesh sliding against each other flashed in his mind. He felt his cock stiffen and his humanlike body flood with need. "Tell me, Emma." He exhaled into her ear and then ran his lips down her neck. "Tell me that you don't need me, that you don't want me."

He moved his mouth to that sensitive spot just below

her earlobe. "Tell me you don't ache to have my tongue inside your mouth, licking every inch of your body. That you don't want the tip of my hard cock slipping inside you, dipping in and out, until I break you of that horrible, distasteful attitude of yours. Tell me you don't want me to fill you over and over again, making you come so hard that I brand myself in your mind. That after I've made you swollen from riding you for hours, how you abhor the thought of me taking you slowly, slipping between your hot thighs until you moan one last time and convulse underneath me. Say you don't want it, little virgin, say it."

Her body collapsed against him, but Emma's eyes were shut tight, her face a fortress of flushed turmoil.

No female could resist the potent pheromones radiating from his body; it was one of his best tricks of the trade. Even better than his voice or the categorical perfection of his male form. All he had to do was focus, and his body turned into a seduction factory. He could hypnotize an entire city block of women with it if he wanted. This was how he would get Emma to return the bond, to need him again like he needed her. Oh yes. He could already smell her pungent desire leaking from every pore in her body, from between her legs. Each molecule vibrated with one unified message: *I want you*, they said.

"I. Don't. Want. You." Emma panted.

What? Guy slammed his fist past her head and into the wall. *Stubborn woman!* She was driving him mad. And she was lying.

"You'll regret saying that," he growled.

"Go ahead." She lifted her chin. "Hurt me. I know you're not capable of anything else."

He took several calming breaths to get ahold of himself. What was he doing? He didn't need her. He didn't need anyone. As painful as it was for him to go back to his old self, it did give him back his freedom—freedom from this painful neediness for a human. *No. This is good,* he thought. *I've lived all but twenty-two years of my existence without being bonded to Emma. I'll be heartless, never again know peace, but fine.*

He gathered himself together, burying his pain. *I still need to protect her. I still need her help.* He suddenly felt drained, like someone had pulled the plug from his body and every ounce of energy had been ripped away. His heart ached, and his head throbbed. He wanted to simply wither away quietly. Alone. Facing eternity as the cold-hearted God of Death and War.

Her eyes flipped open, and her gorgeous mouth held a wicked smile. "It's your move, Mr. War and Death. The bond is broken, and I'm not putting up with your bully tactics any longer. I'm not your plaything, and if you ever cared for me, even with one tiny, arrogant cell in your pea-sized brain, you'd let me go."

"Fine. You win," he said, removing his grip. "You're on your own. I only ask that you do one thing."

"What?" She remained against the wall, holding herself upright.

"Remember when I told you in the car that the other gods are trapped in the cenotes?"

She nodded yes.

He shoved his hands through his hair. "We need you to go back to Mexico and free them."

Her expression was unreadable, and without the bond, he couldn't sense her emotions like before. Was she frightened or just angry?

"Are you serious?" she responded. "That place is crawling with Scabs."

"You were able to free me, so you can free them, too. There is no one else to do it."

"I almost drowned, Guy," she protested.

"We'll take precautions, but I need the other gods free, Emma. I can't coordinate the Uchben, hunt Cimil, and take care of the Maaskab by myself. It's ultimately your choice, but know if you don't do this, women will continue being stolen from their families and slaughtered. Your family will continue to be in danger."

"Sure. No pressure. Can I ask you something?"

Guy nodded.

"Did you ever care about me? Or was it always about this?"

"Emma, I care more than you'll ever know. But you're right to push me away. I'm a coldhearted being, incapable of truly caring for anyone. As soon as this is over, you shall be free from me."

Twenty-Nine

Adrenaline shot through every crack and crevice of my smoldering body. He had each one of my cells aching for him. Yes, I wanted him. So badly it almost split me in two and left me hollow. It took every ounce of strength in my quaking body to lie to him. But I couldn't allow him to further his dangerous, emotional stranglehold on me. Not when it made me feel so weak. Not when I needed to face the reality of my situation. From now on I would belong—lock, stock, and barrel—to one person and one person only: me.

That's what I believed anyway, until I spouted off that phrase, breaking our bond. Afterward, I felt anything but free and strong. It felt like a piece of me had been ripped away. Empty.

Why didn't he feel the same? How could he go from a chest-pounding, feral, seduction machine to Mr. Cool As a Cucumber? Because our link was meaningless to a deity like him. He had plenty other humans he was bonded to, according to Tommaso.

Yes. I'd made the right decision. It had to be this way.

"Fine. I accept. Oh, and there are two conditions."

He waved his hand lazily through the air. Was he bored by all this? Sure, he was. "Go on."

"First, you tell me everything you know about my grandmother. Second, Tommaso has to come with us, and you let him pick his assignment after."

Guy's eyes twitched the moment the word *Tommaso* left my lips. "That's three."

"Yeah, I guess it is, but those are my *three* conditions. Take it or leave it," I said, as if I were in a position to negotiate. Ha. Finally, unquestionable proof. I really was insane.

"Agreed," he said as if utterly uninterested by the whole situation.

What was with this man?

He walked over to the bed and lay down, lacing his fingers behind his head before shutting his eyes.

"What are you doing?" I asked.

He cracked open one shimmering turquoise eye, then snapped it shut. "Now that you've released me, I thought I might enjoy the serenity and relax."

"You're supposed to tell me everything you know about my grandmother."

"I agreed to tell you, but you didn't specify when. So I'm going to sleep. We'll talk in the morning."

Damn that man! Damn him to hell. When would I learn? "You can't sleep there," I said.

"You don't need me, remember?" he said drowsily. "And these are my quarters. But just to prove how gracious of a god I can be, you can have the couch," he mumbled.

"I'd rather sleep in the dirt than be in the same room with you."

He pulled the covers over his shoulders. "Fine by me, little girl. Just stay on the compound since I'm sure the Scabs have people waiting outside, hoping for the opportunity to snap you up."

"Maybe I'll go see where Tommaso is sleeping."

"He's already gone." He rolled over and gave me his back.

"Where?"

He yawned. "I saw you talking to him at dinner and knew you'd insist he go to Mexico with us. So I sent him on ahead to start scouting."

Sneaky jerk. Tommaso hadn't been sent to Siberia.

"What are you doing, Guy? One minute you're ready to tear off my clothes and the next you're—"

"Emma, you've made yourself clear. Take glory in your success. You have no need for me, nor desire me in your life. I concede. And now if you'll let me get some rest, I've been seventy years without sleeping in a bed." He turned off the lamp.

It was almost midnight, but I figured it was worth taking a chance. I knocked quietly on the door and waited, listening for some movement inside.

The door cracked open. "Emma! What a pleasant surprise. A late one, but . . . come in."

Xavier wore a navy-blue jogging suit. I guessed those were his pajamas. "Yeah. I hope you don't mind, but I asked the guards at the gate where to find you. It took me a while. This compound is gigantic."

He smiled warmly. "I get lost all the time. Just wait until you see what we have underground—oh." He placed his hands over his mouth. "I'm not supposed to talk about that. It's such a bad habit of mine, saying things I shouldn't."

I'd definitely come to the right place.

Xavier offered me green tea, and we sat down at his kitchen table. The small cottage had a charming feel despite the piles of books in every corner and the dried-out plant hanging from the ceiling near the soot-coated chimney. In fact, every building I'd seen on the compound had some kind of rustic charm. Everything in Uchben Land—my new name for this crazy place—was remarkably beautiful. Stone walkways, fountains, blossoming gardens with marble statues, and perfectly preserved stone buildings—these people had to have significant means to maintain everything so immaculately.

"So what brings you to my doorstep so late at night?" he asked.

I shrugged. "I didn't really know where else to go. Guy and I don't exactly get along sometimes, maybe never again."

"Ah, yes. He's got a temper, that one, and can be quite arrogant. But they're all that way."

"So you know them, the other gods?" I sipped my tea.

"No. Heavens, I've just read about them. I'm only sixty-eight, and the gods have been…indisposed, as you're aware. However, soon I hope to have the honor. Nothing would satisfy this old man more."

"You're not that old," I pointed out. "Sixty-eight is the new forty-eight."

He chuckled. "Well, my only regret is that I won't meet Yum Cimil. They'll be sure she's locked up when they find her. And from my research, she's the most fascinating. Did you know the Mayans believed her to be a man? I suppose it has something to do with her being the God of the Underworld, but that's not her at all..."

I could tell Xavier might easily talk for hours. He was genuinely passionate about the topic, especially about her. "Xavier? I have to ask you something, if you don't mind."

He rested his cup on the table. "Of course not."

"Why do the Maaskab want to kill me? Why did they take my grandmother?" I knew he had already heard about her and everything else having to do with my life. There were no secrets in this Uchben society.

"That is a loaded question. I wish I knew, Emma."

"I'll accept an educated guess," I pleaded.

He shuffled his fingertips on the table next to his teacup. "We think they're trying to remove the gods and anything related from the picture."

"Lucky me."

"What we cannot fathom is why one of the gods went through so much trouble to make the Payals—the demigods."

"I'm sure it wasn't that much trouble. There must be a lot of women willing to spend a night with one of Guy's brothers."

His quirky little laugh filled the small room. "I'm sure they would, but it's easier said than done."

"Why's that?" I fidgeted with the stone hanging around my neck, sliding it up and down the silver chain.

"That's what makes this whole thing so interesting. The gods can't have relations with humans—at least, not without the human enduring excruciating pain and turning into a vegetable. Even the god experiences some pain, though I wonder if it's more frustration than anything; they are immortal, after all. But there's something about the chemistry of the two species. They're not compatible. It's like mixing—"

"What? He can't have sex?"

Oh my God, no pun intended, but the entire time, I'd thought it was normal for the gods to have relationships with humans, to have children. Mythology was full of stories about demigods—half human, half deity. But was it called *myth*ology for a reason? Why hadn't Guy told me Payals were unique? Wait. How was my grandmother created?

"No, this is not possible for him," he confirmed in a matter-of-fact tone. "That's to say, it was never possible before. And trust me, they've tried. The gods are a lusty handful, except with each other, but someone found a way. You're proof of that. And that means they went through a lot of trouble to figure out how to procreate, including finding women strong enough to bear mixed-blood children. That's another astonishing miracle."

"Yes. A frigging miracle—wait—he...I mean, they can't even make out?"

Xavier gave me a disapproving glance.

"Oh. Sorry," I said.

He continued, "This is one of the reasons I wanted to speak to you. I thought you'd consider letting us study you. Maybe we can figure out how it was done. Just a few blood samples and perhaps a body scan. Nothing painful. We can save the dissection for later." He laughed.

"Sure," I answered absentmindedly.

My frontal lobe churned, frantically processing the facts. *Oh!* Cue giant neon flashing aha. Send information to temporal lobe. Add emotions. *That manipulative, conniving bastard! That lowlife, scummy...* His little erotic play was all a show. A mind game. Then when he saw it wasn't working, he'd changed tactics. "Sure, you can go, Emma," he'd said. But he was working me! *Damn that man or deity, crap—whatever.*

And he hadn't rejected me yesterday. That scorching sensation had been him overloading my circuits. Why didn't he tell me instead of letting me suffer? Oh. Oh. Oh. Hell hath no fury like a Payal scorned.

"Okay," I said.

"Excellent," Xavier said. "We can run the tests first thing in the morning at our clinic."

"You said there were others like me?" I asked. I knew about my grandmother, but I wondered if there were more.

"You're the first we've actually seen. But yes, from what we can piece together, there are others, or there were others. One of the gods—again, we don't know who—started procreating about eighty years ago. Unfortunately, the offspring could all be dead by now if the priests have been hunting them."

I couldn't imagine what those poor, poor women had been through. Maybe I was luckier than I knew to be alive.

Yes, because of Guy, I reminded myself. "Do you think I should go back to Mexico and help him free the other gods?"

"He's taking every precaution to keep you safe. And we've been working around the clock, searching our libraries, databases, everything we can to understand how the Maaskab are creating their powers. Mr. Santiago is also sending hundreds of our fiercest Uchben with you, and dozens more ahead to scout the area beforehand."

"That's good to know. And after, what am I going to do?"

"Don't worry." He reached across the table and patted my hand. "Once the gods are free, they'll find a way to fix this mess. And until then, your bond with him will keep you safe. He won't abandon you."

"Not anymore. I released him," I admitted.

"You broke the bond? Why would you do such a thing?"

Yeah, and it wasn't painless like Tommaso said. In fact, I felt sick. Hollow and sick. Tired, too. I could barely keep my eyes open. "I needed to be free. He was only using me, controlling me."

There was a long, silent pause. Silence? The voices were quiet. Had removing the bond done that, too? I listened for a few moments just to be absolutely certain.

Yes! Silence. Sweet, blessed silence in my brain! No more buzzing. Maybe breaking the bond wasn't such a bad idea after all.

"I've studied the gods for twenty years, Emma. I've read every myth, archive, and every history book. Without a doubt, they are the most conceited, perplexing, and difficult beings on the planet. But Votan always does what's right. He genuinely cares about this world, and that includes you. Even if it means making choices you may not agree with or understand."

"Of course, you'd say that. You're an Uchben," I said.

"Dear, I would never lie or betray my own faith, especially to make the gods look good in your eyes."

"Sorry, I shouldn't have said that." I sipped down the last of my tea.

He said, "Did Votan—sorry, Guy—ever tell you he agreed to stay in his role for eternity just so he could create and build the Uchben society? It was his brainchild, you know."

"No, but there's a lot he hasn't told me. In fact, he tells me nothing."

Xavier left the table and went to the kitchen, returning with the warm kettle to refill our cups. "It was the only way the other gods would agree to partner with humans. No one wanted to inherit his responsibilities, and a rotation of duties was due—they used to change every few thousand years. This was an important turning point in history. Votan was the only god who believed humans could be trusted to drive their own destiny. He believes the gods were created to help humans evolve and that humans weren't simply put on this planet to be controlled like children.

"Little by little, the others have come around to his side, but it took a great sacrifice on his part. He will forever have to be the God of Death and War."

I suddenly felt sorry for Guy. When he'd screamed that he'd given up everything, I'd thought he was being dramatic. But he really had. Nonetheless, that didn't excuse his little power play.

"So you trust him?" I asked Xavier.

He nodded. "I trust he has the best of intentions in his heart. He's also much older now and has had more time to make mistakes, and is therefore wiser. That doesn't mean he's perfect if that's what you're asking."

Xavier was right about that. Guy wasn't perfect—on

the inside, anyway. And why would he trust the entire human race, but not me? Why wasn't I worthy of driving my own destiny? "Thank you, Xavier. I really appreciate you taking the time to talk to me."

"Anytime, dear girl." He smiled.

"Can I ask one more thing?"

"Absolutely." He nodded. "Anything."

"Can I sleep on your couch?"

Thirty

Oddly enough, I slept pretty well, even if it was a lumpy old couch and not the extra-long king-sized bed that felt like twenty clouds stacked one on top of another, which was currently occupied by the man—deity—responsible for causing some of the most painfully frustrating moments in my life. That list of moments was growing longer with each passing day and now included being falsely coerced into hormonal and emotional overload.

I looked at my watch. It was five in the morning and dark outside, but the sleep had done wonders, and I had unfinished business to settle. No matter what it took, I was going to make that man—deity—come clean.

I slipped on my heels and crept out the door, finding two large men in dark gray military garb standing at attention just outside. I shook my head and laughed. "Sure. He says I'm on my own now. Frigging con artist,"

I said aloud and marched toward Guy's quarters, the two men following closely behind.

When I arrived, I cracked open the door and peeked in. He was still right where I'd left him: tucked cozily into his bed, bare back to me. *Uh-huh. Let's give you a nice wake-up call, Emma-style.*

I ran my hand over the side of my head. I still had on last night's makeup and my hair was a mess. My teeth also needed a good brushing. I grabbed some clean clothes and crept into the bathroom, carefully going over the words in my head.

After a quick shower, I dried my hair, threw on a T-shirt and sweats, and then took a deep breath. "Payback is such a Payal. Let's see how you like playing by your own rules."

I opened the door, the soft glow of early-morning sunlight dusting the room, and tiptoed to the bed. I quietly slid under the soft white sheets and snuggled against his bare back. He was wearing some kind of silky boxers. *Yum.*

I slinked one arm around that tight, firm waist, making sure to teasingly rake my braless breasts between his shoulder blades. There was a small jolt of energy, but now it wasn't so intense. Maybe because I was anticipating it, craving it.

Guy's breathing was even, and he remained perfectly still. I reached around and began skimming my hand over his washboard stomach, stifling my urge to snicker. I felt *incredibly* naughty, which felt incredibly good; but gods, he so deserved this. How dare he twist my heart into giant, ugly knots and sexually bully me with his blatant, misogynistic, strong-arm tactics when he was totally incapable of ever being with a human woman. *Jerk.* "Oh, Guy," I feigned like a saloon harlot. "I'm so sorry for everything. Yes, I need you. I want you." I shamelessly rubbed myself against his firm ass, letting out a tiny, low moan. "I'm sorry I ever doubted you."

Surprisingly, Guy didn't move. Was the man dead or simply in shock? Or perhaps scared as hell because he'd have to fess up that his little man show was a sham? All these years he'd taunted me, flashing his tail feathers. *"Look at me! I'm such a big man, and you're nothing but a little girl."* But he wasn't able to touch a woman without hurting her or enduring excruciating pain himself. And that meant he was still... a virgin? I gasped. Of course he would be. And he'd be a hundred times more frustrated than little ol' me; he was much older.

Let's find out how frustrated. Shall we, Mr. Studtastic? Still spooning, I swept my fingertips, light as a feather, across his naked, smooth shoulder and planted soft, teasing kisses over his shoulder blade. I ran my hand slowly down until I reached his waistband. *Still no reaction? Still pretending to sleep, my friend? Okay then...*

I slid my fingers between the silky waistband of his boxers and his bare hip. Just an inch. Then another and another, until my entire hand was inside the intimate domain of his underwear, gliding up and down over his bare skin—hip, ass, upper thigh. Reverse. Upper thigh, ass, hip. *Yum.*

I found myself enjoying my little skin safari way more than I should, but knowing it couldn't go anywhere gave me a certain sense of reckless liberty. "Guy?" I whispered. "I want you to make every one of my fantasies come true. You were right about everything. I want to take you inside me. And"—I squinted my eyes, holding back my laughter—"ride me for hours."

Unable to resist, I began massaging his firm backside. It was perfect. Velvety, soft skin over solid muscle. And his smell was…amazing. I inhaled deeply, letting the complex, masculine scent fill my lungs. *Okay. Maybe time to stop.*

Just as I was about to say something, Guy rolled on top of me, pinning me beneath him, with a hungry, heated look on his face. "What are you doing, Emma?" he snarled, his turquoise eyes boring into me.

"What does it look like?" I growled back, barely able to breathe with the weight of him on top…on top…sooo on top of me. "Blowing your little charade right out of the water," I managed to finish.

"What are you talking about?"

I took a deep breath to gather my thoughts. "Us. That's what. You know what kills me most? It's not that you're not man enough to actually do any of those things you advertised—because you're not a man—or how you made me feel about my lack of experience, but that you're not tough enough to tell me the truth. You're a coward and a bully."

"I am not—"

"Oh, come on! For once, come clean, Guy. Stop pretending and say the truth. You have weaknesses like the rest of us."

"You're right. About everything. I do have weaknesses." Then he bent his head and pressed his full, angry lips firmly against mine.

Gods. They felt so good. So effing damned good.

Before I had a chance to even think of what to say, his

hot tongue parted my lips, and I found myself accepting it indulgently. His thick waves of soft hair fell like a curtain around our faces.

Okay. Annny minute now. That little scorching sensation was going to kick in... and...

His demanding tongue began making rhythmic, forceful strokes against mine—a seductive display of what the rest of his body craved from my flesh. He gripped my chin with his powerful hand and thrust his thumb against my bottom lip, widening my mouth, demanding I take more of him. It was as if he was desperate to be inside me, and I found myself equally as desperate to oblige.

His sweet, hot breath heaved between my lips. I inhaled, relishing the sensation of Guy's scent filling my lungs, his weight on top of me. His smell was intoxicating. *Yes. Man crack.*

His large, strong hand slipped from my mouth and raked down the length of my neck and chest, and then forcefully tugged my shirt up in a crude gesture of entitlement, exposing my bare breasts.

His primal gaze studied my face for one intense moment before his eyes traveled down to my breasts like they were something he'd just hunted and claimed for himself. A prize.

"Mmmm," he said and then dipped his head. His silky black hair fanned over my shoulder as he began working his warm, wet mouth over my nipple, treating my breast like an ice-cream cone about to melt on a hot summer day. Whatever energy pulsed through him now charged though my sensitive flesh, but there was no searing pain like before. This was all euphoric, mind-blowing tingles, irresistible to my poor sex-deprived body. The flow of blood rushed between my legs, readying me to take him. I bit my lower lip with the stark pleasure of it and burrowed my fingers deep in his hair while he eagerly sucked. I'd never imagined that being with anyone could feel so good. But it wasn't just anyone, it was Guy. A delicious, protective, sexy deity. And in the back of my mind, I knew if he went any further, I wouldn't be able to stop, I'd never be able to get enough.

Okay, I'll ask him to stop. Or I'll stop…in a minute, maybe ten. His tongue started dancing in little circles over the hardened tip of my breast.

Let the poor guy have more ice cream. It's sooo hot out, my lust-driven voice argued.

No, Emma. Bad, my rational mind warned. At least for once, the combative voices in my head were my own. Refreshing.

As I was about to tell him to stop, he nudged my legs apart with his knees and ground himself against me with one long, scrumptious stroke, sending a shock wave of erotic tingles through my most intimate parts. I let out a moan and dug my fingers into his shoulders, almost plummeting off the orgasm cliff right then and there.

My moan sent him off a cliff of his own, the self-control cliff. His body trembled as he pushed his thick, hard shaft hungrily, rhythmically between my legs. His heavy breathing turned into primal panting. And that grinding, that delicious ache, the pulsing of my soft flesh begging for him all created a divine pressure building deep inside, the electricity rushing through our bodies.

It was like being sent to another world. *My new heaven.* And we weren't even having sex?

Pull that foot back, Emma. You're not cliff diving with

this man. Back away from the orgasm cliff, Emma. Do you hear me? said my rational voice. But it was quickly losing the debate.

He bathed my breasts with the steam of his breath for a moment longer, and then his slick, hedonistic lips worked their way to my collarbone, his tongue sliding and massaging in tune with his pumping hips. He found that sensitive hollow at the base of my neck, making my entire body undulate as he savored and sucked. All the while, the grinding between my legs and palming of my breasts continued relentlessly.

Cliff! Cliff! Cliff! my naughty voice chanted.

But it wasn't...he wasn't...we weren't...supposed to... Oh, gods, I couldn't think. And his smell...I was drunk with it. "But how, Guy?" I finally managed to whisper. "How? You..."

"I don't know, and I don't care," he panted against my neck. "I've waited seventy thousand years, Emma. Seventy thousand lonely fucking years for you."

The words floated into my ears, sticking like a sacred commandment I couldn't ignore. *Yes,* I thought, *for you. I...am...for...you.* My mind drifted to those shimmering turquoise eyes; that enormous male frame blanketing my body; those warm, sweaty, diamond-cut muscles; his primal grinding against my wet entrance through my sweatpants. My hips urging him on and on.

Okay, okay. But did you see the size of that man's gear? And that was when it was taking a nap.

He returned his full lips to mine and kissed me with such hunger that our teeth scraped. So delicious.

He shifted his weight to my side, and I felt his powerful hand plowing down the length of my torso, working its way to my waistband. He began tugging at my sweats. Down, down, down. All the way down. Leaving me with only my T-shirt pulled up to my neck and my panties.

He looked me over with those wild, lust-filled eyes. "Ooh, the infamous pink thong. I've dreamed of seeing you in those." His eyes shifted to meet mine. "But I've been tortured with visions of you without them."

Okay. Compromise, said rational voice. *You get on top, check things out, and then decide.*

Deal, said naughty voice. I shifted my weight and rolled him onto his back. He didn't resist; in fact, he smiled.

I straddled him and caught a glimpse of his heaving chest. He looked uninhibited and hungry. His eyes were changing to a dark emerald green with swirls of sky blue.

He sat up, pressing his bare chest to mine. He cupped my ass and pulled me into his thick erection between my legs.

"Oooh," I involuntarily groaned. I could feel myself slipping toward the point of no return quickly.

You're not ready for this, Emma. You can't handle a man like him.

We had a deal! Check out the gear, then decide, argued naughty voice.

Now or never. I slipped my hand between us and gripped his erection through the silky black fabric of his boxers. His body instantly jerked with pleasure as I pushed his cock against my wet panties. My fingers didn't come close to wrapping around that girth. He was enormous. He was also beyond sexy and just the thought of trying to slide him inside me started to send me over the edge. So much man. So thick. So ready. So...*mine*. I slid myself up and down its length, squeezing and massaging his cock. The fact I was a virgin no longer registered. I wanted. I needed. I wasn't leaving his bed until I had him inside me.

He suddenly grabbed the hem of my T-shirt and began pulling it off. The necklace I still wore caught in my hair. He gave a quick tug and the chain broke free. The amulet tumbled to the floor. A searing pain shot through me, and I shoved back from him, writhing in pain, screaming.

"Emma!"

I curled into a tight ball as the scorching fire jolted every muscle in my body, making me shiver with excruciating convulsions.

Two panicked guards burst through the front door, Xavier following behind them. "Oh, heavens. We were outside waiting to talk to you and heard screaming—"

Guy's angry words almost blew out my eardrums when he ordered them to leave.

I rolled over, burrowing my head under several pillows.

As the pain dissipated, humiliation took its place. What had I just done? Correction. Almost done?

I heard Xavier and the two men scramble from the room. Guy muttered something unintelligible at the ceiling, then said, "Emma, I . . ." I peeked at him from under a pillow. He was sitting on the edge of the bed, covering his face with his hands. "Why? Why did you do that?" he said.

I flipped over, gripping the sheets, and sat up. "Well—I—Christ, Guy. I didn't mean for that to happen. One minute I was giving you a taste of your own medicine, and then you were—were giving *it* to me."

"But you knew, Emma, we're not compatible. I could have killed you. What were you thinking?"

He was blaming me and acting like he'd had zero participation? "Screw you."

Okay. Not so classy. Or civilized. But come on. I almost gave the man—or deity, whatever—my virginity in a heat of passion, and he was talking to me like a child who'd colored over an original da Vinci with a Sharpie.

"Yes, I know that's what you were about to do, but how?" he asked.

Smug jerk. I began to cry and pulled a pillow to my face, flopping down onto the bed. "I don't know. I don't."

"Shhh. Okay." He stroked the back of my head. "I'm sorry. We'll figure this out. It'll be okay. Just please don't cry. I hate it when you cry."

I nodded but didn't bother lifting my head.

"Stay right there. I'll be back," he said.

I heard him get out of the bed, slip on his pants, and pad to the door.

There was a rumbling of raised voices outside, and then the door opened.

"Emma? Get decent. You need to hear this."

Thirty-One

Guy let Xavier back in, but not before flashing an apologetic glance over his shoulder. Was the news going to be *that* bad? His eyes said yes.

After providing a ten-minute apology for barging in and interrupting what had almost been a moment I'd remember for the rest of my life, Xavier told us about Friar Bernardino de Sahagún, who'd dedicated his life to recording and documenting the history and folklore of Mesoamerica as the Spaniards took over most of Latin America.

Now, don't get me wrong. Xavier had a calling, which I respected to the nth degree. But what it had to do with my almost act of carnal lust with a god—well, I didn't get the point. Until, that is, he explained how the friar recorded a small group of Mayan descendants near the border of Belize who discovered a mine filled with black jade.

Apparently, the jade was believed to have certain mystical

properties, one being it was absorbent. Not like a Bounty paper towel. This stone absorbed dark energy, emotional energy, and—yes, you guessed it—god energy.

As soon as the words left Xavier's mouth, I knew. I looked down at the necklace on the floor with horror as if it were a cootie-infested lollipop.

"That's how it was done," Xavier exclaimed. "He made them wear a necklace similar to Emma's, blunting his energy so he could sleep with these women. They probably wore it through their pregnancies, as well."

There were several minutes of frantic debate between the two as the dots began connecting.

I stared down at the seemingly harmless piece of jewelry. Could a rock really do all that? Then I remembered that while I had it on, I wasn't able to make a significant dent in Tommaso when I punched his stomach. But later that same day, after it had fallen off, I'd socked Cimil across the room. It had muted my strength, too.

Then there was the gray soot that covered the Scabs' bodies. Xavier explained that they were using this material as a shield, which is why they were so difficult for the gods to track.

"So you think the jars are made of this?" Guy asked Xavier.

"It fits. The jars absorb energy. Then when it's somehow released—"

My eyes nearly popped out of my head. "Did you say 'jars'?"

Xavier's and Guy's eyes froze on me.

"Yes. Why?" Guy asked.

"I saw a jar. There was one floating in that pool you were trapped in, and I flung it at that stupid cat."

"But I thought you released me by reciting the phrase I taught you."

"I never got that far. I was a little distracted by that overgrown kitty. Hey, you don't talk to animals by any chance?"

"Emma! It was the jar. Why didn't you tell me about it?" Guy yelled.

"I thought it was garbage somebody dumped there," I answered defensively.

Guy hesitated. "It's a weapon."

"That little thing?" I stared at the offending, lifeless rock on the floor.

Guy snatched up the necklace. "Obviously, Emma won't mind if we borrow this for a closer look." Guy stopped and smirked. "I'll be sure you get it back."

Oh. I bet he would. It was the magic key to Naughty God Land.

Xavier looked sad. "Do you still believe Cimil is behind this?"

Guy gave him a consoling pat on the back. "I don't know, my friend. If she is, she'll pay."

Poor Xavier. He seemed to have a case of hero worship for Cimil.

Guy called the guards outside, who appeared within seconds. "Call the leads in Mexico. Tell them to find Tommaso and ask him where he obtained this necklace. I want to know where the mine is."

He shoved the necklace into his pocket. "Emma, I have to go." He placed his index finger under my chin, tipping my head to meet his gaze. I was still in stun mode from what just occurred.

Shame? Astonishment? Desperation? The wheel of

emotions spun in my head. *Click. Click. Click!* Ah. There it was. Horror. That was a good one.

Necklace or no necklace, that insane display of reckless lust was all me. One hundred percent Emma. *Damn.* What was I doing fooling around with the God of Death and War? This mess had grown far beyond the old predicament of me being obsessed with a seductive voice in my head. This was a whole other ball game—one that I'd never win and end up heartbroken because, I finally realized, Guy was my Achilles' heel and I couldn't stop myself from feeling things I shouldn't when it came to him.

I gave him a rigid nod, trying to conceal the mental breakdown I was preparing to unleash.

"Hey," he said, sensing something was amiss. "I promise, I'll be back as soon as I can, but I have to gather the chiefs. Now that we understand what we're dealing with, we must rethink our strategy. Xavier will stay with you until I come back." He grinned from ear to ear. "And then we're going to finish this."

I swallowed hard. "But, um..." Now that I'd gathered my wits, which had just returned from a joyride in the hormone-mobile, I didn't want to finish it. I wanted to run far, far away. First from him and then from myself. How could I have come so close to having sex with the man who'd used me, tormented me, and manipulated me? *And who I could so easily fall in love with if I'm not careful.*

Oooh. But who can blame you? Look at him, Emma. Cliff! Cliff! the little voice in my head whined.

No, stop it, I scolded myself. This was getting way out of hand. I'd only end up hurt if I entertained any delusions of him ever loving me. I had to remember that. I had an obligation to help Guy free the others so that they could take care of the Maaskab, ensuring the safety of my family, but after that, we were D-O-N-E.

My dream of being normal still existed. It didn't matter if I wasn't 100 percent human. I was still the same person as before. Still Emma Keane. My life was waiting for me to return to it and finally live it! And Guy didn't belong there. Or did he? I suddenly imagined him killing people all day and then returning home to me—the quaint little yellow house in the country with the vegetable garden—where I'd be waiting for him with a turkey loaf dinner on the table.

Then he'd say, "Hi, honey. Give me a second while I rinse off all this blood."

"Sure, babe," I'd respond. And then we'd eat, sip wine, and share stories about our day. Me, I'd talk about my day at the office. Him, he'd talk about inciting death and war. For dessert, we'd eat cookies—okay, that part wouldn't be so bad—then he'd try to make love to me without frying my brain. Dreamy.

And then there was the age gap, a seventy-thousand-year difference. Not so bad, right? If we were fossils.

He had to see all these dead ends, too. Didn't he? And that meant only one thing: that little incident was simply recreational for him. He couldn't see our relationship any other way.

There. It was decided. All doors leading to any imaginable happily ever after with Guy slammed shut. Dead bolted. Security chained. Chair propped against the handle. Closed.

"Don't worry. I won't be long," he said, changing into a pair of black cargos and a black T-shirt. He must have chosen that outfit on purpose. He looked solid, sleek, and irresistible.

On the other hand... who's talking relationship here? Whatever happened to casual sex?

Shut it, little voice! Stop that. I'm not putting that evil necklace back on. "Okay. See you later," I said with a neutral tone.

He planted a possessive, mind-bending kiss on my mouth and ran out of the room, leaving me alone, flushed, with an overly anxious Xavier. No fun.

"Any advice?" I asked. "Besides a cold shower and a shrink?"

"Not really. But you're quite the pioneer. Bedding Votan." He scratched his chin. "And you broke the bond. Lots of firsts. You're a fascinating creature."

"Thanks."

I didn't want to sit around for hours waiting for Guy's return, so I insisted Xavier take me to the clinic for those tests he'd asked for.

I'd imagined a small office with maybe a first-aid kit and a cot, but it was a small, state-of-the-art hospital, complete with surgical ward, physical therapy, ICU, and everything I guessed a modern hospital needed. He said they preferred to have their own facility because it kept their activities under the radar, especially since they treated the occasional bullet hole and Maaskab knife wound.

I spent a few minutes giving blood, plus an hour taking X-rays. He said he wanted a record of my physical makeup for posterity. Then he sent me to go see the resident psychiatrist. Funny. How did he know I needed one so badly?

Unfortunately, Dr. Lugas had no interest in discussing my personal love life, which made me realize how much I missed my girlfriends. Dr. Lugas was all business. Sixty, only a few inches taller than me, and bald, he was clearly a fan of Italian cuisine. The red sauce stain on the lapel of his white lab coat said it all.

"How long's this going to take?" I asked, looking at Xavier.

"He's just going to ask a few questions. He's an expert at evaluating tolerance for stress and he assesses all our guards."

"Mine will be about as impressive as a one-year-old."

Dr. Lugas asked me some basic background questions for the first twenty minutes. Then, when he asked me to describe the most stressful situation I'd been in over the last few months, well, I had a hard time choosing.

Being pushed by a jaguar into a cenote and almost drowning?

Finding out that the man who called my head his home for the last twenty-two years is a god?

How about finding out that my great-grandfather was one of them?

"I'm going to go with facing the Maaskab in Barolo. That was pretty awful."

"And how did you feel right before the attack?" he asked calmly.

"Pretty pumped, actually. I'd just pummeled Cimil, and she flew across the room. I felt powerful—"

He interrupted, "Did you say you hit Cimil?"

"Square in the jaw. She was strangling one of your guards," I added.

"Have you discovered any other abilities?" Xavier asked.

"I've been wearing the necklace, and I haven't really tried. So, no. I guess I haven't."

"And how do you feel since you broke your bond with Mr. Santiago?" Dr. Lugas asked.

Ugh. Did the whole world know now? Of course they did. With a communication network like the Uchben's, there were no secrets. "I can take care of myself."

Xavier mumbled a few sentences in Italian to Dr. Lugas and then said, "That's an excellent idea."

Dr. Lugas stood up and left.

"Sorry?" I asked. "Did I miss something?"

"Let's see if we can teach you to take care of yourself."

I spent the next few hours hooked to an odd-looking box that monitored my brain waves while they made me do everything from meditation to watching gruesome war movies. Nothing happened. Then they put on a slideshow. Every time an image flashed that made me mad, like some a-hole kicking a dog, Lugas's and Xavier's eyes lit up.

"Dr. Lugas, change the slides," Xavier instructed.

Lugas nodded enthusiastically and opened up his laptop, which was running the images into the projector. With a few quick keystrokes, the pictures changed from photos of babies, flowers, war demonstrations, and other random acts of violence to what felt like the evening news. A photo of a crowd beating a helpless shrouded woman in some Middle East country. Soldiers in some African country firing on a group of helpless women and children. The images broke my heart, and with every image, I felt angrier.

"Enough!" I blurted out. "Why are you making me watch this awful garbage?"

Smiling, Xavier turned the laptop screen toward me. It

showed a real-time line graph that looked like it had registered a ten-point earthquake.

"Yeah? So?" I stared blankly at the two gloating men.

"Emma, don't you understand what this means?" Xavier said.

Hello. Look at my face. "Not really."

Lugas said, "Miss Keane, every time we show you an act of cruelty against someone innocent, your energy surges off the charts."

"Okay?" I leaned back in the blue plastic-molded chair, my hands cupped in my lap.

"Emma, this is big. Huge!" Xavier was almost salivating. "You've got their strength."

"Sorry?" I said, turning to Dr. Lugas. Maybe he could speak Emma-ese?

"You are a very, very strong human," Lugas explained. "And now we know how to make more."

"Super-soldiers, Emma," Xavier said. "Think of what that means. For us—for humanity."

What? Were they insane? "Oh no, boys. I don't think so. You're not going to use me to make Uchi-super-soldiers. Forget it. I'm not a baby factory." Heck, I hadn't even cut the ribbon on the factory yet.

"It doesn't have to be you. It could be any woman. She only has to wear the necklace," Dr. Lugas said, nodding at Xavier.

"No, guys. What you're talking about is wrong. And who says the children will grow up to fight on your side?" I argued.

"Emma, your energy only spikes when you see an injustice. It's identical to the gods. They're hardwired to protect. They're incapable of hurting innocent humans."

Right. Famous last words. I could see arguing with the two was futile. "Fine. Whatever," I said. "But so far, I've done nothing other than light up a screen. Pretty damned useless if you ask me."

"With proper training, you could control it, fight like you did with Cimil," said Xavier.

"Good luck with that. If I could ass-kick on demand, I would have done it by now."

They exchanged glances, and something told me they weren't aligned with my point of view.

"Why don't you give it a try?" asked Xavier.

"No."

"You might be able to use it to kick Mr. Santiago's ass, as you put it."

Xavier was very convincing. "Fine, but this doesn't mean I agree with your lame super-soldier idea." I shut my eyes and tried to coax the energy out.

I focused, relaxing every muscle from my toes to the tips of my fingers, but after ten minutes, nothing happened.

"Sorry, gentlemen." I shrugged and then yawned. Boy, being angry took a lot out of me.

"Not to worry, my dear girl, you simply require practice. Right now you're tired. Let me take you back," said Xavier.

I said my good-byes to Dr. Lugas and left the clinic with Xavier. It was a beautiful day, late afternoon. I hadn't realized how sorely I craved a moment of quiet, alone. *Alone.* The thought made me giddy. No voices, no bees, no one asking anything of me. "I think I'll stay here for a while," I said, pointing to a small bench in the garden courtyard with a cherub-topped fountain. Xavier was about to speak when someone grabbed me from behind.

"Where the hell have you been?" piped Guy.

Xavier reached out his arm, trying to pry Guy from my shoulders. "She was with me at the clinic doing tests. Remember?"

Guy growled, "The guards were to stay with her at all times. I gave specific instructions."

"Let me go!" I tried to pull away from his claws, but he didn't budge. "What the hell is your problem, you damned Neanderthal? I'm not your property." I twisted and elbowed him in the gut, launching him back a few yards.

"Ow. That hurt," he whined, rubbing his stomach.

Xavier couldn't have looked more pleased.

"I guess I needed the right catalyst?" I shrugged and looked at Xavier.

"Nice. You've been teaching her this?" Guy asked Xavier.

"All in the name of science, my friend." Xavier lifted his palms faceup.

"Well, take your..." Guy coolly stopped himself from whatever cruel thing he was about to say. "You're needed back in the main hall. We're leaving, and you are on point to debrief the men about the jars."

"We're leaving?" I asked. "Now?"

Guy's wild eyes were pumped with adrenaline. "We, as in myself and the Uchben. You're staying here."

"I thought you needed me."

"Not anymore. The jars are keeping the other gods trapped in the cenotes, and the Uchben are perfectly capable of removing them."

I was supposed to be relieved. Wasn't I? But something unpleasant was gnawing at me. "I thought you weren't leaving for a few more days. What happened?"

"We were only delaying so Xavier could have a chance to dig up information. He's done that, and now there's no reason to wait any longer. We have work to do."

I could see he was hiding something. "There's more. Isn't there?"

The sun shone on one side of his face. The light made his eyes look softer somehow, like translucent, icy-blue lakes, though his expression was hard. A fortress. He was in warrior mode and thinking about bad things, dark things. Maybe…death? And war?

Of course he was. I sighed. He was such a hopeless case.

He ran his hands over the top of his head and down the back of his neck. "The Uchben we sent ahead are missing. We think the Maaskab were tipped off."

I gasped. "Why do you think that?"

"One of the Maaskab answered Tommaso's cell phone and told us so."

If this were any other situation, I would be cracking a joke about a Maaskab talking on a cell. It would fall somewhere in the category of a vampire riding a unicycle. It just seemed funny.

"But it could be a mind game to make you second-guess your own people. Tommaso could have lost his phone," I offered.

"Perhaps, although not likely."

"So you think Tommaso is dead?" My heart thumped loudly inside my chest. No, I hadn't known Tommaso long, but I already considered him a friend, someone I would be forever grateful to for saving my life.

"Very likely."

How could he be so matter-of-fact about this? It was

my fault. Guy sent him to Mexico because of me. Me. Never in a million years did I imagine he'd be in danger. I wanted to die.

My knees were about to take a siesta. "I—I'm not staying here." I reached my hand out and steadied myself against Guy's chest.

"You'll only get in the way, Emma, and if Tommaso is dead, there's nothing you can do."

The tears began to trickle. "I'm not your property, Guy. You can't tell me what to do. This is all my fault, and I should do something to help."

People were now gathering around us to stare and take pictures of Guy.

"Emma." He grabbed me by the elbow, dragging me across the courtyard. "I get it. You're devastated. This is truly a horrible situation. But Tommaso was—is—a grown man and knew perfectly well what kind of life he'd signed up for. He accepted the risk. But are you so naive that you'd believe he'd want to put your life in danger to save him? Or die needlessly? Are you so stubborn that you're willing to forget those monsters at my villa? How about the pile of bodies they left behind?"

I wanted to vomit. He was right about the Maaskab being dangerous. "What about you?" I asked.

He stopped and turned to face me, then laughed in that deep, arrogant rumble. "Emma. Really. I'll be fine. I'm indestructible, remember?"

"Yeah, famous last words from a man trapped for seventy years in a Mayan swimming hole. And didn't anyone ever tell you it's a bad idea to tempt fate like that?"

He grinned. "You're worried for me, aren't you? This is very flattering. Not to mention a first; I don't think anyone's ever been concerned for my well-being. Not even my brethren."

I suddenly felt silly for behaving like an overprotective mother, but yes, I was concerned. How could I not be? "I'm not worried." *I'm terrified.*

"Yes, you are. Say it. Come on, say it," Guy said like a goofy child.

"Oh, stop it." I smacked his arm. "This isn't funny. Those priests are horrible. And dangerous. And they smell really, really bad."

He shrugged casually. "Which makes it just that much more exciting. It's no fun killing pleasant, nice-smelling creatures, now is it?" He smiled.

Okay. Strange response, but I didn't have time to dig deep into that one.

"Guy?" I slipped my arms around his waist and buried my face in his chest. I inhaled that sweet and smoky scent, which gently infused the air around him. I guessed it was what a god in his position should smell like. Dark, delicious, and deadly?

"Yes?" He wrapped his arms around me.

"I want you to put it back…the bond." If he had to leave physically, I could still keep him with me mentally.

He pulled away just enough to see my face. He looked way too happy, one might even say smug. Like he'd achieved some giant victory. "Why?" he asked.

Because whether I liked it or not, being near him gave me comfort and made me feel safe. It also made me feel vulnerable and afraid—a complete contradiction. But this wasn't the time to go emotional scuba diving and add more feelings to my collection. Not when the tiny ledge of sanity I'd managed to perch on was crumbling. Tommaso, who at a minimum I considered a friend for having risked his life for me, was dead. My family was still in danger, and my life was still in ruins. And as a topper to my chaos salad, I couldn't stand being left behind. I wanted to go to Mexico and see this end myself. I wanted to hear the Scabs tell me what they'd done with my grandmother. I wanted to see them pay for everything.

"Oh, stop gloating." I rolled my eyes.

He laughed loudly. "That's my spunky girl."

Girl? Impossible. He was impossible.

"Emma, I want you to know something." His tone shifted from warm to serious. "It has to do with what you said last night. Despite what you believe, I don't know more about the circumstances surrounding Gabriela's fate. But I have every intention of finding out and punishing the Maaskab severely for everything." He looked away for a moment and then stared down at me, as if willing me to see the honesty in his eyes. "I wanted you to know that before I left."

"Thank you," I whispered. "For telling me the truth." Then a part of me thought about how great it felt delegating my revenge to Guy. I'd bet he was really, really good at it. The best.

"Come on." He brushed his thumb affectionately along my lower lip. "We only have a few minutes. We'll have to make it fast."

Thirty-Two

"What do we have to do? You're not going to make me sacrifice a little bunny or something?" I asked as we charged toward his quarters.

He laughed. "No, my sweet."

There were two men I didn't recognize waiting at his door. "Who are they?" I whispered.

"Jake, Alexander...this is Emma." He gave them a nod. "They are tenth-generation Uchben and will be looking after you."

Jeez, seemed like there was an endless supply of brawny, fierce men around the place. They probably grew them in a garden out back. I smiled and greeted them.

"We'll just be a minute," Guy said. He pulled me inside to the sitting area, then headed for the bathroom. He returned with a pair of silver shears, reached around to the nape of his neck, and cut ten inches off his braid. The rest of his thick shiny hair fell around his face. He looked devastatingly handsome, and I couldn't help but gawk.

"Here. Hold this." He handed me the braid. "Now turn around."

"What? You're going to cut off my hair?"

"Sorry. It was your brilliant idea to break the bond."

I shook my head no. "Isn't there another way?"

"Emma, please, honey. It's only hair."

"Oh, Christ." I turned my back to him and felt the swift execution of my red curls immediately followed by his soft lips and rough stubble brushing against my neck. Images instantly pulsed through my mind of his bronzed hard body sliding over me; his thick, strong hands massaging my breasts; his hot, wet tongue plunging in my mouth.

I shuddered and sucked in a deep breath.

As if reading my thoughts, he whispered in my ear, "I, too, wish we had more time, my sweet. There are many things I need to tell you . . . and to do to you."

I shivered again. "Like what?" I said, my breath suddenly moving as fast as my pounding heart.

Again he whispered in my ear, "Like ridding you of that nasty virginity."

Oh yesss. That sounded nice. *Wait. You're suddenly forgetting everything? You're just ready to give yourself to him?* I paused for a moment. Maybe I was.

No, he didn't love me. In fact, I had no clue what I really meant to him. And yet, somehow, I didn't care. Being near him, feeling the warmth of his lips and body completely shut down those rational thoughts telling me it could never work out: He was a god. I was not. And our pasts came with so much baggage that trusting him the way I needed to felt impossible. And yet I wanted him anyway. What if he never came back? What if this was our last chance to be together? Maybe it was time to jump off that cliff and take a risk, take what I wanted.

"Why wait? I mean, how long could it possibly take? Five—ten minutes?" I wanted it to take hours, but I'd take what I could get and I wanted him to say yes.

An awkward moment of silence passed, and then he placed his hands on my shoulders and turned me into him. His thick, strong lips, his fierce eyes, and his black brows all worked together to form the breathtaking expression on his face. Was it lust? Was it more? I didn't care.

He dipped his head and kissed me hard, threading his large hands through my now much shorter hair. "Gods, woman, you look sexy as hell," he whispered in between the demanding thrusts of his delicious tongue.

I leaned into his large frame, wanting him to know I'd meant it; I was his for the taking.

He groaned, signaling that my offer pleased him. His hands moved slowly down my back, and he cupped my ass to pull me into his hard shaft, making an offering of his own.

My body's temperature quickly escalated from hot to inferno. Oh, gods, he felt deliciously male. The friction of his stubble, the strength of his arms holding me to him, the heat of his body, and the…

Ouch! The heat of his body! I jumped back and doubled over. *Dammit! No!*

I heard him groan, but this time with displeasure. "Hell, the necklace is with Xavier."

Oh, gods. Was this the god equivalent of getting down and dirty at Lookout Point in the back of a Chevy only to discover there were no condoms for a ten-mile radius?

I plopped down on the bed and closed my eyes, waiting

for the pain to dissipate. I felt the bed sink as Guy sat at my side but refrained from touching me. "You okay?" he asked.

I nodded and then opened my eyes. Big mistake. Seeing him, turquoise eyes looming with unquenched lust, face flushed, lips red and swollen, only made me want him more.

"When I come back," he said, "we're going to finish this." He brushed the unruly curls from my face and kissed me softly. Despite the lingering heat, it still felt frigging wonderful to be kissed by him, to be wanted by him.

"I need to touch you again to complete the ritual. May I?"

He had no idea how much he may. I looked into his mesmerizing eyes and nodded.

"Brave girl," he said and pulled me into him. He began reciting words I didn't understand, nor could I ever repeat. But they were beautiful, like they'd been created by the wind.

"What did you say?" I asked.

"The Prayer of Loyalty and Protection."

"It was beautiful."

"Tonight, you need to light a small fire outside and burn the hair together," he instructed.

"Our hair? Why?" It sounded so . . . witchy. *Would eye of newt be involved, too?*

He shrugged as if the answer were obvious. "We are sending a smoke signal to the heavens, proclaiming our bond."

Wow. That wasn't pagan at all. It sounded endearing and romantic. Then I remembered the entire Uchben clan was bonded, too. "How do you guys get so much hair?"

"Sorry?" he asked.

"The Uchben, they get your protection, too, don't they?"

"It's not the same. What I've given you is a piece of my essence, a piece of what humans call the soul. It weakens me somewhat, but it enables me to sense how you feel and ties me to you. I gave it to your grandmother when she was five, and I think you inherited it because you carry a piece of her inside you.

"The Uchben, on the other hand, have taken vows, binding themselves to us, to serve us, and to live by our laws. The penalty for breaking their oath is death."

I guessed "Thou shall not kill" wasn't one of the gods' commandments. They seemed more like an eye-for-an-eye kind of crowd. Case in point, Guy's title. But he was clearly so much more than the bringer of death; he had an abundance of compassion, which is likely why he took such an interest in protecting me all my life and why I suspected he bound himself to my grandmother. "Why my grandmother of all the people in world? Why did you choose her?"

He hesitated suspiciously. "I wanted the ability to track her after I killed the Maaskab. I needed to find out how she was made and why."

"Seems silly to weaken yourself right before battling Scabs."

He shrugged. "Well, no one ever said I was perfect or thought things through all the time."

"You say you're perfect all the time," I pointed out.

"See how wrong I can be?" He grinned.

"Guy, now's not the time to be flawed. I couldn't handle it if something happened to you. So, please, don't do anything stupid. Those men, the Maaskab, I swear they're not even human. They're something dark." I shuddered thinking about the shadows hugging the Scab's body.

He pecked me on the cheek. "Emma, I'll be back in two days, and then we'll sort everything out and deal with... your situation. I promise."

He practically floated from the room. If I didn't already know where he was going, I would have guessed he was going to see his favorite soccer team or maybe buy a new sports car. He looked utterly jazzed.

Yes, nothing like a little death and war to get the old god pumping.

Every time I felt like things couldn't possibly get any worse, they did. I found myself wishing I could go back one week earlier when all I had to worry about was a bossy man with a steamy voice living in my head and only one family tragedy to deal with. I'd give the rest of my curls to have that old life back. It's funny how things work out that way.

Now Tommaso was likely dead because of me. Guy was running off to confront the only monsters in the world who could actually harm him. My life and the lives of my family were at risk.

This time, I was not going to ask that stupid, fate-tempting question, *Could things possibly get any worse?* Because if I did... kablam! Fate would find a way to do it.

I spent the entire morning alone—well, except for the other gods whose lovely buzzing voices were still just as incomprehensible as before—pacing around Guy's quarters, cleaning up the mess I'd left on the patio from burning our hair, chewing my nails, and asking Bill and Ted or Bing and Bong—whatever—about any updates from Command Central.

Finally, just before noon, there was a knock at the door. Xavier entered with a long, dread-filled face. I knew it wasn't good news. "I didn't ask. I swear," I said aloud, unintentionally pleading with fate.

"I don't want you to be alarmed, but—"

"Did they find Tommaso? Is Guy all right?" I interrupted.

Xavier raised his palms, cautioning me to slow down. "We don't know what's happening. The last communication we received, the men and Guy arrived and were getting into position. Then there was a lot of noise through the satellite feed, and everything went dead."

"Dead? Oh, God. No!"

"Oh, heavens. I meant silent."

I took a deep, calming breath. *Okay. Okay. Get ahold of yourself.* "So what's next? What are they going to do?" I asked.

"I don't know, my dear. The chiefs are deciding now."

"This is awful." I turned my back, whisking away an escaped tear.

"Emma?"

"Yes? Please don't tell me there's more," I answered quietly.

"I didn't say anything," Xavier responded.

"Emma?"

My eyes moved around the room suspiciously. "There it is again."

"There's what again?" said Xavier.

"Emma, I can hear Xavier's with you. Is there anyone else? Can you go somewhere private?"

"Holy shit, this can't be."

"Shhh. Don't let them know I'm here," Guy said.

I started backing away from Xavier, stumbling over

my own feet. "Nothing, Xavier. I'll be right back. I, uh, forgot to condition my hair." I scrambled to the bathroom, praying I wasn't hearing what I thought.

I shut the door and turned on the shower. "Guy," I whispered. "Is that you?"

"Who else?" he said. *"Don't tell me you've got another god set up on mental IM? That would be so disappointing."*

"Are you okay? Why can I hear you again?"

"I'm sorry to say that we have a little situation here in Mexico. Seems someone has been sharing real-time information with the Maaskab. Luckily, we're better armed, but there are more of them than we'd thought. And since our communication channels are compromised, I voluntarily jumped into a hexed cenote."

"*What!?* You're stuck in the cenote again?"

"Yes, but it's actually a different cenote. This one is quite warmer. A bit larger, too. I wish I'd had this—"

"Un-bel-ievable," I interrupted. "I thought you were supposed to be an all-powerful deity. Couldn't you have conjured up a satellite phone or something?"

"Emma, I am a god, not the Creator. We cannot simply manifest objects in such a way. We manipulate energy, which is quite impress—"

Oh, jeez. I'd opened up the ego worm can. "Well, you're damned lucky I renewed my subscription to Guy Talk before you left."

"Funny girl. Listen, I need you to do me a favor. And please hurry."

Two cutthroat-looking guards, garnished with automatic rifles across their chests, stood in front of the steel-plated door. The larger man, Mr. Dark Buzz Cut—I didn't know his name since they never wore name tags—shook his head no.

"Sorry, Miss Keane. You're not allowed in," said Number Two Buzz Cut.

"But I have an important message. It's for your chief, Gabrán."

"Tell that moron that I'll peel the skin right off his bones if he doesn't let you pass."

"I can't say that. He'll break my arm," I responded to Guy.

"Excuse me?" said Dark Buzz Cut.

"See," I whined to Guy, "this is silly. Isn't there a secret password or handshake? They'll never believe me."

"Why not? They all know that you and I are... close."

Oh, great. Did that mean everyone now knew we'd gotten frisky? Of course they did, dammit! No secrets in Uchben Land. "Fine." I looked up at Number Two. "Listen, Guy says that he'll peel the skin right off your bones if you don't let me pass."

"And that I'll be sure the other walks with a permanent limp."

"Oh, gods. That's so mean," I told Guy.

"Do it!" Guy screamed.

"I hate you." I turned to Dark Buzz Cut and repeated Guy's words in a not-so-menacing voice.

"Sorry, Miss Keane. Make all the threats you want. You're not getting past us."

"See! They don't believe me," I barked at Guy.

"Emma, you have to stun them."

"I can't. I don't know how to," I pointed out.

"Close your eyes and imagine me grabbing you."

"Ugh!" I rolled my eyes.

"Em, this isn't a game. Lives are depending on you."

"Fine." I threw up my hands and then shut my eyes, focusing hard. Nothing happened.

"What are you doing, Miss Keane?" asked one of the guards.

I held out one finger. "Hold on. I'm thinking."

They looked thoroughly amused, but not the least bit worried.

"Emma," Guy said in a deep, hypnotic voice, *"you are stupid and weak! I don't know why I thought I could depend on a silly little girl like you. Of all the humans in the world, I had to get stuck with you."*

"What?" How could he be so cruel? The anger began to blister in the back of my brain, stoking the tiny spark struggling to ignite deep inside.

Oh. Sneaky bastard, I thought as the lightbulb went on. "You're doing it on purpose. Aren't you? Okay. Now what?"

"Now focus on that feeling and imagine it growing. Feed it."

The tiny fire began glowing hot inside my head. I imagined my anger being wound into flaming logs and then being tossed on top of the fire. I let the flames grow and spread their tendrils through my body.

"I'm doing it! It's working," I whispered.

"Push it down your arms. Then—"

I reached out my hands, and both men flew against the steel door with loud, painful grunts and then sank to the ground.

"Oh no." I crouched beside Dark Buzz Cut, who writhed in pain. "I'm so sorry! Are you okay?"

"Emma, what are you doing? Go! Go! Before they get up. They'll be fine, but the men here with me won't be if you don't hurry."

I jumped over the two very unhappy men and then slammed the door shut. There was a large sliding lock, so I bolted the door before turning down the long, dimly lit hallway. At the end was another steel door with a touch pad on the side and a video camera mounted above. It all looked very 007.

"There's a door with a keypad. What do I do?"

"Punch in four, eight, fifteen, sixteen, twenty-three, and forty-two."

"Long enough?" I mumbled while hitting the keypad.

The door clicked open, and I cautiously peeked my head through the crack. Inside was a massive NASA-like control center with a tiered stadium layout. At the bottom was a podium with a large floor-to-ceiling screen behind it. The screen itself looked like something right out of the show *24* with multiple views from different cameras. Everyone was working frantically on all levels, either talking on their headsets or typing at their stations, much too busy to notice little old me.

I cleared my throat. "Excuse me?" I said sheepishly, getting no one's attention.

"Louder, Emma. For gods' sake, this is no time to be polite."

I cleared my throat. "Hey! I'm looking for Gabrán."

Like someone had stopped the music, everyone froze and turned toward me.

"Um. Gabrán? Is he here?" I looked around the room, flashing an awkward smile.

The man to my left blurted out, "You can't be in here."

Next thing I knew, someone sacked me with such force, my teeth rattled in my head as I hit the cement floor.

"Emma, what's going on? Did they hurt you? I'll kill them!"

"Get off me! I have to talk to Gabrán. I have a message from Guy." I grunted my words, unable to take a full breath.

I heard the men screaming to remove me and was suddenly pulled to my feet and then shuffled toward the door by two, maybe three men. One of them wrapped his arms around me from behind. I couldn't turn.

"No. You don't understand..." I struggled, but it wasn't making any difference.

"Hit the man, Emma! Stun him!"

"Oh, Christ. You so owe me." I quickly pulled and tugged on that little ball of energy swirling in the pit of my stomach. This time it came easier, like it knew the way. With my arms pinned to my sides, I wiggled my hand free and touched the man's wrist.

The man fell to the ground, and I swiveled on my heel, holding out my hands in some comical-looking position a child would use pretending to be a tiger. *Grrrr!*

"Back!" I yelled. "I'm not leaving until I speak to Gabrán. Get back or I'll..."

What should I call it? Zap? Stun? That would sound silly.

"I'll...make you wish you were never born." There. That sounded threatening.

"Good job, my sweet. Now, find Gabrán."

An oak tree of a man, with a flaming red beard and equally red hair pulled into a long braid, stepped forward. His eyes, though an icy cool turquoise blue, looked ready to shoot missiles. "I'm Gabrán," he said with a thick Scottish accent. I recognized him from the dinner. He'd been the giant man wearing a kilt, standing with Guy. Only at the time he looked rather handsome and resplendent, in a Celtic relic kind of way. Now he just looked terrifying. "And ya have ten seconds to start talkin', o' I'm gonna have my man put a bullet in you."

My eyes darted up to a small balcony overlooking the room, where a man stood with his rifle pointed straight down at me. I noticed a tiny red dot over my heart. These people really took security seriously. "Guy, you better start talking. They have a gun pointed at me."

"Tell that Scottish bastard that he's a sorry excuse for a chief. And the first chance I get, I'm going to make sure he gets sent back to the dungeon in Caernarvon where I found his pasty, sorry ass."

I cleared my shaky throat and repeated word for word.

Gabrán's eyes lit up with anger. "You tell that slimy bastard he's the worst god of war anyone's ever seen. I've seen better battle tactics from a tree stump!"

I heard a soft chuckle in my head.

"So?" I asked. "Can we talk somewhere private? Or are we going to have a peeing contest now? Because I'm pretty sure I'd lose."

"Come with me, lass. The rest o' ya back to work! Find my men!"

I pushed through the crowd of soldiers encircling me and trotted smugly behind Gabrán. We went into a small drab room with maps and dry erase boards filled with formulas.

"Okay. We're alone," I said to Guy.

Guy began recounting what had happened after they

arrived in helicopters to the planned coordinates north of Bacalar. The Maaskab were already waiting for them, but the meeting place was set at the last minute. This is how he knew someone on the inside had notified the Maaskab. The good news was that he was fairly certain most of his men, having scattered into the jungle to take shelter from the attack, were unharmed. The Maaskab were fast but used mostly archaic weapons like arrows and knives. They didn't believe in anything modern, which got me wondering how the hell they got around town. Evil bicycles?

"Gabrán, there are a few hundred of them, I think. If I manage to round up some men, we could pick them off, but with traitors in our midst, I'm afraid we'll lose too many on our side."

I repeated.

If I thought the chief looked miffed before, he was incensed now. After pacing for several moments and yelling some incomprehensible garble in some odd language, Gabrán turned to me. "Okay. We have to call the men back. We cannot flush out the traitors in the field like this."

"That's ridiculous! We can't leave the other gods trapped. We need to get them out to deal with the Maaskab."

I repeated, but Gabrán didn't look convinced.

"He's right," I said, crossing my arms. "You can't retreat. There's no way to give your men instructions without the Maaskab knowing. They'll be ambushed trying to leave. I have a better idea. Send a message telling the men to stay put, but that you're sending reinforcements to handle everything. Make sure the Maaskab hear some phony landing coordinates to draw them away. In the meantime send a small group from here, your most trusted men, to free the other gods. It will be safer with the Maaskab distracted. Once the other gods are free, then we can kill the Maaskab and round up your men."

Gabrán folded his thick arms, lifting one red brow. "Guy, you've got a smart woman there. Verra well, but I'm leading this."

"And Guy says you need to make sure I go, so I can help coordinate."

"Emma! No! Dammit, you foolish woman. You're not coming down here. It's too dangerous, and I'm not in a position to protect you!"

"He insists," I said sweetly.

"Emma, this is betrayal. I'll punish you for this."

"And he says you should give me a quick lesson on automatic handguns."

"A gun? Emma, are you insane? What are you doing? You're not a soldier. You've never killed anything in your life."

"And two guns. That ought to do it," I added.

"He's yelling at you, isn't he?" said Gabrán, cracking a smile.

"Yep."

"Good. Serves the arrogant bastard right. I'll have my men teach ya, arm ya, and get ya ready to kill those repugnant beasts. I have no problem with ya fightin' with us, lass. Even better, if it fashes your man." He paused, turquoise-blue eyes glimmering, and moved his mouth to my ear. "Did ya hear dat, ya old crusty bastard?"

This man was so going on my Christmas card list.

"Son of a bitch. I'm going to break his legs and then yours, Emma!"

"Yep," I said cheerfully to Gabrán. "He heard ya."

Thirty-Three

I watched with fascination as the dozen soldiers moved with silent precision, loading the sleek camouflaged jet inside the private hangar. They glanced at each other but didn't speak. Were they reading each other's thoughts?

Lifting crates, carrying duffel bags filled with gear, and securing equipment, everyone knew exactly what to do and where to stand at the precise moment for maximum efficiency. Within twenty minutes, we were up in the air and on our way. They even remembered to bring my guns—empty, of course—to teach me how to use them.

Within one hour, the shades were shut, lights were out, and the men simultaneously closed their eyes, going into some disturbing group nap time. The air buzzed with their energy. Very unsettling.

"What are they doing?" I whispered to Gabrán, who was the only one awake, busily reviewing topographical maps on his laptop in the seat next to me.

"'Tis the way the men prepare for fightin'," he responded quietly. "The ancient Seido mediation of the Japanese warrior. Clears the mind."

The Uchben were like a giant melting pot of rituals and traditions, technologies and science, and culture and wealth. "You Uchben seem very…eclectically resourceful."

"It's our way. We come from many countries and different t—" He stopped to catch himself from saying something.

"What?" I prodded.

As if wondering if he could trust me, he turned his head and gave me a quick once-over, sizing me up. "Our strength comes from adopting the best of everything the world has to offer, regardless of when or where it was created."

The answer sounded airbrushed; he'd landed on not trusting me.

"Emma, tell the chief something's going on outside."

"What?" I asked.

"It doesn't sound good, but at least we know there are still loyal men out there fighting. But gods, I can't see shit."

I grabbed Gabrán's arm. "Something's happening."

"I think some of the men are attacking the Maaskab outside the cenote."

I relayed to Gabrán, then asked, "How much longer until we're there?"

"This is the fastest plane we have—nine hours at best."

"Guy?"

"I heard. There's nothing you can do, Emma. I'll keep you posted if I see anything."

I sat back in the chair and tried to mimic the sedate-looking men around me, but every nerve in my body was firing on all cylinders. I had no clue what I was going to do when I got to Bacalar, and seeing these well-trained Uchben, who acted like we were going to a day spa—yes, that relaxed—well, it struck me that I'd be getting in the way. Was I out of my ever-loving mind? Just because I could exude some preternatural energy that shocked people didn't mean I could fight a Maaskab or kill another person. But a part of me, the irrational side, needed this. I needed to fight—for me, for my family, for Grandmother, for those women.

I got up and went into the tiny bathroom. Déjà vu. My airplane conference room. "Guy, what am I going to do?"

"About what?" he answered.

"I should have listened to you. It's obvious that me going there's a mistake. But I couldn't sit back and let this play out while I stayed in my cozy room. It's not right."

"I know."

"You're not mad?"

"Worried, yes. Mad, no."

"You always surprise me. You're so different now. I would have expected you'd be yelling at me or telling me how stupid I am."

"As much as I'd like to do that, it wouldn't help increase your odds of survival."

"Why couldn't you have been like this when you used to be in my head? You were never this calm."

"Actually, I was."

Oh, right. Guy was to calm as Emma Keane was to war. "Then why? You were so explosive and controlling all those years."

"Normally, my behavior is a result of my unbelievable arrogance or insensitivity toward others, but in your case, it was all about strategy."

"A straightforward answer would be nice for once."

"If I'd filled your ears with sweet, kind words, you would have never toughened up. I knew that someday you might be the one to free me. In fact, I think I always knew it would be you since no one had come for me. I had to make myself so irritating that you'd do anything—risk anything—to extract me from your life. Like a painful splinter. Of course, I'd planned to wait until you were old enough to travel alone and strong enough to make the journey, but you sped things along with your little deviation."

"Why didn't you tell me the truth? I might have believed you—helped you. And it wouldn't have caused me so much pain."

He was about to comment but stopped. Maybe being the god of war trained him to think in terms of dominating the opposition, not asking for help.

"I could not risk it. You were my only ticket to freedom."

I was stunned by the bluntness and lack of sentiment in his words. Had I simply been the only tool in his chest? A means to an end? If so, why didn't he change his behavior after I released him? He still acted like a jealous, possessive, controlling boyfriend.

"What about Tommaso?" I asked. "Why did you attack him at the villa? You were already free."

There was a pregnant pause.

"The bond. It makes me feel overly protective."

"Oh." One by one, the tiny pieces slid into place. The way he'd deprived me of any male relationships and enticed me with his seductive voice. He'd been slowly manipulating me, working me into position, where I'd risk everything to either see him or be free from him. And afterward, once he'd been released, his bouts of jealously were a result of the bond.

"So the bond makes you feel territorial. Like I was some stupid bone to fight over," I said, feeling completely deflated.

"Yes, I'm sorry if it caused you any pain."

"And what happened between us yesterday morning?"

"Emma, I wanted to talk about this later in person."

"No. Now! I want the truth."

"Truth?" he said. *"It was simply years of pent-up frustration. I'm sure you of all people can sympathize."*

Of course. I'd been his first chance at sex since…ever. "But before you left, you said—"

"I said we'd sort your situation out, and we will. That doesn't mean we're compatible. We're not. I'm a god. You're basically a human. Your purpose is to grow up, have children, grow old, and die. Mine is to herd the sheep. And right now, I've got wolves—lots of fucking wolves who've been chowing down on my flock. I don't have time to play house. Sorry, Emma."

His cold, hard words hit me like a two-ton block of ice. *He never cared. He never cared. He never cared.* Except when it impacted him. He was so cold, so callous.

I hunched over the sink and grimaced, forcing myself to swallow the pain.

"And since we're on the subject, and you're so eager for the truth, I have another confession. One you should know in case anything happens. The attraction you feel for me isn't real either."

"Sorry?"

"My kind can emit a potent pheromone that lulls humans into submission. In the opposite sex, one whiff

creates a sexual desire so strong that I could get a girl to strip naked in a crowded restaurant, crawl to me on her hands and knees, and then lick my boots. Ha." He chuckled. *"That one never gets old."*

Wha-what? Pheromones? The man crack thing was real? "I-I can't. I don't understand..."

"There's nothing to understand except that after this is over, you'll be free to move on and live your life. Normal. Out of my hair. Just like you wanted."

"Oh," I said again like a complete idiot while his words ripped through me, leaving nothing behind but my tattered heart and a gaping hole where my self-esteem once stood. Had I really allowed myself to believe our connection was more? Had I allowed myself to feel emotionally attached to this being whose sole purpose in life was to kill? He'd seemed so affectionate and caring at times, but it was always about getting what he wanted from me and nothing more. I had let myself get caught up in his selfish agendas. He was a heartless, selfish prick, and I allowed myself to be blinded by his exterior. Really, what woman wouldn't? He was a god. A larger-than-life specimen of male perfection. And a complete ass.

But me? I was worse than an ass. I was a sucker of colossal proportions.

"Em? Is everything okay?"

"Yeah, tired is all. I'm going to try to catch a few hours."

"Good idea."

Thirty-Four

The bustling inside the plane jarred me from my daze. My mind reeled with betrayal and confusion for hours as I went over the discussion, my life with Guy, my future without him. Why was it so hard for me to accept? Did he really believe I was so small and insignificant? Really? It had always been all about his agenda and the bond?

"Would ya like somethin' tae eat, Emma? We've got less than an hour to go until the drop," said Gabrán with an all-too-mischievous smirk.

"Drop?" I questioned.

"Yes, you'll be flying with Brutus strapped to your back." Gabrán pointed to a brawny man, number 322 I'd seen that week. Crew cut Brutus nodded politely, not appearing at all pleased.

"What do you mean by 'flying'?" I asked, already fearing the worst.

"Well, lass, you don't expect us to be invisible if we chopper in. We'll be parachuting our way down tonight."

Parachuting? They'd failed to share this tiny detail. Of course, I hadn't asked. I figured we'd land at a nice airport, hop in some Jeeps, drive to Bacalar, quietly find the cenotes, and do a little bobbing for jars. Then voila! Let there be gods.

"And you'll be needin' tae change your clothes there. Pink is a lovely color, mind ya, but not so effective for cloaking yerself in the dark."

I looked down at my pink sweater and jeans as he shoved a pile of dark gray clothes at me, including a black ski mask.

"Thanks." I stood to head back to the bathroom.

"Christ, woman! What the hell are you doing in here?"

I heard grunting and screaming on Guy's end. *"Get the hell off me. Calm down."*

I almost fell forward but caught myself in between the seats. "What's happening, Guy?"

"It's Cimil. She's decided to drop by and pay me a little visit," announced Guy.

I looked at Gabrán. "It's Cimil. She's inside the cenote with him." I hoped she'd poke out his eyes and rip his head off. She seemed like the sort of deity who did that kind of stuff just for kicks.

The buzzing sound from the voices got louder. It was like a cat in a dryer.

"What's she saying? It sounds awful." I clutched my ears.

"Shush, Emma, let me listen to her."

"Guy, make her stop. She's going to give me a seizure."

"Cimil, stop screaming. Yes. Yes. I know…but…" He paused. More screeching. *"Sorry, Emma, she's hysterical. Cimil, I can't hear you because you're making Emma squeal."* The screeching stopped. *"Thank you."*

"Oh, thank heavens."

I listened for what seemed like an eternity to one side of the conversation that consisted of an occasional *"Uh-huh"* or *"Hmmm. Interesting"* from Guy, followed by a "Buzz. Buzz. Buzz!"

It was beyond annoying. When this was all over, I was sure I'd never want to see another deity or a bee for the rest of my life.

"Anything?" asked Gabrán.

"Guy? The chief wants to know if you have any new information. We're almost there."

"Cimil says that she's been chasing the Maaskab, collecting the jars, and trying to figure out which one of the gods was teaching them to use the jade."

"Cimil's innocent? Father Xavier will be relieved," I commented. "So how'd she end up inside the cenote with you?"

"She was chasing one of the priests through the jungle and thought she had him cornered. He was standing at the edge of the cenote, and right as she was about to grab him, he disappeared. She fell in."

"Too bad she didn't land on your head," I mumbled.

He sighed. *"Emma, I'm—"*

"Shut it. I'm not interested," I snapped and then turned to Gabrán. "Let's get this over with already. I'm ready to kick some ass."

"Oh!" Gabrán chuckled loudly and turned to his men, who were gearing up. "Look at our mighty little demigoddess here, boys. Ready to go toe-to-toe with the witch doctors."

The men laughed.

Well, I meant, "Kick Guy's ass," but what the hey.

"Not to worry, lass. Just a few minutes more. Get those vicious little hands of yours ready to go."

Okay. Parachuting on its own? Maybe not so terrifying. Parachuting into a Mexican jungle at night while strapped to an angry Uchben man named Brutus? An unimaginable nightmare that would haunt my every waking moment for the rest of my life.

In midair, between Brutus's menacing grunts of disapproval at my squealing, I found myself feeling relieved that my parents believed I was already dead because there was no possible way I was surviving this jump.

The sky was overcast, without so much as a speckle of moonlight filtering through. I felt like I was falling down a deep, dark well as the air whistled past my ears, and my brain kept telling me that at any moment, my body would slam into the earth. So when we landed with a muted thump in a small clearing, it was Brutus's lethal-sounding "Hush!" that kept me from doing a victory disco right then and there. He was also strapped to my back.

"Not a sound," he warned as he unhooked the harnesses and slipped his night-vision goggles back on.

We silently wove our way through the trees, and I wondered how the hell we'd find the others. There were no radios, and Brutus didn't make any covert bird squawks like I'd seen in those spy movies. Then I remembered how the men had loaded the plane before the flight. They could read each other's minds. Of course. That's why Guy would want Gabrán to help. Their communication method was difficult to infiltrate. These Uchben really were amazing.

After thirty minutes of tiptoeing in the darkness over the leaf-covered path, we found the other men and began walking in a quiet formation, me sandwiched somewhere in the middle of the Conan conga line.

I brushed my hand over the handgun holstered to my waist and clicked off the safety as Brutus's "brother" had shown me. Then I began focusing on the little fireball in the pit of my stomach, trying to pull it up, readying to draw from it.

"Emma? Are you near? I hear something."

I didn't know what to do. Gabrán had told me to be silent unless it was urgent, so as not to give away our position.

We suddenly stopped, and the men began splintering off into various directions. Brutus gave me the signal to hold still. I couldn't see anything so that meant he poked me in the back of the head.

Then the buzzing sound began growing. I could barely think. Something was riling the other gods. In fact, the last time they'd been that loud was right before— "Maaskab! They're here!" I screamed and felt my body go flat under Brutus.

"Stay!" Brutus commanded and then got up and ran off into the jungle. I rolled over and found myself lying—gulp—all alone? *Holy Virgin of Guadalupe, kill me now.* I gritted my teeth, reaching for the gun at my side. But what if I shot an Uchben? I put it back in its holster, realizing that something was tickling my neck. I leaped up gasping and swatting the furry creepy-crawly thing. My backside bumped into something hard, and I turned right into a tall, dark shadow that smelled like rotting meat. "Scaaab!" I screamed.

His eyes glowed with swirls of red as he glared down at me in the darkness. I think I startled him, too, because he froze for a fraction of a second, just long enough for me to reach out and touch his arm. A shock wave of energy surged though my hands and the Scab flew back.

"Yes! Take that!"

"What's going on? Where the hell are you?" screamed Guy.

"I zapped a Scab with my hand."

"Is he dead?"

"I don't know. I can't see anything, and I'm not about to go and check his pulse," I said.

"Emma, I can hear you outside. You're close."

Suddenly there was a small break in the clouds, allowing a sliver of moonlight to catch the surface of the water. I was only four feet away from the edge of a cenote. It was huge. Twice the size of the first cenote where I'd found Guy. "Guy, are you in there?" I whispered down at the water.

"Yes, hurry up and let me out before the priest wakes or his friends show," he commanded.

"For my family, for my family, for my family, and for one last opportunity to kick Guy in his man gear for being such a repugnant, coldhearted, a-hole," I repeated aloud as I gathered the courage to jump.

"I heard that!"

"Emma?" I heard a voice call from the shadows of the tree line.

"Who's there?" said Guy.

"Oh my gods, Tommaso? Is that you?" I moved away from the edge of the cenote, watching the outline of his familiar shape step from the shadows.

"Yes."

I ran and threw my arms around him, never happier to see another soul in my entire life. "I thought you were dead," I whispered.

He held me tight for several moments. I could feel his breath on my neck; his heart was racing. He released me, and I saw the faint trace of his reassuring dimple-framed smile. "What are you doing here?" he asked quietly.

"I was bored," I said. "Decided to try this Uchben thing out for fun."

"Still the funniest girl I know."

"Can't help myself." I shrugged. "It's part of my charm. So are you here to get them out?"

"Who?" he asked.

"Guy and Cimil." I pointed to the black hole.

"Not exactly."

"Why not?" I asked.

"Jump into the water. Do it now!" Guy screamed.

"Emma, there's so much I need to tell you—so much you don't know about those... demons."

I took a step back. "What's going on, Tommaso?"

"Guy's talking to you right now. Isn't he?" He stepped in and painfully gripped me by the shoulders.

I nodded. Fear and confusion came crashing down while Guy continued bellowing in the background of my head, telling me to jump in the water and free him.

"Don't listen to him, Emma. He's not what you think," Tommaso commanded.

"Tell me something I don't already know," I said.

"He's the enemy, Emma. The Uchben are the enemy. They're killers."

This situation didn't feel right. Not one little bit. "Tommaso, let me go!" I pushed away from him, placing my hands flat against his chest. I felt something odd, like cords stretched across his skin underneath his shirt. "Something's wrong with you," I said. "Did the Maaskab hurt you?"

"No. They've set me free." Tommaso tore open his

shirt, forcing my hand to run down his chest. There were four raised scars running from side to side.

"What are those? What did they do to you?" I pulled away and backed up to the edge of the pool, holding my hands out defensively. If he rushed me, I'd be over the edge in half a heartbeat.

"They showed me the truth, Emma. The Uchben and gods are pretending to protect the world. But it's a hoax. The Uchben only care about keeping their power, their wealth. Guy only cares about controlling humans, manipulating them, and keeping them weak. He doesn't care about any of us. He never has."

"Emma, he's lying. He's one of the traitors. Don't listen!" Guy screamed.

"You've lost it, Tommaso. I've seen the Maaskab, and they're monsters," I said.

"Yes. They are. They're also loyal soldiers. Ruthless. And that's how wars are won, through strength, sacrifice, and..."

Tommaso continued ranting about the rightness, the glory of his self-appointed task of savior of the planet, but Guy's hypnotic voice began drowning him out. *"Emma, do you remember when you asked me why I changed my name?"* he said calmly. *"It was because I wanted the one you gave me. You changed me. Or why I gave your grandmother my oath? I did it because I'd never seen a child with our blood. She was so beautiful, special. Just seeing Gabriela filled me with hope. To know that perhaps I might someday be able to create life instead of taking it."*

"Oh. I get it. Now you want me to believe you have a heart, that you care about anyone other than yourself?"

"Yes," Tommaso answered, unaware the question had been for Guy. "That's what I'm asking."

"Yes, that's what I'm asking," Guy replied simultaneously.

"Shush!" I held up my finger to Tommaso. "I'm trying to listen."

"Did you just shush me?" Tommaso asked.

"Yes. Yes, I did. And I realize how weird that is given we're right in the middle of a rather hefty situation, but I have something to say to Guy." Pause. "Guy, screw you! On the way here, you said your purpose is herding the sheep—that you use your pheromones to do it. You used them on me! And don't forget, you told me it was only the bond that made you protect me and feel jealous."

"I felt jealous because there is nothing more important to me than you, and I didn't want to share you. That's why I tried to keep other men away. I wanted you for myself."

I wrapped my arms around my waist and squeezed back the angry tears. "More of your lies, Guy."

"I admit, I've lied to you, but that doesn't mean I'm not saying the truth now. Please, believe what I'm saying, and if you can't, at least believe that Tommaso is dangerous, and he's going to kill you."

What was with this man? He'd just raked my heart over the coals, but now that he'd discovered his competition—Tommaso—wasn't dead, I guessed the bond was kicking in again. Making him feel jealous. It wasn't real. He'd told me so.

I looked up at Tommaso. "Tommaso, if I leave with you now, what happens next?"

"First, I'll get you the hell away from here. It's not safe. The Maaskab and the Uchben will fight. And when we win, you'll be able to go home to your family."

"Don't the Maaskab want to kill me?" I questioned, whisking away the tears.

"Emma, they want to rid the world from these dictators. If you come with me, they'll leave you alone. They won't see you as the enemy. You'll be able to go home back to your life. Please, Emma, step away from the edge and come with me. I promise to keep you safe. Always." His voice was deep and sincere. He'd never betrayed me, and I had no reason to distrust him.

"Please, my sweet," Guy said in that lulling voice, sending shivers down my core. *"I know I've hurt you, but I'll spend eternity making it up. I can fix this. I can fix this hole I've created between us, the damage I've caused your life. I can fix anything, but I can't fix it if I'm dead! Do you understand? He'll kill you, Emma. You'll end up like your grandmother, and I can't bring you back!"*

"Don't you dare bring her into this!" I screamed at Guy.

Something whistled by my head, and I immediately crouched. Christ, had it been a bullet?

"That's enough chitchat. I need to get you out of here," Tommaso hissed. He grabbed my hand and pulled me into the dark jungle.

"Emma, no! Don't! Everything I've said is the truth." Guy's words were now frantic. *"I know you can feel it. I have bonds with others, Emma, like Gabrán. But why can't they hear me when you can? Think about it! The bond didn't create our connection or my love for you. Or my jealousy. You and I, we are meant to be together. I know you feel the pull, too."*

"Pheromones," I grumbled, stumbling over branches and rocks, scrambling behind Tommaso.

"That only works when we're in the same room. Haven't you felt something even when I'm away? It's because I love you."

"How dare you! You expect me to believe that? After what you said on the plane?"

"I said those things because I realized how dangerous my world is for you. If it weren't for me, you'd be somewhere safe right now. And this situation will only repeat itself. You will never be safe with me. I will always be the God of Death and War, but I don't want you to leave me, Em. I don't want you to die."

I wanted to believe him. Gods, I did. But actions always speak louder than words. His actions told me he couldn't be trusted. And his words were too perfect to accept as the truth; they were exactly what I wanted to hear.

Tommaso stopped. "Just break the bond, Emma. Say the words, and end it right now. Free yourself."

"I don't know what to do. I can't think." I grabbed the sides of my head; the other voices began screaming and hissing painfully inside my skull.

"Did he tell you how he killed Rosa and Arturo? Did he?"

"Guy, what's he talking about?"

Tommaso and Guy started screaming at the same time, and with the voices, I could only catch every other word, but it was enough for me to hear that Guy had savagely executed them.

"Guy? Is it true? You killed that old couple? My grandmother's sister and her husband?"

"Yes, but . . ."

I couldn't make out what words came next, but I heard all I needed.

I clutched my temples. "Stop! My head! Stop!" The voices were like daggers in my ears, drowning out everything else. Or maybe it was the sound of my heart cracking in two.

The phrase "*Kaacha'al lu'um, tumben k'iin*" suddenly

floated from my lips a second time, my mind seeking escape from the torturous noise.

Then there was silence. Sweet, sweet silence.

I crumbled to the ground, trembling. Tommaso's arms wrapped around my waist and pulled me up. "Good job. Let's get you to our camp."

Christ. What had I just done? Maybe I didn't trust Guy. In fact, I felt downright confused and livid, but there was no way in hell I'd join Team Scab. Forget it. I still believed they'd killed my grandmother.

"No, wait." I pulled my arm away. "I'm not going with you."

Though the night obscured his face, I saw he looked irate. "Emma, you're coming with me. Don't make this hard." Tommaso reached for me as I turned and started running back toward the cenote.

"Emma! Get back here!" Tommaso screamed, the crunch of his footsteps following closely behind.

My heart pounded furiously in my chest while I stumbled through the darkness, feeling my way around trees and branches. Emptiness and dread washed over me as once again the bond with Guy evaporated.

"Emma! You can run, but you can't hide!" Tommaso's voice echoed through the air.

Shit! He's using tired clichés. That was a bad sign. I started focusing my thoughts on summoning a little energy and kept on running. But it was so damned dark. Where was that dang cenote? It couldn't be far because we'd only walked a few meters—

Yes! The shimmer of the water's surface caught my eye

a few yards away, just on the other side of two large trees. I bolted in its direction and was halfway over the edge when something plucked me out of thin air. I found myself suddenly surrounded by trees, encased by two dark arms. The smell made me gag instantly. *Ick. Fresh Scab.*

"Release her," said a deep, familiar voice. The Scab flung me to the ground and vanished right before my eyes. I caught a whiff of black licorice as a menacing shadow emerged from the trees. "Emma, it's so nice to meet you in person, although I've really enjoyed our dreams together."

I could barely see his face, but part of my brain, which meticulously catalogs all things to be deathly afraid of, recognized it. *Let's see . . . lions, undercooked chicken, jumping out of planes at night while strapped to angry men named Brutus, dark alleys, venomous snakes, insane people with guns—oops, that's me—and Guy's brother, the sinister sexual predator from my dreams.* My brain hit the Panic Now button big-time.

Igniting the fireball in the pit of my stomach, I stepped backward with my hands extended. I was going to launch that evil deity into the next state if he touched me.

A movement flashed from the corner of my eye, and there was Tommaso, latching something around my wrist. "Sorry, Emma. Can't let you do that."

I felt cold, hard stone pulse against my skin as the power drained from my body instantly. Black jade.

"Get her to the temple," Guy's brother commanded.

Then I knew fate really did hate me.

Hiccup!

Thirty-Five

"Well, great job, lover boy," Cimil seethed. "What the hell was that? *'I love you'?* Did you honestly expect her to jump to our aid with that sad line? Now we're going to be stuck in this festering aquarium for eternity."

"Shut the hell up, Cimil." He meant every word he'd said to Emma, but it mattered little now; he'd failed her, and now those evil cretins were going to end her life. He could not face the thought of an eternity without her. And to think, she'd die alone, frightened, and believing he never really loved her? He'd go mad. He'd fucking go mad.

Dammit! How could he have so sorely miscalculated? Once Emma had made up her mind and gotten on that plane in Rome, heading for Mexico, Guy panicked. He thought of nothing but her safety and how furious he was that the Uchben had disobeyed him.

Instead of telling her the truth, Guy decided that if she

were to survive, she needed to go into battle filled with anger—easier to tap into her powers that way. That was one reason he'd said such coldhearted things to her on the plane.

He also knew that as much as he needed her, she deserved better. She deserved a normal life, to live in peace. That was not his world. Those were things he could never give her. He was the God of Death and War. He always had been and always would be. And his mere presence in her life was a threat to her existence.

Cruelly pushing her away was the right thing to do. So he thought.

Gods dammit! Why hadn't she listened and stayed in Rome? But she hadn't, and when Tommaso tried to lure her to her death, Guy simply had to change tactics. Guy had to tell her the truth. He'd been tied to Emma since her birth, before that even. And although he didn't quite understand why or how, she had become a necessity in his life. She was his fate. Cimil had even foretold it to be so.

Yes. He was silly to believe he'd be able to let her go. He'd had a taste of her light, her essence inside him. He realized that if anything happened to her, he'd spiral into a venomous rage so destructive that the Maaskab would look like a gang of unruly Muppets in comparison to the fucking apocalypse he'd bring to the world's doorstep.

"And where in gods' creation is your pack of Uchi-morons?" Cimil barked, pulling him back from the precipice of his first panic attack ever.

"Shut it. I'm trying to think." Guy didn't have the faintest clue where Gabrán and his men were. They were likely fighting Scabs, but he knew his men could take care of themselves. Emma, on the other hand . . . "They'll be here. Gabrán won't fail."

"That bloated sack of Scottish bull? Honestly, Votan, of all the people you could have picked to be your right hand for all eternity."

"I'm very sorry that my choices displease you," he said with bitter sarcasm, "but you can hardly hate the man for refusing to be your pet, Goddess of the Underworld—"

"Don't call me that! I hate that title. And there is no damned underworld. There's just Las Vegas, and that doesn't count."

"All right. Fine," he continued, "since you're such a plethora of knowledge, I'd love to hear your take on our current predicament."

"Tisk, tisk. Up until now, I've avoided being caught and have been gathering information so we can wipe these bloodthirsty vermin from the earth."

"Did you manage to figure out why they want the Payals?" Guy asked.

"No…no. But I've been able to narrow down the Maaskab's hideout to one square kilometer."

"Did you figure out which one of our brothers made the Payals?"

"Um—no, but whomever it was has been helping the skanky priests—teaching them."

"We know that already. Do you know why one of our own would help them?" Guy asked.

"Well, not exactly. They've been experimenting with those damned jars all over the place, and they're really nasty."

"How impressive. You're a regular goddess of unsolved mysteries," Guy said.

"You laugh, but they've got this entire area warded with those damned black rocks. This jungle is an invisible labyrinth. And those malodorous priests have learned how to create temporary portals and sift in and out of thin air. They can move a hundred meters at a time, maybe more."

Astonishing. So that's how they were able to get the upper hand on the Uchben. Not even the gods could do that. "Any way to stop them?" he questioned.

"No. Other than to snap their necks between sifts."

"You're a wealth of strategic information, my sister," he said.

"Screw you, lover boy. Next time we face the apocalypse, I'm teaming up with Kinich. At least he has his own pyramid and knows how to handle the ladies."

"Ha. You think the parrot god could handle Emma? She's her own force of nature."

"Yeah, and her life is as good as over if she doesn't get away from Tommaso."

The thought scorched his soul. "She will. She must."

"And if she survives, my dear brother, what do you plan to do with her?"

"I'd been considering wiping her memory, her family's, too, so she'd be free to live her life—find a mate, have beautiful babies, and grow old. But now, I don't know. I can't live without her, and I don't know how to be with her. I took an oath to be the God of Death and War for eternity. How do I do that and give her a life? My world is nothing but violence."

"Oh, I don't know. Seems the girl can handle more than you might think. You should have seen the way she came after me. Perhaps you two are kindred warrior spirits."

"I hadn't thought about that."

"Of course not, you're too busy coddling her like a

child. Well," Cimil added. "Personally, I'd be more concerned with her mortality. Have you thought about that? She's going to grow old."

No. He hadn't. In fact, he really hadn't thought through any of this. He just knew he needed her. "What do I do?" Guy asked.

Cimil was silent for a moment. "First, you save her. Then you might try asking her what she wants—let her decide her fate. Isn't that what you're always telling us we must do with the humans?"

Cimil was right. He'd been treating Emma like a child, and it always ended poorly when he did. No wonder she hated him. "You're right, but I think she may have already made her choice. It wasn't me."

Cimil's energy swirled around the cenote. "Well, can you blame her? You *are* an arrogant, manipulative, deadly—"

"I get the point. Can we change subjects? Perhaps focus on what we'll do when we get out of here?"

"Certainly, my dear brother. And your loyal Uchben? What's taking them so long?"

"I'm not sure."

"How about that sweet little Chac? He's still running around the jungle somewhere. Can you summon him?" Cimil asked.

Guy had tried summoning Chac the last time he'd been trapped in the cenote, but the boy was a wild creature and wouldn't come near the water. Almost two centuries ago, the poor boy accidentally drowned in one of the cenotes right as Guy had been passing through. Taking pity, he pulled Chac to the other side of the portal, attempting to reignite the limp body with the light of the gods, but too much time had passed.

When Chac emerged from the cenote, the energy from their world flowed through his veins, but only a fragment of his soul remained. Guy tried to heal him and teach him, but it was useless. Now Chac wandered the jungle like a ghost, frightened by anything that moved. He would always retreat to the area near the cenote, like a rabbit to his hole, but never entered the water.

"I'm afraid not—"

A loud splash startled them.

"Bloody hell. What took so long?" Guy said. He looked at the frail, naked legs kicking under the water. *No, it's not one of the Uchben.*

In less than a second, Guy felt the familiar pull of the water spitting him out. He lay like a limp fish, facedown in the mud, the water jutting from his lungs.

"Could someone please pull me out?" a voice echoed from below in the water.

Guy crawled to the edge of the cenote, panting. The sun was peeking over the horizon, giving the sky a grayish glow and just enough light for him to see the pale little man treading naked in the water. "Xavier? Is that you?" Guy called out.

"In the bare flesh, my friend."

Guy grabbed a long branch lying at his side in the moist dirt and used it to fish the pale man from the dark water. "What the hell are you doing here? And why are you naked?"

"I was in the neighborhood shopping for jars, saw one floating in the water, and decided to go skinny-dipping for it," Xavier said in a deadpan voice, but no one was ever sure when he was joking or serious.

Xavier sighed. "I'm here rescuing you, obviously. And

I didn't want to get my clothes wet when I went to remove the jar from the water. With the humidity, it could take days to dry, and there's a particular species of fungi—"

"Yes, thank you, Xavier. Very interesting, but why are you here?"

Xavier explained that after Emma had left with Gabrán, the satellite images had come in. With communications compromised, he quietly went to one of the chiefs and talked him into authorizing a plane. "I had to come in person and see for myself. We found the mine, and there's something else. It's a very large structure. A pyramid."

"Who's your friend?" Cimil asked with a saucy voice, standing in her fire-engine-red lingerie, wringing out her black cocktail dress.

Guy took an impatient breath. "Xavier, this is the infamous Cimil, who apparently doesn't know how to dress for the jungle or combat. Cimil, this is Xavier, one of our most prestigious scholars—who...simply isn't dressed."

Xavier, too starstruck to catch the comment or notice he was still nude, reached out his hand. "Cimil, I've always wanted to meet you. I'm a huge, huge fan. I know everything about you."

"Really now?" She stepped forward and ran one finger down the front of Xavier's chest.

"Y-yes," he stuttered nervously. "You're an avid fan of tango, you love to play tennis with the God of Eclipses—even though he always wins—and you love a bargain."

"I have to admit a good garage sale does get my juices flowing." She turned to Guy. "I *like* your little friend here. He's amusing. Can I keep him?"

Guy cringed. "Did you bring clothes, Xavier?"

Xavier snapped out of his rock star trance and scrambled over to a tree where his clothes hung.

"We need men," Guy said to Cimil. "But even if we manage to round them up, we'll still be unable to tell the Tommasos from the loyal Uchben."

"I brought twenty men. They're waiting near the fort. Culling is quite easy," Xavier called out from the trees, slipping on his tan running suit. "Check their chests. All Maaskab bare the mark. They must perform the ritual of bloodletting to become one of them."

That little old man was eccentric but extremely bright. Guy might have to make him immortal before Cimil ruined him.

Thirty-Six

"This can't be happening. This can't be happening." I squeezed my eyes shut, hoping when I reopened them, the nightmare would be over. I was locked inside a medieval holding cell, complete with dank stone walls, a torch sconce, and a small bucket in the corner for what I imagined was supposed to be my toilet. Sad part was, there was nowhere to sit or sleep. Could that be because I wasn't going to be here long enough?

"Effing great." I threw up my hands and paced the eight-by-ten room, chewing the distasteful cud of my colossal mistake.

Earlier, after I'd realized that I was quite possibly the lamest person on the face of the planet for not jumping into that cenote when I had a chance, I peacefully went with Tommaso and the two Maaskab who'd appeared out of thin air behind me. I truly feared for my life but tried to remain focused and mentally record everything I could: which direction we were walking in, the direction of the sunlight, what kind of weapons the putrid monsters carried—anything I could to help me escape later.

After zigzagging through the jungle for over an hour, they blindfolded me and tied my hands behind my back. Without them free, I thought for certain the mosquitoes and gnats would treat me like their own private buffet. And then I realized the bugs hadn't come near me since we set out.

So that finally settles it! The trophy in the Evil, Eviler, Evilest Contest goes to—drumroll, please—the Scabs. Not even bloodsucking bugs wanted to get near them.

"Are you going to kill me?" I asked Tommaso.

"Walk, Emma," he'd said.

"Why are you doing this? I know this isn't you."

He pushed me forward. "Walk."

I remembered the four raised lines running across his chest like fleshy speed bumps. "They must have done something to you. Those scars."

"The scars are a badge of honor."

So they hadn't tortured him? He was proud of those scars? "Why four?" I asked.

"I am one of their leaders."

If he really, truly was one of them, then it all made sense now. When the Maaskab were around, the buzzing got louder. Every time Tommaso was around, the same. Their presence must somehow rile up the gods.

I stumbled. Tommaso caught me by the shoulder. "Are you out of your mind?" I asked.

"Yes," he admitted.

"Why?"

"The Uchben killed my family," he said without the slightest hint of emotion.

"Are you sure? It doesn't seem like—"

"I arrived right after it happened. I saw the bodies. They killed my parents, my brothers and sisters, even their children. They shot them right at the dinner table."

Horrible. Just horrible. "Why would they do that?"

"I still don't know."

"Then how? How do you know for sure?" I argued.

"Emma, even I didn't want to believe it, but witnesses saw the men entering the house. They described their clothes, gear, guns, everything. Then I found a record in the Uchben database. It was only an entry with a date and time, but I knew."

"So you joined the Maaskab instead of finding out why?" I couldn't believe he'd make such a drastic leap to the dark side without solid proof.

"No, that's when Chaam asked me to work with him."

Chaam must have been Guy's brother, the sexual predator. I wondered what *his* unique talent was. Maybe hitting women? The God of Domestic Violence. That seemed like a fitting title for the bastard.

"I didn't want to at first," he explained, "but I realized how right he was about everything. The Uchben and the gods only care about keeping their power."

"Do you honestly think the Maaskab and this Chaam guy don't want the same thing? Sounds like they're trying to knock the high man from the totem pole so they can sit up top instead," I argued.

Tommaso laughed. "Oh, you couldn't be more wrong."

"Are you sure about that? Because you're about to kill me simply because I happen to be related to them."

"Emma, you were created for a purpose. Your life was never yours to begin with."

"My life isn't mine? What the hell is wrong with you?" I asked.

"I don't expect you to understand." He flashed a nervous glance at the two Scabs walking behind me.

"Are you going to kill me?" I still couldn't believe this was the same Tommaso.

"No. Chaam likely will, though. Or he could decide to give you a temporary reprieve if you play nice."

"Screw you, Tommaso. This is my life. And make no mistake, if you help them end it, then you're a cold-blooded killer, a murderer, just like the people who killed your family. Period."

He winced and then laughed wickedly.

No, not the man I thought he was. How could I have been so wrong? I saw how he reacted when I'd talked about the pain my family was going through after I'd been taken to the villa. He had genuine compassion. He'd been so kind and so . . . "Wait. It was you, wasn't it? You brought the Maaskab to the villa, when they came to get me."

"You finally figured it out," he answered.

"Why didn't you take me yourself?" I asked.

"I couldn't compromise my position. It's very difficult to infiltrate the Uchben."

"And the necklace? What was that for?"

"Chaam has a particular fascination with you. It was a gift from him. All his women wear one."

"Lucky me." Then I wondered if the Uchben had figured out yet that there was more to the black jade than we'd originally understood. In fact, it seemed like a multipurpose supernatural tool for evil. It could act as a fertility aid to the gods, create watery god prisons, act as a shield from being viewed by the gods, become unattractive pottery, and according to Guy, be used as a weapon. What else could this stuff do? Get rid of toe fungus, cellulite, or pimples? Those were evil, too, right?

"What's next?" I asked. "Do I have hours or days?"

"Now you wait. Get in." He pushed me down onto the cold stone floor. "Good-bye, Emma," I heard him say as he began closing the door behind me.

"Wait! Tommaso. Please!" The door slammed in my face, and now I had nothing to do except replay my mistakes over and over again in my head, fidget with the bracelet, which wasn't coming off without a hacksaw—oh, add tacky, unbreakable jewelry to the list of black jade uses—and think about how I'd give anything to see Guy again.

He'd been right about Tommaso; he did hurt me. Worse than Guy ever had. Sure, Guy didn't play by the rules; he manipulated me, played yo-yo with my feelings, withheld the truth, but he'd always done those things in an effort to protect me out of love. I got that now. Just like I got that my attraction for him was so much more than pheromones.

Because even without the bond, I felt our connection. It ran deep inside my bones and had infused itself in my heart. I couldn't breathe without him in my life, and in this moment, I would give anything to hear the sound of his deep, velvety voice or get one final glimpse of that epic body.

Lord, he was sinfully handsome. The swell of his powerful biceps, the span of his broad shoulders, the endless peaks and valleys of muscles covering every square inch of his bronzed body. I could spend hours reliving the feel of him lying over me, panting, needing me—it made my insides liquefy instantly. But the nail in the coffin was those eyes. The way his turquoise gaze drilled right through me took my breath away. His eyes were a thousand times more powerful than the rush from his scent filling my lungs, the taste of his lips, or the growl he made when he thrust himself between my legs.

And I couldn't ignore that when I removed the bond, it hurt. It hurt like hell, almost as badly as when he pretended he didn't care about me.

But did I love him?

I didn't even have to think it over. Yes. I did. I just didn't know how much, or if I could love him enough to forgive him. I knew I wanted a chance, and it killed me to think I wouldn't get one.

Speaking of being killed, that seemed to be my fate. Guy and Cimil were trapped, Tommaso was a traitor, and the Uchben were off chasing Scabs through the jungle.

No one was coming to save me. Dammit. How had I gotten myself into this mess? I should have stayed in Rome and waited patiently like Guy had told me. Again he was right. I really did deserve that spanking he'd threatened me with so many times.

I could only pray now that he would eventually find a way to escape and kill every Scab walking the earth so that my family would be safe... so the world would be safe.

I had to believe he would. He was a god. He was an extraordinarily dedicated one, too.

And I had to believe that he was the best damned killer on the planet.

Thirty-Seven

"I go alone," Guy said bluntly, leaving no room for negotiation.

"Don't be a stubborn fool, brother," said Cimil. "We free the others first; then we go to collect your precious pet and take down the Maaskab."

"No, there isn't time. They're going to kill her. You take the men to the cenotes, free our brethren," Guy said.

"Cimil's right. You can't go alone," said Xavier.

"I'm not asking—"

"Ay, he's right about that, ya crusty ol' bastard." Looking tired, dirty, and disheveled, Gabrán and his men emerged from the shadows of the jungle. A huge smile swept across Guy's face. "About time, where the hell have you been?"

"Well, funny thing happened on the way to our little party," Gabrán explained. "We got ambushed by a bunch o' filthy Scabs, as your wee lass likes to call 'em. Once we realized they were movin' from place tae place faster than a bolt of lightning, we changed our tactics. Seems they're easy to kill if ya close your eyes an' listen. They make quite a bit o' noise when splittin' air."

"Fascinating," said Guy.

Gabrán explained that he and his men killed about forty or so Maaskab, but as if they'd been called to go home for dinner, the Scabs suddenly disappeared.

"Somewhere important to go, no doubt," Guy said.

He showed Gabrán the aerial photos Xavier had brought. The two men discussed, swapped insults, and rattled on like two spiteful siblings before finally settling on a plan. Gabrán refused to leave Guy's side, so he and his men would go together. Xavier and Cimil would go with the men who'd accompanied Xavier to free the other gods.

"Brother, please reconsider," Cimil begged. "You risk quite a lot to free your little Payal. I've foreseen all possible outcomes and eighty percent result in your failure. Ten in your disappearance forever— Oh! Oh! Can I have your collection of cookbooks and the villa in Greece?"

Guy frowned. "See you in few days."

Thirty-Eight

The door creaked open and in stepped Chaam. He was dressed in a black caftan and wore an elaborate green-jade-and-silver necklace with a large serpent pendant. I stared blankly for several moments. My mind wanted him to be Guy, but even in the low glow of torchlight, I could see he wasn't. First, Guy would never wear that horrible outfit. And second, Guy's lips were slightly fuller, his jawline stronger, and overall he was taller and huskier. Guy was better in every way—even his man gear—although I'd never tell him that because it was way too fun picking on him.

"Let me guess, you were dropped in the ugly, stupid bucket when the gods were made. No wonder why Votan never mentioned you. I'd be embarrassed having you as a brother, too."

He slapped me across the face. "Quiet."

Yep. God of Domestic Violence. "Oh, and what a

bonus. You're socially retarded. You're like the trifecta of losers. In fact, why don't I just call you that?" I shot daggers with my eyes, rubbing my cheek. I hated being told what to do, but being slapped? Hitting a woman was only one step above beating children and kicking puppies. Only the trashiest, lowest breed of pond scum did that.

He raised his open hand in the air, but instead of cowering, I dropped my hands and took a step forward. "Go for it, Trifecta. You're going to kill me anyway, and I'd rather die knowing I didn't do anything to add joy to your life."

Instead of slapping me again, he laughed, lowered his hand, and crudely stroked the side of my face. "You're feisty. I like that about you, Emma."

Ewww. I didn't want him liking anything about me. Then I reluctantly recalled the dreams I'd had of him and the very spicy things he'd wanted to do to me. *Uh-oh.* "Trifecta, what exactly is your special talent?" I asked.

"My name is Backlum Chaam," he said with conceit. "I am one of the four Bacabs, the first gods."

Guy never mentioned that they weren't all born at the same time, but there must have been a pecking order; the way Chaam said Bacabs held some kind of importance, at least inside his bloated, chauvinistic head.

"Being the oldest, I have many talents," he added.

Yes, yes, you arrogant toad. Of course you do. "You're the god of what, exactly?"

He stepped in closer, pressing his body against mine. I wanted to retch. "I am the God of Male Virility," he said proudly.

Perfect. Lucky me. "You *are* going to kill me? Right?" Death wasn't sounding so bad compared to the other possible outcomes running through my mind.

"That will be up to you." He flashed a sinister smile.

Baboon. "I'm guessing there are strings attached to the living option, ones I won't like." *Come on. I know you want to make a sinister chuckle,* I thought. *Wait for it, wait for it...*

Sinister chuckle.

Yep.

"Oh, I promise," he explained. "All of the women I've laid with have thoroughly enjoyed every second, even your great-grandmother."

Double-eeew. Was my great-grandfather propositioning me? "Why in the world would I sleep with you?"

"Aside from the fact that I can show you pleasures only found in dreams..."

My nightmares.

"...We have come to the end of an important era."

He so needed a new title. Perhaps, God of Medieval Debauchery? "You mean you've finally realized you're a complete ass, and you're going to stop killing innocent women?"

He frowned.

"Yes," I continued. "That's right. I heard all about your lovely Scabs picking off the ladies. That's so classy, by the way, but why go through all that trouble to make Payals if your army of Scaby losers murder them?"

"Only the women who prove incapable of carrying my seed are picked off. The priests do so enjoy a good hunt."

I really wanted to hurt this man—being—whatever. He was a waste of good air.

"But the others," he rattled on, "the ones who have the good fortune to carry a child for me, they get to live and raise my offspring."

Oh yes. Good fortune, indeed. Murderous, evil prick! "So you take innocent, young women, virgins, hoping their first baby will be a female like me?"

He made a low, gravelly laugh. "You're right, but don't undervalue the firstborn boys. Ahhh, my boys," he said stoically, "I send them to become Maaskab. It was quite the upgrade for that little band of archaic Mayan witch doctors. With my blood and leadership, they've become most powerful. Such fun."

I'd been right about the Maaskab. They weren't entirely human. *Oh, Christ!* I thought. Was my uncle in California a Maaskab? What would have happened if I'd gone to live with him?

Put it in your Can't Deal with This Now Pocket, I thought. Boy, that thing had to be getting full.

Chaam leaned against the cold, moist wall and crossed his arms. "Sadly, they're lacking in the strategic thinking department, thus the reason we recruit leaders like Tommaso. Quite easy to do with the right catalyst."

Catalyst? "You mean you killed his poor family?" I asked.

"Yes, but that didn't quite provide the result we wanted. Luckily, we've discovered another more effective way to gain people's allegiance."

Oh, goody. Evil confession time, I thought. *I really, really am going to die. Because bad guys only spill their guts when they're about to slit your throat.* "Yes? Go on."

Chaam paused and smiled. "Okay," he said cheerfully. "I'm so proud of this little tidbit that I must share." He clapped his hands.

I suddenly realized that for once, Guy was wrong.

His brother wasn't more arrogant; Chaam was simply bonkers.

"We've discovered a way to liquefy the black jade. We can inject it into any human. They're consumed with a hunger for darkness, and they must feed it, or the jade starts to turn on them."

"You mean, it creates an addiction to being bad?"

"It's damned brilliant!" he replied. "That jade has so many uses."

Poor, poor Tommaso. He'd been injected with foul, demonic heroin. Somewhere, deep down inside, I *knew* he didn't want to hurt me.

"Personally," Chaam added, "I use it to polish my teeth." He smiled and showed me his pearly white smile. "See."

Boy, he really *was* bonkers. And evil. But he did have nice teeth.

Chaam continued, "However, I have to admit, the jade can't do everything. Fuel my weapons, for one."

"The little jars?" I asked.

He had the look of joyful madness in his eyes. "Giant jars, Emma! Those little ones were merely prototypes. We ended up using those to create traps in the cenotes or to distract Cimil—she always gets in my hair. Nosy bitch. But no matter, now we have four colossal structures filled with seventy years' worth of the most potent energy I could find."

He explained in horrific detail how he had the Maaskab kidnap thousands of women. And with the aid of the black jade, he'd slept with them, taken the female children once fully grown, and then coaxed the dark light into their bodies through various forms of torture. All for the purpose of extracting their light, their life force. Their bodies, being part deity, made them more powerful than any human, and their humanity made them mortal.

He was creating Payals for biofuel.

I wanted to vomit. He was beyond evil. And medieval. And he was the poster child for debauchery. He was every single nightmare I'd ever had rolled into one. The poor women. He probably lulled them into submission with his pheromones to impregnate them, only to later steal away their children and kill the girls. His own daughters. Sick. Sick. Sick.

"So you're going to torture me so you can put my tainted god juice in your giant jars? Then what?"

"Well, my dear, this is where you get to make a choice. My vessels of destruction are almost filled now, and I have all the Payals I need. Once I release the energy stored inside the structures, darkness will sweep across the world like a giant tidal wave of decay—devouring any human flesh it comes in contact with."

Oh. Oh no. This was bad, way bad.

"Those who take refuge inside the jade mines will be perfectly safe, but the rest of mankind will perish. In fact, my boys are busy sealing the entrances to mine shafts now. So... will you join them or become apocalyptic fertilizer for my giant jars?"

"Sorry?" I was still trying to grasp the situation. End of my family and friends? End of humanity? Everyone on the face of the planet, except for Scabs?

"This last structure, my pyramid, is waiting for a good topping off." He made a dramatic wave of his hand. "You can choose: die or have a life with me."

"Why would anyone want a life with you?"

"Silly woman. Even after the apocalypse, I'll still have needs. I am the God of Male Virility, and you are by far the strongest Payal I've ever seen, even with your distance from my lineage. Who knows? Maybe I'll let you have a few children and keep them."

Yack. Shudder. Cringe. "That's such a fabulous offer, really; I'm mulling it over this very second. What I meant was, why do you need to kill absolutely everyone else?"

"Humans, Emma, are destroying this world. They're like radioactive cockroaches. I'm simply giving fate a hand, taking out the trash before the planet is irreparable."

I remembered Guy mentioning that the gods were hardwired to protect humans, even if they got tired of it. Chaam's wiring had gotten crossed.

"What about the other gods? What will they do when they get out?"

"They're not going anywhere. And besides, after the energy's been released, what can they do? They can't bring back all of those people. In fact, the other gods might thank me for freeing them from their tedious, eternal duties of rescuing the stupid humans."

"I think you're wrong. I think when Guy is set free, he'll spend the rest of eternity kicking your arrogant, repugnant ass."

He arched one brow and then stuck out his lower lip in a pout. "Oh. The little Payal doesn't like me. I thought you might be a good candidate for immortality and sack play, but alas..." His smile was evil incarnate. "The little primate wishes to join her grandmother. Fine with me, I have a thousand others to choose from."

"Grandmother? *You* killed my grandmother?"

I wanted to jump on his head and pound it into the

stone floor. What kind of sick animal could hurt a sweet, old woman like her? For heaven's sake, he was her *father*.

"Oh yes, Emma. She was so full of light. It amazed me how long she held on. Hours and hours of torture. Can you see it in your mind? Of course, she came to me well primed since her own sister lured her to me and betrayed her. I made sure to repeat that fact several times. The angrier, the better. More dark fuel."

There it was. The answer I'd been looking for. My darkest fears confirmed. My poor grandmother had been tortured and then killed by Chaam. Could I ever tell my mom such a thing? Would I ever get the chance? Not likely. Perhaps it was for the best. Then there was the horrible truth about Rosa and Arturo. They'd lured Grandma to her death. I partially wished Guy'd let them live, so I could have killed them myself.

Oh, sweet Virgin of Guadalupe. I gasped. I was filling with hatred, just like he wanted.

He continued his malevolent banter. "Well, look at that." He bent down and peered into my eyes. "Already turning colors. Once they're black, you'll be all ready to go."

"Fuck you! I hope Guy rips your heart from your body and makes you choke on it."

"Good girl. Let that darkness in." He pounded on the door, and it swung open. "See you at the top of the pyramid, baby."

I felt sick to my stomach. Everything I'd ever loved would soon be gone. And stupid, stupid me. I could have stopped this. I almost deserved to die. If Darwin were still alive, I'm sure I'd get his vote.

Well, I wasn't going to go down without a fight; I'd

claw and kick until my last breath. And if I couldn't fight my way free, I certainly wasn't going to help Chaam by becoming his biofuel. My last act would be one I could be proud of. I would think of everything and everyone I loved, every good memory in my life. Chaam would be hard-pressed to squeeze even a drop of darkness from me.

I planted myself on the floor, sitting with my legs crossed. I closed my eyes and began playing the sunniest memories of my life. I pictured my parents and every wonderful thing about them; how they'd always cared, no matter how bonkers I acted. I thought about my grandmother, her soft hands, the floral smell of her hair when she hugged me. Her laughter. I thought about my friends, Nick, Jess, and Anne, and their outrageous appetite for life, including their relentless belief that someday I'd get a date. Then I thought about Guy singing *Madame Butterfly* and how my lifelong friend, guardian, and tormentor had been a real, live god. I thought about him screaming he loved me.

"If by some miracle any of you can hear me...I love you, too, and I'm sorry I let everyone down."

Thirty-Nine

In all his years, Guy had never seen anything like it.

"It's like that bloody show Emma used to watch, *Star Trek*." Guy scratched the black stubble sprouting along his jaw while Gabrán's men attempted to penetrate the transparent wall with various objects. Daggers, sticks, they even threw a few rocks. Nothing went through, and it was too high to climb over. "Damned evil bastards have a bloody force field."

Gabrán spouted, "Thanks to help from one o' you."

Guy grunted. He still had a hard time believing one of the gods was involved. But Gabrán was right; this kind of energy manipulation was divine in origin.

Guy, Gabrán, and the men were finally forced to weave through the never-ending maze of invisible walls the Maaskab had erected around the perimeter of their village by feeling their way until an opening appeared. Then they walked for hours more until they found another, a painfully slow process. It was well past nightfall by the time they arrived at the outskirts of the Maaskab village.

"Where is everyone?" Guy whispered. The village appeared eerily vacant. The thatched-roof huts were dark inside, and only the crickets chirped.

"I don't know," Gabrán replied. "But we cannot go in tonight. My men need rest before we fight."

Guy couldn't wait; he needed to know Emma was still alive. If he had to, he'd tear the village apart stone by stone with his bare hands to find her.

Stubborn girl, why had she broken the bond? It would have helped him sense her direction. In the end, maybe it didn't matter. The Maaskab would have slathered her in that black powder to block their connection.

Guy looked at Gabrán. "Stay here. I'm going to walk the perimeter and see what that big structure from the photo is."

Gabrán cursed. "Take Brutus, then. That way I ken see for myself whatcha find, and he ken call to us if ya get in teh trouble."

The bond between Gabrán and this particularly unique team of elite Uchben soldiers came in handy for times like these. Like each of the chiefs, they had been handpicked by the gods to be given the gift of immortality and undergo nearly a century of rigorous training. They lived, ate, studied, and sparred as one and were personally taught the art of war, telepathy, and mind sharing by Guy.

For their dedication and self-sacrifice, the elite Uchben, like Brutus, were rewarded with seats on the Uchben Council and would someday become chiefs themselves. To Guy, it seemed like so little—after all, they had to relinquish their mortality, couldn't have ties with the outside world, or take a wife—but their willingness to make such sacrifices spoke volumes about their belief in the Uchben mission.

Guy and Brutus inched their way around the perimeter of the quiet, rancid-smelling village, passing empty huts, unlit fire pits, and vacant stone structures. Where had they all gone?

They continued on until they reached the northern end of the village where the two men stood speechless as their eyes registered the colossal structure in front of them.

"Is that what I think it is?" Guy asked.

Brutus nodded.

"Did you show Gabrán?"

Brutus nodded again.

Guy gaped for several moments. It was nighttime, but he could easily make out the immense black pyramid and sense the darkness seeping from between the black stones. "What in the world could it be for?" The poisonous smell was strangely familiar; it held the odor of evil, death, and hatred . . . the absence of light.

"It smells like the cenote where I was trapped," said Guy.

There was a rustle from fifty yards away. Tommaso emerged from the jungle, moving toward the structure. Guy's eyes locked in on him, and within the space of a heartbeat, Guy was on top of Tommaso, flooding the man's body with a burst of energy. Tommaso fell limp on contact, and Guy dragged him back behind the trees where Brutus was waiting.

Brutus stared at Guy, his eyes wide with shock.

"What?" Guy asked.

"Did you just sift through the air?" Brutus asked.

Guy didn't realize it, but he had.

"Must be something about this place." Guy glared down at Tommaso.

Brutus nodded and then his focus turned to the traitor. He pulled out a long, sharp blade. "Must be Christmas. Here, let me open that for you."

"Not yet, but soon," Guy replied and lifted Tommaso.

Guy stared with lethal fury at Tommaso as he awoke in the dirt and then slowly moved his head from side to side, seemingly oblivious to Brutus emptying his canteen over his head or to Guy who now held a very large knife.

"Where the hell is she?" Guy growled. He jumped on Tommaso, legs straddled over him, and dug the blade into Tommaso's neck.

Tommaso cackled. "Right about now? Dead."

Guy pushed the dagger into Tommaso's flesh, drawing a trickle of blood. "You'd better hope for your sake that she's still alive."

"Kill me. Go ahead. I don't give a shit. Because tonight, the reservoir will be full, and we have more than enough Payals to complete the job."

Job? What job? Guy swiftly raked the blade across Tommaso's chest, cupping one hand over his mouth to stifle the scream. "I'll give you a choice, Tommaso. You can tell me where Emma is, and I'll grant you a clean death." Guy bent over him and whispered into his ear, "Or, my dear friend, you can withhold the information and live a very, very long time. We'll pump you full of medicine. We'll do everything to keep that heart of yours strong and healthy so I can enjoy torturing you every minute of every day for the rest of your life. Your hell will be endless, without mercy. Now, where's my Emma?"

"*Your* Emma?" Tommaso laughed. "Chaam made the Payals—she belongs to him."

Chaam? All this time it was his brother Chaam? He was always competitive and domineering. But never in a millennium would Guy have suspected this of his brother, the God of Male Virility, whose only focus in life seemed to be perfecting the art of seduction, answering the prayers of sad, awkward young men pining for the prom queen, or helping human males maintain their macho identity—tireless, brutal work, no doubt, but regardless, Chaam wasn't the coldhearted type.

Thank the gods that they were not really related—not in the traditional sense anyway—because if they were, Guy didn't think he could handle hating himself any more than he already did.

"She belongs to me! Where?" Guy dragged the blade deeper over the same wound.

"On top of the pyramid. But you'd better hurry." Tommaso laughed wickedly. "Chaam really enjoys making the Payals bleed when he juices them. They don't last long."

Guy suddenly understood. Pyramid. Reservoir. Payals. Juice.

He turned to Brutus in horror. "The pyramid is made from that black jade. It's a giant jar."

Tommaso laughed again. "All this fuss over Emma—she's nothing. Fertilizer."

Guy plunged his knife into Tommaso's chest. "A deal is a deal. Enjoy your death."

Relief swept across Tommaso's face as blood spurted from the gaping hole. "I'm sorry," he muttered.

That was an unexpected response. Guy turned and bolted for the pyramid. He didn't care if he had to face five hundred Scabs on his own. If his body was destroyed, he'd be sent back to the cenote. But Emma—

Guy reached the base of the structure and sifted to the top, where he spotted Emma lying over a torchlit altar with Chaam gripping a knife.

"Stop singing, you stupid bitch!" Chaam screamed, slicing the blade down her leg. "You're going to stop this instant! Do you hear me? Turn those eyes dark, dammit."

Though bound to the altar with ropes, she was wiggling her toes, smiling, and singing—wailing, actually, "Ain't nothin' gonna break my stride. Nobody gonna slow me down, oh no! I got to keep on movin'..."

Matthew Wilder? Leave it to Emma to save herself with corny eighties music.

He shifted behind Chaam and plunged his dagger deep into Chaam's neck. "Get away from her!" The two men rolled to the ground in a blur of fists, blood, and knives.

"You can't kill me, you idiot. I'm immortal!" howled Chaam. "And you won't be able to fight us all."

From the corner of his eye, Guy noted the tall black silhouettes materializing on the platform. "Oh, shit." The Maaskab were coming in droves.

In that same instant, Gabrán's team appeared and began fighting. Brutus had undoubtedly alerted them.

Guy turned his entire focus back on Chaam, whose once-turquoise eyes were now black, empty. No goodness remained in his soul.

Guy's instincts to protect the human world screamed for Chaam's death. And yet, his brother was right; there was no way to kill him. But he could...

As the two continued rolling, each struggling to get the upper hand, Guy's eyes flashed to the gaping black hole the size of a water well opening just under the altar. The reservoir's entrance, he surmised.

If a tiny jar floating inside a cenote was sufficient to keep Guy imprisoned for seventy years, he had to believe that being thrown into the heart of this black jade pyramid would render Chaam completely inert. Maybe there'd be some eternal suffering involved, too. Plenty of stored dark energy from his victims.

One could only hope.

Guy channeled his rage, thinking of all who had suffered at the hands of his cruel brother, including Gabriela. He rolled Chaam onto his back and released the energy from his body. The surge hurled Guy back several feet, but left Chaam stunned. Guy scrambled to his feet, dragged Chaam to the opening, and threw him down.

He didn't pause to revel. Instead, he turned to Emma, who was laughing hysterically. Had she finally snapped? "Emma! Are you okay?"

He looked into her eyes. No one was home, except for the karaoke star. "Wake me up, before you go-go..." she began singing.

Guy cringed. Gods, he hated Wham!

Guy tore a strip of cloth from his shirt and bound Emma's leg. The cut had been inflicted for pain but wasn't lethal yet. He untied her and pulled her into his chest for a quick moment, thinking. He needed to get Emma somewhere safe, quiet, away from the overwhelming energy of the pyramid, but the only way down was blocked. The Uchben were lined up at the top of the pyramid's steps, fighting the never-ending swarm of dark priests.

He thought of sifting, but he didn't know what would happen; this power was unfamiliar to him, and she was already in such a fragile state. *Down the steps it is.* "Emma! Wake up! I need you to wake up, honey! I have to fight with the men, or we won't get out of here." He shook her, but she remained incoherent, singing and smiling.

"Gods dammit, woman! Wake the hell up!" he screamed into her face.

"Oh, Cupcake," Emma said with a giggle. "I missed you. Tell me a story." She poked the tip of Guy's nose.

Was she drunk? He paused for a quick moment. Maybe he needed to try a different approach. He bent down, still holding her tightly, and whispered in her ear, "Emma, honey. I'm sorry for everything. You were right. I'm a lying, arrogant, selfish bastard. And I'm sorry I treated you like a child. I'm sorry I hurt you. I love you, and I'll never do it again. Please wake up? Please?" He gently kissed her lips and then pulled away, grasping her shoulders to see her face.

She snapped her eyes shut tightly for several moments before they popped open, wide with shock. "Do you really love me?"

"Yes. Very much." He nodded and then cupped her face. "And I'll spend eternity proving it to you."

She stepped away from him, confused. "Where the hell am I?" Her gaze shifted to the vicious tangle of Gabrán's Uchben team battling the priests and then to her wrist. The realization hit her. "Oh my gods." She cupped her hands over her mouth. "Where's that bastard brother of yours? I'm going to tear his balls off!"

Guy made a quick sigh of relief. Emma was back. "Honey, please. I need you to listen to me. We need to—"

"No," she interrupted, her eyes filled with rage. "You listen to me! That son of a bitch tortured me. He killed my grandmother and thousands of other women. Take this damned bracelet off me and tell me where the hell he is." She held out her wrist, panting furiously.

He grabbed the solid stone cuff with both hands and squeezed until it cracked, falling to the ground.

"Thanks." Emma rubbed her wrist. "Now let me at him."

"My sweet, he's been shoved down that very, very dark hole underneath the altar, and I doubt he's ever coming out."

"Oh. You mean he's dead?" Emma asked.

"No, but I bet he wishes he was, and so will you if we don't get out of here. Gabrán's men can't hold back the priests much longer. They were already running on fumes when we arrived."

Just then, a priest sifted between them with his back to Emma, a black jade dagger raised toward Guy. In one swift motion, Emma raised her hand and released a surge of energy. With a loud crack, the priest literally ripped in half, down the length of his body. The two sides fell in opposite directions, his innards steaming.

"Holy crap, woman! What was that?" Guy stared down at the twitching right half of the body. He was morbidly shocked and incredibly proud.

She shrugged casually. "Payback. Hell hath no fury like a Payal scorned. Can we go now?"

Guy smiled. "By all means. Please, after you."

Leaving a trail of decimated Maaskab in their wake, Emma led the way down the pyramid, with Guy and the

Uchben following just inches behind. Gabrán joined them at the base of the steps, and having witnessed her awesome display of power through the bond with his men, the chief commented that she'd be giving barbecue classes to all Uchben when they returned.

With Gabrán and his men at their flank, Guy and Emma plowed through the jungle, remaining on the narrow trail that weaved back through the invisible labyrinth. They were miles away from any roads, towns, and transportation, and it was nothing but the thickest, most miserable breed of vegetation.

As they pushed ahead, Emma informed Guy about the bad news: why Chaam had built the pyramids and that there were three more jade structures somewhere in the world. Not good. Worse, she hadn't learned how they were detonated. None of them had a clue. Guy hoped it wasn't throwing a deity down that hole.

Adding to the severity of the situation, other Payals were being held prisoner, waiting to be used as fuel. Guy figured they'd easily find Chaam's harem of apocalyptic love slaves inside the mines, but were there others?

"It's straight out of a futuristic horror movie," she said to Guy. "Chaam's been injecting people with serum made from that crap. It makes them do evil things. Can you imagine what would happen if that stuff got into the water supply? I mean, look what it did to Tommaso—" She gasped and stopped walking.

Guy, following closely behind her, almost rammed into her back. "Don't stop, Emma."

She turned and placed her palms on his chest. "Guy, where's Tommaso?"

Guy looked over his shoulder at the men who were in a

tight formation behind him. "Keep moving. We'll be right behind you," he instructed.

They didn't question and walked around him and Emma, into the night.

"Not too long, eh," Gabrán warned as he passed by last.

Guy nodded and then turned toward Emma. He felt a wave of euphoria wash over him as he looked at her, really looked at her for the first time since he'd left her in Rome. He'd never been more grateful for his nocturnal vision. Gods, she was so lovely. Even in her current state: filthy, tired, and bruised, her clothes covered in dirt and blood.

Yet somehow, she was even more gorgeous to him now. Maybe it was because she'd found the strength to accept herself, her unique place in the universe. Maybe it was because he'd thought he'd lost her. Regardless, he wanted to take her right then and there as he studied her jaw-length red hair, hanging in sweat-soaked spirals. She'd never looked rawer, fiercer, and sexier.

He knew the Maaskab weren't far behind, but he couldn't resist stealing one quick kiss. He bent his head down and captured her lips. Emma slid her arms around him, and his body lit up. Her mouth opened to him, and she began lapping against his tongue, hot and heavy. He tasted the salt of her skin and the sweetness of her breath mixing in his mouth, and he knew life couldn't get much better. Well, except...he gripped her tighter wishing he could finish what they'd started in Rome, but right on cue—

"Ow!" Emma pulled away, puffing out three quick breaths, fanning her face. "Jeez, couldn't you warn me that was coming? That burns." His powerful energy had stunned her; he couldn't seem to keep it in check when he touched her.

"I'm going to get a set of black jade earrings made for you," Guy offered.

"Not on your life, big boy. I'm not putting that stuff anywhere on my body. You're going to have to find some other— Hey! Don't change the subject. What happened to Tommaso?"

The first rays of sunlight crawling into the sky caught her sparkling green eyes—eyes that were encased by red, bloodshot whites. She'd had a really, really rough few days and wasn't going to take this well, he thought. He closed his eyes and held out his hands defensively.

"I killed him," he said, expecting to be shredded into a million pieces as Emma blasted him with her hands.

He waited for a moment, and then realized she hadn't moved. The tears began streaming down her face.

Guy released a slow breath. "I'm sorry. I know you cared for him, but you must not be angry—"

"No. No, I'm not. How could you know? How could anyone know Chaam murdered Tommaso's family to turn him against the Uchben? Or that it wasn't enough. He was too good, so they had to inject him with that jade venom." She clenched her fists. "It wasn't his fault, Guy." She turned back in the direction of the Scab village.

"Where are you going?" Guy asked. "We have to keep moving."

"What does it look like? I'm going back for my friend."

"Emma, honey, he's gone. You're wasting your time."

"Did you see him die? Are you sure?" she asked, not bothering to slow her pace.

"Not exactly. But no one could survive a stab wound straight to the heart."

"I'm going back to make sure. I have to. He saved my

life once, and I'm not leaving him with those monsters," she argued.

"No, Emma. It's too dangerous. Let's ensure the other gods have been freed; then I can go back with them and finish off the other priests. I'll look for Tommaso then."

He tugged her in the direction the men had headed. "Hurry. We must catch up to Gabrán."

She shot daggers with her eyes. "Listen, Guy. I was kidnapped, terrorized, and tortured. And for the frosting on my danger cupcake, I just cracked open twenty bloodthirsty priests like Easter eggs. I think I know all about dangerous. But I can't let one more innocent person fall. No more!"

Guy considered her words. He understood how she felt, and he did not wish to deny her anything, but she was being foolish and reckless. He was tired, she was exhausted, and Gabrán's men were ready to collapse. Immortal or not, they needed sleep and food. Personally, he heard a long, hot bath and a chocolate chip cookie calling his name. He also wanted to bed Emma. Immediately.

He looked down at her, wondering why she wanted to take such a huge risk just to know for certain Tommaso was dead. Unless... "Emma, I know now isn't the time for this conversation, but did you love him? Actually, that's not what I meant to ask. Do you love me?"

Her eyes fixed on her mud-caked boots and then filled with tears. "Yes. And I don't want to be apart from you ever again. I feel so empty, especially after I broke the bond. But will it be enough? Will we stand a chance if we can't trust each other?"

She was right about the trust. He'd broken hers on more than one occasion, which he knew he could fix over time, but her first comment was a monkey wrench. A big one. The feelings she'd described were the mark of their bond, not love. Would he lose her if he told her this? But if he said nothing, she might live her life falsely believing she loved him.

"Emma." He grabbed her hand and placed a soft kiss in her palm. "The feeling you describe is the influence of the bond. I wish I could say it was more. And I understand that without trust, you cannot love me. So now, I have to prove I'm deserving of it."

She cocked her head to one side. "No. You're wrong. I know what I feel, and I love—"

"Oh, how sweet."

Guy and Emma gasped and swiveled on their heels to find Tommaso positioned in front of an army of priests. He was shirtless, his heaving chest caked with dried blood.

"How? How the hell did you survive?" Guy muttered under his breath.

"Did you honestly think a little knife wound to the chest could stop me?" Tommaso asked.

"Um, yes?" Guy threw back flippantly.

"Okay." Tommaso shrugged. "Maybe I did, too, but a little of that black juice"—he rubbed the almost healed wound over his heart—"and never better."

"Could this fucking day get any worse?" Emma groaned as Guy lunged at Tommaso and the Maaskab attacked.

Forty

Add “Can cure fatal injuries” to the list of 101 uses for evil black jade. I swore I was going to rub that stuff over the calluses on my feet as soon as I got home.

I swung to the right and then to the left. My hands blasted anything that came into contact. The first few dozen Scabs fell to the ground instantly cooked, but as I reached Scab number twenty-five, they began falling and getting back up again. I was running out of juice. How or why? Who the heck knew? Two things were certain: I was tired, and they kept on coming.

“Guy!” I screamed. With the swarm of black mud–crusted bodies bearing down on me, I couldn’t see him. I felt a thud against the side of my head and then the warm gush of blood down the side of my face. I continued flailing my arms, but my vision was flickering from the blow.

“Guy!” I screamed again as one of the priests threw me into the dirt and then jumped on top of me.

And what can I say? He was like all the others. Head to toe covered in black soot, long ropes of foul-smelling dreads, rotting black teeth, and barely any clothes. Oh, and one special accessory. I caught a glimpse of the shiny blade raised in the air right before he plunged it deep into my stomach. There was a little pain at first, but then a crippling blaze of agony racked my body. I peered into his black-and-crimson eyes in horror as he lifted his arm once again and hammered down. The air escaped my lungs as the knife sliced another hole through my torso.

Just my effing luck! I'd finally gotten Guy to admit he was a huge, selfish jerk, and I'd realized he really did love me. Sure, he was convinced that my feelings were tied to that idiotic bond, but I knew it was more. It had to be. Why else would I be willing to keep him in my life after all he'd done?

Regardless, I'd been looking forward to making him prove himself to me. I had in mind twelve-hour foot rubs while I nibbled hot dogs and watched chick flicks. Oh, the possibilities.

I was also tickled that the man responsible for my grandmother's death got what he deserved—sort of. Personally, I wanted to see him burning in the fiery pits of hell, but I supposed an ominous black hole filled with anguish from his thousands of victims would do.

And finally, I'd made peace with the whole "being different" thing. Discovering I had the ability to crack bad guys in two with the touch of my hands sure helped.

Only now, after discovering all this, I was going to die? And still a virgin, no less. Well, effing great! Just effing *great*!

When the dark priest raised his dagger for a third

time, a bolt of lightning struck the top of his head. Smoke snaked from his eyes sockets as he collapsed to my side. Cracks of lightning suddenly exploded all around me. One by one the Scabs fell to the ground.

"Good job, K'ak!" I heard a female voice call out. It sounded like Cimil.

A stunningly gorgeous, tall, golden-skinned man, with a mane of silver-streaked black hair falling to his ankles, stepped from behind the shadows of the trees. Aside from the two-foot high headdress, made of intertwining silver-and-green-jade serpents, he was completely naked.

"Hello, Emma." His face glowed, and I felt a wave of heat as his gaze settled on me.

"Cock, I presume?" I choked out.

He frowned. "Kay-apostrophe-a-kay. K'ak," he clarified with what sounded like a perfect British accent. "It's Mayan for heat. But you can call me K'ak Tiliw Chan Yopaat."

"It—it practically rolls off the tongue," I sputtered.

He shot a glance over his shoulder, and how he did it without losing balance, considering he was wearing fifty pounds of jewelry on his head, was anyone's guess. Maybe he'd had a lot of practice? "Votan, get your ass over here. Your human is dying," he said.

I'm dying? Oh yeah. I am.

Guy instantly appeared at my side and peeled away my tattered, blood-soaked shirt. The anguish in his eyes said it all. "Oh, *Emma*!"

I raised my hand to his face and met his stunning turquoise gaze.

Like staring into the gates of heaven, I thought. Then there were those lips, his sinfully rock hard body, and that man gear. I'd never get the opportunity to experience him putting those to use on me or letting our love grow into something more. We could have had an amazing life together because he was amazing. Strong, fearless, and beautiful. But more than anything, I couldn't stand the thought of him suffering because of my death.

"I'm sorry, too, Guy." I swallowed, tasting nothing but blood. "Just promise you won't let this change you. You're wonderful and kind—when you want to be—and I know you'll kill every last one of those fucking bastards. You'll stop them and save my family. I know you will, because you're an awesome god of death and war."

He took a deep, slow breath. "I love you, Emma. I really love you."

"I love you, too," I whispered.

"You do?" His eyes lit up.

Of course I did. I'd tried to tell him that before, but true to his stubborn nature, he didn't listen to me.

I sighed. "Yes."

Brutus appeared over Guy's shoulder. "Sir?"

"Not now, Brutus," Guy blurted out.

"But, sir." Brutus frowned. "Tommaso, he's still breathing. Do you want me to finish him off?"

"No!" I screamed. Then I realized it wasn't just Brutus, but Guy, K'ak (resist laughing), and yes, Cimil gathered around me; there were dozens more. A mixture of Uchben I already knew and…others. They were smiling down at me, glowing with affection. "Who are they?" I whispered to Guy.

"These are my other brethren, Emma. The gods."

They were beautiful—no, they were breathtakingly gorgeous. Their faces were amalgamations of every culture and ethnicity I'd ever seen. Deep golden skin. Large almond-shaped turquoise eyes. High cheekbones. Full, sensuous lips. Some had thick black hair, and others, flaming red or pale blond locks. If I hadn't known any better, I would have guessed I was staring at a pack of very suntanned angels. Except they were naked. Very naked. And they didn't have white fluffy wings. Oh, well, nobody's perfect.

"Please, Guy. Don't kill Tommaso," I begged.

Guy's brows furrowed. "Emma, you don't understand what you're asking. He's tried to kill you twice."

"Please. It's my last wish," I begged. After all, it wasn't Tommaso's fault. He was simply another victim like my grandmother, only this one we could save.

He jerked his head back. "Last wish? Woman, what the hell are you talking about? You're not going anywhere."

"I'm not?"

"Hell, no! You and I are taking a trip to the other side. You'll be immortal, just like Brutus and Gabrán. I can't take this anymore."

Brutus and Gabrán were immortal?

"Emma, the thought of living without you, constantly worrying about you, it's fucking exhausting."

"You can do that? Make people immortal?" I whispered.

"Yes. The other gods must agree, but yes. I mean, if that's what you want."

Well, that was a no-brainer. See my parents again? Be able to help the Uchben fight the Maaskab and free the other Payals? Not die of old age or die a virgin? "One condition," I muttered.

Guy stroked the side of my head. "Emma, can't we negotiate later? The process doesn't work so well on the dead, and we don't want another Chac on our hands."

The little boy I'd seen near the cenote. Chac. He'd been changed after he'd died? Couldn't wait to hear the explanation on that one. *Pocket.*

"Tommaso. Cure him," I whispered.

"What? Have you lost your mind, woman? Absolutely not. Never. No." Guy shook his head.

"Guy," I pleaded. "It's not his fault. He's infected. Doesn't he deserve to be saved, just like anyone else?"

Guy growled, and there was a rumbling of voices behind him. Guy looked at each one of his brothers' and sisters' faces and then turned back to me.

"It's one thing to let him live. I could put him in our prison. But the only way we know to maybe—and I mean maybe—cure him would be to make him immortal, too," Guy said.

"Do it," I said.

"You—you and he..." Guy looked mortified.

"Now it's your turn to trust me. I'm only asking this because it's the right thing to do. Cure him."

Guy nodded solemnly. "Okay, my sweet. For you, I will do it."

Forty-One

"How are you feeling, my love?" I felt a rough hand jog the length of my sternum, between my breasts, and then up again toward the hollow at the base of my neck.

My eyes eased open and settled on an incandescent set of turquoise eyes. I sighed, transfixed by their glint. "I love this dream," I said with a breathy voice and stretched my arms above my head, enjoying Guy's warm, hard body pressed against mine. "It's my favorite."

I reached out and skimmed my fingertip down the ridge of his proud nose, and then trailed the pad of my index finger over his full, sumptuous lips, watching as the corners curled into a smile. A smile that made my heart flutter erratically.

"As much as I love being the star of your erotic little fantasies, my sweet." Guy tucked a stray lock of his chin-length hair behind one ear. "This is real."

Nooo. This had to be a dream. My body hummed with

a euphoric, serene energy. There was no pain or soreness. I was floating on cloud nine except for the noise. It sounded like the loud roar of an engine and was ruining the tranquil, sexy bliss of the moment.

My eyes darted around the large, dimly lit cabin of the...plane? "Christ!" I sat up, whiplashed into reality. "What happened?" Guy was snugly wedged between me and the window, stretched across a fully extended sleeper seat, the kind I always saw on British Airways commercials. Except Uchben sized. That's because we were on Uchben Airways.

The plane was completely empty, except for me and Guy. And I supposed the pilots. "How did I get here?" I ground my palms into the sides of my head.

"Ah, my sweet." He eyed me like a fresh-baked cookie. "We have so much to talk about, yet oddly enough, seeing you like this pushes talking to the bottom of my list. You've taken to your new body with unprecedented success." Guy positively glowed.

"New body?" My hands began frantically hopscotching over the red, silky fabric covering my parts—arms, neck, thighs, heart. Check! Everything was still in its proper place, and I still felt like me.

"Yes. New, but not necessarily improved—one cannot improve that which was perfect to begin with." His gaze lazily savored my curves. "Before my ability to produce a coherent thought dissipates," Guy said. "I must inform you that while you have been infused with the light of the gods, and therefore are technically immortal, you can still die if your body is destroyed. Think vampire. Those SOBs live forever as long as no one stakes them. They're such a pain in the ass."

Vampires? I wasn't about to ask; my mind was still stuck on the word *immortal* anyway. Then I remembered the horrific knife wounds in my stomach. I tore open the front of my robe and released a sigh of relief. No more holes. In fact, my skin was flawless, smooth, and glowing with a slight golden hue. Were my pasty, BullFrog-sunscreen days finally behind me?

I heard a low groan from Guy who stared longingly at my bare breasts, his smile replaced by a hungry, primal blaze—a look I knew, a look I loved, a look I'd do anything for. He reached out his hand and skimmed his fingertips over my nipples. He watched with eager fascination as they pulled into tight little pearls.

Cliff! Cliff! Cliff! my naughty voice began to chant.

"Mmmm," he rumbled, not taking his eyes off his prize.

"Time to cut the ribbon?" I asked nervously.

Guy's attention suddenly shifted. He pulled me down and rolled me on top of him. His erection strategically nestled between my legs.

Oooh, I guess that's a yes. Cliff. Cliff. Cliff!

He devoured my lips with a kiss so filled with frantic need that goose bumps exploded over every square inch of my skin. As he ground his hardness into my cleft, his tongue plunged deep inside my mouth, lapping and stroking, ravenous. His hands floated over my back to my neck and then worked their way underneath the silky soft fabric of my red robe. All I could think of was the flood of arousal pulsing relentlessly through my core.

His hands languidly moved over the bare skin of my shoulders and then peeled away the robe from my arms. The sash, hardly tied to begin with, slid apart, and the thin fabric drifted to the floor.

Gods, his touch feels incredible, I thought as he relished my bare back with his rough hands and then moved them lazily down to cup my ass.

He pulled me into the thrust of his hips, and it took every ounce of restraint I had not to tumble down the orgasm cliff right there. I pulled back, just an inch, and then noticed he was wearing a thin, black—caftan?

"Oh, Lord!" I planted my palms on his chest and raised my upper body away from him. "Take that disgusting thing off! That's what your brother was wearing when he... when he... Are you trying to completely ruin this?" I climbed off him and covered my face. "Take it off!" I shrieked.

I couldn't stand any reminder of Chaam. That beast tortured me in ways that would haunt me for my new eternity. And what was with the gods and caftans? Was there a sale during the seventies and they all stocked up?

"I had no idea, Emma. I'm so sorry." There was a muted rustle. "There. Open your eyes."

Guy was poised in front of me naked, his head bowed against the cabin's ceiling, fists clenched at his sides. Of course, I'd seen him nude before, but not like this. Not fully aroused and waiting for me.

"Um... wow" was all I could manage. My eyes traveled over his buttery, caramel skin. I wanted to bathe in the sight of his raw, gorgeous masculinity. His tight, hard muscles pulsed with anticipation, and his nostrils flared with each rapid draw of breath into his heaving chest. He looked like a wild, adrenaline-pumped lion ready to take down its prey.

I couldn't wait to explore every inch of him, starting with the lean muscles that sloped from his powerful neck down to his broad shoulders. I would work my way down his thick, strong arms and then over the two firm mounds of pecs, jeweled with two plum-colored nipples, which begged to be first in line for licking, closely followed by the rippling muscles cascading down his stomach that faded into a patch of coarse black hair. And last, but certainly not least, his...I swallowed hard and tilted my head to one side as my eyes truly registered the size of his pulsing erection. It was like the rest of him, double the size of any human man.

"Guy? That's—that's really...are you sure this is going to work?" I asked.

He crossed his arms over his smooth, perfectly chiseled chest. Gods, he was gorgeous.

He flashed a devious smile. Then it melted away. "Have I ever let you down?"

The hesitation I felt dissolved instantly. It was ironic when I thought about it: where we'd started, where we'd been, where we were going. There was once a time when he was my protector. As I grew, he became my tormentor, and we fought—for years. It nearly destroyed me. Then I became a woman—a strong one at that. But somehow, I still couldn't breathe without him. He was my everything, and when he looked at me, I knew he felt the same.

So once again he'd been right. I. Needed. Him. I didn't just need him in a sexual or survival kind of way. I needed him to make me whole. "Never. You've never let me down, Votan. God of Death and War, I love you."

He pulled me against him. His thick erection pressed deliciously into my stomach. As he bent his head to kiss me, a thought flickered through my head.

"Wait," I said.

He raised one black brow. “Yes, Emma?”

“I have a question.”

“I’ve been waiting for you my entire existence. Can we talk later?” he asked.

“Where are we going?”

“To New York to see your parents. I’m pretty sure you can take care of any threats on your own now, but I wanted to meet them in person. Time to put faces to those voices I’ve heard for so long.”

Damn. I really love him, I said to myself. “And Tommaso?” I asked.

He frowned. “Now *you’re* trying to ruin the moment.”

I waited.

“Okay,” he said. “Tommaso is safe, healthy, and on his way to Rome.”

Oh, thank heaven. “Votan?”

He rolled his eyes and dropped his arms. “Yes, my sweet?”

“Be gentle?” I asked.

He smiled. “Absolutely not. You’re immortal now, and I have seventy thousand years of pent-up frustration. Gentle is the one thing you will not get from me until the fifth or sixth time.”

Hmmm. That sounded really, really promising. “Fine. But cut the ribbon slowly. I want to remember this.”

After Guy picked up the phone to the cockpit and informed the pilots that disturbing us prior to landing in New York would be a mistake punishable by death, he pulled out several blankets from the overhead compartment and laid them over the narrow bed. It could have been a hammock for all I cared. I just wanted every surface of his body raking against mine. Now. He was meant to be my first, my only. I'd waited long enough.

He led me by the hand, and we lay down next to each other. At first, he took his time, languishing kisses over my aching breasts and sensitive neck. But something wasn't right, wasn't fitting the moment. I felt his body tremble furiously as he held back. God or not, being unable to quench his male thirst for seventy thousand years must have been torture, and to show that kind of restraint in an effort to make the moment memorable for me was truly heroic.

Slowly, he began trailing kisses down my stomach, over my belly button, and to the curls between my legs. His fingers slid up along my inner thigh until they reached my slick folds and exposed my entrance. His tongue dipped inside, and a wave of ecstasy washed over me instantly.

He didn't flinch as my hands ran through his thick, soft waves of hair and dug into his scalp. "Emma, you taste so sweet," he whispered as his tongue plunged inside my cleft. I gasped as he slid his thick fingers inside me, nearing me to the second wave of release.

I then realized his reserved touch was a sacrifice; he was holding back. And he'd waited so long...for me. I wanted to give him everything he needed. It was long overdue, and there'd be years for leisurely lovemaking. "I want you. Now."

He looked up from between my thighs and flashed his trademark, devilish smile. "Okay, but cut the ribbon slowly, I want to remember my first time," he said.

"I knew it! You're a—"

I was about to say "virgin" and make a huge fuss, but he cut me off.

"I was waiting for you." He crawled over me, locking his eyes to mine. He positioned his thick pulsing shaft at my slick hot entrance. "I love you, Emma. You are my light."

He must have known how resilient my new body was because when he thrust, he didn't stop until he was deep inside. And yet, there was no pain, only delicious tremors of ecstasy.

Supporting the weight of his body with his bronzed arms, he raised his head toward the heavens and released a groan so primal, so piercing, that it shook the depths of my soul. The sky rumbled in response with a deafening thunder, and the plane dipped. I couldn't care less; I was utterly lost in the mind-blowing surge of energy pulsing between our two bodies.

My heart literally stopped for the space of one breath, and then began pounding furiously. I felt a powerful burst of light course through my veins, and in an instant, I saw every moment of his life all at once. An eternity of struggle and violence, of fear for the fate of the world. Through his eyes, I saw it all—every battle, every death, every moment he'd lived. Darkness.

Then I saw something amazing. Something I never expected: each moment of our lives together through his eyes. Light.

I heard each word we shared—the fights, the laughter, and the years he listened quietly to the world through me, lovingly savoring each moment. I felt his heart racing as he pulled me from the dark pool, when he saw me for the first time and pressed his lips against mine. My mind vibrated with the passion, desperate need, and the raw emotion he felt for me. I relived his joy as he carried my unconscious body into the portal, knowing he would give me immortality. I would be his forever.

My mind pulsed and ached with the love he held for me, and in that moment, I knew everything about him, every corner of his mind. Finally, there were no more secrets between us.

I blinked and felt my mind settling back into my body and the intense pleasure of Guy slipping in and out. With each stroke of his shaft, he groaned, and I felt a crippling euphoric release. And with each release, I clung to him and begged for more.

He obliged, eagerly filling me again and again, launching my body into a never-ending spiral of orgasms. His body continued pumping against mine, the ropes of his muscles—arms, chest, shoulders, and neck—working beneath his glowing golden skin, while he bore down on me with his fiery turquoise gaze.

Just when I thought I couldn't take any more, that I'd simply pass out from intense pleasure, he climaxed. The plane shook violently as he convulsed inside me and collapsed.

We lay there panting, still joined, the sweat-slicked skin of our bodies pressed tightly together. Even if I could have moved, I didn't want to. Being so close to him made me feel so whole, so at peace, so full of love.

My new heaven.

"Wow. Thank you. And thank you for this new, sturdy body," I said, finally catching my breath. "That was—that was . . . *really* worth the wait."

"Yes," he said with an airy breath. "Thank the gods

we'll be getting an eternity together, because I'll never get enough of *that*."

Ditto. I mean, not only did the man curl my toes, but he made the sky shake.

"Emma, I know that was a little fast, but you are so amazing and delicious, I couldn't help myself. I promise, I will take my time for the next round," Guy said.

Holy guacamole. He actually thought he'd short-changed me? "Are you kidding? It was the best ten minutes of my life."

Even though the weight of his enormous frame didn't bother me—again, thank you, new body—he shifted to my side and pulled me tightly into him. "Ten minutes?" he questioned.

I looked at his sweat-covered brow. Gods, he looked so adorable lying there with an after-sex glow.

The pilot suddenly announced our imminent arrival to JFK over the intercom.

"How about five hours," Guy said with smug, male pride.

"Five hours?"

He nodded, gloating.

"I hope you're absolutely certain I'm immortal. Because if that was your version of a quickie, I think my heart would give out with the extended version."

He smiled and then was silent for several moments before blurting out, "After the wedding, would you wear the ring for a full nine months? I'm not sure it will work now that you've been changed, but I like the idea of having children."

I held up my left hand and noticed two rings. On my ring finger, there was an offensively colossal, princess-cut solitaire. On my pinky, a small silver ring with a black jade stone.

I gasped with horror. “Why am I wearing this?”

“Despite your Payal blood and immortality, your body is and always will be anchored in the physical world, Emma, because your light is bonded to tangible mass. Mine is not. I fear our bodies remain incompatible without the jade.”

I was about to yank it off and throw it at him, but then my brain caught up with me. “Wait. Children? Wait! Wedding?”

Forty-Two

Three weeks later. Barolo, Italy

"Emma, I don't think this color shirt goes with the tie!" Tommaso called out from the great room as I arranged the double chocolate chip praline cookies on the silver tray in the kitchen. Guy insisted that his delectable creations were to be served as appetizers rather than dessert.

"Tommy, what man in his right mind thinks pink doesn't go with black?" I covered my mouth, smothering my laughter. Guy flashed me a disapproving glance and pulled a second batch from the oven.

"Okay," I whispered to Guy, "so pink is tacky. But my girls love the metro look." Anne, Nick, and Jess were coming along with my parents, eager to meet my new "man" and his brother, Tommy. I had made Guy take an oath that he would give the girls a chance; he still couldn't understand that it was normal for women of this day and age to date extensively before settling down. I guess he was still a bit old-fashioned; after all, he'd waited seventy thousand years to "cut the ribbon."

"Emma, stop doting over Tommaso," Guy growled. "He's a grown man and doesn't need your help."

"Wanna bet?" Tommaso's life now depended on me. After my mind-altering sex with Guy at thirty thousand feet, we arrived in New York, thinking I could start putting the pieces of my life—our life—back together. A life that would most definitely include a long, secluded vacation with Guy at his newly renovated Italian villa.

No such luck.

After a very emotional reunion with my parents, which included telling them that I'd been kidnapped by drug dealers, held for a few days, and then rescued by a group of international, clandestine mercenaries who'd been tracking the rogue criminals for months, I introduced my parents to the new love of my life: Guy, one of the mercenaries. He *so* looked the part.

My mom nearly fainted when she saw him, and my dad was utterly speechless. No one even seemed to notice my eyes were a little different—I had on contacts to cover up the turquoise—because they couldn't take their eyes off Guy. Neither could I, actually. Somehow he'd become even more devastatingly handsome. I guess being in love suited the God of Death and War. But the joy of our family reunion in New York was short-lived.

"Emma, we have to return to Rome," Guy announced as I was sorting through my drawers, deciding what I'd send ahead to Italy.

"We just got here!" I whined.

"I know, my love, but Gabrán just called. The Uchben

Council will try Tommaso tomorrow. I'm told they will vote against him, and he'll be given an immortal execution—beheaded."

"What? They can't do that!" I said.

"My sweet," he explained. "Tommaso's grounds for innocence are undocumented. The council can only rule according to our laws, and the laws require evidence. There is no hard proof that the jade made him betray us."

"This is different. They have to see that," I argued.

Guy kissed the top of my head and hugged me tightly. "Someone must be willing to stand up for him and appeal for more time to establish the facts. I am not allowed to interfere in such a way—it will be seen as an abuse of my power. You must vouch for him."

So that was that.

Guy and I went to Rome. I argued on Tommaso's behalf and took an oath to watch over him for thirty days while Dr. Lugas and his team observed his behavior and ran tests on his blood. If they found evidence, he'd be released to my oversight for a year—a sort of Uchben parole—and then set free.

It broke my heart when the council blacklisted Tommaso from being an Uchben ever again. No one truly seemed to blame him for his wrongdoings, but no one trusted him, either. The lingering effects of the jade were unknown, and in their minds—once a traitor, always a traitor.

As for Tommaso and me—well, what can I say? When he and I saw each other for the first time after the battle, it was hard for both of us. My mind still saw the man who tried to end my life. Even though he couldn't remember what he'd done while under the influence of the jade, he'd heard every gory detail during his trial. He couldn't look at me without feeling pain, either.

I assured him that I'd get over it, but I could see the torment in his eyes; he'd hurt so many people. He'd lost everything he loved for a second time in his life. If it was the last thing I did, I'd make sure he found happiness, and I had to believe I could help him pull his life back together.

That's why I asked Guy to publicly decree Tommaso as his brother—a god thing I'd learned about from Xavier. Guy pouted for two whole days, but as a gesture of his trust, he agreed. Tommaso wasn't happy about my plotting, either. Guy was apparently a very bossy brother.

One tiny consolation to this mess—not that Tommaso cared, but he was even hotter now that he'd gained a new pair of turquoise eyes just like mine. Sure, he was no God of Death and War, but nobody's perfect.

So tonight, Nick, Anne, and Jess were not only coming with my parents to meet my new "man," soon-to-be husband, but they were also coming to meet my brother-in-law to be, Tommy. Who knew? Maybe he'd hit it off with one of them. If anything, he might have some fun. They were really good at that.

While I finished arranging the trays in the kitchen, Guy slid behind me and wrapped his arms around my waist. My knees buckled in response, and for the fiftieth time that day I fought my urge to rip off his clothes and mine, then throw him on the floor, and well—you know, make the sky shake. Sadly, we had guests, and considering how noisy Guy got, we would have to behave.

"I can't wait until we're alone again," I said.

"I've already arranged to have Cimil watch over Tommaso after your family leaves."

"Where are we going?" I asked.

"I have another villa in Greece."

Greece? What other secret getaways did Guy own? I'd have to shuffle through Guy's memories later. There were a lot there, and I'd decided I didn't really want to remember them all. I knew his heart, and that was enough.

"Not even my brothers and sisters can bother us there," he added. "Not that they'd have time."

The gods—who were not really blood relatives, by the way, because that would make Guy my great-great uncle, and that would be gross—were busy locating the other three black jade atom bombs, the Payals, and the remaining Maaskab. Personally, I had an itching to fight some more Scabs now that I was immortal. But Guy—as always—was right. We deserved a little time together, some happiness of our own before we ran off to save the world. That job would always be there, he pointed out.

The doorbell rang, and my heart lit with joy. I turned to Guy. "They're here!" I clapped with excitement and ran through the great room toward the front door.

As I yanked open the large stained glass door, I heard both Guy and Tommaso scream in unison, "No!"

It was too late.

There, standing in front of me, was an old woman with glowing red eyes, flanked by an ocean of Scabs. She was naked from her waist up and had thick, black dreadlocks draped over her chest. The smell was nauseating.

I looked into her eyes as I raised my hands, readying to split her in two, but there was something eerily familiar about her.

"Holy Virgin of Guadalupe. Grandma? Is that you?"

THE END (Not Really . . .)

To free himself from the demented queen he serves, Niccolo must turn a human woman into a vampire like himself. But it can't be just any human woman—it has to be the most stubborn, impossible, *irresistible* female he's ever met…

Please turn this page for an excerpt from

Accidentally Married to…A Vampire?

Prologue

July 12, 1712. Bacalar, Southern Mexico

Delirious with hunger, the weary vampire sat hip deep in mud, his broad back against a hollow tree as he glared at the crisp blue sky. The monthlong summer rains had abruptly retreated. Now how much longer could he wait for her? Hours? Days? Sunshine was not Niccolo DiConti's most cherished friend.

"*Magnifico*," he grumbled.

His gaze shifted to the nearby pool. "Where the devil are you, woman?" he growled. Endless days had passed without as much as a ripple on the water's surface. This ancient Mayan ceremonial pool was the goddess's favorite portal to the human world when she came scouting for souls—he'd paid a king's ransom for that information—but she'd yet to materialize.

His shoulders slumped, and he sank deeper into the sticky

jungle floor. Shards of painful sunlight pierced the tree canopy and danced across his face, a face gloriously referred to by many as that of a hardened warrior—dark features, a few character-building scars, and capable of producing a soul-chilling scowl when necessary. Today, however, he could not muster the strength to frighten a small child.

You are a pitiable mess, he thought for the hundredth time.

Struck hard by the irony of his situation, he let out a bitter chuckle. He was legendary for his raw power, intrepid leadership, and ruthless will to survive—no, not just survive, thrive. In any situation. Any century. But as soon as he saw her, he might actually beg like some lowly mortal serf.

Bene, anything it takes, he reminded himself. *And count your blessings that your men are not present to witness your mental shipwreck on the Island of Self-Pity.*

He closed his eyes, attempting to push away his bitter frustration, but his thoughts only swiveled toward his gnawing hunger. *Hmmm, a rabbit or monkey...I must catch a little something to quell the hunger pangs—*

"Well, well. What do we have here?" said a sultry feminine voice.

Niccolo's eyes snapped open to find a dainty woman with long, wet ropes of red hair snaking down her naked body. "*Cristo sacro!* It is about bloody time," he barked.

The woman arched one coppery brow. "Oh my, aren't we a cranky little thing? And dirty, too. Had a little mud bath, did we, vampire?"

With her lean, almost boyish frame, the Goddess of the Underworld reminded him of a delicate fairy. But he knew better than to underestimate Cimil. Not only was she infamous for instigating mischief and being twelve cookies shy of a baker's dozen, she also possessed powerful sight—thousands of years ahead, millions of possible outcomes. She was his last hope. Sad really.

"My sincerest apologies, goddess," he said. "It is my lack of nourishment speaking." He pushed himself slowly from the muck and stretched. "I have been waiting weeks, and as you are aware, the sun weakens my kind." He wiped his dirty hands on his black trousers and then ran them through the length of his damp hair, shaking out the leaves.

She ogled him like a giant confection. "Well, well. If I'd known *you* were waiting, little dumplin', I might have dropped in sooner. But I was deep in a trance, connecting to a future version of myself. Had to catch up on *Dexter*. What a hottie! That guy puts the *errr*," she purred, "in killer. Ya know what I mean?"

Niccolo shook his head slowly, unsure of how to respond to her bewildering jargon. Having lived in a hundred countries and speaking dozens of languages fluently, Niccolo considered himself an educated man of the world. He'd even learned English from an Oxford scholar. Yet he had never heard such colloquialisms.

"Not into *Dexter*?" She looked confused. "Oooh, I see. You're a *Walking Dead* kind of guy!" She winked. "I gotcha." She suddenly jumped to one side, away from a butterfly fluttering past, and then froze for several moments.

Unsure of what else to do, Niccolo cleared his throat.

She instantly snapped to life. "Hi. Who are you? And are you aware that good hygiene has made a comeback?"

Masking his confusion and ignoring the slight on his shabby appearance, he bowed his head and replied, "Niccolo DiConti, general of—" He caught himself and stopped. Perhaps he should not call attention to his identity. The gods might not be on his list of admirers. Although they should be. What was not to like?

Cimil's eyes lit. "*The* Niccolo DiConti? What an honor!"

Niccolo stood a little taller then. "Yes, I seek your assistance."

Cimil rolled her eyes. "Well, no duh. You didn't abandon your queen's side, risking her wrath, to see me in my fabulous birthday suit. Although…" she began slowly, pacing like a slinky cat. "You and I could have some fun together. I don't mind a little dirt, especially on a tasty treat like you." She licked her lips.

Despite her odd speech, Niccolo understood the gist. He ran both hands through his hair once again, this time with worry. Sex was the last thing on his mind at the moment, and the last few centuries, for that matter. Too much killing to do, he supposed. But a coldhearted female like her would never warm his blood, even if he had the urge.

Regardless, she was right. He had taken a substantial risk abandoning his post. By now, the queen was likely hunting him via their blood bond, and it wouldn't be long before she caught up. Indeed, he needed Cimil's help. Urgently. Only it had never occurred to him that she might ask for sex as payment. On the other hand, what woman wouldn't want him?

He squared his shoulders and stared down at her. He could do this. Any price for his freedom, right?

"*Bene*. If that is what you wish, I will bed you in exchange for your assistance."

Laughter exploded from Cimil. "Oh, would you relax, vampire? First off"—she held out her scrawny index finger—"I don't need to blackmail men into sleeping with me." She snorted loudly. "Because I'm loaded!"

Loaded?

"I do not see you carrying anything. In fact, you are nude," he pointed out.

Cimil looked down at her body. "Oh, look! I *am* naked." She frowned. "Heeey, it's not polite to interrupt. I was telling you a story. Let me see…" She scratched her head. "Oh yeah. I was explaining how I'm so moneyed—that means 'wealthy' to you, Bo-Bo—I even bought myself a nice little sultan with a camel just last week." She paused and tapped her finger on the corner of her mouth. "On second thought, he wasn't worth the tiny island I had to trade for him, and the stupid camel doesn't even fit through the bedroom doorway. I *should* go back to blackmailing men for sex. That's a great idea. Thanks!"

Niccolo swallowed hard. *Cristo sacro! I am going to have to sleep with the crazy she-demon.* Perhaps he could secure the return of her island instead? He, too, was "loaded." *Might even have an additional island somewhere to sweeten the pot.* To keep track of such things proved challenging after a thousand years or so of existence.

"And second"—she held out two fingers—"you're really not my type. I like 'em warm. But I will take that shirt and those pants."

Not her "type"? She is out of her mind. On the other hand, if the goddess merely desired his mud-caked clothes…

"*Bene*," he replied. He could easily glamour new garments off a nearby villager later. He slipped off his not-so-white linen shirt and black trousers and stood before her in the buff.

A sly smile stretched across her pixie-like face before she whistled and gave him a leisurely once-over. "I like you, vampire. You have this whole tanned European NBA gladiator *je-ne-sais-pas* man-fusion thing going. I'm totally getting you."

He had no clue what she'd just said, but he did not care to know or to waste more time. He tossed the clothes to her feet. *"Eccolo."*

Still gazing at his nude form, Cimil sighed and then began dressing. "You even smell delicious. Like a hint of chocolate with vanilla, and…"

"Mud?" he said dryly.

"That's it." She slipped on his large shirt and pants. The five-foot woman looked like a child playing dress-up in her father's clothes. "Well, Niccolo, I haven't got all day. Why do you risk life and limb to see me?"

"My freedom."

Cimil froze midway through rolling up a pant leg. "You want to leave the queen's employ?"

He nodded with an uncompromising stare.

"Complicated. Unprecedented. Perfectly insane…I'm in!" She froze for several awkward moments and then sparked back to life. "Wait. Why do you need good ol' Auntie Cimi's help?"

Niccolo hated to air vampire business, but Cimil had to have heard of Reyna, the queen. "There is only one way to be relieved from her service: death. I would like to avoid it."

"I see. You wouldn't happen to have some wildly irrational reason for doing all this, would you? I love acts of futile insolence. They're so whimsical!"

Trying not to sound like a pansy, he admitted, "I no longer wish to kill for her."

"A vampire who doesn't want to…kill? *You* don't want to—" Cimil broke off, laughing hysterically. "That totally qualifies!"

Niccolo's rage percolated as she clutched her stomach and slapped her knee. How dare she mock him! In truth, he had no objection to killing for the right reasons—for example, to protect the innocent from dark vampires, Obscuros—but for far too long he'd killed simply because he'd been ordered. He needed to be free, to know that every death he caused was justified.

Then there was the small matter of the queen's mental instability, which undoubtedly fueled her unscrupulous behavior. The last straw had been when she demanded he blind the maid because the girl did not curtsy properly. He'd had to quickly call in several favors and get her a position with a respectable family where she'd be allowed to keep her eyes.

Sì, it was as clear as the fangs in his mouth; if there were a Crazy Shrew Olympiad, the powerful queen would triumph.

Upholding the Pact between the gods and vampires, destroying Obscuros, those were still worthy causes, but he needed to get far away from Reyna before he ended up killing her—an act that would have fatal consequences for any vampire unfortunate enough to carry her blood, including himself.

Cimil continued howling with laughter and then suddenly spotted a large black beetle strolling past her foot. Her eyes filled with horror. "N-n-no. I think you are"—she swallowed hard—"lovely. I would never say that." She jerked her head up and looked back at Niccolo. "Okay. And if I don't help you?"

Is she speaking to me or the insect? "Then I will die," he answered anyway.

"Live free or die, is it?" she said, eyeing the bug again.

She is mad. Why did I come here?

"*Sì.* That is correct," he replied hesitantly.

Cimil watched the beetle disappear under a rock. She sighed with relief and then continued rolling up the other pant leg.

"You're like a bad bumper sticker," she said.

Bumper sticker? Why does she insist on speaking in code? Niccolo began grinding his teeth.

She stood, grasping the waistline of the pants to hold them up. "Lucky you, I enjoy a challenge. You'd be surprised what dull, predictable things people ask me. 'When will I die? When will the world end?' Blah, blah, blah..."

Niccolo released a quick breath. "Will you assist me or not?"

"Sure, my little cupcake of despair. Now, normally I charge twelve ninety-nine, plus shipping and handling, but in this case I'll cut you a deal. You will be indebted to me, and I will have the right to call in the favor at any time in the future or past."

Past? That settles it. I have found another contender for crazy shrew. Very well, at least I will not have to sleep with her. He hoped. He, too, "liked 'em warm" and with a heart or a soul, for that matter. A little sanity might be pleasant, too.

"Agreed," he said.

Cimil took several steps forward, closing the gap between them, and stared with her large turquoise-green eyes. "Prophecy time, mighty warrior. Kneel."

Niccolo complied.

Baring a devilish grin, Cimil placed her soft hands on his cheeks and rubbed his unshaven jaw. "Oooh. Just like your eyes. So tough and black. The things your stubble could teach my calluses."

Niccolo cocked one brow.

Cimil frowned. "No? Not into calluses? Fine, then." She took a deep breath and then stared into his eyes before softly kissing his lips. She sucked in a deep breath as if absorbing his scent. "Okay. Up, up."

That is all?

"Well?" he asked.

She turned and pushed through the thick underbrush, uncovering an overgrown path.

Niccolo trailed behind her, thoroughly perplexed. "Where the devil are you going?" he bellowed with his deep, commanding voice. "Tell me what you saw!"

"I was right about you, big guy," she said. "You *are* a challenge, and I'm going to love watching you run this gauntlet. It's a delightfully cruel one, at least for your shallow, undead mind."

What the bloody hell?

She continued talking without slowing her pace. "I saw all possible outcomes of your life, and there is a path that leads to your release from Her Majesty's command."

"Is *not* dying part of the equation?"

She kept up the rapid pace. "You're dead already."

Touché.

Cimil stopped abruptly. Niccolo plowed into her back.

"Ow!" she yelped. A small flock of blackbirds burst from the bush to her side, chirping noisily as they fled to the sky. He winced as the sunlight continued to heat his skin and weaken him.

She spun to face him. "Listen, Hellboy, we need to make this quick. I have garage sales to hit and naughty souls to claim. Decide."

"I do not understand." Was this goddess tormenting

him for sport? Why did she call him Hellboy? *How very rude!*

She poked at his bare chest with a razor-sharp fingernail. “You hate taking orders.”

Sì, true. After all, I am a vampire.

“And even if you decided to listen like a good little boy, the odds of pulling this off are slim to none.”

I happen to excel at all things impossible. I am a vampire!

“So don’t come crying if you end up in your queen’s dungeon.”

Vampires do not cry, silly woman.

“Tortured three times a day for all eternity, which is where you have a ninety-nine point nine-nine-nine percent chance of landing if you don’t do exactly as I say.”

Actually, those numbers are quite encouraging. He thought his odds were somewhere between pigs flying and hell freezing over. “*Bene.* I understand. Tell me what you saw, what I must do.”

“First, you will have to find your true mate. Or, more accurately, she will find you. A human, by the way.”

“Human?” *That is disappointing. But, on the other hand, there certainly are more tedious creatures on the planet. Cimil, for example.*

“Yesss.” Cimil narrowed her eyes. “And watch your tongue. I happen to be partial to humans—most, anyway. Clowns, not so much. Those evil bastards never stop smiling.”

Niccolo didn’t know what these “clowns” were, but he made a mental note to stay away if he ever encountered one. Sounded unpleasant.

“I did not say a word,” he retorted innocently.

"Good, because I'm warning you, if you're not in this for the long haul, jump off the Cimil Soul Train now and boogie your naked body home." Her eyes quickly shifted to a squawking toucan perched above on a branch. "Who the hell asked you? You can't even dance. I mean, *really*."

Niccolo scratched his chin, ignoring the bizarre behavior and the urge to wrap his hands around her neck. "My resolve will not waver."

She stifled a laugh. "Even though your kind considers such a fate, to be with a human—your food—a curse?" She began laughing again. "This particular female will be disobedient, demanding, and a pain in your cold, old, naked ass. She's also hotter than an apple pie fresh from the oven."

Cimil's description piqued his interest. "You mean to say...she is beautiful?"

Cimil smiled. "Irresistible. Sharp as a whip. Sexy. Perfect for you in every way."

Niccolo felt his insides twist with anticipation. She would be his? All his? *Hmmm.* "Go on."

She raised her brows. "Before you get all excited, Mr. Studtastic, there are rules. First, you must continue to uphold the Pact. No ifs, ands, or buts. That means you must keep that"—she pointed to his penis—"in your pants...when you find some, obviously. And those"—she pointed to his fangs—"in your mouth."

The Pact had many parts to it, and he knew them all since he'd spent the last thousand years upholding its laws. It was central to maintaining the vampires' existence; as long as they followed the commandments, they would be left alone by the gods to live. Rule one: vampires could not kill innocent humans—Forbiddens—although the queen's compliance to this law was highly questionable. In any case, even the most honorable of vampires were known to lose control in the throes of feeding or passion. Therefore, those activities with Forbiddens were strictly off-limits, too. The only exception was for those mated to a Forbidden—practically unheard of—in which case, a careful, consensual nip here or there was allowed, but nothing more.

"Done," he said. "I will refrain from biting without her permission. Nor will I sleep with her until she has been turned."

"Not so fast, tomcat," she added. "No biting, even if she begs. And she *must* be turned *with* her permission on the anniversary of your third month together. That very same day. Understand?"

"Why three months?" he questioned.

"Hey, buddy, my gig is prophecies and hunting for garage sales. I don't make the signs, I just follow them." She shrugged. "Anyhooo, the rest is up to you." She turned and continued marching forward, quickening her pace. "So. You in?"

Niccolo looked from side to side. "In? In what?"

"Yes. *In*. Are you on board? Ready to throw down. Roll the dice. Ride that crazy cow called life and make her your bitch?"

Niccolo frowned. Her colloquialisms were simply offensive. And this coming from a ruthless vampire. "You are asking if I am committed. *Sì?*"

"Siii." She rolled her eyes.

What other choice did he have? Besides, he did not believe in this ridiculous mate business. He had known tens of thousands of vampires over his existence, but only a dozen or so claimed to have found their true mate. It was extremely rare. And for those few, he saw no evidence they were anything more than contented couples who'd beaten the odds. There was no cosmic force at play.

As for his mate being human, he could find a way to cope temporarily. Sure, humans were only a step up from a cow or goat one would eat, or perhaps keep as a favorite farm pet; however, he wouldn't be the first immortal to bear the shame of coupling with a human. It was manageable. Especially if she happened to be beautiful.

Whoever she was, he would woo her, set her up with only the finest of things, and after the three months were up, he'd have her begging to be turned. Once he was free from the queen, he had ample resources to provide his mate with a comfortable, separate life for eternity. Everyone would win. Everyone would be happy.

How doing all this could possibly free him from being that festering bunion of a queen's general, he had no clue. He'd been warned that Cimil's instructions were cruel at best, fatal at worst, and required an extreme leap of faith. But at this point, anything was worth trying. Hell, if he failed, there was always death. He hoped. The queen's dungeons were notoriously hellish.

But he wouldn't fail. He was the strongest warrior the vampire world had ever known. He had fought and won thousands of battles, upheld the Pact, and maintained the peace between the gods and vampires for a thousand years. This would be a stroll through the park...or jungle. Whatever.

"It's much better than I'd hoped for," he stated coolly.

Cimil's eyes lit up. "All right then. Oh, and there's one more thing..."

Cimil waved her hands and watched the vampire collapse to the ground. She poked him several times in the chest, checking to make sure he was out cold.

"*Bene*, Niccolo DiConti," she said, perfectly imitating his deep voice. "Your mate will not be born for, oh, say, about three hundred years, and I have to entomb you in the meantime. Otherwise, you won't live to see another full moon. Did you know your paranoid, sorry excuse of a queen fears your strength and plans to kill you? Crazy shrew. I wish I could take her out myself. But nooo." She shook her head.

The beautiful, naked vampire lay completely oblivious over a bed of leaves.

Cimil sighed. "You are such a scrumptious man treat. How could anyone think of killing you? But I guarantee, after three hundred years, your queen will only be a teensy bit peeved by your absence, and she will have reconsidered her plot to murder you. You can thank me later."

She leaned down and pressed her mouth to his full lips and then ran her finger along his chiseled jaw.

"Come, my handsome vampire. I have a few things I must do to prepare you. Then I'll put you somewhere safe to await your bride. Oh—I know!" She clapped excitedly. "You can stay inside my piggy bank! And I'll create a dramatastic jungle intro to your lady! How about *Romancing the Stone* meets *Apocalypto*?"

She flung the naked giant over her shoulder and gave him a loving pat on his bottom. "Watching you two will be so much fun! I might have to charge the other gods admission to this show when the time comes."

Penelope needs money—lots of it and fast, to save her mother's life. So when an offer to carry a stranger's baby falls into her lap, and with it, a million-dollar payday, she can't say no. But then she realizes just who is fathering this golden child, and things go very quickly from steamy to scorching…

Please turn this page for an excerpt from

Sun God Seeks… Surrogate?

Prologue

Wondering which screw in her head had come loose *this* time, twenty-four-year-old Emma Keane strapped a parachute to her back in preparation for yet another fun-filled jungle mission.

"Dammit! Stop wiggling!" she barked over her shoulder. "And that had better be your flashlight!"

Well, actually, it was a cranky, rather large warrior named Brutus strapped to her back and wearing the parachute because she had yet to find time for skydiving lessons.

Dork.

In any case, looking like a ridiculous, oversized baby kangaroo wasn't enough to stop her from making this nocturnal leap into enemy territory—Maaskab territory. She had scores to settle.

Emma sucked in a deep breath, the roar of the plane's large engines and Brutus's growls making it difficult to find her center—the key to winning any battle—and not freak out.

Funny. If someone had told her a year ago that she'd end up here, an immortal demigoddess engaged to the infamous God of Death and War, she would have said, "Christ! Yep! That *tooootally* sounds about right."

Why the hell not? She'd lived the first twenty-two years of her life with Guy—a nickname she'd given her handsome god—obsessed with his seductive voice, a voice only she could hear. Turned out, after they finally met face-to-face, their connection ran blood deep. Universe deep, actually. A match made by fate.

Emma rubbed her hands together, summoning the divine power deep within her cells. One blast with her fingertips and she could split a man right down the middle.

"Careful where you put those," Guy said, cupping himself.

Emma gazed up at his smiling face and couldn't help but admire the glorious, masculine view. *Sigh.* She knew she'd been born to love him, flaws—enormous ego and otherworldly bossiness—and all.

His smile melted away. "Please change your mind, my sweet. Stay on the plane, and let me do your fighting."

"Can't do that," she replied. "The Maaskab took my grandmother, and I'm going to be the one to get her back. Even if I have to kill Tommaso to do it."

Guy shook his head. "No. You are to let me deal with him."

Emma felt her immortal blood boil. She'd trusted Tommaso once, and he'd betrayed her. Almost gotten her killed, too. But she'd known—well, she'd *thought*—it wasn't Tommaso's fault. He'd been injected with liquid black jade, an evil substance that could darken the heart of an angel. That's why, after he'd been captured and mortally wounded, she'd begged the gods to cure him.

Then she did the unthinkable: she'd put her faith in him again.

Stupid move.

He'd turned on her a second time, the bastard. Yes, his betrayal—done of his own free will—was her prize on that fateful night almost one year ago when her grandmother showed up on their doorstep in Italy, leading an army of evil Maaskab priests, her mind clearly poisoned.

"If Tommaso hadn't helped her escape, we could've saved her," she said purely to vent, because she really wanted to cry. But the fiancée of the God of Death and War didn't cry. Especially in front of the hundred warriors riding shotgun on the plane tonight.

Okay, maybe one teeny tiny tear while no one's looking.

"Do not give up hope, Emma." Guy clutched her hand. "And do not forget…whatever happens, I love you. Until the last ray of sunlight. Until the last flicker of life inhabits this planet."

Brutus groaned and rolled his eyes, clearly annoyed by the sappy chatter.

Emma elbowed him in the ribs. "Shush! And how can you, of all people, be uncomfortable with a little affection? Huh? You bunk with eight dudes every night. That's gross by the way. Not the dude part. I'm cool with that. But eight, big, sweaty warriors all at once? Yuck. So don't judge me because I'm into the one-man-at-a-time rule. That's messed up, Brutus."

Brutus growled and Guy chuckled.

In truth, Emma didn't know what Brutus was into or how he and his elite team slept, but she loved teasing him. She figured that sooner or later she'd find the magic words to get Brutus to speak to her.

No luck yet.

Accepting a temporary defeat, she shrugged and turned her attention back to the task at hand. She took one last look at her delicious male—seven feet of solid muscle with thick blue-black waves of hair and bronzed skin. *Sigh.* "Okay. I'm ready," she declared boldly. "Let's kill some Scabs and get my granny!"

She glanced over her other shoulder at Penelope, their newest family member. Her dark hair was pulled into a tight ponytail that accentuated the anger simmering in her dark green eyes. Pissed would be a serious understatement.

Emma didn't blame her. What a cluster.

"Ready?" Emma asked.

"You better believe it," Penelope replied. "These clowns picked the wrong girl to mess with."

Guy frowned as they leaped from the plane into the black night.

Backlum Chaam has waited seventy thousand years to meet the woman Fate has chosen for him, and now that she's here, he can't believe his luck. Maggie is brilliant and gorgeous and...in terrible danger. For Backlum has dangerous enemies, and now so does she.

Please turn this page for an excerpt from

Accidentally...
Evil?

One

There has to be evil so that good can prove its purity above it.

—Buddha

November 1, 1934. Bacalar, Mexico

Why is that man... naked?

Dazed and flat on her back, twenty-one-year-old Margaret O'Hare observed the man's bare backside as he stood on a nearby weather-beaten dock, toweling off. Her vision, at first a groggy mess, focused to a machete-sharp point, the pain in her forehead equally knifelike.

Yes. Naked. Really. Really. Naked. She'd never seen such a large, well-built man or such a perfect backside—hard, deeply tanned, and worthy of a marble sculpture. Maybe two. Or five. Too bad she was a painter.

Hold on. Where the ham sandwich am I? Margaret's eyes, the only body part she could move without experiencing pain, whipsawed from side to side. *Jungle. Dirt. Lake. Okay. I'm lying near the lake.* Yes, this was good. She recognized the place. Sort of.

Am I near the village dock?

Her peripheral vision said no; this dock had a tiny *palapa* for shade at the very end.

Then where?

She made a feeble attempt to lift her throbbing head, but her body rewarded her with a spear to the temple.

Ow. Ow. Ow. She took a slow breath to allow the skull-shattering jab to dissipate. *All right. Relax and think. What happened? What happened? What happened? And who is Mr. Perfectbottom over there?*

A sticky blanket of gray coated her thoughts, but she did recall swimming that morning. Maybe she'd slipped on the village dock and fallen into the lake. Maybe Mr. Perfect-bottom had been bathing down at the shore and rescued her.

Or not.

Her clothes were bone-dry except for the sweaty parts. Come to think of it, she felt like a mud pie, soggy underneath and dry on top, baking in the sun. It didn't help that someone—maybe the man?—had placed a warm fur under her head and neck. God, it was itchy.

She willed her hand to make the painful journey behind her ear to give it a good scratch. Her fingers brushed the soft, silky hairs of the makeshift pillow.

How odd. People in these parts don't wear mink.

The mink coat purred.

Maggie sprang from the moist grass and scrambled back a few feet against a thick tree trunk. "Ja-ja-jaguar!"

The glossy black coat didn't budge a paw. It simply stared, its eyes reminding her of two big limes—wide, round, and green. Then the damned thing smiled right at her like some real-life Cheshire cat. God damned disturbing.

"You! Cat!" The man barreled down the dock, each heavy step thundering across the creaky wooden planks. "Leave! Do not return until I call you."

Maggie should have been frightened by the boom of the man's tone, but instead, his rich masculine timbre soothed her aching head.

"Raarrr?" the cat...

...responded? I must be hearing things, she thought, her eyes toggling back and forth between man and beast.

"Do as you are told," he said to the animal, "or the deal is off."

The black cat hissed, whipped its shiny black tail through the air, and dissolved into the shadows of the lush vegetation surrounding the small lakeside clearing.

This is too bizarre; I need to get out of here. Maggie turned her wobbling body to seek shelter in another dream.

"Where the *hell* do you think you're going?" said that deep, rich voice that wrapped her mind in ribbons of warm dark caramel and exotic spices.

Before she could mutter a word, her head cartwheeled and her body tipped. Two firm hands gripped her shoulders and propped her against the tree. "Close your eyes. Breathe."

She suddenly wanted to do just that. And only that. The man's voice was...compelling.

As she sucked in the dank, thick, tropical air, her mind slotted missing memories back into place.

How had she gotten there?

She recalled searching for the path to the ruin where her father spent his days. Little Kinichna'—or Little House of the Sun, as he called it—was the biggest find of his career, the one that would put his name on the archaeologists' map. Ironically, this dilapidated and historically uninteresting pile of rubble had been known about for years, but when her father's colleague asked that he decipher etchings from a rare black jade tablet found not too far away, he'd realized they were directions, an ancient Mayan treasure map. Said map led to a hidden chamber right underneath Little Kinichna'.

"You are now well. Open your eyes," the man's husky voice commanded.

She took a moment to survey her body.

Miraculous. Her pain *was* gone. In fact, she felt downright euphoric and tingly. Especially in the spots where he touched her. Maybe in a few other spots, too. *Margaret O'Hare! You dirty trollop!*

She slid open her lids. Two icy turquoise eyes, just an inch from her face, sliced right through her, their raw, unfathomable depths filled with stark, primal desire.

Applesauce! She jerked her head back and knocked it on the tree. "Ouch!" *Great. Now I have a lump on the back to match the front.*

The colossal man straightened his powerful frame and towered over her like a giant oak, but he didn't release her from his fierce gaze.

Well at least he'd put a socially acceptable distance between their heads. The same could not be said for their bodies; the heat from his heaving chest seeped right through her. And thankfully—or was it regrettably?—or perhaps magically, since she didn't know how he'd had the time?—he now wore a pair of simple white linen trousers. No. It was a definite "thankful." The moment was awkward and unsettling enough without the man being naked *and* staring. Which he was. Still staring, that is. Silent. Suspicious. Studying her with his beautiful turquoise eyes dressed in a thick row of incredibly black lashes.

Why the deviled egg is he looking at me like that?

Maybe he thinks that giant lump on your forehead is about to give birth to an extra head.

"What happened?" she finally asked.

"I'll ask the questions," he said. "Who are you, woman?"

Not the response she'd expected. "Ducky. I'm lost in the jungle with a half-naked rake."

"Rake?" Dark brows arching with irritation, he planted his arms—silky milk chocolate poured over bulging, never-ending ropes of taut muscle—across the hard slopes of his bare chest. Maggie meticulously cataloged the man's every divine detail, like she would for each precious artifact from her father's dig, from his long, damp reams of shimmering midnight hair falling over his menacingly broad shoulders; the cords of muscles galloping down his bronzed neck into said broad shoulders; and his sinfully sculpted abdomen tightly divided into rounded little rectangles, which reminded her of an ice cube tray—a fancy new invention. *God, I miss ice cubes.*

But as impressive as his raw, abundantly masculine features were, it was his height that most bewildered her. People from these parts were not known for stature. In fact, at five foot six, she had a good six inches on the tallest men in the village, and her father, Dr. O'Hare, an entire foot. No. This giant man most certainly wasn't from the sleepy little pueblo of Bacalar or anywhere in the Yucatan, for that matter. But then, from where? His exotic, ethnically ambiguous features didn't provide any clues. He could be a Moroccan Greek Spaniard or a Nordic Himalayan Kazak. *Hmmm....*

"Yes, rake, as in cad? Or if you prefer, savage," she said.

"Hardly. Savages don't save women in distress. They create them."

True. They also don't have wildly seductive, exotic accents. Like one of her parents' Hollywood friends.

Lightbulb.

"Oh my God. You're a picture film actor, aren't you?"

Yes. Yes. It all made sense now. The locals in the village had been talking about a film crew for weeks. Word on the street—errr, word on the pueblo corner next to the stinky burro—was that a famous Russian director was making a movie about Chichen Itza and filming historical reenactments in the area.

"An... actor." His icy, unsettling expression turned into a charming smile inspired by the devil himself. "Yes."

She sighed. "That explains the trained cat. Where's the crew?" She glanced over her shoulders.

"Crew. Errr." He raised his index finger as if to point somewhere, then dropped it. "My crew will be here in a few days."

"Getting into character! Right." Maggie had heard firsthand how actors prepared for their roles. Fascinating business. Of course, acting had never really interested her. Nothing that required work ever had, which was why she'd taken up painting when her parents pestered her to do something productive. Going to parties and dating famous, good-looking men apparently weren't worthy pursuits.

They were right. If only her mother had lived long enough for Maggie to tell her so.

"Now," he said, "will you tell me who *you* are?"

She held out her hand. "Miss Margaret O'Hare of Los Angeles."

"You are a very long way from home."

No. Really? "I'm here working with my father. He's a professor doing . . . ummm . . . research."

A teeny fib. Or two. Who's gonna know? Truthfully, her father wasn't researching doodly-squat; he was secretly excavating. And the "work" she was doing? It didn't amount to a hill of pinto beans; her father wouldn't let her anywhere near the sacred structure. "No place for a young lady," he'd said. Well, neither was this slightly lawless, revolution-ravaged Mexican village, where electricity was considered a luxury—as were beds, curling irons, and those blessed ice cubes.

And chicken coops. Don't forget the chicken coops. The village was plagued with wretched little packs of villainous roaming chickens. *Like tiny feathered banditos who leave their little caca-bombs all over the damned place.*

You'll survive. Some things are more important.

"Well, Miss Margaret O'Hare from Los Angeles, very pleased to meet you." The man bent his imposing frame, slid his remarkably-rough-for-an-actor palm into hers, and placed a lingering kiss atop her hand.

An exquisite jolt crashed through her, causing her to buck. She snapped the tingling appendage away. *Wow. That kiss could combust a lady's drawers like gunpowder. Poof! Flames. No drawers. Just like that.*

The residual heat continued spreading. *Please don't reach my drawers. Please don't reach my drawers . . .*

He frowned and dropped his hand. "So tell me, what were you doing in the jungle, Margaret?"

"Jungle?"

"Yes, you know that place where I found you unconscious. Barefoot. All alone. It has many trees and dangerous animals." He pointed over her shoulder at the lush forest filled with vine-covered trees that chirped and clicked with abundant life. "It's right behind you, if you've forgotten what it looks like."

"Yes. That." *Thinking, thinking, thinking.* She wiggled her bare toes in the mushy grass and looked out across the hypnotic turquoise waves of the lake. Funny how the man's eyes were the exact same color right down to their flecks of shimmering green.

An early afternoon breeze pushed a few dark locks of hair across her face. *Still thinking, thinking, thinking.* She brushed them away and then focused on the grass stains on the front of her white cotton dress. Darn it. She loved this dress, with its tiny hand-stitched red flowers along the hem. Her father had had it specially made along with a beautiful black stone pendant the week they'd arrived. He'd said the gifts were in celebration of his find; everything was exactly where he'd thought, including some mysterious, priceless treasure that would "change their lives." He'd said he couldn't wait to show her when the time came.

"I'm waiting," the man said with unfiltered impatience.

"Waiting. Oh, yes. I was in the jungle because..." *Still thinking...*

Fear. Yes, fear was the reason she'd been capering about. Her mother's recent death had left her plagued with the corrosive emotion. She feared she would never make right with her past. She feared opening her eyes to the present. She feared the future would bring only pain and suffering because eventually anyone she cared for would leave. Fear was like an irrational cancer that ate away at her rational soul.

It was why, when her father began acting peculiar back home—disappearing for weeks at a time, mumbling incoherently, obsessing over that tablet—she came to Mexico. She feared he might simply disappear in this untamed land, evaporate into nothing more than a collection of memories—just as her mother had.

And now she feared that she had failed; her father had not been seen for three days. But she didn't dare articulate this distressing, gloomy thought aloud.

"Because...I am a painter!" she said. "I went exploring for new scenery. I got turned around, and then that giant cat of yours appeared out of nowhere and chased me." She rubbed the gigantic lump on her forehead. "I fell and hit my head. You didn't happen to find my sandals, did you?"

One glorious turquoise eye ticked for the briefest moment. "Searching for scenery?"

"You don't believe me?"

He shook his head and grinned with a well-polished arrogance only found on the face of a Hollywood actor. She quickly wondered if he'd ever met her mother but then dismissed the thought. She didn't want to think about her mother; the pain was simply too fresh.

"No. I do not believe you," he stated dryly.

The nerve! "You did find me in the jungle, didn't you? Wasn't I unconscious?" She pointed to the large lump on her forehead. "And wearing this?"

"Yes, but I believe you were searching for something else."

Nosy rake. "Well, it's been a pleasure, Mr...." *Arrogant Nudesunbather? Mr. Nomanners Perfectbottom?*

"Backlum Chaam."

Backlum? What an odd—oh! He's in character. "Sure, Joe. Whatever blows your wig, but—"

"The name is not Joe, it's Chaam. I just said it."

Margaret blinked. *Deep, deep into character.*

"And I assure you, I do not wear a wig. This is my real hair." He gave his shiny black mane a proud tug.

"I meant—oh, never mind. Listen, it's been great, Mr. *Chaam,* but I gotta skedaddle; my father is probably wondering where I am." She wished. Her father was likely dead. Or injured.

Stay calm. You'll find the ruin. You'll find him...

If only she'd insisted on knowing exactly where the excavation site was hidden. Instead, she'd done what her father had asked—fearing his anger—and stayed near the village, spending her days painting, learning Spanish from the local children, or swimming with a friend she'd made: a young woman named Itzel who didn't speak a lick of English.

"Have a lovely afternoon." She flashed an awkward grin and turned toward the shoreline.

A firm grip pulled her back and twirled her around. Two powerful arms incarcerated her body and smashed her against an astonishingly firm, naked chest. His touch instantly ignited that gunpowder, and...

Combustion!

A wave of carnal heat ripped through her body. *Oh my God. Oh my God. Oh my Gooood...* Margaret felt her face turn a lascivious red. Beads of volcanic sweat seeped through her pores. Every muscle in her body wound up with merciless unchaste tension, like ropes anchoring a massive sail, a sail blowing her ship toward the most delicious place ever. And then...

Release.

Maggie braced herself on the man's bountiful biceps as the tension snapped and silent fireworks exploded throughout her body.

Oh my God. Had she just...had she really just...?

He cleared his throat. "Was it as good as it looked?"

She let out an exaggeratedly long breath. *What the flapdoodle?* "You're not an actor, are you?" she asked, unable to keep her voice from quivering.

He shook his head from side to side. "No. And you are no human."

Glossary

(In No Particular Order Because Cimil Said So)

Yum Cimil: Goddess of the Underworld, also known as Ah-Puch by the Mayans, Mictlantecuhtli (try saying that one ten times) by the Aztecs, Grim Reaper by the Europeans, Hades by the Greeks . . . you get the picture! Despite what people say, Cimil is actually a female, adores a good bargain (especially garage sales) and the color pink, and has the ability to see all possible outcomes of the future. She's also batshit crazy.

Cenote: Limestone sinkholes connected to a subterranean water system. They are found in Central America and southern Mexico and were once believed by the Mayans to be sacred portals to the afterlife. Such smart humans! They were right. Except cenotes are actually portals to the realm of the gods.

(If you have never seen a cenote, do a quick search on the Internet for "cenote photos," and you'll see how freaking cool they are!)

The Pact: An agreement between the gods and good vampires that dictates the dos and don'ts. There are many parts to it, but the most important rules are vampires are not allowed to snack on good people (called Forbiddens), must keep their existence a secret, and are responsible for keeping any rogue vampires in check.

Obscuros: Evil vampires who do not live by the Pact and like to dine on innocent humans since they really do taste the best.

K'ak: The history books remember him as K'ak Tiliw Chan Yopaat, ruler of Copan in the 700 ADs. Really, King K'ak (Don't you just love that name? Tee-hee-hee...) is one of Cimil's favorite brothers. We're not really sure what he does.

Kinich: Also known by many other names depending on the culture, Kinich is the Sun God. He likes to go by Nick these days, but don't let the modern name fool you. He's not so hot about the gods mingling with humans. Although...he's getting a little curious what the fuss is all about. Can sleeping with a woman really be all that?

Votan: God of Death and War. Also known as Odin, Wotan, Wodan, the God of Drums (he has no idea how the hell he got that title; he hates the drums) and Lord of Multiplication (okay, he is pretty darn good at math so that one makes sense). These days, Votan goes by Guy Santiago (it's a long story—read Book #1), but despite his deadly tendencies, he's all heart. He's now married to Emma Keane.

Chaam: God of Male Virility. He's responsible for discovering black jade, figuring out how to procreate with humans, and kicking off the chain of events that will eventually lead to the Great War. Get your Funyuns and beer! This is gonna be good.

Black Jade: Found only in a particular mine located in southern Mexico, this jade has very special supernatural properties, including the ability to absorb supernatural energy—in particular, god energy. When worn by a human, it is possible for them to have physical contact with a god. If injected, it can make a person addicted to doing bad things. If the jade is fueled up with dark energy, then released, it can be used as a weapon. Chaam personally likes using it to polish his teeth.

Payal: Though the gods can take humans to their realm and make them immortal, Payals are the true genetic offspring of the gods but are born mortal, just like their human mothers. Only firstborn children inherit the gods' genes and manifest their traits. If the firstborn happens to be female, she is called a Payal. If male, well . . . then you get something kind of yucky!

Maaskab: Originally a cult of bloodthirsty Mayan priests who believed in the dark arts. It is rumored they are responsible for bringing down their entire civilization with their obsession for human sacrifices (mainly young female virgins). Once Chaam started making half-human children, he decided all firstborn males would make excellent Maaskab due to their proclivity for evil.

Uchben: An ancient society of scholars and warriors who serve as the gods' eyes and ears in the human world. They also do the books and manage their earthly assets.

Book of the Oracle of Delphi: This living, ancient text tells the future. But as events unfold, the pages rewrite themselves. Currently, the good vampires are in possession of this text.

The Gods: Though every culture around the world has their own names and beliefs related to beings of worship, there are actually only fourteen. And since they are able to access the human world only through the portals in the Yucatán region, the Mayans were big fans.

The gods often refer to each other as brother and sister, but truth is, they are just another species of the Creator.

Demilords: (Spoiler alert for Book #2!) This group of immortal badasses are vampires who've been infused with the light of the gods. They are extremely difficult to kill and hate their jobs (killing Obscuros) almost as much as they hate the gods who control them.

Hey there! If you enjoyed this novel and want to let me know, just click those fantastic little stars on the retailer's website, write a review, or ping me directly! (Contact info is below.) I see every note/review and do a little disco dance when they're good. Helpful feedback also welcome! (Sorry, Mean People. You'll just be ignored because Mean People suck. Yeah, you know you do.)

Mimijean.net

Twitter @MimiJeanRomance

Facebook.com/MimiJeanPamfiloff

THE DISH

Where Authors Give You the Inside Scoop

From the desk of Roxanne St. Claire

Dear Reader,

Years ago, I picked up a romance novel about a contemporary "marriage of convenience" and I recall being quite skeptical that the idea could work in anything but a historical novel. How wrong I was! I not only enjoyed the book, but *Separate Beds* by LaVyrle Spencer became one of my top ten favorite books of all time. (Do yourself a favor and dig up this classic if you haven't read it!) Since then, I've always wanted to put my own spin on a story about two people who are in a situation where they need to marry for reasons other than love, knowing that their faux marriage is doomed.

I finally found the perfect characters and setup for a marriage of convenience story when I returned to Barefoot Bay to write BAREFOOT BY THE SEA, my most recent release in the series set on an idyllic Gulf Coast island in Florida. I knew that sparks would fly and tears might flow when I paired Tessa Galloway, earth mother longing for a baby, with Ian Browning, a grieving widower in the witness protection program. I suspected that it would be a terrific conflict to give the woman who despises secrets a man who has to keep one in order to stay alive, with the added complication of a situation that can only be resolved with a fake, arranged marriage. However, I never dreamed just how much I would love writing that marriage of convenience! I should have known, since I adored the first one I'd ever read.

Throughout most of BAREFOOT BY THE SEA, hero Ian is forced to hide who he really is and why he's in Barefoot Bay. And that gave me another story twist I love to explore: the build-up to the inevitable revelation of a character's true identity and just how devastating that is for everyone (including the reader!). I had a blast being in Ian's head when he fought off his demons and past to fall hard into Tessa's arms and life. And I ached and grew with Tessa as the truth became crystal clear and shattered her fragile heart.

The best part, for me, was folding that marriage of convenience into a story about a woman who wants a child of her own but has to give up that hope to help, and ultimately lose, a man who needs her in order to be reunited with his own children. If she marries him, he gets what he needs...but he can't give her the one thing she wants most. Will Tessa surrender her lifelong dream to help a man who lost his? She can if she loves him enough, right? Maybe.

Ironically, when the actual marriage of convenience finally took place on the page, that ceremony felt more real than any of the many weddings I've ever written. I hope readers agree. And speaking of weddings, stay tuned for more of them in Barefoot Bay when the Barefoot Brides trilogy launches next year! Nothing like an opportunity to kick off your shoes and fall in love, which is never convenient but always fun!

Happy reading!

Roxanne St. Claire

♥ ♥ ♥ ♥ ♥ ♥ ♥ ♥ ♥ ♥ ♥ ♥ ♥ ♥ ♥

From the desk of Kristen Ashley

Dear Reader,

As it happens when I start a book and the action plays out in my head, characters pop up out of nowhere.

See, I don't plot, or outline. An idea will come to me and *Wham!* My brain just flows with it. Or a character will come to me and all the pieces of his or her puzzle start tumbling quickly into place and the story moves from there. Either way, this all plays in my mind's eye like a movie and I sit at my keyboard doing my darnedest to get it all down as it goes along.

In my Dream Man series, I started it with *Mystery Man* because Hawk and Gwen came to me and I was desperate to get their story out. I'm not even sure that I expected it to be a series. I just *needed* to tell their story.

Very quickly I was introduced to Kane "Tack" Allen and Detective Mitch Lawson. When I met them through Gwen, I knew instantly—with all the hotness that was them—that they both needed their own book. So this one idea I had of Hawk and Gwen finding their happily ever after became a series.

Brock "Slim" Lucas showed up later in *Mystery Man* but when he did, he certainly intrigued me. Most specifically the lengths he'd go to do his job. I wondered why that fire was in his belly. And suddenly I couldn't wait to find out.

In the meantime, my aunt Barb, who reads every one of my books when they come out, mentioned in passing she'd like to see one of my couples *not* struggle before they capitulated to the attraction and emotion swirling around them. Instead, she wanted to see the relationship build and grow, not the hero and heroine fighting it.

This intrigued me, too, especially when it came to Brock, who had seen a lot and done a lot in his mission as a DEA agent. I didn't want him to have another fight on his hands, not like that. But also, I'd never done this, not in all the books I'd written.

I'm a girl who likes a challenge.

But could I weave a tale that was about a man and a woman in love, recognizing and embracing that love relatively early in the story, and then focus the story on how they learn to live with each other, deal with each other's histories, family, and all that life throws at them on a normal basis? Would this even be interesting?

Luckily, life *is* interesting, sometimes in good ways, sometimes not-so-good.

Throwing Elvira and Martha into the mix, along with Tess's hideous ex-husband and Brock's odious ex-wife, and adding children and family, life for Brock and Tess, as well as their story, was indeed interesting (and fun) to write—when I didn't want to wring Olivia's neck, that is.

And I found there's great beauty in telling a tale that isn't about fighting attraction because of past issues or history (or the like) and besting that to find love; instead delving into what makes a man and a woman, and allowing them to let their loved one get close, at the same time learning how to depend on each other to make it through.

I should thank my aunt Barb. Because she had a great idea that led to a beautiful love story.

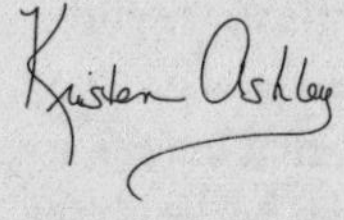

♥ ♥ ♥ ♥ ♥ ♥ ♥ ♥ ♥ ♥ ♥ ♥ ♥ ♥ ♥

From the desk of Eileen Dreyer

Dear Reader,

The last thing I ever thought I would do was write a series. I thought I was brave putting together a trilogy. Well, as usual, my characters outsmarted me, and I now find myself in the middle of a nine-story series about Drake's Rakes, my handsome gentleman spies. But I don't wait well as a reader myself. How do I ask my own readers to wait nine books for any resolution?

I just couldn't do it. So I've divided up the Rakes into three trilogies based on the heroines. The first was The Three Graces. This one I'm calling Last Chance Academy, where the heroines went to school. I introduced them all in my short e-novel *It Begins With A Kiss*, and continue in ONCE A RAKE with Sarah Clarke, who has to save Scotsman Colonel Ian Ferguson from gunshot, assassin, and the charges of treason.

I love Sarah. A woman with an unfortunate beginning, she is just trying to save the only home she's ever really had from penury, an estate so small and isolated that her best friend is a six-hundred-pound pig. Enter Ian. Suddenly she's facing off with smugglers, spies, assassins, and possible eviction. I call my Drake's Rakes series Romantic Historical Adventure, and I think there is plenty of each in ONCE A RAKE. Let me know at www.eileendreyer.com, my Facebook page (Eileen Dreyer), or on Twitter @EileenDreyer. Now I need to get back. I have five more Rakes to threaten.

Eileen Dreyer

♥ ♥ ♥ ♥ ♥ ♥ ♥ ♥ ♥ ♥ ♥ ♥ ♥ ♥ ♥

From the desk of Anne Barton

Dear Reader,

Regrets. We all have them. Incidents from our distant (or not-so-distant) pasts that we'd like to forget. Photos we'd like to burn, boyfriends we never should have dated, a night or two of partying that got slightly out of control. Ahem.

In short, there are some stories we'd rather our siblings didn't tell in front of Grandma at Thanksgiving dinner.

Luckily for me, I grew up in the pre-Internet era. Back then, a faux pas wasn't instantly posted or tweeted for the world to see. Instead, it was recounted in a note that was ruthlessly passed through a network of tables in the cafeteria—a highly effective means of humiliation, but not nearly as permanent as the digital equivalent, thank goodness.

Even so, I distinctly remember the sinking feeling, the dread of knowing that my deep dark secret could be exposed at any moment. If you've ever had a little indiscretion that you just can't seem to outrun (and who hasn't?), you know how it weighs on you. It can be almost paralyzing.

In ONCE SHE WAS TEMPTED, Miss Daphne Honeycote has such a secret. Actually, she has two of them—a pair of scandalous portraits. She posed for them when she was poor and in dire need of money for her sick mother. But after her mother recovers and Daphne's circumstances improve considerably, the shocking portraits come back to haunt her, threatening to ruin her reputation, her friendships, and her family's good name.

Much to Daphne's horror, Benjamin Elliott, the Earl of Foxburn, possesses one of the paintings—and therefore, the power to destroy her. But he also has the means to help her discover the whereabouts of the second portrait before its unscrupulous owner can make it public. Daphne must decide whether to trust the brooding earl. But even if she does, he can't fully protect her—it's ultimately up to Daphne to come to terms with her scandalous past. Just as we all eventually must.

In the meantime, I suggest seating your siblings on the opposite end of the Thanksgiving table from Grandma.

Happy reading,

Anne Barton

♥ ♥ ♥ ♥ ♥ ♥ ♥ ♥ ♥ ♥ ♥ ♥ ♥ ♥ ♥

From the desk of Mimi Jean Pamfiloff

Dear Reader,

After living a life filled with nothing but bizarre, Emma Keane just wants normal. Husband, picket fence, vegetable garden, and a voice-free head. Normal. And Mr. Voice happens to agree. He'd like nothing more than to be free from the stubborn, spiteful, spoiled girl he's spent the last twenty-two years listening to day and night. Unfortunately for him, however, escaping his only companion in the universe won't be so easy. You see, there's a damned good reason Emma is the only one who can hear him—though he's not spilling the beans just yet—and there's a damned bad reason he can't leave Emma: He's imprisoned. And to be set free, Mr. Voice is going to have to convince Emma to travel from New York City to the darkest corner of Mexico's most dangerous jungle.

But not only will the perilous journey help Emma become the brave woman she's destined to be, it will also be the single most trying challenge Mr. Voice has ever had to face. In his seventy thousand years, he's never met a mortal he can't live without. Until now. Too bad she's going to die helping him. What's an ancient god to do?

Mimi